THE BE(K)NIGHTED

BY

MARK HARBINGER

Published by Phoenix T Publishing and Media Literacy LLC

Print ISBN: 978-1-7370110-0-2

"Marian Michaels," "The Butterfly," "Brick Reese," "Slinker," "Animal," "Wild Bunch," "Deke," and "Hell-Rider" are all public domain characters who first appeared in Hell-Rider, issue number 1, by SKYWALD PUBLISHING CORP, in 1971.

Book Cover Design by ebooklaunch.com

~ ~ ~ ~ ~

The fictional lands, names, characters, places, and incidents in The Be(k)nighted are inspired by events, legends, and cultures from various parts of the world (including some that inhabit *only* my imagination). None are intended as a faithful representation of any one country or culture at any point in history.

It's a different Timespace.

~ ~ ~ ~ ~

My deepest thanks to everyone who supported my return to the writing. Special thanks to author Tim Marquitz for his mercenary copy-editing and his beneficent testimonial; to Travis for his wonderful feedback, inspiration, and support; to Kyler and Debbie for their encouragement; to the mysterious Carmen Carter for her tireless beta-reading (hey, somebody had to be first); and to both Dad and Brian, who I should have listened to sooner.

Also, my thanks to everyone who has ever taken the time to try and teach me a damn thing.

~~~~~

For "K Mark"
and "T Mark,"
…My Eternal Aspirations.
:-{D]
~~~~~

Contents

The Be(k)nighted

PROLOGUE, PART ONE

"Incantation Of The Law Against Inept Critics:
Let those who read this verse consider it profoundly,
Let the profane and the ignorant herd keep away:
And far away all Astrologers, Idiots and Barbarians,
May he who does otherwise be subject to the sacred
rite."

—Nostradamus, Century VI,
Quatrain 100

\###

The present.

They both knew he would kill her, and they both thought they knew when.

"So, it turns out Uncle Brick is the one who tells me you died," Marshall reported from the doorway behind her. Marshall ("Butchie" to her) had arrived at her home without warning. But Marian wasn't surprised. She couldn't be.

Marian didn't turn around. Instead, she just stared at the discs on the table before her. "You shouldn't talk like that, Butchie. They let you back off the Fifth Floor because you told them you weren't still having the visions."

"No." Marshall considered that for a bit, wondering just how long this was all going to take. "I just stopped telling them that I was." After another long pause, he said, "I have seen your funeral, Grandma."

Marian said nothing. She was always impressed by Marshall. The way he had overcome his early-onset schizophrenia throughout child-hood. The things he had done. The people saved.

He walked up behind her and placed his hand on her shoulder. "The recordings again?"

"Just the three main ones. Want some tea?" By *main ones*, she meant the ones that delved into the greatest detail about his violent epi-sodes. The recordings were two CDs of sessions from Marshall's past with Dr. Akhem—the childhood and teen years—and a DVD from just a couple years ago, when Marshall was an adult.

"Hm? No." He sat across from her. "Main ones, sane ones. Shhh. Sit down. Let's go here." All the last were just whispers, but Marian heard them as she poured herself another cup.

So, he's back off his meds, Marian noted as she observed him.

Despite the sunlight streaming through the open curtains, to him the walls were dark. His *friends* were close, at the edges, in the impene-trable corners of the room, hovering nearby. *You can't make it happen. She's too dangerous. Kill her! Stand up. You're going to fail. Did she offer tea? Yes, tea. Take it! No, it's poison!*

He knew they were ready to pounce whenever he gave the order, whenever he cast the spell, whenever he chose, *like now!*

He thought he did a good job ignoring the voices.

She watched him glance around. Alert to his state, she sat straighter as if readying for battle, her supple, dark skin a study in contrast to the full head of stiff, argent hair resting on her shoulders like a pharaoh's headdress. No one could have guessed her age from her beautiful ebony face.

Then she took a moment to really look at her boy. Though only twenty-five, he looked twice that. Handsome but gaunt, with a thick, tangly head of salt-and-pepper hair. His face was expressionless despite the permanent frown that remained as though he were a vaudeville pup-pet whose jaw was just shaped that way. The stolid facade remained all the time, except for the occasional half-smile that sometimes flickered forth like sparks from a short-circuit.

And, of course, the perfectly still brown eyes. Always the eyes. *I can see the love there, even if everyone else calls them dead,* Marian had once told the doctors.

For his part, Marshall *knew* that someone had moved all the pictures on her walls, every single one of them, just ever so slightly, since the last time he was there. It was a code. He should know the code, of course, but he didn't. *You're so worthless,* a voice said. There just wasn't time. *Do it now!* No, he needed more time to figure it out. *Grandma Marian can help.* Yes, she would help. He just had to ask her. *You're too late!* Right. No, that was right. Grandma Marian was going to die. He knew that. *Okay, so we can kill her. Let us do it. Get out of the way!* He would kill her. He already had. But first he needed answers. He had to focus.

Let's go here, he suggested to the group. Out loud, "Can I hear one?" He was asking Marian to play a recording.

She got up to get a cigarette. When Marian returned, she had a whiskey instead.

She put the first recording in and pressed *Play*.

Before it could start, he blurted, "I love you, Grandma."

She sipped and smiled at him. "I love you, too, Butchie."

And then they heard Dr. Akhem's voice from fifteen years ago.

PART TWO

RECORDING ONE:
MARSHALL, PATIENT, AGE 10

###

As you hear the doctor's voice, Marshall, you remember how his office smelled of dust and paper, like a public library. And you recall Dr. Akhem's appearance back then. His hair—it was gray back then, too—pulled back into a ponytail and tucked under his sport jacket. A kindly looking old man. He was so skinny. You remember thinking he must have been very old. His handlebar mustache and eye twinkle looked like the Santa Claus in that old black and white movie on 34th street.

But, no, he was too skinny. And there was no beard.

Same vibe, though. Kind.

Judgmental.

"Do you like those blocks?"

Oh, yeah, you remember now … the blocks! You used to just stack them over and over again. Whatever happened to those? You realize he must've brought them out just for you, because most of his clients were adults, and his grandson wasn't born yet at that time. The one you saved.

You even stole a block once and never returned it. The doctor must've known, but he never called you on it.

"Why'm I here?"

Oh, you sounded so young.

"Why do you think you are here?

The sound of blocks falling. Then a pause. "You wanna find out if I meant to kill them."

"Well, the people who interviewed you before told me why. They said you were just doing what the voices told you to do."

A pause. "So, why'm I here?"

"Well, for one thing, I was wondering what else the voices are telling you."

"Nuthin'."

"Nothing?"

"Mmp-mm. The medicine makes me so sleepy. Y'know, I can't think. I—so, I don't hear 'em now." You could hear the *tap, tap, tap* of you rebuilding the block tower.

"What did they used to tell you?"

"The usual stuff. That I am bad. Y'know."

"How would I know?"

"Everyone hears 'em." You remember thinking that back then.

"Really?"

"Yeah, but you all don't talk about it. That's why I got in trouble, y'know? I talked about it before I did it."

"You mean before you killed them."

"I didn't kill them. The gas leak did."

"Well, you leaked the gas, Marshall."

"No."

"No?"

The blocks falling again. You can hear yourself sigh on the recording. "SHE did."

"She? Who Is she?"

"SHE dudn't have a name. But the others have a name for her."

"The others. You mean the other voices? So, some voices talk about this other voice?"

Another sigh. "You don't believe me, anyway."

On the recording, you hear the doctor being very patient. "I believe you, Marshall. You hear voices. They talk about each other. And you're right, some other people hear voices, too. But not everyone. About one in a hundred, if you're interested. Anyway, I am here to tell you the voices aren't real. They're not real people. Do you understand?"

"The Demi-urge is real."

"What?"

"That's her name. She's real. Isn't she?"

You remember the doctor made a face like he smelled something bad. "Well, that's more of a title than a name. Anyway, why do you think that voice is real?"

"Well, the others think she is. And she's the one who first told me I can choose. Choose what the others show me. Or she used to. She, um, um, she dudn't talk to me … now. You know. With stupid meds."

"You don't like the medicine, do you?"

"I dunno."

"Did the *demi-urge* tell you to kill your parents?"

"N'm'prents."

"What?"

"They're not my parents. They're my foster parents … were …" There's a long pause as the therapist allowed you to reflect. "Most of the voices just tell me I'm bad. They tell me I'm stupid, y'know? That I have to watch out. You and the others are part of a secret group, out to get them … and me, too! Like that. But a few of the voices … they're not like that. They talk to me … normal. Y'know, like you do."

You hear pen on paper. You recalled the doctor always wrote a lot of notes.

"And the ones that talk normally to you, do you talk back … to them?"

"With my thoughts. I have killed with my thoughts. I guess I am bad. I mean, I killed people. So, that makes me bad, right?"

The doctor didn't answer. "And do they listen? The voices?"

"What? Ya'. I said I've. Killed. With. My. Thoughts," you said with a *duh* in your voice.

"So, they told you to kill your foster parents? Or you told them?"

The sounds of you getting up, walking around the room. The ankle chains make you sound like a child ghoul.

"They showed me all the different ways it would happen. They show me how my stepparents could get hit by a bus. Or one of them chokes. I didn't like that one. Drowning. Cancer. Those are the quiet ones. Oh, and lots of car accidents. The sound of car crashes, it's just like in the movies—did you know that? Anyway, it's like that: dying of illnesses, sick all kinds a' ways, so cold in their bed. I've seen, I saw them die a hundred times. A thousand. They always suffered. Over and over …

"So, I chose the one that was least painful. They were good to me. I thought I could at least do that for 'em. This way they died in their sleep. Boom. That's it, y'know?"

"Marshall, did you set the gas leaking? Did you start the oven?"

"No!" The chains stop clanking. You catch the sound of the sofa-cushion's whoosh from you sitting back down.

"Who did, then?"

"They did," you said.

"Who did?"

You remembered this part for sure: a long pause as you looked up and locked eyes with Dr. Akhem for the very first time. "My *friends*."

The doctor took a beat. "And I suppose the Demi-urge is your friend, too?"

And you shyly replied, "No, not really. She gets on me, gets on me for listening too much to the other voices, the ones she says aren't real. But she dudn't believe I'm worthless like the other voices do. She thinks I'm okay. Yeah, I'm good, she says. I'm even good."

"But you said you *chose* it. You chose the gas leak. So, you did it?"

You actually remember being annoyed at how obtuse the doctor was being. "Um, look. If you give me meds, you are not the one who gives them to me, it would be a nurse. Right?"

"Yes. I suppose."

"It's like that. I chose. But I didn't do it. They did it. I didn't even tell them … I just … *I chose*, alright?" Another crash of blocks.

You remember, he just sat there and stared at you for a long time. You didn't look up from your blocks, but you could feel his twinkly eyes. "Have they showed you how anyone else dies?"

You sniffed. "Lotsa' people."

"Like who?"

"Like … your grandson."

Another long beat. The sound of a notebook flapping down onto a table. "Excuse me?"

"Your grandson. He's in school … and another older boy shows up at the school with a lot of guns and shoots him. Shoots lots of kids. Lots of blood."

"Well, that's highly unlikely." As you listened to this, you could consider, with the benefit of hindsight, Columbine had been the only high-profile shooting before then, and that was five years or so before, so it would have sounded far-fetched. Maybe the doctor thought you were thinking of old news footage?

The doctor continued, "Besides. I don't even have a grandson. But ah, um, mmm hm. Well, that must be really very scary to see all that death."

Something you say is unintelligible. Now, you can be heard sniffling. "You're right. Highly unlikely." Another pause. "So, I'm crazy, right?"

And then Dr. Akhem said not to worry about that and suggested time was up, and he said this was very productive, and everyone was going to listen to you when he tells them about your voices, and it was a great time meeting you.

But, of course, by that point, all you could hear was the Demi-urge, the one voice that never leaves, even in your dreams. And she hissed at you through the drug-induced fog: *It is him! He is the one! He is our enemy! You must remember that … ALWAYS!*

PART THREE

"Close your eyes! Or lose your sense of sight forever!"

> —Marian Michaels, a.k.a.
> the Butterfly (circa 1971),
> from the 1995 television
> documentary *Heroes or Vigilantes?*

###

The present.

Grandma Marian clicked the recording off. She ejected it.

"Now, Dr. Akhem just signed your latest release. You just spoke to him a week ago, didn't you? How is he?"

"The same as always. He never changes. You know."

"Oh, yes, I know." Marian thought about how tonight was going to, *was supposed to* play out. Part of her still couldn't believe he would hurt her. *But Marshall hasn't been the same since he lost his son, poor Prince.* She had to provoke him with her denials for him to follow through.

Unlike her smooth face, the wrinkles on her hand revealed her true age. Marshall noticed the well-manicured red nails and the large white-gold ring with the inset sapphires running along its length. To help him ignore the voices, he focused on the glimmering of the ring as her hand extended for the next CD.

She put in the second recording and pressed *Play.*

PART FOUR

RECORDING TWO:
MARSHALL, VAGRANT, AGE 14 1/2

###

Your memories of this time aren't as reliable so, at first, all you can do is listen. This recording starts with the sounds of rustling. You can hear the traffic, the trains, and the other city ephemera in the background. It was a hallowed night down by the docks where you were living at the time. You were homeless. In hiding.

There were no meds for you, and there hadn't been for some time. The others who slept around you, in their boxes and blankets, avoided you, but this wasn't because you were violent or mean. Quite the opposite. You remember a lot of laughing and singing to yourself. You listened to the radio and imitated the announcers and the movie trailers. ("*In a WORLD …* ") And you fed everyone. They liked you for that.

But your spells still freaked them out.

That's what Dr. Akhem walked into that cold November night. He just showed up one evening, meandering between the piles of blankets and tents and grocery carts and burning trash barrels. He would call out your name from time to time. Your old name. But no one responded.

But the doctor kept coming. Apparently, he wasn't afraid of the way all the barrels and tents screamed at him. (It was funny how those screams weren't captured on the recording.) Still, you remember thinking at the time, *How could he just walk by them like that?* The barrels, they *hated* him. Could he really not hear their threats?

Then he saw you.

You remember this now. If Dr. Akhem was horrified by your appearance (or your odor), he didn't show it. He hugged you. And he mentioned the strange food disappearances. That was how he found you.

An entire store's worth just vanished! No sign of entry, but the cameras all malfunctioned and showed blurs, he recounted from the news reports. Then something funny he said about the piles of food next to your tent.

But no, instead, you listened to the voices. You pretended you didn't know. Played it cool. You didn't eat hardly any of it, anyway. Too much was poison.

Then he said he wanted to record you. You said okay, but the others, your *friends*, were already gathering. SHE wanted the doctor dead. *Now. Now! Do it!* SHE yelled and banged in the back of your head.

But you didn't want to hurt the old man. Really, you just wanted to send him away for his safety. Or at least warn him.

But SHE wouldn't like that, you knew, so you said nothing.

"AUGH," the recording said. This was the doctor squatting on a crate. "It is good to see you again. Do you remember me?"

You coughed out a laugh and said, "Maybe. Maybe, baby. Were you ever a baby? Is you is my baby?"

"I want to show you something."

You remember it was the tablet with the school parking-lot video recording. Oh boy. On the recording, it was a gray, early morning, but after school had already started. You, wearing a fedora and your flip-shade sunglasses atop a Greenless Grove jumpsuit, walk into the shot toward a particular empty parking spot. Meanwhile, at more or less the same time, a broken-down SUV pulls into that space from a different direction. As the driver gets out of the vehicle, you walk up to him. When he exits the car, you can see he's a young adult, barely out of high school himself. And the video showed you waving your hands at the driver as he reached back into the SUV for a gun. This is where the recording got weird.

There were no witnesses. But from later visits with Dr. Akhem, you knew forensic experts investigating the crime found the following on this footage:

First, from the moment you started waving your arms, Wayne (Wayne Osmond was his name, of course—he was a former fellow mental health inpatient at the Greenless Grove Healthcare Center, where you'd both been committed) is shown on the video as being in slow motion. Enough storage space on the hard disk to record two hours of time instead had been spent on Wayne doing what normally would've been about five seconds of action.

During those two hours of footage, you can be seen walking away, at what looks like normal speed, to hide right next to Wayne on the other side of his open car door.

In slow motion, Wayne turned and fired. This takes most of the two hours, while you just crouched behind his car door, a strange glow coming from around your eyes.

Then, in a practiced fashion, you stood up and released your spell. The gun was knocked free, and the bullet fell to the ground a foot or two in front of Wayne, bereft of any kinetic energy. You closed the car door on him gave him a massive head wound.

You remember looking at his body on the pavement while feeling the *dJinni* all around you. They had begrudgingly given their energy so you could do the spancasting. Some voices murmured their approval. A few others complained. One or two said to finish Wayne off.

Then you went into the school, borrowed a phone so you could call the authorities.

You knew you'd never be able to explain this. And even if you could, you had escaped Greenless Grove to do it. Most of the voices said to run, and you agreed. *Let's go here.*

The cops eventually found several automatic weapons and pistols, with many hundreds of rounds of ammunition, inside Wayne's SUV. He was a former student who had a troubled past and some sort of grudge against a former female friend who still went there. Wayne had bragged about how he was going to get her attention after he got out of the mental hospital.

The physical building housed not only a high school but an adjacent elementary/middle school as well. Your visions had shown you that in that elementary school, in a small room near the nearest door to where Wayne's car was parked, was Dr. Akhem's grandson.

"You do remember this, right?" On the recording, Doctor Akhem was insistent.

You didn't answer.

He continued, "I was worried about you. The way you ... left Greenless Grove. And then when this video surfaced on the news. I just wanted to find you, to make sure—"

"Are you going to arrest me? Just because I kill? That stinks. I stink!" you snapped at no one and everyone.

"No. I am not the police."

"You're worse. You're the enemy—SSHH! Let's go here ... let's go here ... let's go here ..." and the sounds of something, probably your blanket, sliding away on the pavement.

"W-wait! Come back." Then you hear the sounds of him getting up, walking after you, breathing huskily in the chilly air. "I just want to talk. I am not taking you anywhere."

You spun around so fast the two of you nearly bumped heads. "Damn right, you're not."

The doctor stepped back. "I'm trying to thank you! Look, you saved him. *You* did that, did you not? You saved my grandson! Isn't that why you did that?"

Now you were nonplussed. You remember fighting back the voices, even the Demi-urge's screaming, pushed them all back into the background. You turned your head to the side and tried hard to hear only Dr. Akhem.

He continued, "I remember. I still do, Marshall. You said he got shot. It's not a coincidence, is it? You really did see that?"

Cautiously. "M'kay."

"So, you see the future." It wasn't a question.

At first, you just nodded dumbly, then more frantically before, "Yes. Yes, damn it." You remember being angry. How many times? How many therapy sessions had you tried to tell him the past seven years? But he never believed. You remember being so angry, you wanted to let Wayne do what he told you he was going to do. That would teach them all, some voices said. But no, you couldn't do that. You couldn't let innocents die. Wayne had to be stopped.

You were both crazy. But Wayne? Wayne was *dangerous.*

So, you set about escaping. You had already, through good behavior, managed to convince them to lower your dosages. So, not only did the usual background voices return but so did *theirs*. And, of course, SHE was clearer than ever at that point. But SHE didn't approve of anything that helped Dr. Akhem. So, you did this without her. You just focused on the others, the few who liked you and weren't under the Demi-urge's control.

As long as you didn't take their energy, as long as you used your own, they would help teach you. Over the past several years, they had shown you the limits of your spells, beyond just picking the futures they showed you.

You could slow time, in small bubbles of area nearby. This is how you survived so long as an inpatient. And this is how you were able to do so much learning. They thought you just used those piles of books you borrowed for your room as some sort of fetish. But no, you read them. Plenty of time. This sort of thing was strangely easy for you. *Spancasting* it was called.

Inside the bubble, it was like a large boulder being carried down the rapids. Time still moved for those inside, just much, much slower.

Or you could banish objects. This was the trickiest of your spells. You made things disappear. Your friends, the dJinni, said you could replace them with other things, things from elsewhere—something about other timelines. You would work on that later when you got better. You didn't understand that yet. But, theoretically, you could throw a paper airplane, and then, before it landed, pull it from this timeline and switch it with an object from a different timeline—say, one where you threw a hand grenade instead?

Infinite possibilities meant, well, infinite possibilities! The dJinni were always feeding you ideas.

It was funny. As you grew up, the *others* went from being your *friends* to your *demons* to simply the dJinni. Now some were friends, some were allies, and some were neither. You could use them, just as other people tried to use them ... or each other. It was all relative. The more history books you read, the more you realized one person's angel was another person's demon, depending on who got what they wanted from them.

But if a dJinn couldn't be persuaded, tricked, or coerced into using their energy, all of the spells took away your energy, your life force. Over the years, you had used your own life force a lot. You were fourteen when you escaped but, visually, you looked as weathered as many of the others in the homeless encampment.

"Your friends, the demons. What are they telling you now? To kill me?"

"Some are," you admitted.

"So, it really does all come back to your choices, doesn't it?"

Silence. You shifted back and forth between your feet, nodding frantically.

"Listen, I was supposed to bring you back to Greenless Grove. I have bosses, too, you know. They sent me to find you. But, sometimes, I disagree with what they want. Sometimes I call an audible." You didn't get the reference then.

"I have a friend. She lost a loved one … because of my bosses. And so, she isn't a fan of them, either. And she … is like you. In fact, she was once also supposed to be arrested and taken to my bosses. But back then, long ago, someone let her go to start a new life. She can help you. She can help you do the same, I think. It would be a community placement, under her watch. Would you like that?"

"M'kay," you agreed but, deep down, you remember you felt helpless. At least in hiding you made your own choices. Now, it would be more medicines, more doctors, more people telling you what to do.

You'd had enough of that already.

"I will have someone come around and pick you up at—"

"First thing tomorrow morning. At sunrise."

"Ha. Yes, that's right. That's exactly correct."

Then you can hear yourself reciting:

Mountains, sun behind.

Mighty peaks are black at dawn,

but revealed later …

"It's a HAIKU."

You almost shouted that last word. You wanted him to understand how important this point was. "The voices didn't write that, Doctor. I did. They don't create. I do. They just destroy."

This doctor was unafraid. "Well, I think my friend Marian can help with that. But you will need to behave for her and do as she says. Can you do that?"

But you didn't answer. His question was buried in a cacophony of other questions from other voices, and you were getting tired of fighting them all.

Then he offered you meds to help you sleep. He just carried them around in his pocket. And, to his surprise, you accepted. You remember a couple of your neighbors coming up and asking for some, too.

PART FIVE

"Every man is guilty of all the good he did not do."
—Voltaire

###

And it was later that night—or is it tonight?

You are having a strange vision.

An interlude. (Intra-lude, really. If you're going to be a damn time-lord, get the terminology right. I mean, am I right, Doctor WhoTheHellDoYouThinkYouAre?)

Was this during a spell? You don't remember, do you? Ask the voices.

Come to think of it, where are the voices?

You are in a wondrous kaleidoscope of reflective, mirroring planes of light, dangling above a gnarled, vining dreamscape. You cling to the strings of shimmering energy that crisscross above your head. You hang on to keep your balance. Then the one who has brought you, the one the Demi-urge calls the Enemy, appears, a shapeless luminescence whose vibrations only hint at a face:

"Dreams and Spells. And I will see you now." You hear him, even though his vibrating smile isn't moving.

"Chaos and Life. Since you share this moment with me, you may call me the Mehkard. You can always find me here, traveling within the universe's connective tissue.

"Meaning and Work. From time to time (we should enjoy that phrase), a shimmering golden rift-strike splits the murky crystalline land-scape, leaving behind a blinding white chasm. Is that not how you see it?"

Being as you're basically too blinded to see anything but his halo effect, you just wait for him to continue.

"Wound and Empathy. And then we wince, reflecting the illness of it. My pain echoes the energy bleeding from the schism. But after the wave passes, I gather myself, focus on its path, and trace it back to its source.

"Enemy and Ire. Invariably, the source is an event caused by my endless would-be oppressor: the Multitude, the Chaos-bringers—dJinni is what you will come to know them as, but they are mine to name. You must hear it.

"They are the Regnant. And their strategy is the same: implant themselves in a timeline and trend it toward the destruction of all the conscious life therein. Then they move on to the next timeline and do likewise. Again. And again.

"You must see it. They do this to destroy me. This is because it is from the consciousness of all living beings I originate. I am the living embodiment of all.

"Branches and Continuity. Each time I thwart them, I secure life along another thread of the multiverse. In this way, I bolster my power. And each time I am strengthened, the task the next time becomes easier. Yes, I see your thought. My ultimate victory is assured! Or it would be, but for this: the more life, the more different timelines are created by the near-infinite choices of those life-forms. Thus, the task increases to match my abilities.

"This challenge is the beautiful difficulty of tending my universe."

You see the Mehkard tracing back yet another rift-strike when a singular prayer pierces through the noise. The sounds, the ideas, and the spirit-form of the one sending it … they are somehow there with you both.

"Ah, Purpose and Point. What is this, a prayer? So rare, it must've been exquisitely crafted to reach me here, now, while I am working. Remarkable. Perhaps you led it to me?"

But the Mehkard sighs his displeasure at the interrupting human supplicant. And in response to the prayer, the Mehkard forms a single word:

"No."

And like a swatted insect, the person's spirit-essence tumbles away, back to their own Timestream.

Once they are gone, you cannot help but wonder, how will the Mehkard's quick burst of bestowal affect that person's destiny? Will they die? Be horribly disfigured? Suffer madness? Anything?

The Mehkard answers your unspoken question, "It is no matter."

Refocused, you see and hear the Mehkard continue his task.

"Brevity and the Infinite. As I shall say, I save, collect, and curate timelines. But even after I acquire them, some are easier than others to … cultivate. I mentioned my challenge. What is my solution?

"Well, one has to prune.

"Here, I'll show you. This will help you with the voices. In a moment, I am going to ask you just to look at the end of my pen, into the light, keeping your head still but follow it with your eyes. Follow it upward … and hold your eyes there, yes, good, and relax, and focus on the light. All your attention to that light. We have plenty of time. Keep your eyes open, but imagine they feel heavy and slowly close. Now, Marshall, I am going to start counting."

PART SIX

*"You cannot see beyond a future
you haven't reckoned: wherefore?"*

—Revelator Training Curriculum,
*Choiciferor Ethics Code for
Precognitives*: Precept #1
(as pirated from the original,
in the Extirpacy's secret-files)

\###

The present.

Grandma Marian clicked the recording off. She ejected it.

"Are you okay?" Marian shook her grandson's shoulder. The second recording had long since stopped.

Marshall looked at her and swallowed, glancing at his wrist where his broken wristwatch took up space. Of course, its hands weren't moving. They never did.

He spent a moment counting the spots on the skin of her arm. *New patterns,* he noticed. *A new code.* Yes, that fits. It would be soon. Hard to know exactly when.

Marian waited, trying to be patient with Marshall's process of dealing with what he was experiencing.

For his part, he could only think, *It is time to confront her.* He needed to know the truth, once and for all, before it was too late. *Are the dJinni real? Or, after you are gone, will I be truly alone?*

Then he said it again. Because he didn't know if he had said that out loud or not.

###

They discussed much that day, her insisting time and time again that all the voices were from his illness. Finally, a particularly ominous night approached, with a golden sunset peering in just enough to promise dark storms later.

Finally, Marian closed her drapes to the darkness and went to turn on the ceiling lights, but they weren't working. She mumbled something about how the power hadn't gone out in ages, and she lit some candles that were already prominently displayed in the study. She used that light to make a big pot of soup they could sample from the rest of the evening. Marshall ignored all of this and took his meds from his coat pocket to take a dose.

It was okay to take his medicine, now that he had done what needed to be done.

The candles added to the room's already warm orange glow. She brought Marshall some gazpacho from the fridge and placed it before him. It was already room temperature before he even put the spoon in his mouth.

"I have to ask you. Grandma? Here." And Marshall slowly dropped yet another disc onto the table. This one was a DVD.

Marshall and Marian, the reflections in their eyeglasses stared at each other for a moment.

"Can you play that, Grandma? Please?"

She moved back to the all-purpose player and inserted the DVD. She had it hooked to a projector that shot its movies onto a screen on the opposite wall.

This movie was of older videos. Grainy footage. The first couple of pieces looked to be from news reports back in the 1980s. In that footage was a beautiful black woman, flying about the streets of nearby Seattle. She was dressed in a garish but striking costume, with large butterfly wings and bright, pulsing, phosphorescent lights incorporated into the fabric of the material. Underneath the wings and in the boots were some kind of propulsion devices. And she was literally flying.

"Oh, for Pete's sake. Where did you find this?"

"The Internet, Grandma. Everything is there. This was about the time you and Uncle Brick relocated here from Vegas, right?"

"Marshall, this isn't news to you. I already told you I was The Butterfly, way back when."

The news story went on about the rash of costumed superheroes, vigilantes some would say.

"No, I know. It is not that. It is the footage. Here, now watch."

Now it had moved on to footage from a documentary. In this video, she hovered over and around several gunmen, who fired at her. The shots all missed, flashes of gunpowder and ricocheting bullets drowned out by the flares of her costume's pyrotechnics. Then she landed and engaged them directly.

"See? There! And there!"

Marian didn't respond. She wasn't even looking.

"The way you fight, fly around, the way you move. How many dozens, hundreds, of criminals did you fight over the years? There are twenty or so just in these film clips. And it is always the same."

"They were blinded," she offered weakly. "The lights—"

"Sure," Marshall interjected sarcastically, "yes. You fought literally thousands of armed gunmen over the years with just jet packs. And you kept from being shot because of your *strobe lights*. But see here? See here? Like here, this, there, that! *That* is *exactly* how I move when I use them. This is how I had been taught … by the dJinni."

He moved into the stream of the projection onto the big screen, and his face was obscured by the scenes of her past. "You can see the future, too, can't you, Grandma? They help you, too, don't they?"

They were anti-gravity, not jetpacks, she faintly thought, but she kept silent.

When she didn't say anything, Marshall spun aside and around and pointed to two more instances in the video. He'd watched it hundreds of times.

"See, there. You move around that corner instead of straight into the alley. But why? No reason, except then, *there*, you have the angle now." He's satisfied, proud even, at his recognition. "And then, here is the best, the accidental truck pulling out, clobbering him just as he is about to shoot."

Well, it wasn't like this wasn't expected. Might as well save some time. He came here to kill me. He becomes the dJinni's new oracle, replacing me. With my cancer diagnosis, I won't be alive much longer, anyway. It was better this way. My denials infuriate him. So, he tells them to kill me, instead. I've seen it. The dJinni will make it happen. Somehow.

And besides, those old tapes! I hate being reminded how much I've sagged.

"Butchie, okay. Listen, I'm not going to sit here and argue about how I am some kind of magical woman who can see the future. You are the one with the visions that matter, not me! And who is to say whether or not you choose them? I don't know. I don't. But me? And the degree to which you are implying I could pinpoint it? That wouldn't just be a sorceress. That'd be a goddess, son!"

"Son!" he repeated, imitating her voice as he stopped the DVD. "Son." He slumped back into the chair, his voice thick with implications. But he couldn't say it. He just could not level the accusation. He just looked at the table toward that third recording of hers.

The third one. That one has the footage of his own son, Prince, back at the hospital. The one marked *Prosecution, Exhibit 8.*

She understood. So, slowly, very, very slowly, she replaced his DVD with hers and pressed *Play.*

PART SEVEN

RECORDING THREE: MARSHALL, HOSPICE IN-HOME CAREGIVER, AGE 22

###

Now, in this video recording, it is only a couple years ago. The mounted-camera, closed-circuit footage in her bedroom showed you approaching a woman sleeping in her bed, on her side, back facing the camera. You pulled away a propping pillow that was out of place and touched her shoulder, gently pulling her onto her back, and so you were startled by her scream:

"WHO ARE YOU IN MY HOUSE?"

You jumped back. Maggie, who had just asked the relevant question, lay in bed, eyes wide in fear. Those same eyes, recessed into her wrinkled features, had seen over ninety summers come and go. They had seen all her children and grandchildren both live and die. And since, she had been diagnosed with posterior cortical atrophy, and subsequently Alzheimer's.

She had had literally hundreds of caregivers hovering over her bedside. And you had been her daily caregiver for a hundred days yourself but, of course, as sometimes happened, she did not recognize you.

Your smile flickered. She had slept most of the past week, when she was not moaning in pain and mumbling complaints too disjointed to follow. She had again been listed as *nonresponsive* in the nurse's notes when you came in. But she was awake and alert. Maybe this was the day you had foreseen?

"My name is Marshall. Mar-shall. Um, Glasses, remember?" She called you that because of the flip-shades. "I am your caregiver. I am here to help you. Your nephew Brandon sent me. How are you, Maggie?"

She squinted at you. Her mouth opened and closed soundlessly. She lowered her head. You thought she had given up trying to speak, so you were surprised when she mumbled,

"Water."

You held the cup with the bent straw to her mouth. The water was already mixed with the thickening agent so she could swallow it, after a fashion. Once she gurgled and coughed enough that a bit of it had been drunk, she rested her head back deep into her pillow.

She was quiet, so you continued your normal routine. Her living room, where her medical bed sat, was a well-kept library, with walls lined with bookshelves she had long since forgotten.

"Have you gone to the bathroom yet today, Maggie?" you narrated as you checked her diaper. She was dry. The nurse's notes said she had just been cleaned, but they were not always reliable. Then you measured her arm circumference. A slight lessening.

"You have not been eating, Maggie. Do you want some food?"

And, amazingly, she nodded. Even pointed to the kitchen. *I knew it,* you thought. She had been refusing nearly all food for weeks. You remember thinking, *Today is it. Today is going to be the day.*

You grabbed the mashed potatoes from the fridge and scooped a small serving into a bowl. "What is it? What do you want today? We have mashed potatoes. Hm? Would you like some mashed potatoes?" You sat her bed up straight and brought your stool over so you could feed her.

You were all set up and about to begin when she held up her hand and shook her head.

"What is wrong? Do you want another dri—"

"'S cr'm."

"Ice cream! Wow, you really are looking for a treat." She smiled broadly at that and coughed a few times. You wiped her mouth and gave her another drink. When you returned from the kitchen with her ice cream, she had a question for you.

"Hm. Ghh, glasses." A gasp for intermission. "Where? Bran-don? Needs money. Fer tolls."

She referred to a time about forty years prior, when he drove her Charger to and from work across the Sound, but she got her only living relative's name correct. Yes, this was definitely going to be the day.

Do not worry, you assured her on the recording. You would call him over. *He will want to see you for this,* you thought.

You had been working with this family for many months. Margaret Howard was a retired schoolteacher (history), and she had been the matriarch of a tight-knit family. Her son joined the army and was lost in a training accident. Her older daughter married and had two kids. One died in a car accident many decades ago. And the other, the younger one, died as the widow of a wealthy research scientist, but without any children. Her younger daughter's estate paid for her around-the-clock hospice care.

Meanwhile, her brother-in-law and his ex-wife had only one child. That child was Brandon. In his fifties now, he was a retired machinist on disability. He collected trains and, more importantly, he was the family archivist. He was Maggie's only remaining link to the living world.

You knew that when people are about to pass, as they decline, there is usually a time, right before the end, when they get a burst of energy. There are medical reasons, but you were taught it was energy from the land of the dead the person uses to finally sever all bonds to the living.

And it was energy you could help control.

You had the routine down by now. You had done this with nine or ten other hospice patients over the past few years.

It was a small kindness, but you just needed to do it. After the way Dr. Akhem rescued you (without turning you into the authorities), and then how he and Marian Michaels ginned up the phony identification, and with a new surname, *Lastpost*. How Marian adopted you, taking you in as her own. You had to pay if forward.

You had earned your high school diploma. And although largely home-schooled, Marian and Dr. Akhem insisted you spend your last two years in a public high school, just to help you learn how to interact with others.

You didn't like it much. After being shunned and even violently accosted, you learned mostly to keep your mouth shut. You freaked everybody out, and whatever you said when you tried to make friends only made things worse.

Rather than being haunted by voices, you spent all your free time addled by the strong meds and haunted by your classmates.

But you watched enough television and movies to really work on your impressions. In fact, at an open mic fundraiser for the school booster club, you did a bunch of celebrity impressions to a standing ovation. After that, your classmates sort of made peace with you. In the hallways, the cool kids would ask you to do an impression for their hangers-on, and then you did one. And then they'd tell you that you were okay (instead of assaulting you, like they used to). It was all very transactional.

You graduated. Dr. Akhem got you a job with this home healthcare company. In a rare, candid moment, he even told you it was the main healthcare contractor for the part of the government run by the Extirpacy. The clients were mostly family of military or other government agents. And this healthcare company ran the Greenless Grove.

Your job was to provide hands-on care for those in hospice. You were helping those who were going to die. Like Maggie.

You skipped your morning dose. A few hours later, the voices started to murmur again in the background. No words, yet, but their presence pressed with a raw pain against the sides of your mind, like your skull was an ill-fitting shoe.

After you set up an extra phone they had lying around the house (Maggie's, technically) to record the conversation for Brandon's benefit, you spent the afternoon talking with Maggie about everything she might share with a future family member. Sometimes, she talked to you as though you were one of her kids. Other times, she just answered your prompts as you asked her about her life. Some of the answers might've been more accurate than others—it was not for you to say. But now, it was on the record. She didn't have to be forgotten.

Later on, when Brandon regretted not having recorded his last conversation with her, you had planned to give him that. The families always loved that.

You helped clean her after the latest bowel movement, and then you changed her clothes. As she laid back down, you called Brandon and gave him the heads up. *Come over right away*, you said. *You have got to see this, she is back! Bring your bag. Spend the night. She is having a good night, and I think tomorrow will be good, too!* You weren't really that excited, but you remembered a movie scene with that dialogue, so you just did that.

As you hung up, you were grateful. You had the power to extend that gift of that last burst of energy, for the family, from hours to days. That is what you had to do. *So many choices. Life and Death. Along so many timelines. This is just one, one me and one Maggie in this one timeline, but there are countless others. And on that scale, maybe which choice I make is not that important. Right? There's always another me, somewhere, making the opposite choice. Even if I screw up, they must balance out … right?*

It was about an hour later when Brandon showed up. You led him into her bedroom, and they chatted. Not bothering to glance at your broken wristwatch, you looked at the wall clock to mark the time.

You watched from her bedroom doorway and listened to their conversation. It was rote, banal. But it was also love. Love, the behavior. Love, the long, grim joy of responsibility and caregiving. You listened to his routine questions. You listened to her fluttered breathing in-between her answers. She stared over at the television. *Laverne and Shirley*. Her favorite. It was Thursday night. But that channel had that show on every night at that time.

They watched it together as you surreptitiously watched them as the *others* watched you. Finally, from out of sight, you let everyone know, *Let's go here*. The gesture you make is barely perceptible but visible in the doorway of the video.

When you finally entered the room, you confirmed they were both in a trance state, carrying on their conversation but utterly oblivious to you. You started to turn off the TV, but then you figured, what the hell? And so, you began.

You flipped your shades down and found your, *what*, center? The Greek chorus of your madness was perversely cheering you on, as though your spell would harm them. *You are going to kill them! Well done, Killer! They don't like you. They do not deserve to live.*

In response to the voices, you meditated. Each inhalation entered you and was ignited to become a burning energy, like a dragon's flame that expanded internally. This glowing power caused your organs and fibers to expand and relax, freeing the black specks of emotional detritus to exit with each exhale.

When you meditated, eventually, you became your breaths, and the waves of your trance-state washed over you. That time, you could still hear: *Life or Death. Tides of breathing. Schlemiel! Schlimazel!* But mostly the voices faded as your *chi* throbbed and fizzed through your veins.

Finally, opening your eyes, you saw the energy you needed to prime this spell, floating about the room like a mist. None of that is visible on the videotape. It just looks like you're staring at the utterly motionless pair.

For hours.

But you remember what you were seeing. Through the energy veil, you could see two pairs of glowing eyes.

One was located behind Maggie; the other was for Brandon. They were dJinni. They regarded you with all the raw burning emotion your own eyes lacked.

In your mind, they showed you the possibilities. Like a child waiting on Saturday mornings for your favorite cartoon, you patiently watched until they revealed the one you wanted.

Then you chose. You paused for a moment to take in the death scene they showed you. It would be there in the room, surrounded by the smell of hospital latex and linens and tons of books and other familiar family keepsakes no one else will know what to do anything with.

And you could see Brandon standing at her side, crying for the end as we all do. It would be in a day or so … after they've had a long, long talk. They would lose track of the time. It would almost be a miracle that they talked that long—what, twenty hours? Thirty? The recording will have long since stopped.

You mumbled a few more incantations as your *chi* surrounded the dJinni. Among other things, you assured them you wouldn't require their energy for this. You would use your own.

For their part, the dJinni said something back in their own language, apparently annoyed with you. Nonetheless, they complied.

The closed-circuit security camera spotted amber light coming from … somewhere? From your eyes? And you danced about, around the room, waving your arms while the stoic forms of Maggie and Brandon remained still. *Were they drugged?* the authorities would wonder later.

Anyway, this was just one piece of circumstantial evidence, the weird dancing around. It was the other recording later at the hospital that got you arrested.

For your part, using muscle memory, you gesticulated to gather the energy from the air around you. You welcomed the power from the other side directly into your fingertips. It merged with your shallow, pelting breath. *Yes!* You smiled inwardly like recognizing caller ID from an old friend. After several minutes, your heart raced …

… your energy to the dJinni …

… and the dJinni turned to use that energy to knead the very fabric of the Timespace around the room.

Leaning onto the bedrail for support, your breaths now provided the rhythm for the entire room as they slowed. Inhale. Exhale. Inhale. Exhale. Slooow. Slooooooower. The glow surrounded the bed and the patient … slowing it all to almost nothing … your breath, her heartbeat. Like a tendril, your *chi* snakes out to Maggie … her time, her time, time, time time time timetime timetime timetime …

After a while, you remember your trance ruptured like a bubble.

"He's awake, now," a demon told you. *No, wait. That was one of them*, you realized.

You were in a nearby chair (and did not remember falling back into it), and your breathing had returned. You wiped the sweat from your face and neck.

Maggie smiled peacefully. Her eyes were clear.

"Heh. Glasses."

"Hello, Maggie," you greeted her. "How long have I been asleep?"

Brandon walked into the room, almost in a panic. "Oh, my God! You won't believe this … but you just slept … and we just talked for almost two full days. It is noon on Saturday!"

At that, you told them they talked all night until Friday. You came back that night to wake them up. *What, you don't remember? That is odd! Well, anyway, the two of you just kept right on talking as soon as you awoke, and you talked all last night, too.*

They seemed satisfied. Being touched by the dJinni, even indirectly, had a confounding effect of folks. Made them impressionable.

Before you went, you sat down to write your healthcare notes for Maggie, the patient.

"She is going to die!" you were reminded by a dJinn in a harsh whisper, and you almost chuckled to yourself. You considered making that the headline of the note. But no, you entered your typical clinical note.

You then placed your hands on your knees and rocked forward to push yourself up from the couch. Your knees and back were stiff from the spancasting. As you shambled to the doorway of Maggie's room, you interrupted them momentarily just to wish them both good night and goodbye. And then you left.

But that wasn't the end of the night for you. You still remember …

###

You remember your sense of accomplishment was to be short-lived. As you walked up the street to your apartment, the houses on each side of the street hissed messages to you: *Everyone knows what you do! Something's wrong; she will tell them. She'll tell them about your lies! You're special, and they will find you. They always find out!*

You went into your apartment and turned on the overhead fluorescents as you tossed your keys into the easy chair beside the apartment door. Then you went over to your pet turtle's enclosure and turned on his light, too.

"Hello, Little Rich," you greeted him.

Just like the lights in the real world, Mr. Rich's light also created more shadows than illumination. Little Rich and his shadow just sat there in the terrarium. He paid no attention to you.

You picked up the child's building block you stole years before from Dr. Akhem. It was scratched but still perfectly good. You turned it around and around in your hand.

As always, this was exactly what you needed. The silence surrounded you like a cocoon, and you closed your eyes. *Don't answer it,* a voice hissed.

And then the phone rang.

It was the hospital. Your son. Something was happening. Something had changed. He had gotten worse. You had to come in right away.

###

The hospital had cameras, too. The video picks up there.

This footage was appended onto the other at trial. You never liked to watch this portion of the DVD. But you cannot turn away. You see yourself leaning over your son's tiny body, grabbing his hand in the hospital bed, pretending to listen to the doctor as he explained the situation. *"He isn't responding to treatment. This is the normal progression for glioblastoma, although this was a sudden setback."*

You remember you could barely see your beautiful boy through the rage of your tears, your quiet sobs drowned out by the *BEEP! BEEP! BEEP!* of the monitor.

You had performed the spell for him the last time you saw him, just like you did every week.

"The spell, it should've bought him more time." *God damn it, this should not be happening! Yes, Maggie's spell took me away for a couple of days, but …*

"I don't know what spell you're referring to, Mr. Lastpost." It was the doctor. Tall, regal-looking fellow. He tried to calm you down. "Why don't you come with me so we can discuss your … options."

The voices screamed in all directions. You had to get rid of the doctor to do what you needed to do. You didn't really know why you chose a banishment at that point. Instinct probably. Mostly, you just wanted him *away.* He tried to remove you from the room, and you got into a scuffle with him, accidentally scratched his face with your watch. Then he got angry and charged at you. You reacted instinctively. In a flash of amber, the doctor was gone.

The videotape caught it. The flash. Then no doctor. The prosecution made up an explanation about you turning the camera off somehow and a kidnapping. Regardless, the doctor was never found.

You continued to hover over your son at that point. You had seen it enough times before with your other patients. His extremities had discolored. His breathing had inverted. Thank goodness his eyes had been closed. You could not bear to have him look at you, the father who could not protect him.

And thank God his mother, Julia, hadn't lived to see this day. *Julia! I'm so sorry!* Your thoughts bounced back to your own grief over Julia's death during childbirth. Prince never met her. He lived a couple of good years, though he was behind in his development, but then, after the diagnosis, he spiraled downward. A brain tumor.

All the voices you heard your entire life, but you never really got to hear his.

You had used your power to do what you could to extend his life. But now, out of nowhere—what did the doctor call it? *An unexpected setback.*

Various dJinni understood the stakes, saying things like, *We cannot let him go mad from the loss. He will kill us all! No one will be able to stop him. Save the boy!* Then the ones who were followers of the Demiurge tried to enter the boy through the tubes to help him. *Possession.* To keep him going they were willing to use their own energy. *Send him back,* they kept saying. Maybe they enjoyed seeing your suffering.

But you knew better. It was too late. You had seen it too many times before in your work as a hospice aide. Your son was gone. At some point, mechanically keeping the body alive is an abomination.

But the dJinni wanted to prolong it. They didn't even ask you. They just entered the boy.

That, you would not tolerate. So, you fixed it. You cast your spells, arms flailing madly. You didn't need their help, or anyone's help. Not anymore. You summoned your *chi* and wielded your eldritch life-force like a miles-high solar flare of plasma, destroying them, fraying their very essence, buying your son time to die.

The beeping (in no time at all, really) turned into a solid tone.

That tone and your labored breathing filled the room.

Some of the dJinni had actually *fought* you. You never forgave them for that. As if it wasn't hard enough.

Those were your memories.

Technically, after the doctor disappeared, the cameras caught you dancing slowly around your son's bed as he died. And then assaulting several hospital personnel who tried to enter the room and assist. Your rage knew no bounds. You didn't remember that. It must have been afterward when you blacked out. In hindsight, you were lucky you didn't kill anyone else (besides the doctor, though he might have survived whatever timeline you sent him to—no telling).

At Prince's funeral, you were mostly lost to the voices. You had long since stopped taking your meds. And once the authorities saw the footage of your strange behavior at the hospital (as well as a complaint from Brandon, something about drugging him and his mom, with forensics to prove it), you were charged with several counts of … You don't remember. Something serious.

You weren't a very sympathetic defendant, but it didn't matter. Marian and Dr. Akhem had the resources and connections to make sure you were found innocent by reason of insanity and have you referred back to the maximum-security wing of Greenless.

Of course, this time, you had a new identity. Nor did any of the staff there remember you. After all, you looked so much older.

PART EIGHT

—Winner of the 1916 *Vanity Fair*
Haiku Contest,
as adjudged by Aleister Crowley

###

The present.

"What are you here to do, Marshall?" Grandma Marian asked.

He didn't hesitate. The entire time in rehab, back in Greenless Grove, after he was convicted of murdering his own son, it was all he ever thought about. Once he figured out Marian was a sibyl, once he saw the video footage that proved it, the question became obvious.

"Did you know Prince would die?" From the look on her face, this one was definitely out loud. "Did you choose that future? Are you choosing this one now?"

Before she answered, she glanced at the hidden camera on the nearby smoke detector that was recording all of this. Unfortunately, the red light was no longer on.

Marshall didn't wait for her answer.

"All those years you helped me with the voices, Grandma. Your talking therapy sessions and the meds. It was all under control, sure. But also, it was all never really gone.

"And *you* were the one who sent me to spend summers and breaks with Uncle Brick and the Revelator preachers at the communes. It was so amazing. They didn't question my visions. When I was with them, we just smoked pot and summoned the dJinni. One time, I asked Uncle Brick. He said you knew all about what they did there. He said you used to live there, too. He was the one who gave me that CD with all the footage of you as the Butterfly. And him, Hell-Rider. the Wild Bunch … all of you, fighting criminals. Super. Heroes.

"Sometimes they would take me on missions, too, y'know? And I don't mean preaching. There were guns. But I saw the future. I dodged the bullets just like you did!

"But I couldn't save Prince, could I?"

Marshall Lastpost shifted in his chair. He stares at the usual fixed spot on the floor as he spoke.

"You knew what SHE said to me, the Demi? One time, SHE said, 'You can go ahead and let the bullets hit you. It's okay; you cannot be killed.'"

Marshall slowly flipped his shades up and made eye contact with his grandmother.

"At first, I thought it maybe was part of my diagnosis. You know, the *God* voices. Jesus complex, right? I kind of thought that until recently, when I had my strongest vision. You know what that was?

"Your funeral."

Tears welled up in Marshall's eyes. "It was so *real*. Everyone was there. And you are lying there, in your coffin. So pretty." He cried without blinking.

"Butchie, is this really necessary? I mean, you have had many visions before …"

He ignored her. "Then it occurred to me. What if that wasn't what the Demi meant? What if SHE was sayin', 'You can go ahead and let bullets hit you … because someone else has decided you will remain alive'?"

"Butchie, stop this …"

"And so, I demanded from the Demi, I said to her, 'Show me exactly how my Grandma dies … if I kill her. Do I kill her?'"

Marian went silent.

"And you know what? SHE refused to show me. SHE refused!" There was no anger in his eyes, and his voice remained low, but his jaw opened as though it were a scream, "SHE had never done that, before."

"So, I went away for a long while and thought about it. And, finally, I hit upon an idea. I summoned HER again and said I would fulfill one mission for her if SHE would show me this one future. I explained what I wanted. And SHE agreed, even though she had to devote nearly all her top dJinni friends to it, SHE agreed."

Marian could only stare.

"And you know what, Grandma? It is now, Grandma. Right now is when you die. But, so, okay, so, before it happens …" Marshall blinked then, and the tears gushed down his face. "I needed to know why you did it. Why would you let my Prince, why would you let our sweet little boy die?"

Marian had held this conversation in her mind several times. Plenty of chances to rehearse. And she used to be an actor on stage before she was one for the government, for the Extirpacy. She took a deep breath. *Here goes.*

"Butchie. I am not the one who sees the future. That's you. And, in the past, you have convinced yourself that you and other agents of a higher power were players in a future that you had already created … and, somehow, the decision had come beforehand, Marshall. But it isn't real, Butchie. All these recordings, you staged them. Drugs were found in Brandon and Maggie's systems. And Wayne was drugged, too. A blow dart that didn't show up on camera.

"That's not to say it wasn't heroic. I was so proud of you. I still am! But magical? No."

This wasn't easy for her. She didn't like lying like this, but this had to be done.

She continued, "And Prince. Oh, hon … he … he just had a tumor in his brain. He was very, very ill. It was merciful the way you let him pass. It was just confusing to everyone the way you did it. It was concerning. So, Dr. Akhem had you recommitted until you could be treated."

Marshall just stared at her. *She is lying. Right to my face.* He knew this. It just took a very, very long time for him to process it. Then he suddenly gave his head a violent shake. "No. Re-educated, you mean. I saw all the Extirpacy patches on the security guards' sleeves, Grandma. You know what the Internet says. They make entire communities disappear, overthrow governments. You think they can't fake some evidence?"

She continued, "You have to believe me. Dr. Akhem is convinced— well, you fooled him with the remarkable coincidence about his grandson. Ever since that, ever since then, he's done everything he could do to protect you. He even released you just this week, even though you're obviously not— Look, yes, your Uncle Brick and I were quote-unquote *superheroes* a lifetime ago. But you aren't. Your hospice clients die just as they are supposed to. You are a schizophrenia survivor. Now, will you please turn off that light! It's in my eyes!"

Marshall complied, flicking off the little amber light that emanated from the tiny LCD mounted on the nose bridge of his flip-shades. He had pirated that tech long ago from one of her old Butterfly costumes and welded it to his flip-shades.

"I mean, as if! Think about it, Butchie. If you *were* a superhero, they'd have to call you the Precept. Because, in a future where your decisions have already predetermined everything, you'd be God."

At that, the entire room seemed to hang in a moment of déjà vu.

"Or *you* would," he said through his sobs, back to looking at the spot on the floor.

Marian tilted her head, disapprovingly. But she knelt beside him and put her hand on his shoulder, waiting patiently … so patiently. *No, I chose Butterfly, as in butterfly effect. I foresaw your coming, even then,* she thought. *To save the world, yes, you are going to have to be a killer, going to have to kill with your thoughts, as you say, just a few more times.*

They remained like this for an indeterminate amount of time. She hovered behind him, overseeing, as he regarded his choices. It was the metaphor for their entire relationship. The thought should've filled him with rage. But, instead, in his mind, he just saw the Mehkard's penlight and remembered what the voice, the new voice, HIS voice, told him to do.

But first, he needed to explain himself. She deserved that.

"The way I see it, Grandma, there are three choices. Either all of this is entirely in my head, there is no seeing futures or demons or any of it … and I am nothing but a madman killer. But I cannot believe that. I mean, well, if that was true, if that *was* it, well, first of all, I can hardly be held responsible … for any of it. I'm just crazy. But, second, I can just feel the truth."

Marian's shoulders sagged.

"Or *two*, you have the ability to control the future, and your vision controls. And so, if I kill you tonight … well, it's because you've chosen that, too."

Marian's shifted her weight between her feet, back and forth, back and forth. *Damn, why are my feet so sore?*

"Or, three, my visions are real, too. And I can also alter reality. I really can choose. But no matter what I think I do, as long as you might be the one really choosing, I cannot know whether or not it is me who did it or not, can I? It is a conundrum … unless I do kill you, kill you and see if I still can pick visions afterward. That would solve the riddle. I mean, right?"

She didn't react, her expression as unreadable as his.

"But, of course, I cannot do that, unless I really am just a killer with an illness." He flung his arms out wide like a little boy playing airplane. "So, the only way to prove the one also proves the other!"

"Well, you're just going to have to wait until I die naturally then, I guess, aren't you, Butchie?" That came off shriller than Marian wanted, but, after all, how was she supposed to feel? *Imagine him coming into my home and giving me all this talk. If he is gonna kill me, why didn't he just go ahead? In the old days, we didn't talk so much!* She was still pretty sure that was how this was going to go, but she was wondering how much longer it would be?

She was dying, anyway, of course. But there was no way Butchie could know that. No one knew, except a select few of the old gang. And the prognosis was that she still had a few months.

"No. There was another way, Grandma." He started crying more heavily. In between sobs, "It took me a long time to figure it out … you know, a long time. But I have all this power. So, it's theoretically possible. If you control enough dJinni, you can do just about anything. If you are crazy enough."

Wait, what was he was saying? For the first time since his arrival, she felt afraid. Her whole body ached so much she could hardly track what he was saying.

"It's not all that complicated, Grandma. There are a finite number of possible witnesses, so once you remove those—"

"Butchie, please, it's getting late. I'm so tired. Let's go to bed and talk about this in the morning, all right? I mean, you can stay, of course. Your old room is made up …"

Marshall continued, "You just pick a future where all of the witnesses die, too. Or are otherwise indisposed. I made sure the energy was from them, not me. I had the Demi pick some of the ones that were with Prince at his deathbed. Grandma? Am I a killer, Grandma? Or are you?"

That stirred her. She briefly grabbed his hand in hers before standing up straight as if to start performing. "No. Butchie. Listen to me. This is just Revelator talk; it's part of their religion. Maybe it was a mistake to let you spend so much time with them. But they are like my family. Anyway, they believe that they are summoning beings and praying through them and making deals with them … it's all very colorful. And, yes, through those prayers, I've seen people do amazing things. Is it God? DJinni? Dumb luck? Who knows? But as for the future? Well, there are always some who are false prophets, those who do like to pretend to be oracles, who say the future is set. But trust me, your future can always be changed. Always." She hoped that would be his takeaway. "Now, please, stay for dinner and overnight."

"No." Suddenly he stood up. He took a deep breath. "Ahhhhhh, okay. Yes. This was for the best. *SNIFF.* Less suffering for you. It was good. Good. Good, good, good. It was good to talk with you, Grandma. Um, goodbye!" And then he lunged into hugging her so hard she yelped.

But just as quickly he dislodged from her and rushed out, tears again streaming.

He threw the front door open and ran out through the swinging screen. By the time its wooden frame bounced back against the doorway, Marshall was long gone.

She stood there, on the throw rug in her front room, for the longest time.

Then she realized she was cold, and she went to close the front door.

That's when she saw them outside: Christmas lights.

In May? *Oh, my god. What has he done?*

They were across the street, draped from her neighbors' houses, in the distance, farther down the cul-de-sac.

And snow. It covered the long knee-high grass like a ratty, soft, white comforter.

No. No, no, no.

Her driveway was littered with mail overflowing from the box. She looked down at her porch to see a pile of newspapers from the delivery boy. A month's worth, or several? Maybe five? Seven?

She picked up a cancellation notice. There hadn't been any power to the house for months.

Then she clutched at the sudden pain in her chest, suddenly unable to breathe, and she understood.

Seven months of real time. And who knows how long within the bubble, without taking her chemo meds? *Wait until I die naturally*, indeed. Like Wile E. Coyote not falling until he looked down, the pain throughout her entire body was suddenly a hundred times worse.

This was how Marshall had avoided the paradox. He had altered time around them and let her die naturally. *It seemed he would kill me. But not like this. So, what now? Does this count? And if my vision really does fail? From what they showed me, he saves the world by defeating the Mehkard with the dJinni's help. So, now, what happens to everyone? Does this still mean he is the dJinni's chosen one now, or not?*

Her mind spun. *Or has someone else taken over? And what happened to everyone? Everyone? Everyone Happened? Everyone did what?*

Her mind spun as she crossed back inside, where the room was spinning, too. *But wait. Really, how was this even possible? I mean, in all those months, someone would have discovered*

No. He had explained it. He had said:

"It's not all that complicated, Grandma; there are a finite number of possible witnesses. So, once you remove those …" Then she looked back outside again, past the glare of the lights. And she saw one neighbor's body lying in his driveway. Another's was inside their car, the garage door still open. A pizza delivery car stalled in the middle of the street. *My God. What? A plague? Germ warfare? A strange confluence of coincidences? What in hell?*

Then she figured out who had done this. Marshall didn't think like this. But she knew who did. She knew who had taken over the future. Marshall's future—and hers.

What was left of it, she thought as she collapsed to the ground. Now her body blocked the open front door.

She leaned at the threshold.

And so, in the few seconds left to her, through the searing pain, as Ms. Marian Michaels sat against the doorway, she prayed. She prayed to the one behind this. For the first time, she foreswore saving the human race, foreswore the future. She even foreswore her own plans, laid out so many years ago. She simply prayed for Marshall's protection.

It was a perfect prayer.

Suddenly, the gas fireplace kicked on. In its very center, its little plastic yule log glowed amber cheer at the scene and the season, if not the reason. There was a rushing rumble of air from its black belly. *Oh, that's right, the propane had been prepaid through the year. How nice.*

Or maybe what she heard was her final breath, the rattle of all her choices tumbling out.

Either way, it sounded a bit like the word *no*.

PART NINE: THE END OF THE PRECEPT'S PROLOGUE

"I was running with joy on the demon's trail,
Though I knew what I hunted was no true God."

—Robert Frost,
"The Demiurge's Laugh" (excerpt)

###

The next day.

Inside his office, Dr. Akhem slowly loaded his belongings into an empty liquor box. The picture of his grandson was gently wrapped in a towel and placed in between some larger books. A coffee mug had *Je Ne Care Pas* written on it, while the stress pendulum sat loosely atop the pile, its work done for now.

"Where will you go?" said Marshall, from behind him in the doorway.

"You mean you don't already know?"

"I told you over the phone, I don't see futures anymore." Marshall stared at the floor between them. "Which means I was right about Grandma Marian. She was the one choosing the futures. She just chose one where all of my choices happen to be the ones she had already pre-ordained."

The doctor might not have heard the younger man over the sound of his paper shredder as he destroyed all his notes. "Okay, well … really, I go wherever I am most needed. With my luck, my next case is probably on the other side of the universe."

After the shredding, but before their ears stopped ringing, Marshall challenged, "I won't let you leave."

"Yet, I will be gone, nonetheless."

"I can't do this without you."

At that, the doctor paused. "Do what?"

"I am going to put an end to all of it."

Now, the doctor was intrigued. He turned and invited Marshall to sit down.

"Explain."

Marshall continued to stand. He towered over the elderly doctor, who looked at him from his ratty wingback chair. "Grandma was right. It's too much power. If someone can control the future … killing myself wouldn't help. Someone else will just come along."

"Go on."

Marshall paced back and forth in the doctor's office. His hands were firmly clasped behind his back. "The dJinni are the key. They show you the futures, if you're attuned to them. We have to stop using them altogether."

"Now, you sound like them." Dr. Akhem pointed up, meaning *corporate headquarters*, "The group who ran the hospice you used to work for, Marshall. The one that controls this place. The Extirpacy. The ones who hired me.

"Long, long ago, they wanted to capture your grandma. Just like they wanted to capture you. That is their mission: capture and re-educate. So that special people with abilities like Marian Michaels won't become a threat. She was already a hero, but once they found out she was a Choiciferor, they tried to get her. She escaped them, with the help of her friends, the Revelators, as you know.

"Look, Marshall, I have always been sympathetic to what Marian was doing. You had to be protected, just as she had been. They may have brought me here, but I don't have any illusions about the Extirpacy. And neither should you."

"No, Doctor. You misunderstand." Marshall paused and turned to look down at the other man. "I am not going to stop the Choiciferors, or the Revelators who protect them. No, I am going to stop the dJinni."

"Oh, and how are you going to do that? You cannot choose futures anymore. Isn't that what you just told me?

"I still kill with my thoughts."

Dr. Akhem's expression was unreadable unless you believed he could be proud.

"Marshall, I am glad to have met you. And I definitely hope you accomplish your goals. Believe me, you are not the first patient I have had who has wanted to kill their demons.

"I just wish I could be there when I see your full recovery. Anyway, checking yourself back in here was a good first step." Then he nodded to the two orderlies, who came up from just outside the doorway and led Marshall Lastpost, still wrapped in the modified straitjacket with his arms behind his back, from the office and back toward his room. But before they left, Marshall stopped them.

"W-wait, wait! Doctor. Listen, Doc! Before you leave, look in the box on your desk. There is a gift. For you." There was an unmistakable amber glint in his eyes.

The doctor got up and moved back over to his desk. He looked in the cardboard box and, sure enough, there atop the pile was something new. Instead of the stress pendulum, there was a single wooden block. And it had something written on the side. In tiny, tiny handwriting there was something. It was a haiku.

> *Time thinks for itself.*
> *But Minds leave life, flowers,*
> *next to a tombstone.*

The doctor stared at the writing for a very long time.

Then sounds of astonishment spun him around. The two orderlies were still standing there, but now they held nothing but empty space between them. They yelled, "Where did he go? What happened? He just disappeared!" But the good doctor ignored them.

He merely looked back at the block and held it aloft, this time seeing through all the possibilities, all the timelines. It was not a hand grenade, not his grandson's ear, nor a love note from Marshall's patient transference in a timeline where he was gay, not Marshall's flip-shades. No, and no, and it was not this, and no, not that either, a turtle? And so forth.

So precious, the kindness. And it had been the same with Marian's death. He didn't kill her. Rather, he just let it happen naturally. The future he chose was a long, pleasant visit where they were never interrupted … that localized *plague* in her neighborhood was nonfatal to the potential witnesses, and the accidents that disposed of the rest? Almost all of them were nonfatal.

On the other hand, he was rather ruthless with the Regnant. The good Doctor Akhem smiled to himself. But, after all, it's never possible to pick a future where *everyone* lives, just the more the better. Choices are important. Sparing the innocent is something to be proud of. He kills with his thoughts, yes, but people may also be saved with those same thoughts.

Choice and Command. Amid the timelines, there are those who are selected to be my champions, Dr. Akhem, the Mehkard, thought. *This Marshall Lastpost shall be my champion, a Champion of Life and Order.*

It is always important to find a champion in each timeline. A quick glance into the future of this one: *Is he actually wearing a cape? Or is that more of a burnoose?*

Then the doctor placed the stress pendulum back in the box and departed.

The Be(k)nighted

BOOK ONE—CHAPTER ONE

PALLA

Actually, I have already died, you know. In fact, I was born dead. Stillborn as it is aptly named.

Funny story about that (or at least no more horrific than the rest of Marshall's tale): in a small rural patch of India, I was conceived to a Dalit family. That is, in India's caste system, I was, entirely by virtue of my birth family, predetermined to live an existence of abject poverty and shame.

In India, the Dalit are not even considered a caste. They are below the caste system, without station, the *unclean*. They are to be ignored, never touched. The Dalit are the ones who work cleaning latrines and sweeping streets and handling all the materials of defilement (blood, excrement, and so forth) that are not to be touched, according to Hindu law.

But I had the last laugh. I died right away to avoid all that.

First, my mother reached the hospital while in labor, in the middle of a shift change. Due to a mix up, she was forgotten—unconscious and immobile—for most of a shift. Upon rediscovering her, they tried to find a heartbeat for me, but there was none. However, they couldn't do a C-section because I had already moved into the birth channel. So, they used forceps. Meanwhile, my neck had gotten caught in the umbilical cord, which served to cut off any remaining oxygen I might've gotten as I was extracted. I came out a pale, chalky blue-gray, unbreathing, and with no heartbeat. They tried to resuscitate me. Nothing. They decided I was dead (because I was, medically speaking). Dear old Mom (whoever she was) was alive but barely hanging on. They didn't have the heart to tell her about me. So, they literally put me in a box, y'know, for safekeeping.

But during the next thirty minutes, two things happened.

Mom stopped breathing and died.

And I started breathing on my own.

My story gets really tragic from there, because then it played out largely as it was supposed to. I was freely given, at the age of twelve, by my extended family to be a *devadasi* (i.e., sexual offering) to Yellama. So, spiritually, my servitude was to feed the Earth Goddess. But on this plane, my family got the equivalent of four hundred fifty dollars, and my body was now for the use of the Brahmin teacher who ran our village. He would pray and summon the spirit of the goddess to consecrate the very bed where he'd raped the other girls. He kept a rotating harem of such girls. That was my home for five more years until a search and rescue operation by the police from a nearby city. That mission was led by a missionary from my current employer.

Nowadays, only my eyes are light blue (to match the logo on my sharp *company* blazers). But that's because of my designer contact lenses. My skin and hair are milk and dark chocolate brown, respectively. The ID badge says my name is Palla Kalrajan. I am executive director of the Blue Rooks Foundation, which is the umbrella management organization of the Blue Rooks Church of Entropy and Revelation. ("Blue Rooksters Forever!" I mean, wouldn't that make a great football team name?)

Anyway, my title is more impressive than it sounds. In fact, my days consist mostly of being personal assistant to, and taking care of, the nearly octogenarian author (of bestselling self-help books) and founder of our church, one Bartholomew Richard "Brick" Reese. And he was the one who I was accusing of *killing me*, to catch you up.

"Stop being so dramatic. You millennials are a bunch of snowflakes," he scolded. The old man had meandered over to a dartboard, which was hung conspicuously next to the mantel. He held up the three darts he'd just plucked from the board and retreated, like a dueling cowboy. He was, per usual, shuffling about in his shiny black silk jammies, with a single cigarette dangling from his mouth. It wasn't lit. He often forgot to light them.

"Okay, first of all, *not* a millennial." I pointed to myself. "Generation X, thank you very much. I just happen to have good skin. Second, how much longer are they going to have to wait for your decision, Brick? Seriously. Eventually, the board—"

"The board can fucking sit and spin!" he said. *Thunk!* A dart hitting double twenty. He was full of piss and vinegar tonight.

I continued, "If you want to help the city with their bid to host the convention while at the same time delaying the event, we need to commit to reimbursement funds for the city," I said over his *thunk!* Double twenty. "And they needed an answer yesterday—ten yesterdays ago, to be exact." *Thunk!* One. "Honestly, I don't understand the hesitation …"

Brick got that weird, pained expression on his face every time we talked about the convention. But, full disclosure, the delay in decision-making was as much due to me as him. I hated talking with him about it. He was so back-and-forth. One day, gung ho to have it, then wanting to put it off indefinitely for some kind of tortured rationale.

"Palla, I told you, my hesitation is that our seers have already seen there is to be a *successful* terrorist attack at the convention. I mean, for spirit's sake, why host it when we know we can't protect everyone?"

"Didn't these same seers tell us the market was going to top out at eight thousand?" I asked.

"I'm not talking about the pretenders who do our media newsletters. I'm talking some actual Revelator priests, true sibyls."

"Okay. Okay." I mentally rolled my eyes and began pacing at the other end of the room, mirroring his movements unconsciously.

I was taken aback, even as I always am every time he starts in with all the magical-prayer, soothsaying mumbo jumbo. How could such a sharp man be so foolish with the religious stuff? Well, I guess, at some level it was comforting that he actually believed in the religion he started. "Okay, Brick, but if this is your final decision, then I have to stop stalling and just announce that's what we've decided. And then I will focus on damage control on all of our cancelled contrac—" The *CRASH!* interrupted me, and I looked around to see Brick on his backside, over a broken end table next to the sofa, behind which he'd been throwing from. "Brick!"

"Uhhhh, damn, damn. I'm okay ..." He gasped, trying to get his breath. "Wait! Okay, can I just get a chance to catch my breath?" I helped him to the couch. I looked him over, and there were no cuts, although he had some fresh bruises to go with the liver spots on his arms and back.

Once he caught his breath, he continued, "Look, just let me talk with the board tonight. In executive session." *That meant Revelator members only.* "Come later to the meeting. Trust me, Palla. There may be a deep divide on this one. Between the timelines. Big choice. Big choice."

Whatever. I wished I'd known what the hell he was talking about half the time. "Okay, Brick." I sighed. After a pause, "Anything else?"

"Clear your calendar for after the meeting, too. There may be a special assignment."

The board meetings generally went until 9:00 p.m., but there was no point discussing it. He knew as well as I did, I had no social life to interrupt. I agreed and tried to make some more small talk, just to normalize the evening. But it was too late. He fell into the chronic depression that always plagued him after his weak spells. "Damn drug," he muttered repeatedly as I tucked him into his chair under a throw by the fire. Hopefully, he would be fine after a good nap. Sometimes, the drug would kick back in after that. If not, I had better be prepared to conduct the meeting without him.

I wondered what special assignment he had in mind.

I stopped by my office and reviewed my messages with my assistant. I delegated the key communiques to my staff. And then I went home and changed into pajamas and retired to the bedroom, drawing the drapes, all as though I were actually going to take a nap.

I seldom fell asleep when I did this, but this daily afternoon pause, this de facto meditation, had been a part of my routine for as long as I could remember. At various times in my life, I have used back alleys, friends' lavatories, my car, overgrown foliage along highways, public washrooms ... even an abandoned drainpipe. I appreciated anywhere I could be alone and uninterrupted.

Wh-wh—hhmhph? I woke to my black cat, Sebastian, head-butting my cheek. *Oh. I must've dozed off.*

Sebastian was so smart. *Wake up, Mommy.* He had learned meows would be ignored, and bites would be punished with a random swat of my hand. But a headbutt? A warm headbutt was just gentle enough for the desired effect.

Like me, Sebastian was a Bombay. Although his short, shiny black fur made him invisible in the dim room, his caramel eyes glittered, nonetheless. He nudged me in the direction he wanted. *Get up, Mommy.* And again. *Time to get up.* I opened my eyes and met his simple gaze.

Food me.

So, I sat up, hunched on the bed, and grabbed the tiny bell that sat above my headboard. Sebastian knew what that meant. He left for the kitchen. Mission accomplished.

My bell rang an awkward *clernk* as I grabbed it. But once I cupped it properly, I launched a salvo of long, onerous mini-chimes. As each *ringggg* lifted into the air, I mentally recited the name of a young girl who was a *sister* back in my home village. They weren't sisters by blood but by circumstance. They had all been offerings … all been the chattel of the sex fiend who ran our village.

I had kept alive by manipulating both my sisters and the man who was our captor and master. I was a precocious child. Within months of being sold to him, I had demonstrated my worth by acting as his major-domo, running his household and personal affairs. And I did the same when it came to the *shows*: the auctions. I helped make various decisions, but one thing was constant: I always made sure that another of the girls, not me, was sold to one of the men from the city.

I also stayed clean of the opiates the others were fed. And I seldom was present for the actual rituals. But I do recall the times when I was there. I recall the eyes. Eyes in the darkness, watching and waiting. Like I was supposed to do something.

The rituals consisted mostly of me pledging my allegiance to my Master, and his friends and clients, all hidden in the shadows. I would then introduce them to the main entertainment. Then the other girls would enter. I passed around refreshments and drugs to the people closest to the stage.

The most remarkable thing was that he never actually raped me. Nor, for whatever reason, did he allow anyone else to touch me. It wasn't my young age, many of the girls were prepubescent. Later, after I flowered, I was told it was because I was ugly.

But I think it was because I was *cursed*. A couple of the neighbor boys tried to force themselves on me a couple of times, but they always met with a bad end. Bizarre accidents. Sudden disappearance. I never remembered details. I just assumed it was my Master who had them dealt with. When I thanked him, he took credit. Then I would go off and try to vomit up my shame. I was ashamed of how I gamed the system for my survival. I made myself his favorite. And all of those who weren't his favorite, they all suffered for it.

One of them, one of the youngest, Ahasa, she gave me this bell. She said I was her gift from the goddess, and that this bell was in return for the way I'd helped her and looked over her.

But, when it came time, I allowed her to be taken, just like all the rest.

I will never forget the look in her eyes as she was led away. I was only a child, but I felt responsible. Curse them all to make me feel responsible.

And so, each bell ring was my invocation. Each one was a prayer for forgiveness. Forty-eight rings. Forty-eight names. Forty-eight times asking for forgiveness. Tears filled my eyes in the mirror reflection beside the bed.

While the ringing sound of my shame still hung in the room, I wiped my face and took a deep breath. I got up and fed Sebastian. He rubbed an affectionate hug against my legs. *Oh, thank you, Mommy*, he trilled. He was very patient.

As he began eating out of his dish, I washed my hands and applied some of my CBD cream. I've never counted, but I apply it every time I touch anyone or anything. So, on any given day that adds up to … well, a lot of CBD cream. I use different brands, different scents. But, regardless of which I use, its smell reminds me of how my life has blessed me. Once my hands reeked of feces and ash, sex and death. Now, I live the very life of a goddess. I earn more of a wage in a day than my entire village did in a year. My lowest ranked assistant similarly lives the life of a king compared to most of the world.

Yes, religion was all a game. But just as the game could be played for evil, I decided it could also be used for good. So, that's my mission. Here. Now. With this church, how many others can I pull up? How many others can I save the way I was saved?

The Revelator who rescued me asked me if I saw the eyes in the darkness, the demons, during the rituals. She said she had done battle with them for me. And the Blue Rooks Church teaches those demons were to be dealt with, bargained with.

But I know better. We humans are the real demons. That's who we all need protection from: ourselves. If there are demons bargaining with us, they do it at their peril. External demons are perfunctory. We make our own monsters.

The question was never far from my mind. Our missions against human trafficking were a very real focus of the church. Could I ever save enough?

I had been hired to cleanse this organization of the scandal of its own sex cults inside its disparate congregations. And that work continued. My afternoon naps were bracketed by a similarly long overnight session of sleeping. And the rest of my hours that weren't spent watching over Brick, I devoted to saving all those victimized children. Somehow, I would find a way to save them all. I had confidence I could.

At least, I had a better chance of doing that than of keeping Brick out of trouble.

I took my time in the shower to clear my head. I didn't exit until I was finished. Maybe the board could start the meeting, but they couldn't finish it without me.

BOOK ONE—CHAPTER TWO

—Brick Reese, later a.k.a. "Hell-Rider" (upon meeting "The Wild Bunch," 1969)

"Step out, bro!"

Heychuck Langston Smith, the lay minister and stepbrother of Marshall, called Marshall out while he stood in the hallway. The hall that doubled as a local inner-city church sanctuary was outside the entrance of the second floor, which laid atop the Chinese restaurant. Marshall could never sneak up on his big brother, even back when they were kids.

"Hello, Heychuck." Marshall stepped from the shadows into the flickering light of the makeshift sanctuary. The entire room, and its reddish-tan painted walls, were dimly lit by a combination of candles sitting on the long plastic banquet table and the one fluorescent bulb in the ceiling fixture that still worked. "How have you been?"

"'Fine." *Except for the arm I can barely move*, he mentally amended. The previous night's job had been bumpy. Heychuck's reputation was usually sufficient to avoid actual violence. He made the rounds and collected the monies due. A routine, like a paper route, only one where he was delivering veiled threats instead of newspapers. Last night, one *customer* decided to sample his own stuff and hadn't come down yet when they met. So, he had to touch him up a bit to get his attention. He had used Romans 13:7 for emphasis: *Render therefore to all their dues: tribute to whom tribute is due; custom to whom custom; fear to whom fear; honour to whom honour.* He wondered if the guy would remember the citation when he woke up in the hospital.

Heychuck came by his ecclesiastical knowledge honestly. He was a certified lay minister at the nondenominational community ministry located atop this Chinese restaurant in Seattle's International District. The building was a long, skinny, faded brownstone in between two different book company's warehouses, located near the I-5 and I-90 exchanges.

But lay ministry wasn't what paid the bills.

Marshall held up a sack. "I brought you some soup, Heychuck, from downstairs."

Heychuck Smith stood up and took it without saying thanks. As he sat down at the table, he asked, "Hey, bro, you got the time?"

Marshall smiled wanly but didn't answer. Nor did he check his watch like he used to do as a child. Every wristwatch Marshall ever wore always eventually stopped. Even the digital ones. It didn't matter what kind. No one could explain it.

"Man, you used to always fall for that," said Heychuck. "'Cause you're not too bright, right?"

Marshall's internal voices echoed their agreement as Heychuck began eating his soup. Marshall joined Heychuck at the table, despite his brother's warning glare.

Heychuck Smith had been through so many foster homes in King County that his real name was lost in the records. As a toddler, he sort of idolized one of the older children named Chuck. He would follow Chuck 24/7 like a puppy dog and say "Heychuck" so often that all the kids, and even that set of foster parents, started mocking him by calling him that. And thanks to a mistake in one social worker's paperwork during a transfer, it stuck. Now, it was his legal name. He liked it, too. In fact, he went to court to make sure of that.

"What the fuck do you want, bro?"

"I just wanted to let you know I am leaving town for a while … a few weeks."

"Told you last time, I'm not watchin' y'damn turtle."

"He is coming with me."

Heychuck wiped some spilled soup from his lip and onto his long bushy beard. He was dressed in several layers of sweaters and hoodies. His jeans had holes on the knees and butt where the thermal underwear was visible.

"Before I go. I … have a confession to make."

If Heychuck cared one way or the other, he didn't show it.

Marshall continued, "I, well. Um, I … you remember the explosion, right?" Heychuck's eyes flared as he stared in response. "Well … Heychuck, I think it was my fault. Technically. Sort of. Look, I had you take me out of the house to get some candy. But that was just a trick. Really, it was because— You know of my voices, right?"

"You mean the ones you don't hear any more?"

One or two of them popped up to dispute that in Marshall's head. *I know*, he told them, *let's go here*. "Well, no, that is not correct. Sometimes I do. Still. Yes. But, well, here is the thing: some of them are real. And some of them can make things happen. You know what I mean?"

"The fuck?" The older man squinted at Marshall.

"Okay. So, there are real … beings who talk to me. And they told me our parents were going to die, but they said I could choose which way they died. I was just a confused kid … I didn't know any better. I thought I had to choose. So, I did."

Heychuck just sat and looked at him.

"These beings … they told me to take you out of the house … so you wouldn't be hurt, too. Then they caused the leak and the explosion. It was painless. Painless for Jesse and Gertie. You know, M-mom and Dad."

Heychuck just kept looking, blinking. Something like sadness seemed to wash over his angry eyes.

"That was the key … all the other ways they were going to die were more painful. But this way, no pain. I was just a kid … say something … please."

"They caused the leak? You mean *you* did. You killed Mom and Dad?"

"No. I mean, yes. I kill with my thoughts … the dJinni, they take my thoughts and make them happen. Look, I had to choose …"

Heychuck sat and processed this for a minute. "You crazy mother… What if I told you some genies wanted me to kick your ass right now, hm?" He stood up so suddenly, the smaller man fell off his chair.

It is so strange not knowing what people are going to do! Marshall thought. In the past, he had gotten used to reflexively letting the *others* give him hints of visions of the future all the time. It wasn't always easy to sort the ones from the *others* from the ones that came from himself, via his illness but, eventually, he figured out that usually he could by the *specificity.* When a voice or a vision was really from the *others* entire scenes would play out … and it usually involved conflict. Something bad happening. So, that meant that, if he was going to have any kind of altercation, he would always get some kind of advance preview of it. And when he summoned his *chi* he could pick and choose, to avoid that happening.

But now there were no more previews.

Heychuck's having been ordained via an online certification a few years back had done nothing to check his innate aggression. As he stood over Marshall, he displayed the cold, angry muscle memory of an executioner.

Marshall nodded. "You should kill me," he said matter-of-factly.

That broke Heychuck's rage for a second, and he rebalanced backward. "Why you tellin' me this now?"

"I wanted … Heychuck, I want your blessing. I plan to make it so no one can ever do that sort of thing again. No more voices showing me, or anybody. That's my plan. But … before I do that, I wanted to give you the chance. It's up to you. I made a choice for you all those years ago. You had been with them longer than me. They really were Mom and Dad to you. And you have never been the same since. I made that choice, and it hurt you. But had they died those other ways … I figured then it would have hurt you, too … but I always thought you would be okay."

"Okay? You crazy sonofabitch. My life. Without Mom and Dad … Dude, your voices aren't real, bro. Damn! You killed them. You deliberately killed our parents for no reason!"

"No. There was a reason … they were dJinni, demons. You believe in them, right? You are a reverend …" But Marshall knew better than to say anything else. He had already said too much. He thought he would probably be killed now.

Good! You're guilty, voices intoned in his mind. Marshall felt completely vulnerable as an involuntary shudder ran through his mind. *Is this how everyone else feels all the time?* he asked the group. *Is everyone else always afraid of the future?*

The chorus answered in their own way. *People aren't stupid like you. Yes! They only see now, not out to the ends of their lives. Life is short.*

Regardless, even if Heychuck chose to kill him, he figured Heychuck deserved that choice. Everyone did. That was the point. No more clerics making other people's choices for them.

But the larger man didn't harm him. At the sound of the word *demons,* Heychuck remembered himself, his calling. He turned his back and walked over to the podium next to his desk.

Marshall's chorus: *He wants you to leave. Don't turn your back; it isn't safe. He's got a gun under that stand! Yeah, a funny gun, with a flag that says,* Got the Time? *Making fun of you, see? Made ya' look. Stupid!*

Heychuck stood there looking at the large mural on the wall behind the podium. It wasn't professional quality, but it wasn't bad, either. Marshall noticed it, too. He could make out Jesus, and Mary, and what looked to be Samson, pushing over some columns. And, on one side, there was a large caricature of Michelangelo's *Hand of God* pointing to a bright white spot in the tapestry of colors, wherein a quote was written on the wall, with a thick black Sharpie:

> *I know thy works,*
> *that thou art neither cold nor hot:*
> *I would thou wert cold or hot.*
> *So then because thou art lukewarm,*
> *and neither cold nor hot,*
> *I will spew thee out of my mouth.*

> —Revelation 3:15–16

Finally, Heychuck said, while still facing away, "You know, at least you've got your voices. You left me with no one."

Marshall stood mute. For some reason, he glanced at his watch again.

Then Heychuck turned around. "All that time we, I mean, Mom and Dad, spent trying to help you with your schizoid shit … and then? They were just gone! Guilty by reason of insanity. Everyone knew you set the leak. But to hear you confess it like, like you actually have an excuse—it's just that I wasn't expecting that.

"But I blamed myself, you know. I saw you playing near the oven earlier that night. I should've known! I should've smelled the gas! Years. I blamed myself." He remembered silently for a moment: drug addiction and juvie, release, relapse, inpatient treatment (twice), and sure, finally, he found God. But part of him always doubted. *Probably only 'cause God didn't see me first.*

"I mean, I eventually stopped hating you. But I wasn't going to be responsible for you anymore. Fuck that."

Marshall pleaded, "Look, Heychuck, I want to stop it. I want to stop all those … beings being able to do that anymore. No more showing futures. No more people like me choosing. But, before I did, I just wanted to tell you, you know, what I was doing. And know that you approved, somehow."

Heychuck looked at his stepbrother like he could *not* have possibly been more disappointed. "Okay. Now you've told me. So, you can go. Go on! Get the fuck out of here." Then he thought, *If he kills someone else, maybe I can give him up in exchange for something else from the police, in case I get caught for something.* "No, wait! Wait, what are you going to do? Where are you going?"

Looking at the floor, where a spot of soup had spilled, Marshall replied, "I'm going to visit some extended family near Chicago. They have special … specialists there, who will help me with all this vision business. You have to believe me. I just wanted your blessing."

"My blessing, hunh?" Heychuck walked up to Marshall and looked down at the shorter man. *Deliver me, I pray thee, from the hand of my brother, from the hand of Esau: for I fear him,* he thought, instinctively leveling the threat. But, instead, he said, "Okay. I give you this. John 15:2: Every branch in me that beareth fruit he taketh away: and every branch that beareth fruit, he purgeth it, that it may bring forth more fruit."

Marshall nodded and repeated, "That it may bring forth more fruit," imitating his brother's voice as well. Heychuck rolled his eyes, as he always had mixed feelings about being mimicked by Marshall.

Marshall asked, "What does it mean?"

"It means those followers of God who aren't doing what they're supposed to will be cut off, so those who are left can better succeed, like pruning dying vines."

Marshall nodded and quickly left, saying he still had a plane to catch and that Uncle Brick had summoned him. But there was one more stop for him to make. He would stop by home first, and then the next visit would also be his ride.

After Marshall left, Heychuck reflected as to the rest of the lesson. The part he left out. The verb that translated to *taketh away* also meant *to lift up*. So, one should first at least *try* and prop up the vine to the sunlight and nurse it to health before removing it.

But he was too angry to lift Marshall up. He couldn't even lift himself up.

He reached into his pocket and clutched the greenies he'd confiscated the previous night and wondered if the pain of this world would ever stop.

###

The large, long limousine pulled up smoothly to the curb and parked. As Marshall approached, he noticed the image of the Needle, along with the several ubiquitous construction cranes downtown being reflected, upside-down like a Pollock painting, on its black roof.

The driver got out and opened the nearest back door, and Marshall ducked inside.

Across from the bench seat, there were two people. The first one he noticed was a voluptuous blonde in a short white dress and a heavy fur coat. Her cleavage featured a large pendant of emerald gems set in silver.

Beside her was Marshall's last appointment before he left town.

This man looked for all the world like a Beverly Hills hipster from 1985. His jumpsuit, gathered at the waist and ankles with elastic was navy blue, with barely liminal black and silver pinstripes. His collar was open at the chest and flared beside his head. His jumpsuit slacks hung loosely like basketball sweats. Like Marshall when he brought his flip-shades down, this man also wore sunglasses. But these shades were more like a stylized ebony visor, of angles and inclines, tailored to cover the eyes from any angle.

This man radiated *power.* Not the kind of power of the dJinni. No, this man radiated the utter confidence of having his instructions followed without hesitation or insolence. He was some sort of higher up at the government agency Dr. Akhem always talked about, the Extirpacy. In the past, the doctor had referred to this man, with no small measure of reverence, as the Agency's Visiting Analyst.

Out of the blue, the Visiting Analyst's secretary had called Marshall just after he left Dr. Akhem's office and offered him a job interview. Killing two birds with one stone, Marshall agreed—provided they would drive Marshall to the airport, too. They agreed, offering to actually have the interview en route.

Now, all together in the car, to Marshall's surprise, it wasn't the Analyst who spoke, it was the beauty. Her face was buried in a manila folder. "Mr. Lastpost, first name, Marshall. Age twenty-five. Has an extensive history of ... criminally insane behavior. He has been committed for inpatient mental health treatment numerous times. Diagnosis: paranoid schizophrenia, early onset. He believes he has ..."—she looked up from the folder as she closed it—"powers." She spoke to the Analyst, not Marshall.

But then, "Mr. Lastpost, welcome. My name is Brianna Carson. And I would like to ask you a few questions. Do you know what job you are interviewing for?"

"No." Her breasts were enticing, to be sure. But her legs contained the message. The stockings she wore, their marble pattern showed hieroglyphs. He knew the message, but if the light was better, he could confirm it ... *Get out! She'll kill you. They want something. It's too late, now ... now or never, never get in a car. Stranger Danger. Danger, Will Robinson!* Even though the car was climate controlled, Marshall's back sweated, and drips formed all around the trace of his hairline.

"Of course you don't." Brianna continued, "We are interested in recruiting you for our Exorcism Task Force. Do you know what that is?"

That word centered him. "Exorcism. Is that still done? Like in the movies?" *Aw, no. They can't get rid of us! You can't either. Stupid!* Marshall shook his head to the accusation only he heard.

She utterly ignored the question. Instead, she asked another. "Are you on medication right now, Marshall?"

"I've been out of my meds for a while."

Then she seemed to lose interest altogether. She took out a phone and texted someone. They all sat there. Suddenly, the car started to pull away. Marshall hoped it was toward the airport. But he didn't mention it.

Now the Analyst spoke. "Your last name. The word *lastpost* means *nuisance* in the Netherlands."

Marshall didn't know what to say to that. He had learned from dealing with bullies in high school that sometimes the best response was none. The hairs on the back of his neck told him this was one of those instances.

Then the Analyst stated another non sequitur, "The sunny season in Seattle is just about over. Five months of non-stop sunshine in a city known for rain. Best kept secret in the continental US, don't you think?" Marshall again didn't answer.

Finally, the Analyst took off his expensive sunglasses and met Marshall's gaze. He had a faint scar down one cheek, but his blue-steel stare was friendly, if vaguely condescending. "So, what can we do for you, Marshall? We're already taking you to the airport, as you can see out the window. And you have an interest in, shall we say, exotic demonic interactions. So, the good doctor thought it only natural we keep you in the fold. A man of your talents can be useful."

"What do you know about my talents?"

"Well, you seem to have a real knack for disrupting video equipment." His smile was profound.

No one will look for your body. Why are the windows tinted? He's in the mob. You're being kidnapped. Nobody knows where you are. Marshall looked away, ill at ease. His flip-shades were up, but he kept sneaking glances from over them at the beauty, Brianna. Marshall didn't get to see that many gorgeous women all made up and up close like that. *She'll have sex with you and kill you, like a spider. That's how it works. Does your dick even work? All work and no play.*

She was still engrossed in her phone, a small smirk on her face at whatever she was reading.

When Marshall looked back at the Analyst, he momentarily locked in on the deep blue eyes and the perfect jaw, framing a sharply pursed mouth with a timely five o'clock shadow around it. Then the Analyst repeated his smile. And while his eyes narrowed, the eyebrows up-ticked understanding and wisdom. *Yes, this is a man you can trust,* said that smile. Plus, he looked familiar. Marshall had probably seen him on television or the news. He was a celebrity, maybe.

"No, I control time," Marshall corrected him, "and I speak to demons."

"Of course you do. So, that's right in line with what our organization does. You see, our part of the government, we find special jobs for special individuals like you. If you have a special skill, there is no reason you should be working as a home-healthcare aide and only helping one at a time when you could be helping … what, hundreds? Or more, all at once, as part of our team? You see what I mean?"

The younger man nodded, even though he didn't.

"Would you like to hear more?"

"Yes, please."

"Fine. I know you are going to be leaving town … er, uh, don't you have anything to pack besides that?" And the Analyst pointed at Marshall's black jacket.

Somehow, the man had figured out what you had hidden in your jacket. Maybe he saw movement. So, Marshall produced Little Rich from inside his jacket. His own smile flickered on for a second at the sight of his pet.

"No, he is all I need."

"Very good. I will see to it that you have a pet carrier in the seat next to you for this flight. We've chartered the flight, you know. Brianna?"

"Carrier. I'm on it." She texted something, but she glanced at the reptile with obvious disgust. Marshall's heart sank a bit.

"Why did you pick me?"

"You tell me you control time and speak to demons, and you have to ask why you were picked?"

Marshall found that logic to be sound. But in a wave of just-enough candor to make his pitch believable, the Analyst added, "Plus, you have access to the Blue Rooks Church in a way we could never have."

"What do you mean? Why do you care about Uncle Brick's church?"

"Ah! Well, that so-called church and the cult behind it, even your famous UncaBrick, they have a lot to answer for, Marshall: Tax evasion, illegal labor camps, children put in harm's way on armed missions, weird scientific experiments with kids. You have seen the stories, right?" He nodded, and Marshall nodded along.

"Some say there are demonic rituals taking place. And you have witnessed that, too, haven't you?" Marshall had to keep nodding.

"And when you were there, as a minor, were you or were you not exposed to potential dangers? Doesn't that constitute negligence for a child's safety, a form of child abuse?"

Marshall, of course, wanted to argue, but he couldn't. It was true. Another nod.

"Now, not everyone there is a criminal, we know that, but several of them have active warrants for their arrest that predate even their formation of the church. Did you know that?"

Marshall's dead expression stared for a moment. Then he slowly lowered his head in shame. *When you put it like this ...*

"So, all of this is to say ... yes. Marshall, that is *precisely* what we want you to do. We plan to arrest the Revelators. And we want your help."

And now, Brianna smiled at him, too. Marshall thought he saw her lick her lips just like his turtle did from time to time.

She waited for the right answer, no doubt.

Later, after the chartered return flight to DC, the Analyst returned to his lodgment, rolling in about 8:00 a.m. the next morning. He hadn't slept. He never could sleep while traveling.

"Honey, come to bed! I missed you!"

Since she yelled from the other end of the hallway, she was shielded from view of the eye roll. "Be there soon, honey!" The Analyst of the

Bureau of Indigenous Security Enhancements was in no hurry. He could hear the alcohol in her voice. She had started early this morning. She would be asleep again very soon whether he came to bed or not.

He sat the broken wristwatch down on the chest-o-drawers in the foyer. It was an exchange he suggested to the Lastpost boy right before he exited the limo.

> *"The doctor told me about your broken watch. Most employees only get a gold watch after many years of service. But I will give you one ahead of time. Here, take this gold pocket-watch … there, that's it. It latches right onto there, sure, yes, use the buttonhole. Good. Now, it goes right in there. There! How does that feel? I guarantee that it won't stop on you. Ever. All I ask is that you keep it on you at all times, okay? Can you do that for us?"*
>
> *Marshall took it and hesitantly exchanged the old one. "So, this is a tracking device?"*
>
> *"That's right, Marshall." The Analyst had lied to the boy. And then he gave him his Extirpacy badge and told him it would gain him access to the Agency headquarters, or any Agency facility, really.*

He had kept his composure. His Master was correct to admonish him right before the meeting. It was everything he could do to keep his rage in check, seeing the Lastpost boy again.

After what that insignificant boy had done to him, no revenge would be too great. But that meant he could wait … until he could exact it in the *greatest possible* way.

He finished his routine bedtime ablutions and started to retire, but before leaving for the bedroom, he picked the watch up again and regarded it. He pored over every scratch, every nick. The cheap name brand, the cartoonishly visible gears there for decoration, the peeling paint. And as he stood there, the shadows gathered around the Analyst in no particular order. As more and more of them arrived, the lights of the room continued to exist but, nonetheless, gave way to the darkness, like a black-lit scrabble walkway in a darkened theater.

Pretty soon, the darkness was the light.

Is that his? one of them, their leader, finally asked.

The Analyst did not answer. Not because he hated their leader, although he did. No, he was lost in memory. He just turned the broken wristwatch over in his hand, again and again, forcing the immobile hands inside the compartment to move, around and around, resembling the orderly act of measuring time, but really just tumbling along, and alone, across the dimensions like someone who had been banished to a chaotic, timeless torpor.

BOOK ONE—CHAPTER THREE

PALLA

###

I stepped with grim purpose toward the building. Board meetings always put me off.

"Good afternoon, ma'am," Brad the security guard said as he held the door for his boss's boss's boss's boss.

"Hello, Brad. How're the kids?" I put my purse onto the belt and emptied my jacket pockets, even my bell, into the plastic bowl before I placed it on the belt as well.

The banal conversation tumbled mechanically through the inevitable platitudes about Christmas shopping as I grabbed my purse off the belt and proceeded through the outer gate onto the grounds.

As always, the courtyard was populated mostly by professional landscaping. The various walls of trees throughout the courtyard were pleached so obviously that their verdant beauty had somehow been transformed into a tacky maze of insecure pretension.

The building itself was old stonework from a century ago. It used to be a bank. The doors were heavy, multilayered glass, with thick, square wooden planks for handles, bolted with ridiculously large rivets. I pulled the first one open and the second one shuddered in anticipation.

In the foyer, the smell of dust and lemon cleaner welcomed me to the headquarters before yet another security person did the same with a wave. *Ugh.* This time I just waved back and walked to the side stairwell rather than engage.

Yep, I was in a mood, all right. My dress shoes were in my purse, but I thought I might leave my tennies on for this meeting. *Screw 'em,* I thought as I lunged up the stairwell.

###

Two hours later.

"And that is all I have," I said, my signal that the board meeting was over, as I closed the binder and reached inside my bag for my CBD cream.

After a Robert's Rules motion to adjourn, Brick said, "Thanks, everybody. Have a good weekend. Palla, if I might have a moment." He was using his professional-timbre voice for the benefit of most of the directors, but I could tell from his lack of boisterousness during the meeting that his energy had not fully recovered.

As the room cleared out, including even the Revelator members, I scooted down from the opposite end of the table and sat in the chair two away from him.

"You remember me telling you about my godson, Marshall?"

Here we go. I nodded, suspiciously.

"He is arriving at the airport in two hours. I would like you to meet him there."

"That's what this is all about? Now, I am a chauffeur slash babysitter?

"He is no baby. Do not make that mistake. Although his manner is sometimes a bit simplistic. I mean, he has issues."

"Of course, I remember the stories." *And read the file.* "But—" Now, we talked over each other.

"But that's all. But he was also a member of the Revelators. He's done as much mission work as most of the active members you know, even though he was only a teen at the time."

"I don't think I'm really equipped. I mean, you have drivers, and personal—wait, you sent him on missions as a child?"

At that, Brick shut up, his face an expression of regret.

I went in for the kill. "So, in the middle of a half-dozen child endangerment lawsuits, you decide it's a good idea to have your CEO hobnob with opposing counsel's star witness? You are insane if you think—"

"Look. It's Marian, damn it! She's dead." He blurted it so fast I almost missed it.

"I am going to …" And then I stopped. While I stared, my brain shrunk in my head, and my eyes refocused on a spot somewhere inside me. I couldn't talk.

"Palla, it's true; she's gone. She'd had cancer, I am told."

I sat and thought. I instinctively reached my greasy hand inside my jacket pocket for my bell, clutching it for strength. All those years ago, the lead agent of the team that extracted me, the mission leader had, of course, been Marian Michaels, in full butterfly regalia no less. To this day, the houses in all the villages for miles around still decorate their front doors with butterfly designs in memory of her.

In those early days after the rescue, it was not only Marian's strength but her kindness that gave me the emotional compass to guide me from my old life to an entirely new one. Later on, she took me in and gave me a home, if only for a short time.

I called her Amma (pronounced ah-*MAY*), which meant *mama*, and also *elder woman* in my local tongue. Marian liked that.

Choking back tears, I asked, "How long have you known?"

"Known?" He leaned on a chair for emphasis, the word *was* a loaded one.

"You know what I mean, damn it."

"I was told it was coming up months ago. She had a cancer."

"Yeah, you said that. Why am I just now hearing this?"

"There was a chance that … the cancer wouldn't have gotten her. She didn't want to worry you. Neither did I." He stood up at and leaned over the table. And, so help me, for all the world, his head bobbled loosely and drooped on his neck like a damn marionette. I had seen him at his worst any number of times, but now, for the first time, I suddenly noticed his breathing. The way his chest never fully compressed, but it just bounded on the surface.

He didn't look like the former superhero and religious leader, media icon of his time. He just looked to be a very, *very* old man.

But I was a trained JD. So, I also read something else in his voice.

"No. That's not it. You've always known. This was it, wasn't it? This was the long game you two cooked up all those years ago. And the convention is caught up in it, too, isn't it? It's all about your schizophrenic godson isn't it?"

At that, he locked eyes with me. I'd seen that look before, that mixture of anger and pride. He forgot how smart I was sometimes, until I showed up several steps beyond him on something. Suddenly, he stood up straight and walked directly to the nearest door. Then, with a sigh, "Yes and no. A lot changes over time. But the basic idea is the same."

"And what idea is that?"

"That you and your brother, Marshall, really need to get acquainted."

Before he reached the door, he stopped, turned on his heel like a much younger man (*his energy was kicking in, again)* and put this out there, "And don't make that mistake, either. He isn't just a schizophrenic any more than you are just an orphan. It's only that he hears voices … and it's really important that he hears yours."

"Important … to you?" I challenged.

"To the church."

"Fine, fine. You had me at airport. I mean, who doesn't enjoy that ride?" I snarked.

"Oh no, you have to drive it. Take a nondescript company car. Pay tolls. The whole bit. You know, 'cause you weren't wrong about the star witness bit."

I got up and took the crook of his arm to join him in exiting the room. "Brother, huh? I never had a brother."

"Well, Marian did largely raise him."

"As she did you. Tell me, is he as annoyed with you being a total jackass all the time as I am?"

"Oh, you bet. And then some."

BOOK ONE—CHAPTER FOUR

3:00 a.m., six hours later.

Brick sat up in bed. He gracefully pulled the CPAP mask from his face and hung it on the bedpost as the machine shut down. Taking the moment to look around the shadowy bedroom, he appreciated the quiet. The air was chilly, but that was mostly from the ceiling fan evaporating his night-sweat-soaked pajamas.

A lifetime of metabolizing and remetabolizing the after-effects of the Q-47 serum he'd been dosed with as a young man had done a real job on his liver. Night sweats were just part of the deal.

He leaned up to get to the bathroom. This was trip number four this evening.

HellFuck'n'Fire, anyway.

Mechanically, he relieved himself and exited the bathroom. Its lights turned off as he left it, and he chuckled, suddenly reminded of an old joke. The punchline was, "Dad, you're peeing in the fridge … and it has to stop." His eyes took a second to adjust, then he shuffle-skidded his footsteps so not to accidentally step on one of his cats. *Where were they, anyway?* Normally, there was at least one on the bed with him, but not tonight.

It was a big old house. They were probably chasing spiders.

He sat back on the bed. Tomorrow, Marshall came home. *His guy.*

Brick's chest swelled with pride thinking about his godson. He glanced at the hand-drawn picture of himself and the other Revelators that hung over his bed. Even in the dark, he could make out the white pitchfork symbol on his helmet in the picture. Marshall had drawn it for him on his birthday many years ago, when Marshall was still a child and cared about birthdays. The picture was a copy of *The Last Supper* with Brick at the center. "For my Godfather," he had written as a caption on the side. Those were good times.

It helped to think of that instead of being overwhelmed by the sadness. The other seers, besides Marian, amongst his friends predicted many things, many different visions, but for months and months, they all agreed on one thing being locked in: Marian would die on the date two days ago. Her body would be discovered today (along with all the other victims along her cul-de-sac) and identified by the authorities in about a week.

Despite his trust in fellow Revelator Choiciferors, he grabbed his phone and dialed her again. No answer—again. Her husky voice on voicemail—again. He cancelled the call rather than leave another message.

He teared up each time he heard her voice.

He also knew he should put the local authorities on it for a wellness check, but no. What was done was done. She knew what she wanted. Had known, he mentally corrected the tense.

If anyone had, she had.

Right now, Brick just wanted to focus on the positive. Marshall had texted him earlier that day that he was getting on the plane, en route.

Brick was worried about whether their plan, or his plan, any damn plan, would work. He thought about the old days, with the Wild Bunch. And later, as the Revelators. They were always so cocksure. But he was anything but sure these days.

He had turned it all over and over in his mind for years, decades! *In the end, I just wasn't strong enough.* That's what it came down to. *Damn old drug.*

With all his money. With all his powers. *They called me a super-hero! But* I *never did. I just called myself Hell-Rider, 'cause come hell or high water, I would make it work. And, for a while, I did.* Brick remembered gaining allies. Building a following, and then a church, training new Revelators, saving people from other false religions and cults.

But what did it all come to? His own church doing some of the same things.

Still not enough. HellFuck'n'Fire, 's'never enough.

Damn old drug.

He also refrained from the other call he wanted to make. He wanted to call the Extirpacy again, for the umpteenth time, and ask if they'd finished the goddamn *new* drug, yet?

But he managed to let that rest, too. He didn't feel like dealing with that jackass VA.

Instead, he just let his head fall back onto his pillow as he thought about the future.

Tired of not being strong enough.

BOOK ONE—CHAPTER FIVE

PALLA

###

Same time, O'Hare Airport.

At first, I didn't know it was him. He just caught my eye because he was so odd looking, the skinny bum skidding slowly down the terminal walkway, sort of ricocheting off the wall again and again as he walked, like a moth on a billboard.

The mise en scène was a bit comical. He wasn't just eschewing the mechanized, free-moving walkway on the far left, he was hugging the far-right wall, avoiding even the others who walked on their own, down the middle. Even those folks walking solely under their own power moved much faster than him.

He stopped several times to study an empty spot on the wall, in between two works of art. Just strange. Eventually, I just sensed this must be him.

He was still maybe thirty yards away when I saw him take out his cell phone and start talking into it. Maybe he was supposed to call me? But when I reached for my phone in anticipation, I saw that his was … round? A CD Walkman? No, I didn't see any headphones, so?

A turtle. He was talking to a turtle.

As he got closer, I noticed he looked much, much older than his age. An unshaven, angular jaw and curly, dark mullet framed a large-eyed face. Fortunately, I got to see him smile a lot at this turtle before he noticed me watching. He had a big smile, and, despite the thin face, he had rubber cheeks that emphasized whatever direction the corners of his mouth pointed. This was nice for me to see because, in all our time to-gether in the years afterward, I seldom got to see that. During smiles, his eyes remained sad, like sunshine during a rainstorm. Even so, those rare smiles lifted my spirits years later when it would matter most.

He looked at me as he approached. When he got close enough to hear, I said, "Hi, my name is Palla Kalrajan. I work for your Uncle Brick."

He stared at my offered hand for a moment before approaching and taking it. "What do you do for him?"

"I run his company, the one that oversees all the churches," I answered truthfully.

"It is funny. The people you run into at the airport," he mumbled to his feet.

It took me a second to realize he'd cracked a joke. He didn't seem to realize it, either; his delivery was so awkward.

"I am supposed to drive you to your hotel. C'mon." I turned and walked toward the parking lot, and he followed.

"How is my uncle?"

"He's all right." I changed the subject because I just realized he might not know about Miss Michaels, and I didn't want to be the one to tell him.

"How was your flight?"

"No casualties."

Now that was definitely a joke. So, he *was* funny. Maybe this wouldn't be so bad.

"Well, if you don't count my Grandma Marian," he continued.

I slowed my walking and turned back around, backpedaling, trying to think of what to say.

"Or the others I had to do away with. But I have a new life now, a new path. No more killing."

And then he smiled, the first time he smiled *to* me. Okay, so a small correction: the *very first time* he smiled to me, it was terrifying. It was *the rest of them* that were rainy sunbows, or whatever the hell I said.

Honestly, my mind raced. *Omigod, Brick. Did you just assign me to chauffeur some kind of psychopath?* I mean, I had read his file, I knew his background. But everyone in the Revelators spoke of him as this wonderful, innocent child who had suffered through a tremendous illness and who wasn't responsible for any of the deaths around him … not really. I didn't always track their religious apologetics, but I knew at least they wouldn't condone murder.

What in the fucking world was I supposed to do with him now?

I must've been gaping. "I can see I have upset you. I should explain. I did not kill anyone, not really. Well, except the dJinni. But for the humans, I just controlled Timespace, and they died, naturally. If I had a whiteboard, I could—"

"COULD YOU JUST wait right here a moment, hm? I will be right back. Just gonna go, go to the washroom. Okay? Thanks!" And I shuffled around the corner to make a call.

Brick's phone went straight to voicemail. So, I called one of his closest friends. One of the original Revelators.

"Yeah, Palla," said Reverend Slink Paxton. Of all the original Revelators, "Slinker" had been the one around the most in the years when Marshall had spent summers with them all. And he was a night owl.

"Reverend. I think I need help. Brick's nephew … he just told me he killed people."

"You read the file. That is part of his illness, his hallucinations." He could tell by my lack of response I needed more. "And even if it were true, look, you know the types of missions we used to go on. We've all employed our fair share of violence. I can tell you this: Marshall is a good boy. If he hurt somebody, or worse, he had reasons. It would have been self-defense."

"He mentioned Marian is dead. Like he knew about it. Or did it. And there were others. Recently!"

Slinker paused a long time. "I stand by what I said. Whatever he's done, he had reasons. Look, he was before your time with the organization. But you can trust him. He is no danger to you. Just bring him home. You will be fine." When I didn't say anything, he continued, "Or we can send a team to escort you."

"Would you mind? No, wait. No, I will be fine. I am probably overreacting. He is just … odd. You know?"

"I do. But he's one of us. Believe me."

"Okay. Thank you, Reverend." I always use titles with religious figures. Even Slinker. My upbringing.

"Of course. See you tomorrow. Good night, Madam CEO."

"Good night."

Marshall said, "Did you call the police?"

JEEZUS, I jumped ten feet! Marshall had come up behind me to ask.

"Don't you ever do that again! Sneak up on me like that! What is wrong with you?"

"Well, early-onset paranoid schizophrenia, with associated secondary psycho-social affective and mood disorders." He frowned at a nearby trash can as he rattled off his report. "Plus, I am hungry. If you did call the police, can I eat real quick before they get here?"

"No. I mean, yes! I mean, no, no police. I just was—look, I called Reverend Paxton to ask … what he thought about what you were saying. You were just awfully causal, talking about Marian dying."

He flickered a smile. "Slinker. I always liked him. Sorry, it seems like death has always been a part of my life, every step of the way." He caressed his turtle as he spoke. "You probably did not have to worry about death growing up, though, did you?"

That stopped me. "Actually, I had to worry about it every day." And then he looked up, and the look on his face was a sincere outpouring of … nothin'. Absolutely nothing. It was unbelievable. I mean, that was where you would expect a note of surprise, shock, mockery … something, anything.

But no. Instead, he just leaned in, shook his head and said, "All those years, I never saw you die, like I did with the others. I never saw you at all! I wonder what that means?"

Now, given everything else he had said, I know the logical response to *that* sentence would be a fucking hard pass on anything else having to do with this man. I get that. I really do.

But, instead, the exact opposite happened. Suddenly, I wasn't afraid of him at all. Now, I just wanted to understand him.

"So, you're hungry? Plenty of great places to eat in Chicago. C'mon. Let's go."

###

A little while later, I was able to pull out my notebook and begin the interview proper.

"So, do you have … what, what is it called, *total recall*? Photographic memory?"

"Mnrph." He had to finish navigating the most recent slice of Chicago-style deep dish pizza before he could answer. "Nmn, you mean like Rain Man? No, you are thinking of autism. On the spectrum and all such. No, schizophrenia is not on the spectrum. It is a common mistake. My flat affect and disconnection from social cues around me are very similar to those with autism, though, and I am also a very good driver." The impression was world-class, but he once again mumbled it to his shoelaces instead of out loud, so, again, I almost missed it.

Nodding with a smile, I took out a small notepad and pen from my purse and took some notes. I was in full business mode now. I wished we had someone from legal to ride shotgun right then, but this would still be a useful informal interview to see what he knew and what he remembered.

"Marshall, Brick told me that you used to go on missions."

He nodded.

"How many did you go on." He had to think about it for another few bites. Finally, "A couple."

"You're sure?"

"Maybe it was three."

"Brick made it sound like it was many, like … many."

More chewing, and then his dead stare at me over his flip-shades. "Eleven. There were eleven."

That was when I noticed he kept turning a gold pocket-watch over and over in his hands and looking around over his shoulders like he had stolen it or something.

"Okay. I was just wondering, since you were a minor at the time. Were they always during your summer visits with your uncle Brick?"

"I guess."

I flashed him a concerned look, and then closed the notebook and leaned back in the booth. "Did you enjoy the missions?"

"Yes."

"Which mission was your favorite?"

Marshall put several pieces of the kale he'd asked for onto the table in front of his turtle's mouth. The turtle fiercely attacked it with his head but otherwise didn't move. For a moment, I locked eyes with it, and the turtle just stared at me as he chewed. Then I looked up, and Marshall was also staring at me, and giving me his answer.

BOOK ONE—CHAPTER SIX

THE STORY OF MARSHALL'S FIRST MISSION, BEGINNING

###

Back then the petite, Asian-featured Mother Po was about your height. You were only sixteen—no, fifteen during that first one. Yet you always looked up at Po. Or perhaps she was always looking down at you. Her round glasses sat loosely atop the very tip of her nose, like the way you wore your flip-shade glasses now. And it seemed her gaze was always over them, or beside them, never through them. Her head always tilted slightly downward. She loomed at the world.

At this particular time, she was looming at the road. She drove much as you'd expect, cautiously, turning the wheel very slightly left-right-left-right-left-right in a quick rhythm that had the effect of keeping the car in an absolutely perfect straight line, with no variance.

You looked out and, other than the occasional road sign ("Falling Rocks"), you didn't appreciate the Upper Peninsula Michigan landscape.

"Dat it?" she asked in her Jersey accent.

You looked at the gas station, with a giant, faded Paul Bunyan statue off to the side, maybe thirty yards away, and you had to admit, "Yes."

That was the one you had seen in your vision, the vision you selected. The one where you were a hero. That was where it was going to happen. You were nervous.

Mother Po pulled in and parked alongside the station, not for gas, but as though for supplies. She glanced up the roadside hill that was behind both Paul Bunyan and the gas station and saw a lone house way up in the woods atop the treacherous slope of slag heap. "And now, you are supposed to get me a candy bar. Snickers! Two!" She grinned at your obvious subterfuge.

"Check again, little one, I think ya' vision was for snack nuts," she joked in reply. "C'mon, let's go the bathroom and get you those treats."

As you opened the door, you mumbled, "I think *you* are a snack nu—"

"What wazz'at?"

"I said I would love some snack nuts!" you said in earnest.

After you both got some refreshments, and she asked the clerk about how to get up the hill behind them (she said she was a photographer, which was actually true), you both got into the car again and followed those directions.

Po used the walkie-talkie to confirm the location of the gas station to the rest of the team. This was the first one you had joined them on, but Brick's Revelator team (him, Slinker, Ruby, and Po) had been using your dreams, successfully, to plan missions all summer. It was quite the advantage, picking a mission you not only knew would succeed but how.

At the time, you never asked how the other team (Grandma Marian, Shaman Storm Breather, and Deke) worked up their plans. But now, you realize Grandma Marian must've sussed them out whenever you weren't there.

Anyway, you remember the mission going like this based on both your memories and your visions:

After Po finished her recon report for the rest of the team, her next conversation was with the owner of the house up on that hill. She drove the two of you up to his house, back and forth along the winding road, until up beyond the tree line at the top of the hill, where the road ended at a dirt driveway that led to that house.

Before you finished pulling into his driveway, she momentarily got out and slashed her own tire. Then she took out her camera with the telephoto lens and put it over her shoulder, and you both set about pulling up to the stranger's house, to ask for *aid* in fixing the flat.

###

About thirty minutes later, a van pulled into the gas station for gas, just as your vision had predicted. There were closer stations to the compound, but this was one of the few stations in the area that also sold animal feed, and the petting zoo was the compound's *legitimate* source of income, so this crew from the compound came fifteen miles out of their way to fill their tank and get some food.

Two large male passengers stayed at the pump, talking while the tank filled. One of them had some kind of rifle slung over his shoulder. The other had a pistol sticking out of the back of his belt line.

The driver walked inside with two young, stumbling, pale-skinned female passengers who had been riding in the back. Even after their eyes should have adjusted, they kept blinking. At first, they didn't take any notice of the three elderly bikers standing next to a couple of choppers over beside the giant Paul Bunyan statue. But then they heard yelling from the female member of the trio. She and the tall, handsome one with the graying hair yelled something at the third one, who was a stocky, misshapen figure with his back to them. He was jumping ape-like up and down and gesticulating wildly. But no words could be made out at that distance. It must've been some kind of argument. After a few seconds of watching the histrionics, they lost interest and went inside.

"Sounds like …" And Slinker nodded, and then continued tugging on his ear a second time. "Sounds like … sounds like?"

"Sounds like … ear!" Ruby answered. Slinker nodded and jumped up and down in excitement.

"Forty … beers? On the wall?" Brick didn't watch many movies, so he wasn't really sure where this was going.

"Forty year?" And then, in response to Slinker's wide-grinned nodding, Ruby figured it out. "*The 40-Year-Old Virgin*!"

"Yes!" Slinker confirmed as she jumped up and down and clapped to her own success.

Then Ruby got serious and scolded the other redhead, "I though the category was movies and not personal histories?"

"Very funny, chickee. You know, as a female in this here biker gang, you need to learn your place."

"My place is behind you with my foot up your ass, Slink. And don't think that, just because I don't fit as easily into our old colors as I used to, that I can't take your sorry ass out in a fight."

Slinker laughed. "Heh, you'd split the crotch in those pants on the first kick. Which isn't to say that couldn't be entertaining."

Brick, who'd been staring intently at the storefront the entire time, interrupted their banter. "Okay, they're inside. I make out two at the pump. We'll head in. You're up, Slink."

Without missing a beat, Slinker yelled, "FUCK YOU!" This time, the yell was unmistakable at any distance. The guys at the pump turned and looked as Slinker stormed away from Brick and Ruby, walking his bike over toward them and the pumps.

"Man, I can't believe it. You ride with someone you think you know 'em, right?" Slinker shouted ahead to the two men at the pump as he aligned his own bike for a fill up. "But then he GOES AND ACCUSES YOU OF SLEEPING WITH HIS GAL! Like she don't already belong to all of us." He yelled that one bit over his shoulder at Brick and Ruby, as they were ignoring him and strutting into the gas station. She hung on Brick's arm like a high school squeeze. Slinker continued, "You know what I'm saying?"

But the two men just stared back at him like mutes.

"Aw, man, it's prepay without a credit card. And I don't have any cash. Either of you boys …?" And the ugly glares from the two men convinced him to cut that thought short. "Right. Well, I got enough to get me to the next station, I reckon." And at that, he started his bike and rolled it slowly forward in a big half circle, as though he were heading out the opposite direction from where he faced.

Before he took off, though, he paused and reached down, as if adjusting something in the gear on the back of his bike, while he waited for the signal.

###

At that moment, inside the store, the other two one-percenters, wearing their dung-and-dirt-encrusted leather vests adorned with bright blue "Wild Bunch MC" (Outlaw Motorcycle Club) three-piece patches, screamed at each other to the distraction of the clerk.

Ruby, despite her small stature, still had enough authority in her voice to hold her own in a shouting match against Brick. The clerk had come around the counter and was yelling at both of them to simmer down.

Meanwhile, the van driver with the two younger ladies was getting impatient at the counter, where the two girls had loaded up their stuff. "Hey, fuck them! Ring us up, will you?"

"Just a moment, sir."

"Now!"

The clerk complied. The compound's reputation for violence preceded him.

As the clerk removed himself to back behind the counter, Brick yelled something incomprehensible at Ruby, and then struck her with a theatrical blow, making the slapping sound against his off hand, while Ruby launched herself backward into the van driver, knocking him into the counter.

Ruby screamed something through her dyed-red hair back at Brick and steadied herself against a nearby rack display. As she stood up, she brandished the display behind her head, clipping the van driver again in the face with her backswing.

Brick took the display from her and tossed it behind the counter, hitting the stunned clerk full in the face. And then he threw an exaggerated punch, which she easily ducked under, but which caught the driver standing behind Ruby square in the jaw. Brick's Q-47 enhanced strength wasn't what it used to be, but it was plenty to knock this guy cold.

And then Brick picked up the stunned driver over his head while Ruby grabbed the two confused girls, one by each hand, and walked them behind the counter. She momentarily looked down at the clerk on the floor and asked, "The backdoor, is it locked?" She wondered if she'd have to kick it down.

He shook his head, so she hurried them out back. Quickly, she asked the two girls their names. The first one answered just as they all heard the sound of the driver being hurled through the gas station store's front window by Brick.

That was the signal.

There was actually a fourth compound member asleep in the truck. So, he awoke, and all three rushed toward the store to investigate their fallen friend. One lagged behind to check on their fallen comrade while the other two approached the front door slowly, guns drawn.

But the sun was at their back, and the glare meant they couldn't see the cabinet flung at them until it, too, came crashing out of the store, this time through the door. They dodged it and fired their guns randomly in defense, but Brick was no longer inside. He'd followed his companions out the back.

The four stunned compound members reeled and gathered themselves out front of the store, making sure they were all okay. Meanwhile, they didn't notice Slinker had ridden his chopper around back to pick up two passengers—the two girls.

Brick and Ruby got onto a third motorcycle (Brick's was still back next to the Paul Bunyan) that the Wild Bunch / Revelators (for their *colors* were legit, they truly had been charter members of the Wild Bunch motorcycle gang, four decades before) had left behind the shop earlier. And so, without a word, they split up. Slinker took the two girls onto his hog and headed out on the open road. Their baggy white shirts fluttering in the wind. And Brick and Ruby seemed to leave on a separate hog, going the other way.

The four compounders entered through the broken front door and windows. Once the shop owner pointed them to out back, they hustled out there only to see the two motorbikes, with passengers, leaving in the two opposite directions. After firing a few shots, they hurried back to their van and gave chase to the bike with Slinker and the two *kidnapped* girls.

This was all except for the driver, the cleverest of the group. He took a pistol and hot-wired Brick's chopper and gave chase to the other two going the other direction.

As the sounds of the various screeching tires and combustion engines faded into the distance, the shop owner walked out front and surveyed the damage. He scowled, wondering if the insurance claim would cover this. But as he entered, his face lit up at the sight of the large roll of $100 bills someone (the handsome biker?) had left behind.

Of course, that wouldn't stop him from filing his insurance claim.

###

Slinker was far ahead of the pursuing van, but he wasn't fully open on the throttle. He cruised so that he could be heard over the engine and the rushing wind.

"Don't be afraid! We're going to help you! You're safe now! Just hang on!"

"Wh-where are you talking me?" the first girl on the back screamed.

"Someplace safe!"

The van floored it. And it was gaining. The first girl kept spinning her head around and trying to look behind them, but the other girl held her fast. "Don't! You'll fall!"

They came upon a side road after an outcropping of trees, and Slinker turned onto it. "This'll work!"

After another hundred yards or so of riding down that road, they could hear the van screeching around the same corner. Slinker slowed his bike to a stop, pointing it sideways, and let the second lady off.

The first girl screamed, "What are you doing? They'll catch us!"

Slinker idled the bike and assured her, "Just watch."

The second girl, who had traded her jacket and bandana for the other compound victim's white shirt, was actually Ruby. And she calmly got off the back of the bike and walked toward the oncoming van as it charged forward.

"C'mere, you," she said as she mentally recited the Litany. *As is One, As is All …*

Plan A was this. Three gunmen in a van against Ruby, by herself, unarmed.

They didn't stand a chance.

They only reason they went to all this trouble was to get the battle away from any spectators accidentally getting caught up in it.

Ruby wasn't a banisher, she was a Spancaster. Her dJinn was willing. So, with a thought and a dismissive wave of her hand, the four tires aged several hundred thousand miles in an instant and burst all at once, disintegrating into dust. They managed to keep the van from flipping over or hitting a tree beside the road as it skidded to a halt about fifty feet from Ruby.

This was an old van. Metal. She concentrated a bit harder on the energy her dJinn provided, and the entire chassis oxidized and rusted out in ten or so seconds, which meant that, instead of rusting, it burst into flame. Now, the men inside stopped moaning and started screaming.

She ran around to one side to check the driver. He was dead. His neck snapped as his head hit the dash. She heard the large sliding door open on the other side.

She dropped to the ground and glanced under the van. From their feet, she saw the two men stumbling from the burning van. One just crumpled to the ground. He had been essentially carried out by the other. The other one, the largest, who had been carrying the rifle, now picked it up and walked around the van, looking for Ruby.

He walked slowly around the front and saw what he thought was a glimpse of white shirt on the driver-side mirror. He rushed around and fired several rounds at it, but it was just hanging there, limply, off the mirror.

"Keeey-YAA!" Ruby launched herself off the top of the burning van and landed a flying kick at the large man's head. He crumpled to the ground, and she landed and rolled.

She got up and walked over to check his pulse. Also dead.

He never thought to look up. Maybe he never considered someone would climb onto a burning van.

The fire caught within the van itself. So, she ran around to the other side and dragged the only surviving compound member in this group (the same one Brick had already cold-cocked) away from the burning wreckage. After a moment, she went back and put the large guy back in the passenger seat, and then ran back away just in time before it blew.

No evidence.

After the explosion, she and her captured compound member just lay there, on the ground. She eventually got up on one knee as they were approached by their target and Slinker. For his part, Slink just looked at her, and then looked down and smiled.

"What?" she demanded. The adrenaline had worn off, and she was too tired to try and figure it out.

And then she realized he was right.

The crotch of her jeans *had* split.

###

Brick was suddenly exhausted. This was how the Q-47 serum always worked. He had super-strength right up until he didn't, when it cut out. Then he was weak as a babe. At some point he couldn't even continue riding. He just pulled over to catch his breath.

If this girl was upset about his stopping, she didn't say it. She was much younger than the other one was. Which made sense. This was the kidnapped girl. The other one was an embedded reporter who had been working undercover for a story, right up until she was too drugged and brainwashed to do anything about escaping from the cult at the compound.

The Revelators had some expertise about such things—having conducted rescue operations like this since '95, the past fifteen years. Although cults weren't as popular as they used to be, the Internet had caused a recent resurgence. In fact, in certain circles, on certain chat rooms, the Revelators had made it known that they were available for hire, if someone in one of those cults needed a hand.

In this instance, the family of a reporter had hired them to break their nineteen-year-old daughter free from the cult. And it had no doubt been a success.

But as he heard the familiar hum of his own bike coming down the road at him, he wondered whether this last bit of the mission would work. Would his godson come through?

About twenty minutes prior. Back up on top of the hillside overlooking the gas station and roads.

"Sil, please," he said after he had introduced himself as "Silvan."

"Mr. Sil." Suddenly her voice was completely oriental-sounding, her head bowing slightly as she spoke, "Thank you very much for your offer of help. We just need to change the tire."

"I can do it, Mom," Marshall said, playing his part.

"You ever changed a tire before, boy?" asked the man.

"No."

"You better let me have a look-see then."

As he led you both from the porch, you asked him about the huge, metal branches with leaves hanging on the front of his house, on his porch. "Oh, those. Yep. Plenty of copper mines around here. You can get wall hangings like those for twenty bucks at the local gas station. Like the one at the bottom of the hill. You know, you look online, you know what they'll charge you for that? Two hundred!" You gazed in response as he put on his shoes and grabbed his hat from a hook just inside the door.

Then he continued over his shoulder as he walked past you. "Except I charge two-fifty on eBay. Ha ha!"

You didn't get the joke. You really weren't familiar with the Internet commerce at that time.

"Very good, Mr. Sil. You will help jack up the car. And after you change it, but before you let the car back down, you will go inside the house to make us some coffee, because you hope I will stay and visit, right?" said Po.

Her tone was fake, but otherwise absolutely normal. Nothing was done, no gestures or other such things like with magic-use, but you had seen her do this before. She was an empath. ("Highest Order," Grandma Marian told you. That meant powerful.) And so, after he had changed the tire, he came up with the idea.

"Yeah, that sounds good. Would you like some coffee? Or tea, maybe?"

"Mr. Sil, you are too kind. Tea would be lovely. Son, run along."

The time you teased her about the ethics of it she told you that she couldn't make anyone do anything they didn't already want to do. She said it was similar to how the Revelators got the dJinni to do their bidding.

She compared people's minds to their homes. Once they invite you in, they have a much harder time telling you to not breathe their air, or walk on their floors, or explore their rooms. In that sense, an empath is always invited in.

Still, you weren't always sure it was right.

As he went inside, she said, "Okay, you wanted to do it this way. Concentrate just how Ruby showed you."

She always said that. And while, yes, Ruby had trained you, you actually always did better when you were with Po. Something about her way gave you confidence. Ruby rooted for you, but Po just expected you to do it. She always used to say, "Best way to beat stress? Get the damn job done."

You walked to the edge of the cliff and looked down. You mostly just saw trees. But you knew from your previous vision the spot you needed to focus on.

You already had used some of one of the dJinni's energy, though you didn't recognize which one, in order to select the vision, the future you all were now on. The Demi-urge and the various dJinni were somehow okay with that. You knew that.

But you had never crossed this line before, using one of them to cast your own spell when it came to spancasting. But the other Revelators did it all the time. They prayed to these beings, and their prayers were answered. And they said you could come along, but only if you did it this way. No more using your own energy. They wanted to help you preserve yourself.

And you wanted to go on a real mission. So, you agreed.

First the usual voices. The ones from your illness. Dummy. Don't be Po's little pet. You can't do it this way. Use your chi, chi-cheater? Run and play! Throw her off the cliff, that'll teach her. The student is now the Master. Chi-chi-chi-Chia!

You navigated those well enough. Not responding but just accepting them. They weren't real, but they weren't fake, either. The trees all around you confirmed you were their chosen one. A lot of time, those voices, the ones coming from the trees now, weren't heard so much as understood, like the way certain subjects were understood in English. Automatic comprehension. Instantaneous. Like magic.

Anyway, those were the fake voices.

But their insults, their commands, still had to be dealt with. For instance, they could be put off. At least for a while. It was a matter or prioritizing, you just had to move along to something else first.

"Let's go here," you told them, instead.

Typically, that was the signal. That's when the Others' voices would bubble up. That's when you would see their eyes, the ones you always felt. You saw their shadows, too. Or rather the shadows of their shadows, like the accidental bits of background left around the edges of a photograph you are cutting it out of with scissors.

But it was their voices you focused on. Like a chamber-pit orchestra tuning before a show, no one dJinn could be heard over the others. They all just clattered and murmured into a cacophony of chaos. But it didn't matter, you didn't need all of them.

Only one.

BOOK ONE—CHAPTER SEVEN

PALLA

###

"So, you hear two sets of voices. The ones from your schizo—from your illness. And another set. And the other set are real?" I made a note to look up the criminal statutes for an insanity plea in whatever states we found out the Revelators took kids on missions.

"Yes, that's right."

"And you can tell the two different types of voices from each other?"

And he nodded as if to say yes, but what he said was, "I believe so. But how would I know, really?"

Good point, I thought. But I just held a professional smile in response to his perpetual frown.

We sat there like a pair of theater masks for a moment. Then he finished his story.

BOOK ONE—CHAPTER EIGHT

THE STORY OF MARSHALL'S FIRST MISSION, ENDING

###

With a sharp thought, Marshall, you lashed out, like a snake strike, and tagged one, not far away, that was behind you. The dJinn was surprised, and it screamed. Now, its voice was the one you heard.

No! NO! You will not!

Tiny beads of sweat gathered on your forehead, and you started to apologize. But Ruby's voice was somehow echoing, perhaps from previous lessons, in your head, "Say the words."

And so, you did. It was a snappy little rhyme:

> *As is One, As is All.*
> *As Angels fly, and Demons Call.*
> *By Holy and Profane,*
> *I Summon the Provincial.*
> *Avert! And Attend!*
> *And You may, then, Dis-*
> *enthrall."*

Now, whether those words were the key or not, you could not say. But there was no doubt the effect they had upon the dJinn. It stopped struggling and seemed to go along, allowing a small but steady stream of its *chi* to pass from it to you, and then, as you pointed the way, on to the rocks below.

Faster and faster, Timespace rolled forward, until *the inevitable over time* became just *the inevitable*. And in the distance, between and amongst the trees, you could hear the rocks begin to slide.

###

A few seconds later, the driver bore down on a helpless Brick and his guest rider on their motorcycle. The van driver was in the process of slowing down and pointing his gun. This was when his motorbike engine became quiet enough for him to first hear the roar. And, by then, it was too late.

The rockslide hit like a tidal wave, several large boulders took his bike out from under him, and a bunch more smaller ones pummeled him into unconsciousness. It all took only a few seconds.

Brick breathed a satisfied sigh. He walked up to the unconscious gunman and checked. He was alive. He looked back at the scared girl, who still sat quietly—probably in shock—atop the bike. Then he radioed to Po.

"We're done. Come pick us up."

BOOK ONE—CHAPTER NINE

PALLA

###

"You saved your uncle Brick's life," I said, pointing out the obvious highlight.

"Probably," Marshall agreed as he finished off the last hunk of pizza. Then a thought occurred to him. "Does he still get weak and get the shakes?" he asked me.

As he had aged, Uncle Brick's Q-47 serum's physiological cycle had become less of a super-soldier-to-a-weakling-and-back proposition and more of a remarkably-agile-elder-to demented-convalescent-and-back journey. I answered, "The good days outnumber the bad ones, but the bad ones render him essentially bedbound. You know, I say days, but, sometimes, it comes and goes all within an hour or two. Or he can go weeks in either state." Then I changed the subject. "He is really looking forward to seeing you."

"I'm ready," he said, standing up suddenly.

"I'll get the check, and we can go to drop you off at the hotel."

Marshall Lastpost left and cradled his turtle under his windbreaker. I thought of my Sebastian as I mentally reviewed his story. Various Revelator priests had couched their invocations of their angels as more like supplications for sustenance, like we were pets asking to be fed. But Marshall's description of his spancasting was more coercive than that. I wondered if this reflected his inner personality, since I was of the opinion it was all bunk.

Later that night, in my hotel room, I thought more about it.

At various times, I had asked the others why I couldn't see these angels and demons. Or why they couldn't just perform some of these spells so I could witness it for myself. But they refused, saying that, unless I was magic sensitive, I couldn't see the spirits. And that they couldn't offend the spirits by performing such tricks.

Whatever.

I mean, yes, Brick and Marian had been costumed heroes back during the Wild Bunch days ... but all the rest, the praying and the angels and the Revelators, that was obviously just Brick's way of mollifying the others, making them feel like they were a part of his and Marian's scene.

And the religion? A tax dodge. I mean, can we just say it? It doesn't mean all of these believers are bad people. But this culture of incredulity was ripe for the abuse we later saw.

That's why they needed me. I thought of all the prayers that the other victims in my home village had tried. Just another comfort, another totem.

But even so, I knew that, at trial, people's attitudes could mean just as much as their actions. I made a mental note to approach Slinker and ask about the ethical implications of these prayers. After all, claiming to be religious or spiritual because you were willing to enslave a spirit wasn't very exculpatory.

My sleep was not very restful.

###

The next day, I picked up Marshall at the pre-arranged time in front of the hotel. If he had changed clothes, he didn't look it. He wasn't carrying any luggage. I asked, and he confirmed he had none. So, I took a sharp inhale and smelled the scent of bar soap. He had hand-washed yesterday's clothes in the sink.

As we drove further into downtown toward our headquarters, I couldn't help but feel some anticipation. I knew this would make Brick happy, which would make me happy. Or, in the alternative, this would drive Brick crazy, which I was good with also. I enjoyed walking Brick back from the proverbial ledge as much, maybe more than anything. I *was* devoted to the church. And the church needed its leader. And when its leader needed me, well, all was right with the world.

And, yes, I know how fucked up that is, given my history. I am not clueless. And even if I was, I had seen plenty of therapists over the years who had pointed it out. But this was different from my childhood. I wasn't seeking approval from a father figure by aiding and abetting their sins. Nor was this me trying to perpetually assuage my guilt.

All other things being equal, I was making sure an organization that truly tried to do good, kept doing good as it scaled larger and larger. That was the thing. These so-called holy people and their church were, at heart, still a bunch of do-gooder former Robin Hood bikers, for crying out loud. They needed someone to run the show from a business standpoint.

Had I always succeeded? Jury was out on that. Well, possibly multiple juries, coast-to-coast. More on that, later. *This* was priority one for me at the moment: How was this new, crazy person of a nephew going to recalibrate the mix? Or the mission?

Like I said, I was enjoying the anticipation.

###

We were back in the boardroom. Brick wanted to meet here for some reason.

Marshall no longer needed me to guide him, and he proceeded at a leisurely pace, looking to and fro down the long cross-hallways like a small child as he walked.

As he entered the room, Brick spun his chair around from at the far end of the table.

"My guyyyyy!" Brick's face showed a grim joy, and he stood up to approach.

"Hello, Uncle Brick." Marshall couldn't hide the slightly horrified look on his usually blank face. That look when you notice your dad is old for the first time.

"Let me look at you. My god, boy: You look like shit."

"And you just smell like it."

"OH! Aaaahhh, ha ha ha ha!" He acted in mock shock, and then hugged his nephew warmly. This exchange was obviously something they had shared many times before.

Now, they were looking at me.

"Does she know about the button?" Marshall asked Brick, flat-faced.

"No," Brick said.

What the hell are they talking about?

They both smirked. I just stared defiantly.

"Go ahead," said the older man with a resigned shrug.

And I'll be damned if Marshall didn't walk over to the edge of the boardroom conference table and slip his hand along the underside of it, slowly, slowly, until you could hear a *click!*

And a particular bookshelf along the far long wall popped open, revealing a hidden walkway.

Brick explained, "Before it was our headquarters, it was a gentrified multipurpose combination housing and retail complex. And before that it was a bank. Everybody knows that, because that bank's name is still chiseled into the front of the building. But, before that, long before that, it was a speakeasy during Prohibition. And there are a fair number of hidden doors and passageways throughout the building.

"C'mon!" Like a child, Marshall wanted to go wherever that hidden passageway led.

"No, Marshall. Put the shelf back. Like I taught you. You know there is nothing down there except dirt and spiders."

As Marshall latched the bookcase shut again, he blurted to no one in particular, "I was the family champion at hide and seek."

"You still are. We hadn't heard from you in years."

"I had some church business to *attend* to," said Marshall, with more than a little bit of hostility in his voice.

And this time the impression was unmistakable. He sounded *exactly* like Brick.

And then Brick got serious. He took Marshall by the shoulders, and he said, "I know. Marshall, Butchie, in case you needed confirmation, it's true. Marian is dead. She's dead, son. Her funeral is next week, here in Chicago. The service will be out there in the courtyard, out front of this very building."

Marshall just held onto Brick as the two men stood silently within their grief, tears forming on their faces. I still wasn't entirely sure what was going on. Nor did I know what was going to happen, about Marian, or with Marshall. But once it was clear we weren't actually going to get any substantive business done, I excused myself.

I made it all the way to the elevator before I started weeping for my sweet Amma.

BOOK ONE—CHAPTER TEN

"Our foster parents weren't perfect. I mean, they deserved better than they got. But, still, they were pretty negligent. One of the main ways they failed was how they left me to raise Marshall. So, his bedtime often became my responsibility. This was because he really only listened to me.

But, sometimes out of spite (as I resented, at some level, having to do it), and sometimes out of the normal exhaustion or frustration over being 'parental,' I would foist it back onto Mom. Getting her involved nearly almost always triggered an incident. But even if I didn't involve her, there was still a chance that Marshall would start in on one of his tirades.

He would bash his head against the wall. He would scream. He would claim that he wanted to sleep, and that we were keeping him up, but then as soon as we left or turned the light off, he would scream some more. And, at some point, Mom or myself, or both of us, would lose our temper and scream back. Or we would hit him. Which would engender more screaming. Even as he tried to close his eyes, he'd suddenly be started awake, screaming again … at something …

I just wanted the screaming to stop.

For the longest time, I had trained myself to keep all our windows closed so that the neighbors would not hear all the screaming. It's a testament to the indifference of neighbors that no one ever called the cops, since I am quite sure that the screaming was still audible throughout the neighborhood. Certainly there were days in summer when I forgot.

At any rate, this would continue until he got too exhausted by it all. It's funny: for all the hundreds of times that scene played out, I cannot remember what it was like at those precise moments when he actually stopped. But suddenly everything was normal again. It was all like a dream. A nightmare."

—Heychuck Smith,
The Truth About the Precept
(*NYT* bestseller)

Rufepirts was just a janitor.

As always, his mind raced. This body didn't know any other way to proceed. He waxed the floor and saw the backward reflection of himself down below. *I can still read it. My tag says,* Maintenance.

"Maintenance!" he screamed at himself.

He yelled loud enough for it to hurt, and that was great. It stung. And then, even after it felt better, it would feel raw again when he ate or drank. He liked feeling the pain. He screamed it again, louder, and the word echoed in the empty lab building, *Maintenance! tenance. enance. enance. ance. nce.*

For his part, Rufepirts was happy to be working here, or working anywhere, really. He had come from a long way away. And he had what they told him—well, what the *Master* had told him—was a good job. It was one of the few jobs where his outbursts were permitted … since he was completely alone.

He said it again, out loud for measure, "The Agency's Visiting Analyst got Rufepirts a job! What the what the Whaaat?"

Whaat? aaat? aaat, aat …?

He held the tall floor buffer by both handles. He was still getting used to maneuvering it. He still tended to press his body against it for torque, instead of letting its centrifugal force steady itself as it propelled. So, each night there were new bruises on his stomach from it.

The bruises hurt when you pressed on them. Sometimes, he couldn't stop pushing them. All night. More fun than sleeping. *The Lost,* even in human form, didn't dream, so sleep was boring.

And sleep *deprivation?* Oh, it was marvelous. He had gotten halfway through his shift before realizing that he had forgotten to comb his hair that morning. It stuck up like a … no, don't know that word, yet. But he kept dropping things and bumping into things … sleep was important in this form, it turned out.

The floor buffer hummed a tune he couldn't place, but that didn't stop him from singing along with it as he grappled with it. He thought it was called "Because the Sky." It was beautiful, and he tried to sing it just so, just like Marshall, like Butchie used to mimic, long, long ago.

In that song there were multiple voices, but they worked together perfectly. This was unlike what Marshall usually heard. Usually, Marshall's voices were shouting over one another.

It was no wonder he liked the song so much.

He liked remembering the visions he and the others had shared with Marshall. Now that he was on the same plane as the boy, he wasn't sure which memories were his and which were the Marshall's. Many times, Rufepirts had offered his own visions to Marshall. He especially helped him with banishing.

Rufepirts excelled at banishing. Even the little banishments out and back in, the ones where you ended up within the same Timespace *What was the word? Teleporting! Yes, that's it.*

But it *was* weird to not hear any of the voices of his fellows. Now that he was severed.

Severed.

He missed his own people. The Regnant, they named themselves.

They were demons. Daemons. Marshall called them the dJinni of the Ancients.

"… with the light, brown haaaaaair … !" *hair! air, air, air …*

Rufepirts decided he was mad now.

Mad. Yes.

Rufepirts was one of the *Lost*. Once you were *severed*, that is what you became. Although there were those among his people who said he'd become mad even before that. Those who said that said it was because of his ties to Marshall. He knew that wasn't correct. His madness was because of that one dark-skinned female human. *She* was the one, the one who lived with Marshall. *She lived; I live.* Happily ever after.

"Awwwwww!" he bellowed to no one.

Because she was bound to Rufepirts, he knew her mind, her power, or rather his power, was as one with Marshall's, looking over him, protecting him. *Through time … what, sideways? No, backward. Only he could have managed that. Backward.*

Yes, well. It was all very confusing.

Anyway, they said to Rufepirts that his power came from his madness. And that sounded about right to him. Only backward.

He wondered if that were true with all beings.

Anyway, the thing was, he couldn't remember causing the severance. Not exactly. It felt as though the severance was forced from someone else.

Someone extremely powerful.

Once that happened, he joined the *Lost* amongst his people … wandering all the disparate threads of Timespace. Until, finally, he bumped into the Master, no, the Analyst. *Have to remember to call him that, or else he gets angry.* The Analyst had been sent there, to the void. Banished. *Just between you and me (whom? and who?), he was going mad, too.*

But Rufepirts didn't like seeing any living being suffer. So, he saved the Analyst. *(My power is powerful.)* And then he showed the Analyst, you know, the way. Stuff.

The Analyst was grateful for that. And then the Analyst hit upon a plan. Since they could travel Timespace, the *Lost* can theoretically wander forever … but, instead, they had helped each other get out. So, they could execute their plan.

Now he had a purpose. He was here, on this here Analyst's world, a janitor, dJinnitor *tee hee,* with a purpose.

The black floor was so shiny after his machine went over it. He loved to look at his reflection in the floor and make faces. *This face is a* moue …

But more of that later. More to do, he thought as the rotor pad on the floor buffer *womp-womped* as the outcast demon sang along.

BOOK ONE—CHAPTER ELEVEN

PALLA

###

I joked with Slinker that there were enough Blue Rooks luminaries at Brick's house to fill a dozen tabloid articles.

"Well, as long as they call us luminaries and not illuminati," he quipped. He was polishing his glasses with a white cloth handkerchief he carried around in his slacks, as he often did.

"Isn't that the same hankie you blow your nose with? Gross."

"I have two, dear. One in each pocket."

"And are you sure which one is which?"

He started to answer, then momentarily held a puzzled look. "Let's just say I am."

"Like I said. Gross."

This was less a party than it was a family reunion. Some former board members and leaders of the Blue Rooks community arrived just to see Marshall. Or, at least, that was their excuse. I noticed that, after the initial greetings with the strange young man, they tended to cluster around Brick. These were people from the very beginnings of the church—when the original Wild Bunch found religion (and learned their clerical magic-use) at the foot of the great Shaman "White-Feather Al" Storm Breather, who was father to the Wild Bunch's road captain, Ian "Animal" Revelation Song.

Here's how the story was told to me: Animal was killed by government agents, who specifically sought out Animal for capture. They said it was because of his abilities. But he had no magic-use abilities. His father had not shown him the ways of the ancients.

The shame of having his son die due to his own unwillingness to teach him was almost too much for the Chief to bear. But Brick came up with the idea that they would learn the ways of magic-use from the Shaman and call themselves the Revelators. And instead of working for hire, or to right random wrongs, they would focus their mission on saving other natural apostates (or NAs for short—Innies as the derogatory, which is what the government called those who were sensitive to magic). This led to more direct conflicts with the *Extirpacy*, who had set up several enclaves under the guise of religious cults, to ensnare and *create* their own clerics, though the introduction of various drugs and stress training (read: brainwashing). So, that's how the Revelators got in the business of rescuing people from cults.

The main topic of conversation was that night, of course, Marian. Strangely, they didn't discuss her death. (I wanted to bring it up but didn't feel comfortable.) Instead, they mostly recounted her tremendous heart, skill (both as a performer—she was a stage singer and actress—and as a magic-user), and, especially, her *attitude*.

Can you believe that one time when she …? was how most conversations started.

Slinker especially had a good time telling various stories centered around how it wasn't so much the bright lights on her Butterfly costume that confused criminals in battle, as it was the skimpiness of her costume. ("She once explained to us that her main superpower, was, how did she put it? Side-boob!")

Several of the visitors brought family with them—a significant other, a child, or grandchild—who had never been to Brick Reese's mansion before. And those plus-ones also brought tertiary visitors, a sort of pyramid of access and glamour. Babysitting that group of excess licensees was my unofficial duty.

I had just finished regaling them with the story of Marian's extraction of me from my village, when I saw Marshall sitting by himself. He had been there about an hour at that point. And he hadn't said much.

"You okay?" I asked.

"Uncle Brick promised me a team meeting. I need to share what happened and discuss what the plans are, moving forward."

"Yes. Okay. We will meet."

"It needs to happen now. Why are we not meeting?"

I sat down beside him. "Your Uncle Brick is a public figure. So are many of the other people in this room. When enough of them get together, it is news. There needed to be some official function, some excuse," I explained. "So, tonight: this is a presentation by Ruby's manufacturing company."

His excited look flashed. "Is Ruby coming?"

"No. She is too ill, I'm told. Her son will be giving the presentation."

Dead eyes and a pause. "But there is no presentation, right? It is just our meeting?"

"That's right."

He seemed satisfied, but there was still something troubling him. Finally, unprompted:

"I told you it incorrectly. I did not kill Grandma Marian; time did."

I leaned back into the couch and got philosophical. Talking with Marshall was a lot like the discussion my college friends and I had when we got high.

I never fit in with all of the trust-fund socialites who were going to law school to leverage their Daddy's firm's guaranteed job at the end, and so I had glommed onto some of the other outcasts in my class. And they and I would often get into these sorts of discussions at the end of our study group sessions.

"They say we're all dying; just some are more honest about it than others," I said to him.

"Who are they?" he asked.

"Philosophers. Counselors. And Blue Rooks missionaries, among others. The idea is that if you remember that you are dying, you will live the right way. That's why so many sermons are about death, I reckon."

"So, if someone figured out a way to stop dying, that would be an open invitation to live the wrong way?"

"I suppose so."

Then a large man with a British accent approached. "'Aha! The two of you, then! Why the long faces? You keep acting like this and the strippers I ordered are going to think they're in the wrong place! Ha ha! Look, but seriously, listen. *Butchwald*: Brick told me all about it, lad. I must say, you did what you had to do, mate. Marian would be proud."

This was Sir Boris Pesskin Wyskald. He was Ruby Wyskald's only son. After she left Brick in the early '80s, she married into British lesser royalty and had him. Only after he was grown did she rejoin the group, now as a Revelator, in 2002, about halfway through their twenty-five-year run.

Maybe it was an old soul–young soul thing, since we were about same age, but I was always offended by how he always acted like the drunk at the office Christmas party and yet somehow everyone always gave him free reign. I suppose he had earned that kind of respect, over time.

He deserved props, though. For sheer efficacy in running something, I took a back seat to no one. But he would have given me a run for my money. He got things done.

That night he wore a loud sweater-vest over a (somehow sparkly) reddish brown Henley and, as always, he was holding a drink. His chubby cheeks were prominent. And his round, ginger-bearded, prematurely-bald head rotated side to side as he talked, giving the effect of being an animatronic build-a-bear.

Yet, despite his ribaldry and seeming foppishness, he was not a buffoon or an irrelevant aristocrat. He was just shy of his fortieth birthday, but he was both a serious Blue Rooks board member as well as a full-fledged Revelator. I don't put in for all this *magic* business, but Brick of course believed in it, and he described Boris as "At any given time, the most dangerous cleric in the room. And you see, that's because, as Ruby's son, he received both her natural talent and her training. His banishing skills are Highest Order."

To me, he was just annoying.

"Hello, Boris." I greeted him with a smile. You did have to smile at his act (at least, at first).

"Love," he said, nodding, to me, and then said, "Butchwald! C'mere, lad. Give us a hug, eh, what?"

Marshall awkwardly stood and allowed the bear of a man to squeeze his arms around him.

Sitting back down, Marshall said, "You seem to be right. As you say, I had to do it. But if I had to do it, then why do I feel so bad?" I think I saw his dead eyes watering a bit. Can there be such a thing as dead tears?

"Look, lad. Don't get wrapped up in the philosophy of it all. All we can do is the best we can do, yes?"

Personally, I was getting annoyed with how everyone was sort of implicitly encouraging Marshall's blaming of himself for his grandma's death. But, as condolences went, this was acceptable, I thought.

Marshall nodded.

"Right, I'll see you both inside," Boris said before excusing himself. And as fast as he arrived, he was out of our party orbit.

"Butchwald?" I asked.

Marshall shrugged. "He thinks it's funny."

"But you don't."

Marshall looked at me, utterly emotionless. "Oh no, I do." And then he let his gaze drift back down to his shoes. "Butchwald!" he repeated under his breath at precisely the same pitch as Boris.

Finally, a few minutes later, I asked, "Hey, did Brick show you any hidden passages here at his house, too?"

Marshall shook his head, lost in thought. Giving up on cheering him up, I absent-mindedly grabbed a few mints from a coffee-table basin in front of us. *I hate mints,* I thought as I ate them.

Then I grabbed some more. And when the silence between us started drowning out the background noise of the party guests, I switched senses entirely and applied some CBD creme to my hands. *Mmmm, lavender.*

###

As I sat at one end of Brick's enormous dining room table, a strange shudder ran through me. *Chilly old house,* I thought. I mentally reviewed the meeting participants, just as I would any board meeting, although this was no such thing. Surrounding the many, many baskets of muffins on the oak table were:

Brick, nestled at the opposite end of the table, with another unlit cigarette in one hand.

Next to him, on one side, was Reverend Sally Radisch, board member and the church's religious director. Dressed in a sweater and mom-jeans, she was a sweet downstate Illinois gal who was best known for being extremely good-natured and earnest. She was always very soft-spoken, timid even. Sally always tended to try too hard and failed upward as everyone gave her the *A* for effort. For some reason, Brick made her head of Blue Rooks security with regard to the upcoming conference. We had some discussions about it, but he assured me I was unofficially overseeing her, so I said fine.

But over the past few months, Sally had given me a different vibe. Like she'd made a decision to promote her own agenda. I was still working on figuring it out.

Across from her was the aforementioned bombastic Boris Wyskald, board member, Revelator, and the polar opposite of Sally. He was self-assured to a fault and, if anything, underrated in terms of his effectiveness. He ran and had greatly expanded his mother Ruby's holdings as she had retired back to live with the Tribe in recent years.

Next to him was Reverend Thomas "Slinker" Paxton, former Blue Rooks Religious Foundation religious director, original Revelator, and Wild Bunch contemporary of Brick. He was the one who sort of mentored me in my current position. A kindly O.G. who didn't take any nonsense.

Seated back across the table, next to Sally, was Reverend Ben Storm Breather, Choctaw medicine-man, Revelator, and younger brother of "Animal." And the only surviving son of the Shaman who trained the other original Revelators. He and I never had occasion to talk much. But Brick bragged of his prowess as a cleric, just as he had with Boris.

Plus, Reverend Ben also brought his elder charge, the dementia-riddled elder, one Alcethra Anthony ("A.A." or "Tony") Jones. He was former FBI/Extirpacy who fell in love with Marian and ended up helping the Original Revelators. Sort of their Bosley. For his troubles, the government maimed him, destroyed his psyche (and erased his official identity), and canceled his pension. He has good days and bad days. But Reverend Ben is now his legal guardian, either way.

Finally, besides Marshall and me, there was Wesley B. Maske, Marian Michaels's second cousin and a friend of Brick and A.A. He was also a board member. And I hear he was a Revelator confidante back in the day, but, otherwise, he was just an interested family member. He was also executor of Marian's estate. As it turned out, during the latter part of her career as an entertainer, he was also her manager. I found that out in the chitchat, as we all waited for the meeting to get started.

Normally, I would start it. But this wasn't a Blue Rooks meeting. As I said, this was essentially a Revelator reunion.

"Thank you all for coming, tonight," Brick started. "I wish Marian could've seen and heard all of us tonight, gathering and praising her."

"She prob'ly did." That was Boris as he lifted his drink in a mock toast. Chuckles from the group.

"Wes, are the arrangements all made?" Brick asked.

"Next Saturday night is the visitation, in the auditorium. Speakers include Reverend Ben here, you, and two or three of her costars from *Bastion Hill* have been invited. Some or all of them might say a few words. The burial is the next day, in the courtyard on Sunday, at high noon."

"Is Mason going to do his comedy?" This was Slinker asking. Mason King was Marian's costar on *Bastion Hill* (he played her son) and he was, for a few years back in the '90s, the hottest young African-American singer/comedian/actor in the country. He had a history of making … unusual … public remarks, taking every opportunity to promote social justice policies. One time, he spoke at a fundraiser for the family of a young black victim of a police killing. In his routine, he was dressed entirely in bright orange hunter's gear, with the bottom of his pants apparently shot out ("License and registration? Of course, officer. Right here. Oh, and one more thing: please stop shooting my black ass!").

Brick tried to set Mason and me up a few years back. It was doomed to fail on account of my allergy to successful relationships. But at the time I blamed him. *Not giving me enough attention* was my excuse. I mean, he was a movie star for crying out loud. Did I think he was going to stay home and wait by the front door for me to come home every night?

"There will be children in the audience. I will make a point to remind Mr. Mason of that." This was Sally, *always playing the prude*.

"The more brothers can speak, the better. Marian was all about free expression." This was A.A. Jones, who had roused himself from his dementia.

"That's exactly right," his guardian, Reverend Ben agreed.

But as the seated participants all issued their various opinions on how Marian's services should go, I refocused my attention on Marshall.

At some point, he had started rocking forward and backward, seemingly agitated. Now, what flickered across his face were less grins than grimaces. He took several really deep breaths and then ran fingers through his hair, stopping halfway as if to pull himself out of his chair by his hair, and then quickly transformed into a relaxed, arms-crossed, legs-crossed professionally seated repose.

It was tiring just watching him cycle through the various states. And if they were a reflection of whatever was going on inside his head, I shuddered to think the energy it took him to … just sit there.

"What is it, Marshall?" This was Boris again. His question ended and cauterized the discussion. Boris had also been watching Marshall the whole time, wisely waiting until Marshall was finished with his internal dialogue.

"We are being spied on," Marshall announced in his usual loud monotone. Then I realized Marshall had been struggling with a decision ever since he stepped off the plane. And, finally, he had made it.

"By who?" I asked.

"By me." At that, Marshall pulled the pocket watch, the one he'd been fiddling with back at the airport, from his jacket and flung it onto the table. It clattered and spun to a stop.

"And what is that?" This was Brick.

"A spy device."

Brick nodded to Wes, and Wes picked up the watch to inspect it.

Brick asked after a moment, "Well?"

Wes, who, for some reason, had miniature tools in his shirt pocket, explained, "It's a railroad watch. Open face. Circa 1930 or so. Illinois is the manufacturer; nice wind indicator; good condition." He removed the back plate. "Hm! Synthetic ruby end stone. Fairly high end."

"And …?" Slinker asked.

"Worth two grand, maybe three." And he left it at that.

"Wait. No, did you check it for spy tech?" Marshall leaned forward into the question.

"No need. You have been staying all day in the quarters just down the hall, with the party hosted in the room around the corner. This entire wing of my home blocks everything, no signals get in or out, son," Brick explained.

"But, as a tracking device."

"There is no high tech in this device, Marshall." Wes seemed confident. He had already largely disassembled it.

"Who gave it to you?" someone asked. Marshall started to reach into the inside pocket of his windbreaker to show them the temporary Extirpacy badge he was given by the Analyst's assistant.

But Brick answered, "It was the so-called VA, wasn't it? The goddamned Visiting Analyst of the Extirpacy." Several people in the room were obviously shocked by this notion. Sally and Reverend Ben actually stood in alarm, as though the enemy were at the gates.

Out of nowhere, the elder hunched-over form of Mr. Jones said from his wheelchair, "Best go back underground, kids."

Everyone ignored him.

"How did you know?" Marshall's face registered surprise. "Do you know him?"

At that, everyone settled down as Brick explained.

For Marshall and the others who had been less involved recently, Brick Reese then recounted how the government, and especially the Extirpacy, had been engaged in an accelerating campaign against the Blue Rooks Church. It went beyond just legal attacks against the perceived wrongs of the church.

The Extirpacy used public relations techniques. It funded documentaries and journalistic exposés against the church. In these shows, it accused the church of doing what it had historically done: cultish practices and illegal labor work camps. The Extirpacy planted moles within the organization to commit sabotage, both white-collar undermining of the church's finances and human resources practices and actual domestic terrorist activities. I had sussed out and fired a couple of those in my first few months.

And, finally of course, first and foremost, the Extirpacy, through its own cadre of special (magic-using, according to Brick) agents, the E-Dogs, still continued to engage in actual paramilitary violence against the traditional leaders of the Blue Rooks Church, under long-standing warrants against some of its original leaders: the Revelators. The very people in this room.

That was who had hired Marshall Lastpost.

I looked at Marshall, and he just looked back with a haunted expression before lunging forward and scooping up all the parts of the timepiece on the table before him.

"Another broken watch," he muttered.

BOOK ONE—CHAPTER TWELVE

"The Extirpacy" (the E) is a government-sponsored but now privately-run, black-box budget operation. Its first official name was the Indigenous Security Enhancements Directorate. It is part of the FBI's National Security Division. Its mission is to find and end all naturally occurring magic sensitives (called "Innies," which is a corruption of the original abbreviation of NAs, which, in turn, was short for "Natural Apostates"—although, for reasons explained below, people often think it refers to "Native Americans").

Founded sometime in the mid-nineteenth century as a secret society, it was an offshoot of early colonial groups of puritanical demon-hunters. At first, the original policy was that anyone who exhibited powers should be killed (as witches, etc.). This often dovetailed with Native American genocidal programs.

It became an official department of the Executive Branch around 1920. It was subsumed into the FBI during World War Two. But by then it had become more sophisticated. This was because scientists from Nazi Germany defected and revealed that they had been able to forcibly create NA-type sensitivity through a mixture of drugs and torture, and that those thus-created were able to use their own life-force for spell fuel, as it were, rather than the life-force of those around them. Hitler eventually rejected the plan (mostly because the subjects killed themselves in short-order, and were notoriously difficult to control in the meantime).

Meanwhile, records show that, under the FBI, sometime in the early 1970s The E developed a less strenuous (if no less immoral) regimen involving only the use of experimental psychotropic and opioid drugs and ritualistic trance-state re-education on volunteers, to create the first class of "E-Dogs" (special agents who used their skills to hunt Innies). This ultimately mimicked Native American Shaman, who had been achieving such effects for some time. Eventually, the mission became to recruit and retrain Innies rather than kill them. [ALSO Note: forcible re-education of Innies who did not take to the drugs replaced termination of subjects as a backup protocol in 1979.]

Meanwhile, some of the escaped early German experimental subjects fled to create havens for NAs around the world in subsequent eras. Despite their madness, some experienced great success in their new endeavors.

Some among the Revelators believe that it is one of these subjects who has risen through the ranks of the E and become its de facto Director (a.k.a. its "Visiting Analyst"), a notoriously savvy opponent with various Highest Order skills (perhaps in all three areas).

As mentioned, indigenous tribes were often enclaves of NAs. Occasionally, tribal Shamans would share their secrets with outsiders. When the son of a Shaman who ran with the "Wild Bunch" got killed, the Shaman honored his son's memory by attempting to train his late son's compatriots. This planted the seeds for what later became the Revelators / the Blue Rooks Church.

One of those compatriots was Marian Michaels. She was born (1944) with powerful Choiciferor abilities, which were further refined after she was trained by the Choctaw Shaman. Later she fashioned herself into a costumed superheroine (The Butterfly) and fought organized crime in the western portion of the US during the 1970s and 1980s.

After she retired, her whereabouts were unknown … this is my love's story.

—A.A. Jones, "Lost Wings of the Butterfly"
(Beginning excerpt: the only portion that he finished)

Marshall hadn't really been sleeping, two nights later, when the Native American, Ben, came calling. But the staring match between Marshall and his pet turtle was like unto a waking dream.

Marshall envied the way the turtle's eyes flared with life. Sometimes, Marshall liked to pretend that Little Rich had cosmic insight. In fact, Marshall prepared a joke whereby he shook and turned him over like one of those old Magic 8-Balls to give a prophecy. The punch line was: *Ask again later. Until then, feed your turtle.*

Ben's knock on the door came again, louder and more insistent. Marshall opened the door, and Ben stepped inside with his typical magisterial bearing.

"I don't mean to disturb," said Benjamin Storm Breather.

"You are not disturbing me."

Ben was dressed in a white turtleneck sweater and jeans. He was a muscular middle-aged man, with tawny skin and hawkish features. His black hear was tied in a bun and his sideburns were long enough to entirely frame his square jaw. He regarded the room around him with the same vague expression that he always carried: one of bemused comfort. When you live as though you are one with everything, you are always "home."

"It is Mr. Jones."

"What about him?"

It would have been an awkward pause for anyone else, but for the Shaman it was typical. Several breaths later, "He wishes you to be present for a very important ceremony."

"What ceremon—?" Then he quickly realized what Ben meant. Ben winced internally, thinking about how it had always been young Marshall's destiny to be next to death. But that was clearly his path.

Marshall nodded and the Native American Indian bowed deeply, saying, "Please come."

Extirpacy headquarters. Two of the beautiful people, a man and a woman, walked the halls in silence. As they walked, the man remembered his time spent in the ether and feeling the faiththunder of the Regnant, pressing against the back of his mind, like a jingle he couldn't forget, or truly remember. Until he summoned them and relieved the pressure, like singing the tune out loud.

"Are you okay, sir?" It was Heather, his other most trusted agent, besides Brianna.

He ignored her, lost in his reverie.

At first, while he had been banished, the faiththunder was just like a never-ending string of nightmares. Vivid. Stark. Rapid-fire visions of death and destruction. There was no forgiveness in those visions. Dreams of being tortured by loved ones. Dreams of torturing them. Others dying in every way possible.

One time, he was burned alive in a house fire while his old classmates in medical school watched from just outside the doorway. Then he was chased off a cliff by wave after wave of his former patients. Then he fell, through partition after partition of reality, plummeting from the sky to break through a barren desert steppe, only to plummet through storm clouds to emerge above a thicket of thorny bushes on a mountainside, and fall through that into another dreamscape. This went on for what seemed eternities. Normally, any of the impacts would wake a person, but these just happened to him, and he had to endure. Forever.

Finally, he snapped back to reality.

Heather had returned to her smartphone, waiting patiently for the Analyst's orders.

"Let's retire to my private quarters … you know, to plan the attack," he said with a wink. The joke being, of course, that Brianna had long since planned out the attack in excruciating detail.

Smiling, she lifted her gaze to him, hungrily. Her dark, curly hair bobbed suggestively across her gaze. "Of course."

The Reese Mansion, in the hallway just outside the guest quarters for Shaman Ben and A.A. Jones.

Ben and Marshall turned the corner to find Boris was already standing there in front of the bedroom door. Boris wore a thick velvet robe, tied broadly at the waist.

"Look here! I was having quite the kip when the most remarkable event occurred. Suddenly, I bestirred and felt rather compelled to *visit you*. I say, did you *summon* me here in an act of bloody absapience?"

If there was an edge to the question it was probably due to both Boris being groggy and because the two of them had always enjoyed a rivalry. They were likely the two strongest Banishers on the planet, but Shaman Ben always had had an edge due to his also having some limited skills as a Choiciferor and Spancaster.

Ben regarded him warmly. "Absapience? That really a word?"

"It means *away from wisdom*, as in *to be unwise*, or may my heraldic crest rust and blow away."

"At some point, I will check with Mr. Maske to confirm my strong suspicion that you have made that word up. Until then, on behalf of Mr. Jones, I want to thank you for being here, both of you. This ceremony is what had consumed me for the longest time. I am not the sibyl that Marian was, but in my own small way, I have managed to see to it that A.A.'s wishes were kept. He wanted you two here for this."

Boris's perpetual smile turned quizzical. "He wanted me, you say?"

"Yeah, I don't understand it either. What can I tell you? You're comic relief."

The two men chuckled, and then they turned to Marshall, as if it were his decision.

"Let's go," he finally said.

Here, a dim voice inside his mind finished.

Then the three of them entered the room of Marian Michaels's dearest friend and former lover.

###

Storm Breather walked in first, regarding the scene as though he'd never been there before. The walls quivered yellow with anticipation in response to the flickering of the various candles. The colored containers for the candles themselves also glowed: blue, red, and green, all arranged on the dresser like a shrine.

It was a pleasant smell, unlike most deathbed rooms that Marshall had frequented the past many years. The window was ajar, and a slight breeze of cool, crisp air seeped in, infusing the room with the anti-odor of early winter.

Boris pulled his robe's cord tighter, thinking that his presence at this deathbed ceremony must've been a mistake.

Mr. Jones wasn't in the bed. He stood, his back to them all as he looked outside that window into the darkness.

He spoke to everyone's reflections. "It's good of you two to come. Is this how you saw it, Ben?"

"Yes."

A.A.'s broad shoulders slumped, and his head dropped. "My papers are all in my bag in the closet. My story. And Marian's."

"Mr. Jones," Marshall suddenly blurted, "I just wanted to say I'm sorry."

"For what? It was never your choice, boy. It was hers. You need to remember that."

"Yes, I will. I do."

"What are your plans?"

And Marshall Lastpost stammered at that, not answering.

"This is an emotional time for all of us. He will find his path." It was Boris, not Ben Storm Breather, who came to the young man's defense.

"Drug runners, human traffickers, phony cults, real cults … all the way down to petty criminals. She was the first, but the work wasn't completed."

Ben turned to look at Marshall. In his vision of this, he had always assumed that these references to Marian were eulogistic; now, he thought they may have been more of a sermon for the boy to consider … a call to action. With him and Boris there to bear witness.

Mr. Jones turned to look at all three men, his eyes glowing specks in the gloom. "Deke, will you take care of her? Take care of them both?"

The three men all turned and looked at one another, unsure to whom he was talking. Back in the day, "Deke" was the only African American member of the Wild Bunch bicycle gang. Later he, Marian, and A.A. shared the bond of their shared heritage, but Deke had rejected Brick's new church and just remained with the Tribe. Everyone assumed he was still there, but no one knew for sure. Deke may have already been dead. But a few years back, around 2014, Ruby and Brick had a falling out, and Ruby reportedly went to live her retirement back with the Tribe, also. That marked the unofficial end of the Revelators. Many thought Ruby had rejoined Deke.

Finally, after the awkward pause, Boris stepped forward and gave the older gentleman a large hug, after which, he held him up at arm's length and gently shook him as he said, "Mr. Jones, it has truly been an honor."

"Sir Boris. Your mom is proud. Don't forget to say goodbye to her."

Boris nodded, but his face was unreadable as he stepped back. Then Shaman Ben stepped forward and gently guided A.A. Jones over to a chair. He placed a blanket over his legs and gently kissed the older man on the forehead.

"Will you all stay with me?" Mr. Jones squeaked.

"Of course," his three friends all spoke as one.

Marshall and Boris sat side by side on the made bed, while Ben stood off to one side of the chair, arms folded like a colossus.

And over the next hour or so the three of them watched A.A. Jones sit, eyes closed, and calmly move on.

There was no litany. No spell. Instead, Shaman Storm Breather softly hummed the songs of his people, a hopeful repetition of chanting tones, preparing the way for his friend to make this next journey.

Marshall would never remember how long they all sat there. Hours, certainly. But how many?

Toward the end, the song could no longer drown out the labored, gurgled breathing. A.A. gasped and rocked gently as he struggled for more air. *The agonal breathing has begun, it won't be long now*, Marshall thought.

And it wasn't long.

Or short, either.

It was exactly the correct amount of time until the end.

BOOK ONE—CHAPTER THIRTEEN

PALLA

###

The next morning, Ben Storm Breather announced what had happened that night to us at breakfast. Other assorted guests were also present for this and, without hesitation, Brick Reese announced that the funeral would be a joint one.

And a double funeral was only appropriate. Marian and A.A.'s relationship was part of Wild Bunch/Revelator lore. According to some gossip I had gotten years ago, after Marian had a brief fling with Brick, Marian and A.A. eventually rejoined and became soul mates, although they never could quite mesh as a couple. As elders, their bittersweet break-up-cum-friendship was an example for everyone around them.

I hadn't known Mr. Jones as well as the others. Most times I had conversed with him, he was quite out of it. But I had heard all the stories. He was the backbone in the beginning. He was their majordomo, their tactical leader. He developed their plans for their missions. He was the one who had the history with the government, the FBI background. He located the targets … the victims who needed rescuing from all the cults and other secret societies that kept popping up. And he was a double-agent. In the end he even outplayed the Extirpacy. And he paid the price.

He had saved the Revelators from the E.

And now he was gone.

Maybe that should have been my first clue.

But I didn't have much time to reflect over the past. I was in charge of the future. And that meant making sure the funeral went off without a hitch.

It was not announced to the press, yet. But that wasn't enough. At least two different false leaks would be issued. Arrangements had been made for faux construction to be taking place this entire week, right on through the weekend, on the street in front of the headquarters entry gate. The invited quests would be trickled in through various clandestine means throughout the week and actually stay there, on the grounds, leading up to the weekend services.

I had to ask about whether any new guests would need to be invited due to Mr. Jones's passing. And I had to ask Sally about any last-minute changes. Just as with the convention, I regarded her role as having more to do with social event management than physical security. But she gave me assurances. So, overall, I felt as secure as anyone could be that the event would be held undisturbed, as intended.

Yeah, I know. I really do.

BOOK ONE—CHAPTER FOURTEEN

—Lao Tzu,
Tao te Ching, Chapter 45

###

Brick thought it was unseasonably warm that next Sunday evening for the funeral. But the winter weather in the courtyard didn't so much hold its breath as it kept it in reserve, only unleashing it every once in a while, with sharp, frigid thrust, like a rapier's staccato. When the wind wasn't blowing, the earthy, comforting smell of the evening primrose and flowering tobacco arrangements hung in the crisp, tangy air.

"It's going to rain," Sally announced at one point. She had grown up in rural Illinois. She had smelled so many storms come and go over the endless, shapeless horizon that it was second nature to announce the next turn. "But, in any weather, Marian would have loved this beautifully decorated courtyard, very much."

She was speaking to Brick, Ben, and Boris, among a few other guests.

The church had sorted out a relatively open spot in the maze of trees in which to hold this ceremony. The caskets were positioned just off to either side of the main walkway to the building, while a tall partition, decorated with lights (arranged in the shape of a butterfly, of course) backlit the scene.

Actually, she would've insisted on more bling. This is too understated for Mar, thought Brick, *and A.A. probably would've skipped it altogether. That would've been a fun fight to watch.* But Brick just nodded his agreement. He reflected on the shared past of the deceased. During Marian's crimefighting career, A.A. was her Man Friday. He was at the FBI, and later the E, during her early years as a heroine. He was instrumental in her success every step of the way, realizing a love he harbored for her long, long before he ever explicitly shared it.

Brick continued to scan the scene. Farther down, the walkway was bracketed by two battalions of chairs. Farther out to one side, a string quartet played a soulful arrangement. People stood in small, scattered groups, gently discussing everything except the subject at hand: death. The sunset seeped over the westward cityscape horizon and through the treescape, giving it all an argent overlay. But strings of bright white lights were tastefully wrapped around certain trees at the far corners of the clearing.

"It is quite beautiful," Ben agreed with a grim smile. "Perhaps we can get the ceremony done before the rain gods have their say."

Brick looked over at Marshall, standing by himself in a nook, wondering how the boy would hold up.

###

Sally followed his glance to Marshall. Mr. Maske had loaned Marshall a golden necktie and helped him tie it into a proper Windsor knot. It was framed behind his typical black jacket. He was actually a fairly handsome young man, she reckoned.

In anticipation of this day, all throughout the week Sally had helped Marshall work to keep his voices at bay. He already blotted them out with instrumental music. (Lyrics tended to contain coded messages, he had told her.) And she introduced him to meditation. They meditated together several times in the headquarters' chapel.

As the visitation progressed, she watched Marshall walk about, eyes closed and humming, so as to avoid the various messages he was hearing from his surroundings. She saw him mimic the sense of satisfaction that Palla and Brick and their friends were emanating. He had good examples. *If there is a thing the Blue Rooks Church could do, it was celebrate death,* she thought.

Shaman Ben left to stand over Marian's open coffin once again. He soaked in the sharp jaw, the metallic, light-blue lipstick and the heavy, dark-lashed, colored-to-match, closed eyelids.

Ben wore a brown leather tunic with bright red and green ceremonial beading over his formal suit. Boris was in a dark purple suit. Most everyone else was in funereal black garb.

As he stood there, Marshall walked up. And then Marshall took the light from the nose-bridge of his glasses—the one that he pirated from one of her old costumes—and placed it in the coffin. *To light the way,* Ben thought, in a reflection of what Marshall must've been thinking.

But, as they shared the moment, Marshall was actually thinking, *Funny how I was the only person present for both of them at the end.*

Eventually, Brick signaled everyone should please have a seat, and then Ben walked up to the casket and carefully removed his ceremonial tunic and placed it upon Marian's feet. Underneath, he wore a sharp, almost shiny, obsidian double-breasted suit, with silver buttons. He paused for a moment to take one last look at his old friend, and then he stepped over to A.A.'s coffin, wherein he placed some special trinkets that only he and A.A. would've known about.

Then he stepped to the podium. *He is the perfect person to do this for Grandma Marian,* Marshall thought to himself.

The musicians finished the bar they were on and then stopped. It was time to make a few remarks before opening it up to others to speak:

"The world is incomplete, but perhaps, in its own way, there is perfection in its incompleteness. For it is the flaws that give meaning to our lives. So, our lives, and this work, and this world, needs no one to finish it so much as it needs someone to take up the work of maintaining it. Marian Michaels did that and more. She made the world a ...” And then he trailed off as he gazed at the gatehouse behind the seated guests, toward the edge of the property.

Everyone turned around to look. And as Marshall looked, he saw, from the gatehouse came walking three, no, four—FIVE people. Two, dressed as guards, scooted ahead of the others, apparently to try and give the assembly some warning. The other three strangers confidently walked toward the crowd, apparently unconcerned about anything. The two strangers flanking on either side were attractively shaped females, wearing traditional funeral dress clothes and even wide-brimmed hats with veils to cover their faces.

And in the middle was the unmistakable form of the strange man known to all as the Analyst. He wore dark, angled sunglasses (even though it was dusk) and black pinstripe, sweat-suit looking clothes underneath. But his form was dominated by a long, white burnoose that billowed behind him as he walked. In step, he took off matching gloves and handed them to one of the ladies, who put them in her purse.

And now that their attention was turned, for the first time, the crowd noticed the flashing red and blue lights being reflected from behind the front wall of the courtyard. The Analyst and his assistants had brought company.

The guards came running up to Brick, and one turned and said, “That’s far enough!” leveling his weapon at the intruders. They complied, stopping some thirty or so feet away, while the other guard handed some papers to Brick. The intruders still appeared unconcerned.

“It’s a warrant for your arrest, sir. And for the arrest of a few others. And it is a warrant to search the premises for ... for, drugs, I think. Sir.” He was huffing. The guard was not used to real action.

Brick pretended to read the paper, but Marshall could see him share glances with Mr. Maske and Reverend Sally. At that, Mr. Maske called for the various visitors to step off, far away, to one side.

Sally just moved toward Marshall and Palla.

Got my Cheez Whiz, boy? an individual voice blurted in Marshall’s head.

The man with the stylishly angled shades raised his hands. "Please! I am so sorry. It wasn't my intention to interrupt anything! Do finish! By all means, it looks beautiful. I regret not being on time." He sounded so sincere.

"How *dare* he!"

"Who is that?"

"What's going on?"

"He's taller than I pictured."

"I've seen him on TV."

The crowd offered every conceivable answer in reply as Mr. Maske shuttled them aside. Marshall was so used to ignoring voices, he reflexively did so again. Instead, he kept looking to Brick for guidance. Brick, in turn, just full-on faced Mr. Maske, who stood by the crowd he had repositioned but looking up to the sky. Brick seemed to be awaiting a signal.

Then the Analyst turned his attention to where Marshall and Sally were standing. "Good work, Marshall, leading us to your family." He strangely emphasized the last word.

Marshall was about to answer when Mr. Maske, via his high-tech eyeglasses, spotted what he'd been looking for. "There! Drones!" he blurted.

And he no sooner said it than a rain of gunfire came spraying upon the courtyard. A bunch of small projectiles bounced off the ground near Marshall. Most of them seem to have been aimed at where the various Revelators stood and not where the larger crowd was.

The Analyst's companions—Marshall recognized one of them as Brianna—crouched in action poses. Their hats fell from their heads, and then you could suddenly see the small, dark gas masks that they were wearing. They both took small canisters from their purses and threw them to the ground. Each canister landed with a *BANG, hisssssssssssssssssss,* and blinding light seared into your brain, followed by the burning stench of some sort of tear gas.

The Analyst smiled, ignoring the sudden melee of darts and screams. "The *Others* still speak highly of you, Marshall. Do you miss their song, Marshall? Can you really not hear them now, Marshall? Does the medicine really work for you, Marshall? They are so close, Marshall! They yearn to have you back, Marshall!" The remarks had the rhythmic effect of a lion-tamer's bullwhip in the center ring, while the circus paraded around him.

Even those who weren't blinded by the initial flash would soon be unable to see much due to the smoke.

Marshall fell over in the initial melee, and now he blindly struggled back to his feet. But before the flash, he had seen Ben drop to one knee at the initial incoming gunfire from above. Something had been jutting out of his shoulder. *Tranquilizer dart!*

Over the melee, he could hear Palla calling his name.

Sally also heard Palla yelling as Ben screamed for everyone to take cover. By the time Sally's sight had returned, she and the others had managed to kneel by a row of trees for cover.

Then Sally saw Marshall just standing there, by himself, looking with blurry vision at the chaos before him.

She saw him watching the two females that had walked in with the VA. They were fighting to protect the Analyst. At their feet, lying unconscious, perhaps dead, were the two initial guards who had heralded them. And they were engaged with Brick Reese.

Brick artfully dodged their kicks and parried with his own. One landed on the brunette, and a second shot, a backhand, hit her neck, audibly snapping it. She crumpled to the ground.

At that, something with the other one, the blonde, changed. For the first time, her professional smirk was replaced with a grim determination. She quickly landed a couple of blows of her own, and as her body armor mostly absorbed two of his glancing counterstrikes, she managed to snag his leg long enough to deliver some sort of shocking touch weapon. With a loud sizzle and flash, Brick cried out and fell to the ground.

Then everyone heard a rumble and, off to toward the front gate of the complex, everyone could see the entire front wall shimmer and crumble in a clatch of debris and dust.

Behind it were several black sedans and vans with flashing lights atop them. Many of which now drove in through the breach.

Just behind them, standing side by side, was a cadre of men and women all dressed in matching brown and black body armor. They all wore helmets with obsidian faceplates. There was no way to see their faces. They had just worked in conjunction to speed up the withering of a maybe thirty-foot section of the stonework wall.

Marshall just stared back and forth at it all, apparently overcome with guilt. He could be heard crying no above the din. Sally quickly ran up to Marshall and pulled him back to cover. Once they were both behind a tree, she tried to gather her thoughts. *What do I do? How did this happen? No! No time now, I have to think …*

Meanwhile, the E-Dogs walked forward in unison, past the black sedans that were now parked inside the courtyard. Sally had never seen one before, but she'd seen reports. By themselves, each one was weak. They would only have been able to affect a much, much smaller portion of the wall. But the E-Dogs, the special magic-using agents of the Extirpacy, specialized in synergistically using their spells in unison.

Sally froze. *I was responsible for this. Wait, I need to summon the internal guards!* she realized. But before she could, other, armed *regular* soldiers, guns drawn, began streaming out of the vehicles and into the courtyard, firing at anyone who moved. They were shooting the guests! Or were those more tranq darts?

BLAM! No. One shot immediately hit Slinker in the head, and Sally screamed at the blood and brains exploding from the exit wound.

No! No! No! Slinker had been crouching on the ground and entering something into his phone, probably signaling for the security personnel from inside the headquarters to come out immediately. He had delayed getting to cover because he was doing her job. Boris cried out and checked Slinker to see, but it was obvious he was dead. Sally could only stare in gaping horror.

Reacting with a snarl, Boris's response was swift. She couldn't believe it. She actually saw him angrily summon two of his favorite dJinni. *How does he do that so quickly?* she thought. *And more than one!*

Even to sensitives, they typically appeared as barely noticeable tricks of light. Here they appeared beyond Boris's shoulders, their own broad outlines reflected in the smoky gloom. To anyone else, or security cameras, all you would see was Lord Wyskald's regal purple form crouched as if to attack.

The others always argued with Sally that she could be a true cleric. But she didn't seem to have any talent for it. She could sense things, but it was never clear, never easy. But Boris was so powerful, Sally could literally hear the echoes of his spell in her mind. Using *their* energy, he proceeded to banish a couple hundred cubic yards of the courtyard ground itself. Sally watched as hundreds of tons of stonework, topsoil, earth, and roots under the impeding troops all shimmered, and then were dispatched from this Timespace, with a flash of blacklight and an audible *snap*, like a tree breaking, over the noise.

Then the soldiers, E-Dogs, and vehicles all tumbled forward as Sally realized what he had done. The earth he'd dispatched wasn't square, but rather a wedge shape, maybe twenty yards wide by fifteen yards long, with the depth sloping: zero at the far edge to thirty yards deep at the near edge. So, in a couple of seconds, all the troops, and their vehicles, fell and slid down out of sight. They'd be able to run back up once they get their bearings, but, for the moment, they were out of action. And Boris did this at a far-removed distance. *Unbelievable.*

All the while, the Analyst had been continuing to shout his taunts at Marshall as he approached. But when Boris suddenly dispatched his troops, he turned to face the purple dandy.

There was no speechifying. The Visiting Analyst merely raised his hands and yelled out, apparently to Marshall? "I know you can hear them, boy! Listen to what they say now!" And then Sally could hear the spell he was casting in their minds, clear as though he whispered it directly into their ears.

But they also heard something else. The dJinni that surrounded Sir Boris suddenly started yelling, gibbering. And not like all dJinni whined when they were first selected to give some *chi* for a spell. No, this was something else.

Terror.

Again, not out loud, but in their heads, Marshall and Sally were sure they could hear them … they took form, they begged for help, clawing at Boris, who spun around and started frantically yelling back at them,

"Wait! Stop, no! You must not!" He seemed to be beseeching to them, or to the Analyst. You couldn't tell. But you could see that the dJinni reached out and held him fast. Ultimately, they spun him back around to face the Analyst, who slowly walked up and raised his hands, gracefully arcing them through the air as if to brush away fireflies, or welcome providence. His smile grew broader with each line uttered:

"As is One, As is All.

As angels fly, and demons Call.

Boris shuddered, his eyes wide and his face covered with sweat, a look of terror held him. His breath became more labored.

"By Holy and Profane,

I Summon The Provincial.

With one hand, Boris clutched his chest. Sally heard them. Marshall heard them. The dJinni were not just holding him, they were removing his *chi*, stripping away the natural, normal protection that all living things have from having such spells cast directly at them. There was a reason clerics only banished *things.* Banishing people was suicide. And you weren't supposed to be able to spancast a spell directly at another living thing, either, like making their *liver* age, for example … only the space around them. Which was difficult enough.

They heard others screaming.

Sally's mind was numb. Friends. Family. She knew he had to do something. Storm Breather was screaming something, too. Sally frantically tried to get Marshall's attention, to go to Ben.

But Marshall couldn't stop watching the Analyst with Boris.

Avert! And attend!

And You may, then,

The spell was straightforward enough. It was cast directly at Sir Boris Wyskald's heart. However much time, however many more beats it would have had, they were gone now.

Dis-en-thrall!

And then the shimmering suggestions of preternatural beings disappeared, letting the dandy's inanimate form drop to the ground.

Marshall's voices shouted above the din, all about in the gloom and the smoke and the dusk. And they left no doubt as to who was to blame for this:

He killed him, but you killed him. This is your fault. Your friend Boris. He was your friend, and you led the others right to him. This is your fault.

Your fault.

You knew this would happen. Your fault. Fault lines. Frankensteins. You're a monster.

Stupid monster. Aunt Ruby will blame you. All your fault. She will hate you.

While Marshall's voices pummeled him with their accusations, the battlefield paused for a moment, seemingly for dramatic effect. For his part, after the fact, Marshall would recall that he could clearly see every detail on the Analyst's face from twenty yards away. The scar above his left eye on his forehead was alabaster white, matching his weird hooded cape and his preternatural grin.

Then shock troops from both sides emerged both from the below-the-ground wedge and from the headquarters, respectively. The bullets started firing. It was an open firefight.

Sally watched in horror as she saw several soldiers, as well as many party guests cut down.

Boris! Spirits! I am so sorry.

Ben Storm Breather heard himself through his own drug-addled fog, screaming for others to take cover, to get behind him. *I must protect them. Spirits, why didn't I see this?* But he already knew the answer. Forces were at work above his station. It had been a long time since he'd been truly surprised like this.

He tasted a faint hint of metal on his tongue as the tranquilizer dart's chemicals coursed through his system. It was everything he could do to keep his feet as he watched Boris turn back the enemy soldiers. *Such bravery!*

And then he saw the Cloaked Devil turn Boris's own spirits against him, casting a spell on his enemy's very heart. *My brother!*

And for a moment, the fog cleared, and Ben just stood and stared at the corpse of his dear friend on the cracked ground.

Then he staggered backward onto his knees, even as he screamed, "IMPOSTER!" Ben shouted with deep rage from his very core. Only his voice wasn't just his own.

At that, the Analyst's cape rotated aside to reveal his shoulders spinning around toward the staggering Indian. The Analyst flipped the cowl back and started. In fact, you could see his head flick back and forth to consider this new challenge because it wasn't just the Shaman.

Ben wasn't alone.

Sally and Marshall—all the sensitives and clerics who were present—could see them, too. Ben was surrounded by dJinni ... and they weren't being coy. They didn't displace the reality around them, no light refraction, no cloudy images. No, they stood, their dragonlike forms plain as day, arranged in a tight phalanx behind their old friend and companion. (They were singing, no *shouting* their loyalty.) There were maybe a dozen of them, stretched out behind and to either side of the Shaman. Just as with Boris, you hadn't seen them appear, they were just suddenly there.

###

Marshall, for one, had never seen them manifest themselves so clearly. Their backs were to him, but he assumed their glowing eyes were the same. These dJinni weren't shadows, or refractions of light, or any other such tricks ... they were corporeal golems—each one standing seven or eight feet tall, man-shaped, with broad shoulders housing muscular-but-short arms. They had massive hind legs, along with self-important spiked tails that snaked along behind them, flicking to and fro as though looking for their own victim. They were dinosaur-men hybrids. Demons. Wraiths. Shed. Spirits. Dragons. Angels. Efrit. Iblis. dJinni. So many names they had had over the years, those forgotten subconscious dragons from the dark recesses of our shared cultural memories.

These dJinni were Ben Storm Breather's spirits, the spirits of his people, come to life.

While the Analyst was distracted, Ben attended to the troops. Despite the gathering darkness behind his eyes, Shaman Storm Breather had only to think and point—no mantra—and his dJinni understood.

BLAM! BLAM! KAPOW! This spancasting spell was aimed at the firearms of the government troops. Their guns all jammed at once. Some exploded in their soldiers' hands. State-of-the-art weapons were suddenly aged such that their components inevitably failed.

Once they realized that they couldn't fire, they, and their E-Dog compatriots, decided to regroup back below the front edge of the wedge. The Blue Rooks security commanders barked some orders as they started to deploy and move forward through the courtyard grove, to outflank and surround their foes.

But it wasn't long before the skirmish was equalized. Brianna fired several grenade missiles from a contraption that apparently had been strapped to her back, under her formal attire. The grenades scattered the Blue Rooks security troops, just as the drones which had originally fired from long range swooped down and engaged the front of the church HQ. Within a few minutes, the Blue Rooks security troops had also been forced to retreat, back into the building.

Once that firing had started, the Analyst had actually rushed over and scooped up Boris's corpse up as a shield from Blue Rooks security's live fire as he crouched next to some overturned buffet tables. But once Brianna and the drones had the situation under control, he stood up and tossed Boris's body aside to address his main foe.

Mr. Maske even snuck up behind Brianna and courageously hit her with a wooden chair leg. But this wasn't a television cop show. So fast she was just a blur, Brianna effortlessly disarmed him and shot him point blank through the chest with a pistol.

Meanwhile, the Analyst advanced on Shaman Ben.

"Indian. You are under arrest. I am rather counting on you resisting, though."

At that, Ben suddenly looked directly up.

"Go ahead and pray. Bring as many of them as you want. They'll all answer to me, too, Indian!" the VA chided.

From nearby, Marshall and the others were worried, at first, that Ben's health was failing, but then they could hear him, again, in their minds. It was his song.

He was chanting.

And his dJinni were, too.

Call and Response, thought Marshall.

Even the usually unflappable Analyst was a little nonplussed. The Analyst's expression was one of pained disbelief. *The Indian had been tranqued! How is this cursed redman even conscious?* his expression seemed to say. The Analyst marched forward to finish off his enemy.

But before the VA could launch his next speech, Ben suddenly raised his hands, and the entire scene was smothered in a blinding light, with a cracking *THA-THOOOOM!* that shook the very ground.

When the light disappeared, Sally and the rest could see what Ben had done. He had quickly chosen a future where that lightning strike would happen. Everyone's ears popped from the sudden changes in barometric pressure and many were warmed by the static electrical charge that had dispersed. A couple of the nearest trees were still lined with glowing vermillion scars.

No one noticed that it had begun raining, a freezing drizzle that revealed the steam coming off the trees and the various combatants.

The Analyst laid flat on his back on the smoldering, scorched ground where the bolt had hit. He didn't seem to be dead and wasn't directly hit. But he was close enough that he was stunned. He tried to roll from side to side, flailing with one arm to prop himself up.

Ben swayed … and then fell over. The drugs had overcome him. He lay prone on his side. His dJinni momentarily also just stood there, slumping from the exertion.

"Ben!" Sally and several others shouted at once. They finally ran to Ben's side, avoiding the beings.

Palla ran up, too. The dJinni all moved aside at her arrival.

Ben Storm Breather was still conscious. And he said just three words:

"It won't work."

At that, Marshall could feel a presence leaving. And then they realized what Ben was saying.

Sally didn't feel the dJinni leave, she was still focused on Ben. They stared at each other as though exchanging a silent message. But Marshall could see it all explicitly, and he started narrating what he was seeing.

"Ben's dJinni … they are all responding to the Analyst now! Sally, they are moving over to him. They are … Oh no! No, Sally … the dJinni? They are switching sides."

Finally, the dJinni all encircled and hunched over the Analyst, who started to move more surely. Then even Sally could see what was happening.

They were reviving the Analyst.

BOOK ONE—CHAPTER FIFTEEN

PALLA

###

The question just kept repeating in my mind. *How could this be?*

The dirt turned into mud as our friends were being slaughtered before my eyes. And there was nothing for me to do. I was frozen by my own utter failure. *How could this be?*

Sally and I had been painstaking. *I* had been painstaking! The secrecy. The security guards. The fortifications. The guests were triple-vetted. No detail ignored; no rock left unturned. We. Made. Sure.

What the VA said about Marshall helping them, betraying us …? That rang true. Someone had betrayed us!

But Marshall? Mr. Maske had assured everyone that wasn't the case.

Not that I took that on faith. I personally made sure that everything Marshall had done since getting off the plane had been surveilled in one way or another. Color me paranoid, but he was way too much of a wild card to leave to his own. From that surveilling, sure, I knew that his meds had completely worn off since he had gotten off the plane in O'Hare over a week ago. But there was no evidence of treachery.

One of the guests? No. The security scans were clear: No one, not a single guest, was wearing a tracking device. No phones or devices were even allowed. Doppelganger agents matching Brick's description had attended two other phony services earlier in the week to throw off undercover reporters.

Sally, on the other hand? If Sally was equally shocked and ashamed, she didn't show it. She sternly held me down in a crouch, trying to avoid flying gunfire and the rest. I would have to investigate later. Right now, we were all going to die.

I yelped aloud as Ben dropped to his knees in prayer, thinking he had succumbed. It was weird how he lifted his hand to shield his eyes even before that bizarre lightning strike. I hadn't even noticed that it had been misting. But the sudden thunder and lightning shook the entire scene to its roots.

We all had gone down at the blast, but still, the VA was not dead. That Jedi-cosplaying motherfucker with the hipster sunglasses was rolling around, still tryin' to get up.

At least his goofy white cape was singed.

Then my attention was pulled back to Ben when he fell over.

Sally and I followed Marshall to Ben's side. Ben said that it wouldn't work, and Marshall once again started lamenting as he looked over at the VA's prone form.

The VA struggled to lay on his side as he locked eyes with Marshall. And the VA smiled.

"Sally, take them somewhere safe." We all looked down at the Shaman, who, unbelievably, was still awake. Sally nodded, and they met eyes. She knelt next to him, propping him up on one of his own elbows.

The Shaman looked about and breathed a deep breath of satisfaction, and with his exhale, he lifted and swung his free arm around in a grand gesture and then, unbelievably, I was, we were … somewhere else.

###

Then the three of us were running up a stairwell inside the HQ, about halfway up, maybe the third floor. I tripped for a second at the sudden feeling of being in a different spot. Sally fell, too. But we all staggered back to our feet.

The stairs were along the outside front of the building, so the first thing we could see was a birds-eye view of the battle. Mostly it was hidden from view by the tall maze of trees. Then I heard Sally. "Are you all right?"

A wave of nausea had to be forced back down. My entire body was shivering, and I was breathing faster than when I had been down on the ground below.

"The battle. It is the same. But it isn't. Is this …?" Marshall asked Sally as he surveyed the scene.

"Yes. He was truly a miracle man. He once hinted he could do something like this, but I never …" Something in her voice was there that told me that he was more than a mentor to her. Of course, Marshall didn't notice.

"So, it is possible. He did it?"

"Yes."

"What? Did what?" I asked, annoyed.

"Reverse Choicifering, essentially banishing someone else. In this case, the three of us—to an alternate Timespace thread," Marshall intoned, with reverence. And then he blurted, "Maybe I could. I just haven't tried it!"

Answering one of his voices, I decided.

Nonetheless, I was just totally lost. After much mute staring, I finally managed a heartfelt, "Huh?"

"Time-travel," he said matter-of-factly.

###

I didn't have time to ask any more questions as Sally insisted that we keep moving upward.

At the middle-point of the fourth-floor stairwell, she stopped running and started feeling the inside wall. She asked, "Marshall, where is it?"

"Here." Marshall kicked the wall and bounced off so hard he nearly fell over the stair railing. But the kick jarred the section of wall loose, and its edges were now evident, with the action of another careful shove causing it to spring open. Another secret door?

Just then: *BOOM!* There was some kind of explosion from outside the building that shook it, and us.

Without discussion, we decided to leave. We all staggered as we entered the secret passageway. And Sally took the time to close the door behind us, with the latch giving a loud *click!*

The small, thin walkway smelled of moist sawdust. It was literally inside the interior wall of this floor of the building. There was no light except a faded glow from around the corner in one direction.

"Where to?" Marshall asked.

"Sub-basement. There should be a boat tethered in the sewer system," Sally explained.

My mind was racing. *How the hell did she arrange this? And why?*

So, he led us in the opposite direction of the light, around the next adjacent corner contour of the building. Between her careful demeanor and Marshall's stoicism, all the thoughts I had in my head to say sounded like ravings, so I kept my mouth shut.

After he turned the corner, he stopped so suddenly we both bumped into him. He reached down and found a small chain, which he then used to pull open a hatch in the floor. There was a light at the very bottom.

It had been covering a large tubular tunnel downward, with a ladder on one side. The ladder stretched for as far as we could see in the gloom, straight down.

It was then that I remembered hearing of this contingency, but it wasn't for the funeral. The sub-garage exit was for those times that the Presidents of the United States from previous administrations had visited. Back in the Blue Rooks' glory days. Of course, even for those plans they wouldn't have used the secret passage. Sally showed remarkable resourcefulness to remember this.

Wordlessly, Sally and I descended before him.

As we got closer and closer to the bottom the smell of sewage became evident.

At the bottom (what was, presumably, this sub-basement, as she called it), there was a stonework landing running alongside a huge storm drainpipe.

And there, as promised, tethered to a stake was a small boat sitting in the river of bespoiled wastewater and sludge. All we had to do was get on board.

Best go back underground, kids.

Yep.

###

I threw up any number of times, but, eventually, we emerged from the sewage by stepping out of a large drainpipe that abutted the warehouse district. My toes squished from the shit and mud as my shoes had been lost during the climb up the stairs in the first place. And my sides ached from all the retching.

Nearby, at the edge of the drainpipe's opening was a cell phone in a plastic bag, buried in the mud. Sally picked it up and dialed someone and said a few words before putting it back where she found it.

"Our ride will be here soon. This protocol was originally meant for a terrorist attack and not government warrants, but it'll do. I'm just glad I swapped in a charged phone yesterday."

I just stared at her until she decided to answer my unasked question.

"I prayed hard about this funeral, and, finally, my prayer was answered. I saw us three in a dream. One of my special dreams."

"You are a Choiciferor, Ms. Radisch," Marshall scolded. "They are not dreams. They are the chosen reverse-images of the futures you choose to avoid." *As if that fucking made any sense at all!* I screamed internally.

But Sally just nodded like Marshall had sagely said, "E equals MC squared," or some other truth.

She had never been trained as a cleric, but she started, about twenty years ago, as a young divinity student who attended Blue Rooks during an internship and grew to become the top pastor in the entire organization. Her skills as a minister were suspect, if all you cared about were the keeping the bills paid and the business of a church running. But her over-the-top earnestness was a hit with the congregants.

But more relevant at the moment, she had also demonstrated her ability to predict the future many, many times over the years, too. I thought of it like a cool parlor trick.

Like in the village where I grew up, there was an old woman who always knew when visitors were coming the next day. Like that. Some people were just naturals. I know it's funny. I didn't believe in spirit-wielding superheroes, but at some level, I had no problem believing in village witches who told fortunes.

Because I'd known some.

Of course, they were all horrible people, otherwise. Truly selfish and manipulative. That was just necessary to survive as an older woman in my village. As likely to slit your throat as praise you when you weren't looking.

Of course, they acted sweet as can be.

Maybe that's what I had against Sally. She reminded me of them.

Nonetheless, she had her own explanation, which she repeated with a twitch of her nose: "My prayer was answered."

"Yes, by *them*!" Marshall snapped, uncharacteristically.

If Sally was offended, you couldn't tell.

"Sally. Where are we going? To the authorities?" Me, trying to refocus us. Plus, I didn't trust that she wasn't taking us into another trap.

"Where I saw in my dream." Then she hesitated and glanced at Marshall, as though he were still bugged.

"Can I go back and get some belongings?" I wondered.

Marshall, to nobody in particular, as though leading a caucus: "Yes, I want to go back to the courtyard. Yes, I can help them. No, I know. Yes, Rich is fine. No. Let's go *here*!"

"No. It's too late for that." *Was she answering me or Marshall?* "In the dream, we go and meet with Ruby. She's at the camp at Barn Grier. We'd best be going there."

Me again: "Wait, what? Barn Grier? It was shut down … what, nearly a year ago."

Barn Grier was the location of our most spectacular failure. A cult popped up in one of our larger rural congregations, in rural Minnesota, right under our noses. And it had burst into the news before I knew of it.

"Um, well, there's still a skeleton crew there …"

"Why? And why wasn't I aware of this?"

"Palla, please. You have been through a lot …"

"Yeah, well, let's talk about that." My voice trended up an octave into my hysterical range. "First off, I want someone to explain why or how I was drugged, because I don't remember even going back into the building! Did you do that? And *then* someone can tell me why you set up a super-secret sewer escape route without telling me. And then, once we've gotten past those preliminaries, we can all sit around and *laugh and laugh* about how our quote-unquote *safe place* from the government agents trying to murder us happens to be the one spot that is *ground fucking zero* for the unauthorized labor camps that triggered all of the litigation that has been the bane of my existence for the past six months, and is, by the way, no doubt—especially if we have somehow kept it open—fully under government surveillance right now! No, really. Go ahead. I'm listening!"

My fists were planted firmly on my hips to emphasize just *how open* my ears were to her.

Off to one side, Marshall sat down, cross-legged in the muddy grass, mumbling something softly to himself. Something about,

"… well I imagine I could, I guess."

Sally had a small tic that was sometimes evident as she spoke. She would subtly twitch each cheek, in quick succession, under her nose while almost blinking with each eye. Like a cute little otter. Or that gal on *Bewitched.* It was an oddly dignifying twitch.

I'd seen videos: Often, in sermons, it preceded her next verse of wisdom, so it registered like a professor gathering her thoughts. The effect gave her an air of importance, despite her schoolmarm looks and mundane manner.

This time, she twitched her cheeks and waved her hand, apropos, since some of her hair had fallen from its bun and was actually in her eyes. She seemed to be considering her options and then, finally, to have reached a decision.

"I know you are upset about all of this. We've all seen horrible things, and we're all still in shock. But sometimes in life things go badly. We cannot change what's happened. But as we stand here, we are in danger. We need to move forward, and you're the leader, our leader. We don't know what is going to happen to Brick, or the other board members. Some will be arrested. Some will be dead. We don't know. So, it just makes sense that we touch base with the *ex officio* board members. As to what we're going to talk about, that I don't know. All I know is what Ruby told me, herself, when I last saw her. And I think that it is best if I let her do that for you, too.

"Except for those specifics about what's going on now at Barn Grier, I'll be happy to answer whatever questions you have along the way. But, unless you have a better plan, let's go meet her now, okay?"

Ruby. That's just great. Ruby's lineage with Brick and the church was ever-present, even though she hadn't been active in nearly a decade. I was feeling like rank had been pulled on me, but I reluctantly agreed. I probably wasn't geared up to process whatever crazy explanations she was going to give me, anyway.

Something, an orange light, caught my eye, and I turned to see what it was.

There was no light. But Marshall's shoulders were slumped more than usual. Worried, I leaned in to see what was wrong?

He was hunched over a turtle.

Oh*! He found a turtle—no, WAIT! Was that …?*

Marshall smiled. It sure looked like Little Rich.

How is that possible? Was he in Marshall's jacket the entire time?

Marshall noticed he was being watched. So, he looked up to us, and smiling a satisfied smile, presented Little Rich to us, as though it was proof that everything was going to be all right.

BOOK ONE—CHAPTER SIXTEEN

*"One just needs a little alertness to see and find out:
Life is really a great cosmic laughter."*

—Osho

###

Once an aide brought them the car, Sally and Palla drove (with Marshall in the back seat) all night to get to rural Minnesota. They were approaching the site of the Blue Rooks Church's greatest shame. But it was important that they go there, Sally thought. *Palla needs to hear what I've heard.*

That next morning, the sunrise came at about 7:00 a.m. Marshall looked out the window with an inscrutable stare and Palla was asleep, mashed up against the inside of her passenger-side door. She had driven the first shift, well to almost 3:00 a.m. For the longest time, she pelted Sally (and sometimes Marshall when she doubted Sally's explanation … Marshall was misguided about some things, but he wasn't a liar), and then the adrenaline seemed to wear off, and she passed the wheel to Sally.

"When will we arrive?" Marshall asked.

"We're actually almost there," Sally said as she approached the exit off US-14 West that would lead them to the farm in unincorporated Ambrosia County. The last time she had come here, it was only a two-hour drive from Minneapolis, a much shorter proposition. Barn Grier was only about twenty-five minutes from Flandrau State Park. Like the state park, most of the year it featured the lush greens of both the wet prairie and the flat-leaved, jittery hardwood forests. This time of year, though, with the leaves fallen, the trees just stood in gnarled repose.

Similarly, now that it was winter, the native bluestem tallgrass (what Sally had called Turkey Foot back in Illinois) had all turned light tan, but it had lost none of its height. It stuck up out of the ditches on either side of the country roads, like bumpers along a lane for child bowlers.

###

As Sally drove, she mentally reviewed the background story: The commune was called "Barn Grier" by the press covering the scandal. To anyone who had ever covered cult behavior, the story was a familiar one. Jason Van Grier originally opened this particular Minnesota facility under the auspices of the local (tri-county) Blue Rooks Church. He was especially loved by his original congregation. By all accounts, he was an energetic, empathetic minister. He seemed to have a knack for reaching young people, young couples, and the occasional older professional looking to reset their life.

Over time, he had opened a series of self-policing drug rehab facilities and people would sign up for short-term inpatient treatment with the county and live in one of the facilities. These were under a 501c3 nonprofit sanctioned by the church and largely funded by the state and local governments.

The Grier House was originally the plan B for those participants who dropped out of treatment. Their particular house master would report them, and then the local authorities would drop them off at Grier House.

Grier House had an excellent success rate. At least that was the reputation; no official audit had ever been done with the state.

But the court case documents revealed many details: occasionally people, recidivists, would report to the authorities of strange, ritual programming being applied to its participants. But rather than investigate, the authorities would take the clients back to Grier House. (several of the well-connected placed their family's black sheep there; it made an excellent resolution to the problem of the family meth-head.)

Forcibly bound and baptized, and rebaptized as often as necessary, the participants were used as forced labor ... being paid as little as five dollars for a fifteen-hour day. The work was grueling, ranging from farm labor to woodwork to lab work (creating products of various types, legal and illegal, to be sold), as well as the various menial services needed to keep the isolated community of two hundred people self-sufficient as a community.

Also, in the court files were descriptions of daily life: The middle of each day, roughly 10:00 a.m. until 2:00 p.m., was devoted to two smaller meals, bracketed by *re-education*. For the kids (and there were kids there as young as nine and ten years old, working the same hours), this meant Blue Rooks *bible studies*, wherein reading and writing were covered. For everyone else, it generally referred to group therapy sessions whereby Mr. Grier and his closest acolytes would hold court on all things personal, sociological, political, and spiritual for the benefits of the group members.

No media or entertainment from any sources outside the commune were permitted to the rank and file.

Finally, the midnight parties were the most publicized feature of adult Barn Grier. (The largest building of the compound, the barracks building reserved for the ruling council of the commune, was vaguely barn-shaped, so the name stuck.) Those parties were essentially orgies, with the idea of permanent coupling socially more or less removed from social life.

There was a caste system, women served the men, and children served all.

As a theologian by training, Sally could look at it holistically: The key feature of Blue Rooks religious education, which is to say its focus on religious liberty ("Your create your own Spirit Guide"), was a natural outgrowth of its origins. This was because it arose as an amalgam of *two* things: the freedom and individualism of the outlaw motorcycle gang biker culture (indeed, regular, local meetings of such gangs have always been called "churches"), *and* the animistic, mystical teachings of the off-shoot of Choctaw that the New Revelators originally fell in with. They combined into a remarkable blend of respect for nature and for human freedom and worth.

It's worth noting that one thing that these two traditions shared was a healthy disrespect for law enforcement. For the most part, that did *not* come into play: local Blue Rooks congregations played by the rules, and the headquarters didn't deliberately run afoul of the law.

But the HQ also was a laissez-faire overseer of its local ministers. So, from time to time, a local leader would take advantage and go rogue. Mr. Van Grier was that.

Again, according to multiple witnesses, he started conducting special sessions for newly pubescent girls, while preaching a philosophy of "free love." Stories of mandatory sterilization were whispered about on the early days of the Internet. The adults weren't allowed to live with or socialize with their biological children … the children had to undergo the ritual of *the program* before they could be allowed to socialize with any adults as anything but laborers.

Sally knew it was all especially galling for the sleeping Palla, beside her in the car. For her part, Palla Kalrajan, after she was promoted to CEO of the Foundation, truly did make a priority of dealing with those isolated incidents. Authorities were cooperated with. For tactics in civil court, she relied on her legal team and followed their lead. Structured settlements were reached, paired with robust nondisclosure agreements ensured that no one incident became the sort of scandal that could hurt the entire Foundation.

But Barn Grier was different. Its final mission was an actual raid on a federal facility. So, the federal government had responded with a sting operation, and one of the Van Grier acolytes was a plant. And there was lax enough record-keeping, cross-training, and cross-pollination of operations and board activities that the legal case against the foundation was irrefutable.

Van Grier was taken away in shackles on national television (after an armed standoff). And the entire facility was made the subject of several TV and Internet documentaries.

The entire place shut down. Locked down. A security company had been hired to police the grounds to make sure it wasn't disrupted thereafter.

And that was how it was supposed to be, even though Sally knew better. She'd been in contact with Ruby for some time, and she knew the truth. She had a feeling that neither of the passengers would take the news well.

She smelled the smoke before she saw it. When she got to a gap in the tree line, she didn't see the rows of buildings under the hillside barn-shaped mansion barracks. Now, it was all smoldering ruins. "No." *Oh no—no, NO, NO!* She braked suddenly enough to wake up Palla. And Marshall bounced off the back of the front seat, too.

"What is it?" he asked.

"Something has happened to the camp!" Sally shouted. "I saw it through the trees!"

"Is Ruby there?" he asked.

She backed up, but the scene through the trees looked normal, now. Instead of answering, Sally sped up down the road to go see.

###

But it wasn't what she thought.

Ruby and the rest were still there, and all were healthy and whole. The only smoke was from cookouts being attended by the riders of a caravan of motorbikes, cars, vans, and even a microbus.

Sally was baffled. *But I saw it.* However, she let it go as a trick of the light. She looked in the rearview mirror to see Marshall's expressionless frown looking back at her.

As Sally's car approached the camp, a cadre of bikes and a car cut her off before she could get to the compound. Ruby got off one of the bikes and limped toward the stopped car carrying a rifle.

"Sally? Oh, my God, Palla! Marshall? Is it really you?" She looked in each window, smiling, to which Sally and Palla smiled in return.

"It is me, Aunt Ruby!" Marshall said out the back window, with a distinct note of excitement in his voice.

Sally said, "Ruby, we have to tell you. They struck at us. At the funeral."

Ruby asked, "You mean?"

"The VA. And E-Dog team. Special agents. An entire company of soldiers."

"Spirits!" Ruby seemed to be reeling a bit.

"Uncle Ben banished us …" Marshall offered from the back seat, to try and get to the point.

"Banished … you?"

"… forward!" added Marshall.

At that, Ruby and Sally exchanged a somber look. Both started to tear up.

Palla, who was still skeptical, had nonetheless spent much of the early ride peppering Sally with questions about the so-called magic being used. Sally had explained that banishing one forward really was sending them to an alternative timeline where whatever difficulty they were currently in was bypassed. In this alternate timeline, for example, perhaps Sally had taken Marshall and Palla inside prior to the arrival of the strike force.

She said that one problem of that was the side-effect they were experiencing. They effectively replaced their doppelgangers at the moment-in-time when they appear. But they only can remember what happened in their original timeline so, for all intents and purposes, it was like having amnesia for whatever the intervening time period was.

Come to think of it, she never mentioned the second problem with it. Oh, wait, I think I understand, thought Palla. But to be sure, "Why are you guys both giving each other that look. Is Ben okay?"

Ruby looked at Sally, who nodded and explained over her shoulder to the others in the car. "That prayer is fatal to the Banisher. You may not know who else survived the attack. But, in this timeline, the one here and now with us, Benjamin Storm Breather is most certainly dead."

Sally let that sink in for a moment. She also took a moment to be silently proud of the subtext of that message ("You may not know who else survived"), because soon, they would have to tell Ruby of Boris's fate in the fight, and it was important she know that maybe that wasn't how it went in this timeline.

Finally, Marshall broke the silence. "You know. Tomorrow is the fourteenth, the very *first* of the twelve days of Christmas."

During that painfully awkward pause, Palla had to think, *Are you sure you're not autistic?*

At that, Ruby shook her head as though clearing it and said, "Right. Why don't you all come inside the Barn and drop off your things—"

"All we have is a turtle," said Marshall.

"—and get cleaned up and rest. We can go over everything later today. And then I will talk with the other road managers. Probably, we can stay here and celebrate the holiday with all of you. Would you like that?" She was looking at Marshall.

He just kept frowning and said nothing.

###

"Do you know why I do this?" And he pushed the button, releasing the slow drip into Brick Reese's body. Brick's prone form stretched and writhed beyond the boundaries of its own flexion. Brick needed to scream but refused to give the bastard the satisfaction.

The man known these days mostly as the Analyst watched for a while. And then he toggled off the spigot again, letting Brick rest for a moment. The Analyst maintained a bored expression on his face.

"'Cause … you're a … uh"—Brick could barely breathe, let alone speak—"sadistic … prick."

"Ah, I should have been more specific. Pardon me for forgetting your legal training. Yes, that's precisely correct. But no, I didn't mean why I *personally* conduct these sessions. No, rather, I was referring to *my mission*." He didn't wait for an answer.

"It would be amusing if it wasn't so pathetic, Mr. Reese. You lack the sight to know the holy ones. And you lack the strength to control those under you that do have that sight. Just because you found *god* smoking vision-weed during a long summer with the Choctaw, you presume to lead an entire *church* of those with true vision?"

The Analyst circled the table upon which Brick Reese was bound. His speech was aimed at the ceiling as though giving a lecture to freshman university students.

"I have read your pathetic little opusculum, your collection of third-rate parables about humanity and freedom and good and choice and—*well*, I can tell you for sure, Mr. Reese, while you were slumming with the Choctaw, I have been *there*, Mr. Reese! I have lived among *them*! The Regnant do not care about any of that, Mr. Reese. They only understand power. They want more of it, not less. And that is the choice my Master gave me. He merely asked the questions: Did I want to live? Did I want to get my revenge? Yes? Yes? Good. He asked, just *what* was I willing to do to get what I wanted?

"And he showed me a simple truth. I had been sent away in violation of order. *Order* was the solution. And for someone like me, I could now speak the special language of the Lost ones. Suddenly, those rare dJinni who were shunned and homeless, the *Lost*—now, they had a friend, a leader. Someone with vision. And I showed them where they might find a new home.

"Your little band of idiot clerics presume to persuade, or even control, the mighty Regnant? Since you run an entire organization of magic-using clerics, didn't you think that it would *behoove* you to learn a thing or two about magic, Mr. Reese? See now, since it was one of your greatest followers who tortured me with the misuse of his power, I suppose I can go ahead and favor you with a lesson: anytime someone isn't using their own synergyte dJinn, the *Lost* ones will be the first to answer. Did you know that? No?

"And here's another. Those *Lost*? They belong to me."

Then he pushed the button again. And this time, Brick did scream.

The Analyst wondered if that scream would somehow mute the voices of the *Lost*, the ones that never stopped screaming in the back of his mind. But no. Instead, all the screams merged into the slow, deep harmonic chords of torment that were the stuff of Order. Of course. *No one will escape it, Master. I promise. I will bring Order.*

Pain was truth. That was the reality that he carried from his previous life, from the way he died.

BOOK ONE—CHAPTER SEVENTEEN

PALLA

###

This is my life? I asked the mirror.

A week ago, I was CEO of a respected religious foundation, living in a high-rise in Chicago with my cat and doing work I could be proud of. Now, I'm a Minnesota gypsy, on the run from the government—well, not so much the government as an unaccountable shadow-agency who is hounding my employer with, natch, lethal paramilitary force.

The day was spent eating in the mess tent and meeting some of the inhabitants here, and then eating again. After that, we were introduced to our respective guest rooms. I couldn't speak for anyone else, but I fell asleep almost immediately and slept a good sixteen hours, until about 4:00 a.m. After that, I just sat around with a bout of insomnia, periodically trying my cell.

For some reason, my cell service wasn't working there, so I wasn't able call anyone to let them know where I was. Nor could I text my cleaning service, but they would be at my place late this afternoon, anyway. Hopefully, they would see to Sebastian. He gets out of sorts if he his food dishes aren't replenished regularly. The thought of my cat made me smile inside.

The room I had slept in was a sparsely decorated beige on beige, and the floors were an unfinished wood that was beginning to darken with age where it was most walk worn. There was one bathroom on either end of the building per floor. The one whose door was open on my floor was closer. Inside, it was already stocked with soap and toiletries, including feminine.

Ruby offered me some of her clothes … she was smaller of frame than me, but she still had a large, shapely bust. She told me she had lost some weight, and so the clothes she gave me were too baggy for her. I put on an outfit and checked myself out in my room's standing mirror. The jeans were high-tops that showed a bulge in the pocket where my bell resided. The top was a red flannel blouse.

The dresser beside the mirror actually had some costume jewelry on it. I was taken by an especially shiny, silver set of four rhinestone mini-snap-clips. I wrapped my hair around and back and used all four of the snap-clips in a row to hold my hair down on one side. My eyes had bags the size of silver dollars, and I had no makeup to speak of. But, overall, I didn't look as bad as I felt.

I had hand-washed my bra, but I had no way to dry it and so I left it hanging on the rib-cage radiator by the window. *I guess I am free-wheeling it today.* The radiator was clanging its steamy outpouring of heat. *Had it been doing that all night? I must've slept soundly for that to not wake me up.* I left my purse behind in my room and went outside to see what in the world I had gotten myself into now.

Last night I had spent a fair amount of time in bed reflecting on the ramifications of what had occurred. I couldn't help but see it through a legal lens first—warrants for searches and for our arrest. The grand jury must've returned an indictment on the most recent case, in the Northern District of Illinois. Okay. Jeez, they had moved fast.

How were we found? I continued to suspect Sally. *Who else could it be?*

I wanted to share my theory about Sally with Ruby, but those two were hardly ever separated.

At one point, the very first day we were there, Ruby thought to ask Marshall where his favorite watch from his childhood was? After he admitted he had given it to the Analyst, Ruby suddenly stood up and went to instruct the various lieutenants in her little band to evacuate the camp, posthaste.

It was about then that Sally and Marshall realized what had happened. Certain the spirits could be prevailed upon to locate people if they were given an item that that person had worn, they all believed that Marshall's old watch was how he was traced to the HQ.

After that, Marshall left for his room. He seemed pretty upset (at least by his standards—no emotion, but more verbalizing and fidgeting).

I felt a little bad for suspecting Sally. I felt even worse because I sort of still did.

I mean, for these two to blame Marshall just seemed insensitive to his condition. He was already going through so much. How could they do that to him? Unless maybe they were hiding something?

I resolved to go by his room if he didn't show himself by lunch time.

As part of my prep for meeting him, I had researched schizophrenia. For most people, it began (the symptoms—hearing voices and hallucinations) in early adulthood, or perhaps a bit earlier. But for a small percentage, it was early-onset, essentially from birth. Studies showed that infants as young as two months old were seeing visual hallucinations.

For anyone, and nearly everyone, who got schizophrenia, it meant the end of having a *completely* normal life. For a small percentage, perhaps one-fourth, who got proper support and treatment, they achieved a sort of balance whereby they might function in society, hold a job, and so forth. At least over periods of time. Relapses were common because, once the patient felt better, they usually took themselves back off their meds. Another one fourth could live independently but couldn't really function in society. And the rest were doomed to live on the streets, in a constant state of anxiety and fear.

I remember watching a YouTube video that simulated what a psychotic episode looked and felt like from the perspective of the afflicted. It was terrifying. And that was an adult, me, watching an approximation, knowing full well that it wasn't real, and that I wasn't going to be affected. It was hard to imagine what someone with the condition, who heard voices and whose hallucinations *felt real,* was feeling. How would you know what was and wasn't happening, or was going to happen? How could you ever feel truly secure or safe?

And then, to consider what it would be like for a person like Marshall, whose onset occurred he was a child? My god.

He's the real goddamn hero, Brick said to me, the last thing before I left that final board meeting.

God, *final* board meeting. Ah, Brick. And, as always, this line of thought, of course, brought me back to the entire use of him (or any child) on Revelator missions.

When I started as operations director back in 2014 (right about the time the Revelators disbanded), there were a handful of stories that various ministers at Blue Rooks had gone rogue—essentially starting cults in their own name. This was the ultimate irony for an organization whose founders, the Revelators, had specialized in rescuing people from precisely that sort of situation from other religions. Part of the reason that it hadn't been dealt with by my predecessor was that the entire organization was in a state of denial. It *couldn't* happen here, with one of our own.

I certainly never gave it much thought when I took over. Even when I was named CEO in 2017. Instead, I focused on making the relatively informally run foundation a truly professional organization. Lots of layoffs and inserting our own, *my* own people. And then when there were bumps in the road, I just followed the lead of our legal team. (My background as a JD taught me better than to second guess a good attorney, once you had one.) We worked hard to resolve them whenever they would occur, like Whac-A-Mole ... but, over time, we felt like we had gotten the handle of it. The reports came less frequently and then, eventually, not at all. For almost two full years, we had no such incidents.

Then the Barn Grier stories made the news. It was an old scandal, from January of 2014, before I was hired at all by Blue Rooks. But I still felt responsible ... I had never uncovered it.

I mean, I had never considered the structural problem underneath. Yes, it was a good arrangement, having an entirely separate foundation and so forth ... but it further isolated the churches from the central HQ.

So, this was the question that Ruby had challenged me and Brick with when the scandal first hit: so, what if a particular local church just kept continued conducting missions? Not Revelator missions, not condoned or coordinated with HQ, or even with Revelator knowledge. But missions, nonetheless. Mercenary. Illegal. Whatever they wanted. Like the old biker gangs in the old days ... outside *the law*. Was the church responsible? Legally? Ethically?

###

I entered the mess tent for breakfast, and Sally was already there with a couple of Barn Grier regulars that I had met yesterday but whose names I didn't remember. We were reintroduced as I brought my tray of food and sat down.

"So, we don't have cell service here?" I began.

"The whole camp is too remote from any towers to get good coverage." This was Bill. He had lots of names, but everyone just called him Bill.

He was a Choctaw who also wore colors of a biker gang, I didn't know which one. Up close, those cool jackets were, in fact, quite nasty. Brick once told me that, in the old days, the gangs deliberately soiled them with feces and other unmentionables and made a point of never laundering them, as a sort of ritual of, what, I don't know, toughness? But I, too, spent my younger years as an unmentionable, so I empathized with the sentiment.

Bill was very fit, bald, with a salt-and-pepper van-dyke around his chin that was waxed to a shot point. Under his biker vest, he actually wore a checkered dress shirt, but with the sleeves rolled up tightly over his large biceps. He had a military bearing and projected leadership. His voice was the deepest baritone I had ever heard, but he spoke softly, almost with a purr. And the final touches were the black leather flat cap and pince-nez eyeglasses (what was it with eyeglasses in this community?), with a single black leather strap that secured them to an inner pocket in the biker vest.

The bottom line: he was confident and handsome, the tattoos were tasteful (vines up and down one arm), and there was always something about a man in leather ... I was momentarily reminded how long it had been since I had gone on a date and quickly decided to suppress those distracting pangs.

Sally jumped into the pregnant pause. "Bill here runs the security. He was born Choctaw and met the Revelators during their heyday, helping them from time to time ..."

"More the other way around. I found young people who were trapped in bad situations. And Brick and the group got them out."

Sally continued, "Bill was later the sergeant-at-arms of the Montana Madmen. Now he's a consultant. He has worked for us. And he's worked for the government."

"So, you're a mercenary?"

"Not exactly. Most of the time, I don't work for pay, at all. My allegiances are ... individualized."

"Bill is a child protection advocate," Ruby interjected. She approached and sat with us. "He was the one who brought it all to our attention. The rot at the core of what the church had become."

"And what had we become?"

"We had become the enemy." Ruby was sure of herself. But I was rested now and had time to think of some questions.

"Why not bring this to Brick?" *To me*, was what I really meant.

Ruby didn't hesitate to answer my real question.

"I didn't know if you were to be trusted. I still don't."

I don't blanch easily, but I did at that. I shouldn't have reacted so badly, but I was proud. Except for Brick (and most of that was all in fun), it had been a long time since anyone spoke to me like that. Truth was, at this point, I was used to being boss. Now I felt like a chided school child, and didn't like it one bit.

"Oh, screw you. I have done nothing but be loyal to this organization. And what have you been doing these past years, except hiding off away from everyone and undermining everything we were—*I was*—trying to do to reform things? You think my own *private* internal audit didn't reveal that your nonprofit was the indirect funding behind the Barn Grier mission that got us plastered on the evening news? But did I give your name to the authorities? No, I did not. So, instead of your accusations, I think the words you're looking for are *thank you!*"

"I thanked Brick. That was his decision, not yours."

"If you think I just automatically just do what that doddering old man says, you really are out of touch with the church."

I could see by her expression that got to her. She and Brick were contemporaries and former lovers. So, by mentioning his age, I was calling her old, too. But instead of yelling, she just scoffed. "Hmph. *The church*. The church was always just a tax dodge ... you think what Blue Rooks preaches is even a vague approximation of the religion that we learned at the old Shaman's feet? Hell, it's not even an approximation of the book that Brick wrote about it! You might want to get yourself a clue."

"And now we are relitigating a very old argument." Sally was smiling warmly at Ruby. "Palla here has done tremendous amounts of good for the organization. And the organization has done tremendous good for tens of thousands every year since it was formed. It has changed lives, and I have been privileged to be a part of that. I have seen the good works.

"But, sometimes, there are bad people who need to be brought to the light of justice. And some of those times the official channels aren't enough. That's why you and Bill here, and all you've been doing, has also been helpful. We are all on the same side." Her nose twitched once, twice, tightening in another tremor, but her warm smile didn't dim.

"I just felt it was important to remind everyone of that."

Sally's heartfelt monologue had the desired effect. Cooler heads prevailed and Bill suggested that everyone reconvene at the meeting room on the first floor of the barracks in an hour.

Give them a chance. You know me. I'm not some dreamy revolutionary. But after Bill made his presentation to me, I was convinced. I think you will be, too, Sally said to me after the mess tent talk.

At that point, I didn't trust any of them.

I had worked hard to make sure the church had become something I could be proud of. I wasn't going to let a bunch of reactionary cooks undo all my hard work.

###

It turned out I didn't to go far to find Marshall. As I left the mess tent, I could see him talking with a younger girl—maybe teenage, maybe older—and Bill chuckled from behind me.

"I see my daughter, Kinta, and Marshall, have met," Bill intoned.

"Your daughter? She's beautiful." She hovered around Marshall as he walked from the barracks.

"Thank you. We're very proud. I enjoy traveling with her. I tell her she's my good luck charm, to ward off the evil spirits."

"'Let me ask you. What do you think of Marshall?"

"The Minko Puskus? It doesn't matter what I think. He is a force of nature. He is well known to the Tribes."

"Minko Puskus. So, that's his Choctaw name? What's it mean?"

"Child Chief."

"Why would the Tribes know Marshall?"

"Oh, everyone knows of his visions and how he would help Ben and Ben's friends help others in need."

"So, you knew Ben. How?"

He held a strange expression on his face for a beat too long. More than just missing his friend. There was a story there. "He was one of my oldest friends; really more like an older brother to me. In fact, I again go now to try and pray for him. Would you like to pray with me?"

I told him how sorry I was for his loss and that, of course, I would pray with him.

I thought we would go to a special grove or a room or something. But, instead, we just stayed there in the middle of the walkway. He stood very still and began singing, in a clear deep voice, something that sounded like: *Chay-esh No Wah Chay Ah-kah-ah,*

Chesh Nah Ko Bee-ah-nah,

T'ey Mah-ha T'ee A-nah-lay …

He nodded for me to join him, and I did—haltingly at first—but then, with repetition, I was able to sing right along with him. At one point, I even adjusted my voice so as to create a natural harmony. I am not sure how it happened, but it started sounding quite nice.

At first, as I sang, I was so focused on Bill and his approving glances that I hadn't noticed the crowd gathering. But after a few verses, I saw them all grouped around us.

And the very first, closest audience member was Marshall.

But he wasn't looking at us. He seemed to be looking past us, behind us. Around us.

I turned to see what he was seeing, but all I saw was a gathering storm above us in the sky.

Bill's eyes were closed as he intoned the prayer over and over again. At one point, as I continued to sing my part, he branched off into another verse. We sang right alongside each other as though we had been taught to sing the song together from the very first.

Marshall's big, dead, unblinking eyes were big as silver dollars and darting about, as though he were expecting something to happen. Bill's and my rendition seemed to hold everyone transfixed.

"Kee-you-oh-oh-ooohs,
Kyuu-oo-pah-ah-lay …

Marshall was edging closer, almost involuntarily, protectively, but I just kept singing:

"Chay-esh No Wah Chay Ah-kah-ah …

I felt lighter than I had in months. I felt alive and closed my own eyes in the enjoyment of the moment. It was a sad tune that we were singing, but it contained the joy of the man for whom the song was about.

I thought back to the various memories of Ben that I had, mostly revolving around conversations about my past. He was one of the few ex-Revelators that I felt comfortable opening up to. Along with Amma, of course. And, to a lesser extent, Brick and Slinker. But Ben was one that I could call upon for even personal advice. He had experience with overseeing a large community, as a tribal Shaman. But in today's age, a native American leader also had to be a very practical, earthy actor, in order to protect the Tribe's interests in the United States of America. I thought he played that part well, and so, early on, when he offered advice for me, unlike the others, I would listen to him.

And now, like Amma, and A.A. Jones, he was gone. Brick and the others might be dead, too. Or worse. It was unfathomable. What else was this Analyst capable of?

So much loss. And a true passing of the torch moment, at a time of crisis for this band of "brothers," this entire movement.

I felt a newfound sense of responsibility to lead this group. But in order to do that, I knew that I had to come to terms with the schism that existed. Ruby, maybe Brick's closest ally, next to Marian herself, had apparently left the fold and set upon her own path. Now, her path and mine converged. What way now?

Probably I had to find out what happened between her and Brick. And what in the world was going on here at this camp? What were they doing?

My eyes popped open after I felt the first raindrop. Eventually, I stopped singing, and the rain started getting heavier.

I turned to Bill, who had stopped singing and had a strange expression on his face.

I laughed. "Did we do that?" I joked, referring to the rain.

But Marshall was shaking my arm (Did I really not notice him lay his hands on me?), and he said while staring at our feet, "You shouldn't. I don't know if we could have stopped them all." *Was he even talking to me?*

Having no earthly idea what that meant (and a little annoyed that his crazy had interrupted my joking mojo with Bill), I pushed him back. "Get your hands off me! What the heck do you think you're doing?"

He just stared at me and stammered something I couldn't hear. (The rain was starting to get stronger and make some noise.) He looked mortified that I'd yelled at him. But he had to learn not to go touching people.

I started to run back inside the tent where the food was. I felt like some dessert, before our meeting on the next hour.

"Thank you for your song!" Bill shouted to me as I scampered inside.

"Thank you!" I replied with a wave.

"You're welcome, Chitokaka," Bill said in a normal voice.

What did he say just then? I wondered as I kept backing away. I would have to ask them what that meant sometime.

"The key is the edible, the Blue Joy," Ruby explained.

The edible, Blue Joy, was essentially a biscuit that was infused with hemp derivatives and a few select ingredients from Q-47 (the experimental drug that Brick had been given to save his life during Vietnam, the source of his *powers*). One, I wasn't surprised this was all about that. Blue Joy was scheduled to be rolled out as a promotion during the upcoming convention we were going to host in Vegas. Two, Ruby's company, Quaruous Manufacturing, was the drug maker, and (this part they didn't realize I already knew) the Q-47 that was used in the manufacturing was obtained during a secret mission that originated right here at Barn Grier.

The Barn Grier mission that was uncovered and became our greatest scandal: it was the actual task-force that infiltrated the Pentagon and stole the Q-47 serum from the vaults. (Actually, it was a basement closet, and it was inside an abandoned medical facility in West Virginia where druggies and squatters had been hanging out for years, but what the media's version lacked in accuracy it made up for in pizzazz.)

Part of my job as CEO had been to make sure we won the court case and were therefore allowed to create Blue Joy, even though some of the underlying chemistry was obtained illegally. Our settlement with the government included a *fine* that represented a royalty from all the sales of the drug the next twenty years. It was a groundbreaking legal solution.

And when our lab reported that the Blue Joy drug prototype had been developed, Brick wanted to rush it to market. But I held him off until it was tested (although we got the FDA to expedite things) and, once it was approved, we set up the upcoming conference to announce it.

We can take the lead, Brick said. *Offer it to the other denominations for free, in exchange for sole purchasing rights. It won't matter that their congregants become sensitive, since we're the only ones who understand the curriculum. Only we know how to truly pray. Eventually, there will be an exodus … to our church.*

It was a bold plan. I liked the part where only Quaruous Manufacturing manufactured it, me being a bottom-line sort of gal. Our legal and organizational ties to that entity were secure—

"It doesn't work," finished Ruby.

I had totally missed what she'd said. "What doesn't work?" I asked.

"Blue Joy." She shook her head brusquely. "Doesn't work."

"Of course, it works. Our lab trials confirmed it—"

"Doesn't work!" Ruby was adamant. "Brick was in too much of a rush. The Tribe has looked into it. It doesn't work. It makes nonsensitives *feel something,* but it is transient. People can see the spirits, but no communication is possible."

I closed my eyes so my eye roll wasn't visible. *I swear, if I have to hear about the so-called spirits one more time …*

But I gathered myself. "Well, for the sake of argument, let's assume that the goal was just to get people to feel spiritual, for just a bit. And you know why we should assume that? Because it was. I mean, I was there. That *was* the goal. And if none of the people taking it can see the future or cause tires to blow out, well, they're just going to have to live with the disappointment, aren't they?"

Okay, in retrospect, that came out cattier than I wanted. But I was really annoyed.

But Ruby was so determined she literally gritted her teeth. She marched right up to me as I stood up straight, in defiant response. *Did she want to fight? I'm not going to hit an old woman, no matter what she says. Or might I?*

I instinctively gripped my bell in my pocket, as though it were a weapon.

That helped center me. After all, this was a woman who just (despite her clinging to the hope that we were magically in an alternate timeline) lost her son. So, I quickly added, before Ruby took a swing at me, "Ruby, please. Just tell me what is going on." The thought flashed through my mind that I had missed several of my daily rituals.

To my shock, Ruby choked down sudden emotion. "The drug isn't—look, it isn't just that it doesn't actually make people non-sensitives suddenly aware of the spirits. It works for that, if only temporarily. No, the problem is that it does the opposite to nearly 95% of those who aren't. It cuts them off from the spirits. And that effect doesn't seem to be temporary. It would mean the end of the church. The end of all of it!"

At that, Marshall, the forgotten man in all of this stood up and repeated that, "It would sever the connection between us and them?"

"Yes. It appears so. Bill?"

Bill stood up and somberly admitted, "When we first heard of this drug, we asked Brick for a sample. I trusted it on no one else and took it myself. And, within moments, I was suddenly unable to enter any vision quests. Later, my spirits responded to my prayers only sparingly and, eventually, not at all. After many weeks and months, it became clear what had happened. The spirits would no longer answer my call. My prayers are now just songs. When I pray, now, I sing as though to an empty room."

Bill said nothing. No one did. And, as I'd taken to doing during awkward pauses, I watched Marshall. None of the signs of him being upset were there. He didn't pass his hand through his hair or against his forehead. His eyes were still, as always, but there was something … what was it? Then I saw it, the way he was shifting his feet back and forth: *excitement.*

"How long has it been?" this was another tribal leader, named Pharell, from another part of the country, who had arrived and who was sitting in on this meeting for the same reason that Palla and Marshall, to get up to speed on the protest. All you could notice about him was his mohawk haircut.

"I stopped taking the drug three months ago. There's been no change. I fear that I may never be one with the spirits again. My friends, my feeling is that this is the work of the Nanishta." He glanced at Palla for a moment. "I fear that we have seen the last summer, and now are in the long winter, when our children's hair turns white and the soil no longer grows: the *Third Removal* when the great spirit, Nanishta, returns to take us to higher ground."

Marshall nodded. "Let's go here," he mumbled, like he was ending a sacrament.

"What is the plan?" And this was me, gently nudging us back to the real world. I wanted to get to the punch line.

"Okay. First, we propose to protest, in a high-profile way, the creation of the drug itself. It was done using inhumane practices; it is toxic; it was created as part of a scandalous act of domestic terrorism, etcetera."

"But that will decimate the church's reputation!" I argued.

"Second," Ruby continued, "we, the remaining Revelators, and friends, are going on one final mission. We intend to destroy not only the lab, but all the specs for the drug's development."

"What? Are you crazy? There are people in that lab. You will kill dozens! And the plans are in the cloud or something …"

Now, Sally stepped forward. "Oh! Um, no, they're not, Palla. After I met with Ruby here last year, I decided to help them. The final prototype was developed in a compartmentalized way, no one group of researchers or technicians have a complete set. The only complete set of specs is on my personal server."

"You mean the server back at HQ that was just impounded by the federal government?"

"No, I had that server moved to a private residence."

"Where?" I demanded.

No one answered. Sally crossed her arms, looked at Ruby, and sat back down.

"Look, you weren't able to trust Brick, I wish you would at least trust me …" And then the looks on their faces told me what I should've already guessed.

My jaw hit the floor. "Brick knew?"

"Dear, this was *his* plan. I mean, *the Revelators ride again*," Ruby said as she waived her arms and projected her enthusiasm like she was in a school play. "Doesn't that just sound like him?"

So, the schism between Brick and Ruby had all been a ruse. And this was why she wasn't at the funeral. Brick needed deniability, and so Ruby planned the protest/terrorist mission on her own.

From that point on, my resistance crumbled, and I focused on just finding out as much as I could about the details of what was supposed to happen. This was not because I agreed with it, necessarily, but I'd be damned if I would continue to be outside the loop, anymore.

As the meeting wrapped up, I silently offered up my own prayer. *Brick, if you are still alive, I am so going to kick your ass.*

BOOK ONE—CHAPTER EIGHTEEN

"I am the punishment of God… If you had not committed great sins, God would not have sent a punishment like me upon you."

—Genghis Khan

###

Almost time for another debriefing, the Analyst thought as he glided in a brisk walk toward the conference room.

But before the debriefing, there first had to be this posturing to his profane *superiors.* The very notion that he should answer to anyone (especially on this plane) offended him. But it had been a small price to pay to achieve his current position at the leverage point of End Day. And the leader of the *Others* had told him that it was necessary for the ultimate goal. He, personally, could never see that far, so he took it on faith.

In fact, the Analyst seldom saw beyond the next debriefing. Each one created new avenues for his visions, visions that lasted only until the next. And so on.

"Gentlemen," he said to the assembled screens displayed on the various tables across from him as he entered the conference room.

"Analyst," they all said in unison. *Order.* He deftly settled into the high-backed chair to meet the quartet of his advisory board at eye level.

"The results of our raid were quite remarkable. We have the key leaders into custody," he began, obviously measuring his words.

"Any casualties? I haven't heard about anything on the news." This was Reverend Bitters, billionaire televangelist on screen one.

"And you won't. My friends have all agreed that this armed conflict with the security at the church was local news only." This baritone from screen four belonged to Mr. James, the magnate who either owned outright, sat on the board, or had family on the boards of eight of the ten major media conglomerates in the US. *My friends* was basically code for *the media.*

"There are several individual social media accounts that are accurately reporting that the raid took place. Was it really necessary to use drones? Live ammo? All of this paramilitary, gun-toting is not only unseemly, but counterproductive." The group gadfly, Acting Secretary of State Vance Itiorvic on screen two, being his ever-present posturing self. *When would he learn that there were no votes to be had, here?* several members of the group thought. "But, not to worry, we have our disinformation bots discrediting all of it."

"We needn't be too concerned. The faithful will understand that this is necessary to fight the greater Evil. We are all born dead, depraved, but only those whom the Lord has chosen shall he protect." Reverend Bitters, repeating the same words he uttered, more or less, at every meeting.

Of all the tenets of the Reverend's raw, militant Calvinism, the tenet of Unconditional Election was the Analyst's favorite, so he said it aloud:

"You have not chosen me. I have chosen you." It basically meant that you were prechosen by God and nothing you did, not good works, not finding Jesus, nor anything else, much mattered. For if there were anything any person could do to change the divine reckoning, then all glory would not be to God.

"John, chapter fifteen, verse sixteen," the Reverend affirmed. Although the Analyst had a different higher being in mind when he had said it.

"One of these days, we need to continue our own, ah, theological discussion, Reverend." This was screen three, the Chinese-American investment banker and presidential hopeful, Bryce Gerald ("B. Gerry") Lee. "Perhaps in another nest of underage pretty boys like the last time." And then he laughed the heartfelt laugh of someone who knew he was beyond danger. He had invited so many magnates, politicians, and other movers and shakers to events with *peculiar entertainments* at his private palaces the past several decades that it seemed he had gathered compromising dirt on most of the ruling class. Apparently, the Reverend was one of them.

The Analyst had seen: During the next election, Mr. Lee's miraculous "out of nowhere" rise to a major party's nomination would be a long-since foregone conclusion by those in the know. He'd appeal to the younger voters would be the storyline. Getting them out in record numbers. But the voting machines were mostly built with tech that was easily hacked and his allies had the code.

While the minister flustered, Secretary Itiorvic said, "Don't be foolish, Mr. Lee. This may be a secure channel, but you should mind your manners. There is no telling how such, um, jokes might be misinterpreted if they came out."

"You're the foolish one for thinking your government is even capable of a secure channel. But fear not, Mister Itch-YEEOR-vick, my government has secured it for you." And Mr. Lee laughed some more.

Mr. Lee is in rare form today, thought the Analyst. *Rumor had it that the Chinese government had their own cadre of clerics. Perhaps that was something to be explored in an alliance with him later on?*

All the better to have them removed from the board. There can be only one champion. Ah! Enough with distracting thoughts. I need my debriefing. "Gentlemen, I trust that the hand-delivered, encrypted tablets that I am having sent to you will give you all the relevant details you require—both as to our raid, and as to part two of *Operation Rapture.* At that point, after you've reviewed the materials, and, hopefully hearing no objections, I will humbly ask that I may be allowed to continue with the plan. Are there any questions?

"Very good. May the Lord continue to bless us all, gentlemen."

As screens went dark and folded downward, disappearing into their respective tables with a metallic hum, the Analyst stood up and walked to a closet. He took out a white, hooded cloak that he had just finished hand-washing that morning. *The faint stains from the battle in Chicago were glorious, like hieroglyphs or the fragments of memories of battles won.* He had spent almost an hour scrubbing it clean. After the laundering, he spent a while watching the skin on his waterlogged, prunish hands recalibrate itself to normal consistency.

He fastened the cloak around his neck with a flourish and took out his phone.

"Send them in for the debriefing." He spoke to Brianna, who awaited his call.

As he waited, his mind drifted to a different time, a different place, where he had found the Truth.

Three men walked in. They had been dressed in black body armor during the operation in Chicago, but they now wore nondescript blue blazers, dress shirts, and khaki dress pants. If not for their military bearing and their standing at attention, they might have been techs at a local PC repair shop. *So young,* he thought. *Much younger than I was. But their role is much more limited.*

These were the mission leaders of the Chicago Innie raid. These E-Dogs performed well enough to merit bonuses. He had promised each of them a well-earned vacation.

If they were alarmed by their boss's dingy argent cape and cowl, they didn't show it.

For they had no idea that right after Brianna had shown them into this room, she had sent the letters to these men's nearest relatives informing them of their unfortunate deaths during a training incident.

The anticipation was killing the VA. *I need this now.* He missed the visions. His numbers had dwindled, and he needed to replenish them. He took off the ubiquitous shades and looked hungrily at his underlings in a sort of ghoulish reverie.

"Sir?" one of them—Jenkins, perhaps—said.

But now they all looked past the Analyst, over his shoulder at the shimmering outlines of the *Others,* the shoulders, wings, towering over them all in the room. Before they even thought to defend themselves, the Analyst turned his shoulder and pointed at the three men …

There was a FLASH! A rippling feeling rushed through the room like a venting hydraulic press. The Analyst dropped to one knee.

And he was alone. The three men? Banished. For what would seem, for them, an eternity.

It's like being paralyzed, trapped in your own body, but it isn't that you aren't moving. You don't exist. You move about, in that other place, but no matter what you do, or what you encounter, you feel, with your very soul, your BEING, you no longer exist. You are trapped, unable to breathe because you are dead, gasping, screaming, clawing at the landscape. It doesn't matter. You are dead. Dead.

You panic, of course. Driven mad straightaway. It feels like days. Maybe weeks.

But that is only the first madness. It is fleeting. Useless.

As the months and years drag on, you eventually come up with new madnesses, as coping strategies.

You stab out your own eyes so that you cannot be tortured by everything around you that you can see but know isn't real. You talk to yourself but the only voice you hear is the distant hum of the others you will never understand, so you shove sharp objects into your bleeding ear cavities so that you cannot hear, either. Nothing really stops the pain.

That's the best you can hope for in that other dimension, to be a cosmic geek without a safe word.

Occasionally, one of those beings takes an interest in you, though, and thrusts their pain into you, merely for a bit of recreation, while you soundlessly scream.

Then you start to like the pain, invite it. That's the beginning of the Final Madness. That is when your eyes see once again. When you begin to understand: ORDER.

Eventually, they might understand that the ones hurting them are also trapped. They might learn to turn their oppressors' aggression against them. To seduce them with the idea of their own escape.

Eventually, they might organize enough of them to get the Master's attention, himself. The one who can fashion the proper loophole in the rules to escape, the same way I did ...... but no—I can't give them that chance.

In the office conference room, the handsome man in the white burnoose pushed himself back up into his chair and then concentrated. It took nearly all his *chi* to facilitate this. His own breathing stopped, his heart slowed, his mind checked out.

And then the deed was done, and the three men were before him once again. They were all huddled together in a lump on the floor. The look in their eyes was vacant, empty.

With what strength remained, the Visiting Analyst drew a pistol from under his jacket and shot each of them so they were also dead of body and not just of soul.

And then he felt the rush of power from behind him … not the depleted lost ones that had helped him in Chicago, hangers on—no, three new, STRONG lost ones. *Dead of soul. I like that. Do you like that?*

The lost ones from those three corpses didn't reply. Rather, they responded by showing him every dream, every possible rapacious future, he had ever wanted. As always, he would navigate through this day, and every day, using the infinite visions.

He let his eyes roll back into his forehead as he put his shades back on.

No. I will not help you.

Those six words were all he said. It was day three of their stay there, and it was one of the many planning sessions for the upcoming protest/strike. But when they gave Marshall his assignment, he simply informed them he wasn't taking part.

Ruby reacted like he had slapped her. Then she tried everything, invoking Brick, loyalty to the Revelators, even Grandma Marian's plans. But she didn't understand. This drug was his way out. Now it wasn't all on him. He didn't have to kill anyone, or even do anything.

Plus, he was very annoyed that they just assumed he would help. Just because they told him to—like he was still a child.

Then Palla, who had had a change of heart, tried to support Ruby about it. She proposed a third way, wherein he would have had only limited involvement. She had projected her own concerns onto him and thought that he was just being risk-averse.

But Marshall flared into open (if deadpan) anger.

"I said no. You pretend to be something you are not. You say you do not believe in any of this, but you summon them all so easily … why did you not do that at the funeral?" And he noticed Kinta, Bill's extremely pretty daughter, who often stood off to the side of their meetings, smiling her encouragement at his righteous anger. So, he continued:

"I am not helping with this mission because I do not believe in it. It is that simple. That is all."

As he walked out, Marshall noticed that everyone in the room had shocked looks on their faces, none more so than Palla, whose jaw just sat open.

After that, they left Marshall alone. And so, without so many meetings to go to, he was free to wander about the camp.

A few days later.

"Hi Marshall!"

"Hello." He looked up from his notebook where he had been doodling to see Kinta, Bill's daughter, again. Every day she would try to strike up another conversation. *She's one of them! She hates you. Stupid.*

She quickly sat down next to him and peered at his notebook, playfully asking, "What are you drawing? Can I help?"

Don't say anything. She'll find out you're stupid! "No," he said. But he didn't close the notebook, either. So, she looked at it.

"So, you draw the spirits?"

"They are not—that is not the word." He took a deep breath, out of sequence with his words, giving the effect he was gasping, or bored. He did that from time to time.

She plowed forward. "What word do you use?"

"DJinn." When she didn't respond to that, he explained, "I have read a lot about them. Everything I could get my hands on, growing up. From all different cultures through history. Most cultures called them 'demons' in their own language. Everyone thought I was emo for obsessing about them, drawing them all the time. Anyway, I think the far Eastern cultures get it right. They describe them the best. And their word is 'dJinn.' 'DJinni' is the plural."

"Like the genie in a lamp."

"They feel like that, some of them. Trapped."

"Hm. Your drawing looks more like a medieval dragon." She let that sit there for a second before saying, "You talk like you know them."

You don't know anything! Why are you even talking to her? "Yes."

"I've seen them, too. But in vision quests. During my initiation rite. During family prayers for our departed. They were just shadows, I think. But they never talked to me."

"They probably tried. It's hard to hear them. In its native language, *dJinn* meant 'to conceal, to hide.'"

She looked at him approvingly and nodded at his lessons. She'd heard about the spirits, of course. And she knew the great Marshall Lastpost's reputation within the tribes.

He went back to drawing. He started to sketch the one that was talking to him now, this girl. She seemed so familiar to him. It felt like one of his dJinn was near him right then.

She's fake. You're dreaming her, his voices offered He looked at her tight dress, focusing impolitely at her chest as it moved in and out while she breathed. *We're the real ones! Not all these people you talk to. Think about it! If they were real, why would they only talk to you while you were awake? Stupid.*

Wait, she is saying something again. "Hm?"

"I said, come play a game with me! I am bored here. All the other guys here are boring. They just want to ride bikes or, you know, make out. They can't carry a conversation. My father doesn't let me hang out with them. But I think he likes that we're talking. He trusts you. You're like a celebrity, anyway. C'mon!" Kinta said.

She pulled him up by the hand, and he tucked the notebook into a pack that he had taken to carrying. The pack had a strap that he put over one shoulder and the flap had some native American beads. It was a trifle, but he liked it. Little Rich was in there, too, much of the time. Along with some antibacterial soap for always washing his hands after handling Rich.

They walked toward the barracks, and they stopped in a large library on the first floor, behind the main stairs. Marshall already knew this room well. He had spent much of the last few nights in this room, reading instead of sleeping. The voices had been keeping him awake. Or he was afraid to sleep when the voices couldn't be controlled as well.

"I heard you yelling at the boss lady."

"It is irresponsible. For her to have so much power but to not know how to use it."

"She acts like she doesn't even believe in any of it."

"She doesn't."

"Wow! Why doesn't someone just show her? I mean, perform a trick or something?"

Marshall sighed. "Every time you do something with your own *chi*, no matter how big or small, there is a small chance that it will deplete all of your *chi*. All or nothing. And it cannot be predicted. Some people go years on end depleting their own *chi* and that never happens. Others, it can happen on one of their first attempts. Some think that that was what happened to Brick."

"Really? But what about when you don't use your own energy? Most of our prayers, we use the spirits?"

"To use a spirit to try and convince someone of the existence of the spirits is considered blasphemy. Besides, a disbeliever who isn't sensitive to the magic that you are trying to convince them of never really buys into it. Like when people who have Capgras Syndrome believe that time has been altered or their loved ones have been replaced with imposters; they always believe some other explanation. I suppose that's what this drug does … it messes with that part of the brain that is or isn't hard-wired to have spiritual thoughts."

"Oh, okay. Like my dad. He still has all his knowledge, but he can no longer make the prayers work. So, big picture, Palla is a waste, I guess. But, to hear my dad tell it, a lot of CEOs are like that."

Marshall thought, *What does Kinta have against Palla?*

She continued, "But you seem like you are sad a lot of the time, if you don't mind me saying so. Anger, sometimes, is just pent up sadness. Are you mad at someone? Are you mad at Palla?"

There was a long pause. They sat quietly at the big table, while she started rifling through some board games, while waiting for his answer.

He said, "You mentioned your dad. I wasn't a very good father. It makes me said to think about that, but I think about it a lot."

"Why?"

"I had to let my son die."

Kinta paused, but she wasn't fazed. "Have you sung his song?"

"No."

"Why not? Don't you know how?"

"Ben tried to teach me. But music ..." he trailed off. Music reminded Marshall of all those times the counselors tried to reach him through various means. Once, after the gas explosion, they had a board-certified music therapist visit him and play and sing harshly strummed songs at him and then go ahead and ask him questions about how the song should change in order to make him feel better. But this was when Marshall was on meds and didn't feel much of anything.

Later his condition necessitated utmost emotional control. His flat affect wasn't just a symptom, it was a choice. Like a defense mechanism. Who wouldn't choose numbness to abject horror every day? Easier to deal with the voices when you were under control.

But there was happiness, too, he had to admit. He liked talking there with Kinta. She was cute. She seemed to not think Marshall was too crazy. In some ways, she reminded him of his time with Julia.

Julia had truly understood Marshall. She was the only one. She knew that being numb prevented some happiness, too. And she was okay with just that reduced amount, as long as she could've been a part of it. Her dad had been autistic.

This Kinta girl, she was still talking to him. "Which game do you want to play? *Clue?*" she asked.

Marshall was startled out of his trance and sat, staring at the pretty girl across from him. Kinta just looked back at him, patiently. Eventually, she stopped waiting for a response and started setting up a board of checkers.

Kinta's long, dark straight hair fell to one side of her dark and tan smiling face. Her dark almond eyes sparkled with the light from the window behind where he sat. She didn't need makeup, as her natural beauty was evident from her smooth unblemished skin, full cheeks, and her red lips. He had found out her age when they first met. Both of them were surprised at each other's numbers. He thought she was twenty-six, not seventeen. And, of course, she politely didn't say how old she thought he was, instead of his actual age of twenty-five.

She was shapely. A little heavyset, like Grandma Marian was, but her ample breasts were much firmer, not so saggy. Big, thick-rimmed glasses. He was sure that she noticed him staring at her that first time they met, so he mostly avoided looking at her at all.

Until now. He held her gaze for a long moment. And then he said, with a perfectly straight face, "I don't need to give you a clue. I can just tell you."

"No, *Clue*, the game—wait. Aaaahhh!" And she laughed so hard he couldn't help but smile along with her. "Good one! Does anyone else know you're funny?"

"Funny? You mean, like I amuse you?" Marshall said to his feet.

Again, the laughing, since the impression was on point. "That was good! Who else do you do?"

For a second, he looked around to see who the audience for her was. But it was just her. Not since Julia had anyone asked him to do his impressions because they enjoyed being with him.

And so, he did another. And another. And the afternoon was filled with laughter and quiet talking afterward.

For just a while, the only voices he heard were between him and his new friend.

They eventually went for a walk around the compound and ended up next to a small building whose sign said it held a well.

Marshall asked, "So why are you here? I mean, do you not have to be in school, sometime, what with you being *a little kid* and all?" The good-natured teasing came surprisingly easy between them.

"I was home-schooled, jerk. Although, that was only this past year. I finished that. My family travels so much, we registered with our native state, Mississippi for the home-schooling diploma. It should be in our mail when we get back. I've got enough credits.

"At first, my Mom passed away, two summers ago. At first, after that, he came home to stay with me, took a local administrative job with the Tribe. But we were both miserable. So, I suggested that he go back to traveling and his old job (whatever that was) as long as he promised to take me with. It's been great. Although I am often bored, left behind when he is involved in the actual meetings. Sometimes, it seems like he knows everyone ... but I've been all over the country."

"I still do not understand what he does as his job," Marshall said.

"He is a consultant. He used to work for the government when I was younger. Look, you were a Revelator, right? Basically, he's one, too. Only he is legal and administrative. He doesn't go on rescue missions … he researches them and helps set them up. Find who needs to be helped, when there's a cult or an abusive pastor someplace who isn't being checked and where innocents are being kept. He helps get them out. I'm not supposed to ask you this, but he said you used to be involved in actual missions. Is that true?"

Marshall thought, *So he was A.A.'s replacement?* That made sense. "Yes. I helped plan them. I guess." But he wasn't allowing himself to be diverted. "No, I mean, why are you and he here? I mean, here, in Minnesota? Now?"

She frowned past him. "I think we should ask him that ourselves, don't you, Dad?"

And Marshall was startled by her father standing right behind him.

"Marshall, I have been telling my flower she is a little kid for most of the last year, but she refuses to accept that. Some nonsense about *aging,* and her *growing up.*"

"I have grown up!"

"Bah! I don't approve."

"Dad, I do all of the driving and most of the thinking for us both. Face it, you're just an older model. I'm the upgrade! Now, I'm not saying you don't have any place where you couldn't be useful … some kind of museum, perhaps …"

"Museum?" he said as mock rage built in him. Marshall briefly smiled at this, he recognized acting when he saw it.

"Y'know. For people to remember how things were done in ancient times," Kinta explained.

"ANCIENT? Why, I oughta—ah! Here we go, a water bucket … let my museum plaque read, "As our forefathers used to douse their children, so, too, did Bill," he said as he headed for a bucket sitting next to the well house.

"Aaaahh!" Kinta squealed in laughter as she launched herself up and away from the scene at a sprint, with her father chasing after her.

"They need your help in the kitchen, little flower!" Bill called after her. "I will entertain your young friend for a minute!"

"Okay! See you later, Marshall!"

"Bye!" he responded.

"May I sit with you, sir?" Bill asked as he set the bucket down.

"You are a good father."

Bill's smile was broad. "I try to be there for her. She reminds me so much of my beloved. She must have told you about her mother's passing? Yes, but I wanted to answer your question." He sat down and clasped his hands in a formal fashion on his lap in front of him.

Marshall noticed Bill had matched his own posture, and they now saw at precisely the same eye level, too. He wondered if that was a conscious or instinctive thing for Bill.

"Marshall, I am here because I believe in this mission. So, I wanted to ask you why you don't want to help."

"I just don't."

Bill continued, "Hm. Well, you should know. Most of the teams have already deployed. This conference in April—the first of its kind—was a brilliant-but-scary idea. Think of it, the Blue Rookers hosting dignitaries from all the major denominations in a retreat designed to hammer out what amounts to a drug cartel. The idea is that it will go the way of legalized cannabis … the people and the states will permit it, while the federal government turns a blind eye. If it is being promoted by the religious community, you preemptively removed the number one obstacle."

"Makes sense," Marshall agreed.

"So, why do you not like Brick's plan?"

He's a liar. They're all liars. Stab him with your pen! Marshall heard as some of the voices returned. But Marshall wasn't going to be derailed at that moment. Just mentioning Revelators snapped him into a hyper-focused mode. "First, what steps are being taken to shield us from them finding us through me, again?"

"Hm? We discussed that … oh, that's right. You left the meeting. That won't work across timelines. When Ben forward-shifted you into this timeline, past the battle, that effectively cancels the dweomer. Cuts it off." *He lies. He's one of them.*

"Has anyone heard from Brick or the others who were at the funeral? Do we know what the result of all that was?" *You killed them all! Stupid.*

"On the news. Just a little while ago. That was originally why I was coming to see you. They said that Brick was arrested and taken into custody. Ben was so amazingly skilled … he not only shifted you three into a timeline where you bypassed the worst of the battle, but Brick survives. Maybe other changes have taken place, too. That spell is so dangerous—fatal, as you know. But stories are told of ancient practitioners who could pick timelines with amazingly subtle changes."

"He's alive?" Marshall repeated the salient fact.

"Yes."

"The others?"

"No word yet. Business operations at the headquarters were suspended and everyone who has the authority to restart them has either already resigned"—Bill made a sweeping gesture—"or is here."

"Whenever one of us was ever left behind, we went back and got them," Marshall pointed out. Then Bill launched into a long explanation for why extraction from federal custody was impractical, after which he returned to trying to convince Marshall to help with the mission again. At the end, Marshall said he understood, and he promised to give helping the mission some more consideration.

It was a lie.

A small one, like the ones his family, Grandma, and Uncle Brick told each other in order to keep feelings soothed in a sort of agreed, blissful ignorance. *You're not taking the boy on missions, are you? Now does that sound like something I would do?* Like that.

It seemed to work. "Well, it's good talking to you. I'll let you get back to your drawing. Oh. But, by the way, I expect you to behave with my daughter, Mr. Lastpost. Do you understand?"

Marshall nodded dumbly.

As he walked away, Marshall decided, whatever happened, he had one advantage: no one here realized that he could no longer see futures. *You are so weak. You never had any power. Tool.*

All the missions. His entire life after she adopted him. Grandma Marian's visions determined Marshall's future.

You're a tool. Fool. Too cool for school.

At that point, Marshall's focus was on rescuing Uncle Brick. There was no way he was leaving him behind. *But who can I go to that could help with that?* Marshall thought.

"Marshall?"

It was Palla. She had snuck up on Marshall.

"Truce, okay? Hey, listen, you want to go for a ride?"

"Where to?"

"I have a few phone calls to make, and I can't get a signal here. We need to see about where we can find your godfather. On the news they showed the federal holding facility in Chicago where he is, as of right now. I have some friends who might be able to tell us if and when he is transferred—y'know, where to find him. We need to talk to him. At least I do."

"Why do you want me along?"

"Well, during the car ride here, didn't you show me an Extirpacy badge?"

BOOK ONE—CHAPTER NINETEEN

PALLA

###

I thought the badge was a heckuva good idea. But Marshall shot it down. *That won't be enough. But I believe I know someone who will be able to help us get in.*

And that was how I first met Mother Po.

No one knew her age. And no one agreed as to when or how she first started assisting with old missions. Everyone knew (and old newspaper articles confirmed) that she was a local psychic for hire that the police had called in for a missing persons case, a young girl. When that missing girl was pinpointed by one of A.A.'s investigations into a religious commune across the border in Tijuana, she literally showed up at A.A.'s doorstep to offer her help. (The Revelators, as nongovernment actors, could do operations across international lines with proper deniability for US law enforcement).

As I said, no one knew her age. But she was already an old woman when she joined the group back in the '90s … many decades older than anyone else. She had to be at least one hundred now, just doing the math. No one had so much as mentioned her to me since long before I was promoted to CEO.

Honestly, I had assumed she had died.

But instead she was at a long-term care facility that was managed by the church, also in Chicago. So, it was *on the way,* anyway.

This time, it was just me and Marshall. I didn't feel I could trust Sally quite the same way for this. We drove back into Chicago (after trading cars with someone else at the camp) from Minnesota during the evening. On the drive in, I stopped at a small town and withdrew a bunch of cash at an ATM and bought a flip phone. That was the last time I used that credit card. I dumped that and everything but my ID into the back of someone else's pickup truck.

Then I used the flip phone to call my executive assistant's home number—a land line. Once she called me back, I made the necessary arrangements. Before entering Chicagoland, we paid cash to stay at a hotel near the interstate.

The TV didn't work. But there were two beds, and that was all I cared about. But as I turned in, Marshall just sat in the little chair next to the desk. He was looking at me.

"What are you doing?" I asked him before I turned off my light.

"Nothing. I am on watch. It is okay. I do not sleep much, anyway. I will sleep in the car again when we leave."

"No, sleep now. I can't sleep if you're sitting there just watching me."

"Well, you are going to have to. It is too cold for me to wait outside."

"Damn it, you're creeping me out, and I need my sleep! At least sit in your bed and not there."

He complied and went to sit in his bed. For a while, each time I glanced over to see if he was still staring at me, he would turn his head, giving the illusion that he had been looking at me the entire time, even though he wasn't. We had turned into a Laurel and Hardy routine.

As I drifted off my mind actually latched onto the idea that I was alone in a hotel with a man for the first time in … ever. *Looks, intelligence, Integrity: you can pick two*, my college pals and I used to say. And then we would decide which of the guys that we were dating, or wanted to date, had which two.

But *always* two. If someone wanted us to think he had all three, they were going to have to prove it.

Of course, the fourth one, *sanity*, was always assumed. Which had proven to be a mistake on more than a few dates.

He's a nice guy, this one. Kind of pissed at me right now. I wonder how long a schizophrenic holds a grudge? I ruminated. I thought about how he might be the only person I'd ever met who'd been damaged more as a child than me. Maybe we were both stronger for it?

Well, anyway, it is impressive how he's managed to stay … productive … over the years; and the way he takes all of this weird stuff in stride.

I glanced over once again and this time he didn't look back. He was still sitting up in bed, but he was asleep. I got up and put a blanket over him. And then I got back into my bed and finally drifted off.

###

From the outside it looked like a luxuriously decorated two-story hotel. Inside was a lopsided lobby off to the right side as you entered. Faux-wood paneling and mounted drapes that covered sections of the walls surrounded us. If you rotated yourself off to the right about forty-five degrees you saw that the far-right edge of the opposite wall had a small window cut into it, right between two of those hanging cloths.

Meanwhile, to the left or straight ahead was what looked like a closed restaurant. Round tables with sets of matching ice-cream chairs were scattered about under chandeliers that were turned off. The room trailed back into the darkness. When we walked up to the window, I saw a large room beyond. Desks and other office equipment. But no people.

We stood there for a while and waited for someone to show up. No one ever manned the small window, or was even visible in the room beyond. From time to time a person would walk past us, entering the lobby from one side door on the right and pushing a wheelchair into and through a door, behind us, off to the left.

We just stood there for a few minutes. There was no bell to ring.

"Have you been helped?" This was one of the orderlies that had pushed a patient around behind us earlier. I guess she had come back through the door on the left, but we didn't actually see from where she emerged.

"We're here to see a Margaret Po," I explained.

If the employee recognized that name, she didn't show it. She just nodded and said she'd be right back. She disappeared back through the dining area somewhere and re-emerged behind the little window. She had us sign in on a clipboard (I debated but decided to leave off the CEO from my name, for now), and she handed each of us a visitor sticker.

"Okay, she is in room fourteen. I'll buzz you in." And then we heard a *buzz* and a click from a door that was right next to the little window but was hidden by a curtain that was mounted on it.

We went in, and she led us down a long hallway. The facility turned out to be huge. We took a staircase down into the basement. The rooms were marked with little note cards taped to the doors. And numbers written on the cards with marker. Classy joint.

I made a mental note to visit and audit all these facilities, assuming I still had a job when this was done.

"Third door to the right," the nurse (for now I'd seen her badge up close) said.

"Thank you." And Marshall walked ahead of me, actually knocking me aside a bit. I guessed he was excited to see another of his old friends, but his manhandling was starting to really annoy me.

###

Po was a disappointment. At first, she was basically catatonic. She was propped up in a wheelchair, with an IV attached. I looked to see what medication was listed on the IV bottle, but I didn't recognize it.

He kneeled next to her and spoke to her in a normal tone for a few minutes. When she didn't respond at all, he then seemed to get very depressed. He flipped his shades down and lowered his head further, touching it to hers, forehead to forehead. He sort of spoke and sobbed under his breath for a few minutes and, at one point, her eyes flicked to looked over at him, but he didn't notice. She closed her eyes back just as quickly, but took a loud, deep, deep breath. *Oh, God. Don't die on us,* I couldn't help but think.

But she wasn't dying. If anything, she looked better as Marshall stood back up. Now, for the first time, she looked directly at me and gave me a little smile. And then she looked over at Marshall and said, "Good boy."

And then, as if that was all he needed to hear, he turned to leave. I gave him a puzzled look, but he didn't hesitate. He turned back around and said, "Thank you." And then he added to me, "We can go." And then he started to walk out.

"What? What are you talking about? What was all of this about? What in the world …?"

At the threshold to her room, he turned back to me. "It is more magic mumbo jumbo. Do you really want an explanation, or are you ready to see Brick?"

Yep, definitely still angry with me. He hadn't spoken that directly to me before. And, I have to admit, once I suppressed the urge to knock his block off, I kind of preferred that to the weird, shy version of him. Now, he was more similar to the sorts of people that I dealt with in my job … a pleasant veneer over a deep well of hostility.

Anyway, this detour had only taken us about an hour off what I expected for the day's schedule, but now, it seemed like wasted time, and that was what was annoying me as much as anything. I hated wasting time.

But I didn't argue, and we left to meet my assistant at a prearranged location. That was going to be for a change of clothes for me (back into some of my own, more professional, attire) and for a satchel for Marshall, to help with his "disguise." Also, some more cash and another burner phone. I gave her instructions for how to reconstitute the board with new members, enough to at least get a quorum for a meeting about early next month, in January.

I thanked her, and then we went to see the most prominent father figure in either one of our lives. While he was still in local custody.

"Know your enemy," somebody said, sometime or other. And so, I did. Even back as operations director, I knew enough about our relationship with federal authorities that I adopted a war-room mentality about it. That meant knowing about them. For example, I knew that the federal facility where he was being held was an adjunct to the local FBI branch office. And all of it was in an abandoned L train station, just a few blocks from the current L station at 35th and Archer. It was an elevated tower of a facility, with no discernible entry but a couple of barred metal doors on either side and no signage.

It took some investigative work, but we had found out that the front door to the facility was actually in a small residential home next door to it. Presumably, there was an underground tunnel between the two buildings.

The entry process wasn't unlike what had transpired at Mother Po's nursing home. This converted lobby was a former living room, barren, except for a gray-on-white floral design wallpaper, with slick gray plasterboard up to the chair rails. The furniture was strictly art deco, not out of a sense of style, but because it always had been. Apparently, it had been repurposed into lobby furniture.

This lobby also had an internal window, and a procedure—filling out a visitor questionnaire and signing a clipboard.

The clerk behind the desk wore green camouflage fatigues. He acted almost giddy to be having visitors. His good humor tended to have the opposite effect, like when you're pulled over by a cop for speeding and they try to be perky. You'd rather they be sullen, to match your mood. This was like that.

The soldier said, "Merry Christmas," and made a joke about what to get Jesus for his birthday. I laughed dutifully. But Marshall gave him a very square-jawed glare (that breathy voice, was he doing a Clint impression?) and presented our badges and instructed the officer to let us in to do our jobs.

The desk clerk seemed to take offense, so I leaned in and gave the soldier a good view of my cleavage and displayed my own polish at navigating the mindset of the modern gatekeeper ("Tell you what. Let us in for a quick wellness check on the prisoner, and I not only promise not to take too long, 'cause I know you're shift ends here in a few minutes, but also I won't mention any of this delay from you to my superiors when I get back to DC. How does that sound?"), and pretty soon we were approved for that wellness check.

As we stepped inside, my soul flinched. This, of course, was the normal reaction when anyone walks into a detention facility. An almost preternatural fear seeped into my consciousness as I struggled for a few seconds to keep composure.

Meanwhile, Marshall also seemed to be affected, but not the same way. He actually seemed *at home.* He walked a bit straighter and even more confidently than his previous act had been. He was positively strutting now. Anyone casually observing us would have believed I was his assistant.

Large doors clicked impossibly loudly as they were opened, one after another, until we were finally brought to a large room with several cafeteria style tables. Some had been pushed together. But a single small one, about the size of a park bench, was in the center of the room. And on the other side of *that* table is where we saw him.

My God. He had obviously been tortured. His white hair was slicked back like a gangster's, but no other indication of grooming was visible. His face was swollen and bruised. The eyes therein were vacant, bloodshot, and edged with some sort of goo that had hardened, maybe a mixture of blood and tears. His arms rested awkwardly on the table before him, at an odd angle from his torso—like a Muppet who'd been tossed aside. He appeared broken, in every sense of the word.

But when he saw us his bushy eyebrows lifted into an expression of surprise and then lowered back down over his eyes, and suddenly now his expression was reset, there, under that swollen face.

We left the guard behind at the doorway to the room. No one else was inside. We sat down across from Brick. It was everything I could do to not cry.

Marshall said to him, "You look like shit."

Brick began, "And you smell …" but couldn't finish their shared in-joke.

"You okay?" I asked, reflexively.

He looked around and shook his head gently, no.

Then my eyes did tear up.

Marshall told him, "Think of her."

Brick just looked at him.

Again, he said, "Think of her. The bond. Use it. She will hear."

Brick's eyebrows again, up and down. He tried to shift in his chair, and I saw that and helped him to sit up.

"No touching!" the guard said.

"Look, he needed my help!" I started. "He was choking. I was just checking his airway—this all goes in my report …" And I just kept on saying whatever I could think of to say. This was because Marshall and I had already worked this out. For this little bit of mumbo jumbo on his part, he insisted that he needed a distraction.

Marshall surreptitiously grabbed one of Brick's hands on the table while I walked toward the guard to argue with him. I could hear Marshall mumbling something as I walked away.

The guard cut our visit short soon after that. But Marshall had assured me that he had only needed a few seconds. And it was definitely just as well. Brick was in no condition to answer any of our questions, anyway. Besides, I don't think I could have borne staying there much longer, seeing him in that condition.

As we left the facility and walked the several blocks to where we parked our car, I asked him, "Did it work?"

"We will know when we get back to Mother Po. But I was able to give him some help. Both he and she now have some *chi* with which to communicate. Her mental abilities were mostly empathic, but she and Brick had a special connection, close almost to telepathy."

"How will that help us?"

"If she can see with his eyes, it could help us quite a bit. Did your assistant check her out?"

I checked my phone. "Yes. She's been checked out AMA and transferred to my custody under a new POA. Let's meet up with her and go back to Barn Grier. There's a lot more I would like to do back at the office, but we are better off if I do it remotely rather than show my face, I think—"

Then I heard,

"Oh-nnh!"

I looked back, and Marshall was crumpled up on the ground, doubled over in pain.

I helped him up, and he said, "I didn't summon any … I just used my own chi, did not want to risk summoning inside their facility … it just takes some … effort. Sorry. I am fine. Sorry."

"Don't apologize. If this works, you'll be a hero to the entire camp."

Then his face did a smile, and he said, "Really? Hm. I wonder if Kinta will think so?"

###

When we returned to the Barn Grier camp late that night, I was struck by how deserted it had become since our initial arrival a few days ago. No more groups of motorcycles and piles of trash outside of the various tiny houses. Most of the larger tents had been folded up and put away, with only the food tent (and of course the barracks house) still dominating the compound.

I sensed a level of excitement in Marshall about our return. Plus, he always perked up when another of his former Revelator mentors was around. They were like obviously like extended family to him. And we had one of them in the car with us. Mother Po was seated in the car up front next to me, the unmistakable smell of elder people—mothballs and dry skin—filled the car.

Once she started talking, I took an instant dislike to her. This was because, a couple of times during the ride, Marshall actually tried to talk to her about what he had been going through—he told her about the incident with his grandma, and about the government's attack during her funeral. I was surprised. Several times I had asked him about what he was feeling, and he wouldn't open up. Now he offered to share his feelings with her.

But instead of engaging, she just kept looking at him like she was slightly offended by his weakness.

"So, you froze up during the attack?" she actually accused at one point, implying *what?* That he should've stopped it somehow? At one point, he stopped sharing with her and just sort of rocked quietly side to side in his seat—I could see part of his head bobbing into and out of sight in my rearview mirror. He stared out the window at the passing empty fields of the Midwest.

Eventually she locked in on her own needs. For example: "Does anyone have anything to eat?" and "I have to use the bathroom." Both came up more than once. I was having a hard time understanding how she was going to be the key to rescuing Brick.

###

Ruby and a couple of others who had been roused at our arrival greeted us and helped Po out of the car and up to the barracks for whatever she needed.

A few minutes later, the larger crowd of about twenty (probably everyone else that was left) came out to see our return, too. Apparently, news of our abrupt, unannounced departure had caused quite the stir.

I wasn't able to avoid the disappointed look of Sally, who stood off to one side and was obviously upset that I had struck out on my own without checking with her first. But I delayed that confrontation to observe Marshall walk up to Kinta amongst the crowd. He said something to her and then she dismissively turned and walked away, replying something over her shoulder.

I walked up to him and asked her what he and her had just said. He told me that he had said that he had gone on a rescue mission and asked her if she wanted to hear about it. In response, she'd said, "No. Not really." And then she'd walked away.

Of course, he didn't understand. He thought she hated him now. He thought he had done something wrong. Depressed, he walked away in a daze.

So, he really didn't have a clue about women. *Hm. Turns out he's a fairly normal guy, after all.*

###

He spent a lot of time in his room the next few days. One time I knocked on his door and he, very calmly and very evenly, told me to go away.

Nor, of course, was he present for the briefing with Po. Ruby and Po basically talked it through with Bill, two other motorcycle gang road sergeants named Stan and Snake (hot take: thuggish men of action), Sally, Pharell (the mohawk guy, quiet but nice), and me. Of all the leaders, we were the only six left to talk with Po about next steps. Po was much more energetic by then.

As she learned what had been going on, Po was—at first—visibly angry about the very idea of the drug and the convention. But then, later, when she learned that Brick meant to destroy the drug so that things would continue as they were before, then she was all for it. "Good boy," she said, apparently meaning Brick.

Not counting the knee-jerk nature of her involvement, it soon became clear she was a very, very sharp lady. At one point, she corrected the others on several key points about when and where they should stage the protest for maximum media coverage. And Ruby actually put her on the phone with Pharell (who was their media liaison) in a call to local law enforcement, to secure the various permits necessary.

She had done her fair share of high-media-coverage missing persons cases, and she knew the drill, get the local sheriff on the phone and then follow his (usually a "his") lead as to what they wanted to maximize for their own personal glory while minimizing the chances for things actually going south on the big day. Sheriffs liked to hold press conferences announcing their own (genius) preventative steps ahead of time. She suggested several to them that they hadn't already thought of so they could announce those.

At first, Ruby was disappointed in me leaving with Marshall, but Po's presence seemed to redeem everything. I also took part in their highest-level command meetings. The same seven that had met before continued as the de facto brain trust. Po's presence changed things. Somehow, she was able to report to them about Brick's … I don't know, state of mind. She didn't claim to read his thoughts, but she would comment as to how he was *feeling*. For three straight days, he had been getting better. Healing. Maybe even well enough to travel without constant care.

Then, something happened, and he was almost *gone* again, emotionally. They all assumed that he had been beaten again. So, if they had plans for him and weren't going to kill him, it probably meant that he wouldn't be transported until after Christmas.

Now this was a step beyond fortune telling back in my home village. I certainly didn't count this as valid intel. But, on the other hand, I totally got how everyone tended to follow Po. I mean, she was *utterly convincing*. I understood how she could've succeeded as a psychic for hire in police matters.

The other reason that I agreed that this week—today was Monday and Friday was Christmas—was probably a wash, and we were in no hurry to try some sort of action with regard to Brick, was that cross-county, high-profile prisoner transfers were actually much easier to do under the radar during a week when all the civil servants were fully staffed. During a holiday week like this, something like Brick getting moved from the (almost invisible) place that he was now, was sure to attract someone's attention.

I still made daily trips to the nearby towns to purchase other burner phones and call the office to keep directing the foundation, remotely. Sally chose to focus on holiday preparations (naturally). And we all knew at some point we would have to try again to get Marshall to suss out some specific tactical choices for us. He was still in hiding after he had been given the cold shoulder by young Kinta, so that was postponed for a bit.

Basically, we all had a week of down time. To regroup.

And *I* also took the chance to reflect and return to my routine of afternoon naps. What can I say? This was going to be a holiday like no other.

###

It was Christmas. Some people in my home country call it "Badaa Din" (which translates as "Big Day"), but that was up north. In our particular southern village, we were too remote to be exposed to such Western ideas, even though it *was* a state holiday.

Sally insisted that everyone wear the Santa hats. She had literally made a special trip into town to buy them. I think I almost saw a flash of anger in her eyes when I refused, and that was so terrifyingly out of character for her that I immediately submitted and said I'd happily take one.

Some of them didn't fit right. It was so late in the season that there wasn't much to choose from at the store, Sally explained.

Marshall's was too big and kept sliding down over his eyes. Eventually he got frustrated enough with it that he rolled it up so that there wasn't any white showing around the edge. So then, it bulged and looked ridiculous. But no one laughed because he had been in such an obvious (for him) funk lately.

Fortunately, Kinta decided it was time to let him out of the dog-house and started to make fun of his pimple hat, calling it a *whitehead* and offering to pop it. He was just so relieved that they were talking again, he happily unrolled it and wore it pushed way back over his head, so he could see.

Bill had a vinyl collection (of course) that he took with him on all his travels, specially packed, always, into a firm plastic saddlebag on the side of his bike. The barracks game room had an old record player, and a few extension cords later, we were all enjoying vintage records out in the mess tent in an actual, honest-to-goodness party.

The Christmas dinner was cold cuts and other convenience-store fare, as well as a lot of beer. But that didn't matter. Everyone was enjoying themselves. The mohawk guy, who was an impressive baritone, sang a couple dozen songs for the group, and since the men outnumbered the ladies about three to one, my dance card was full once the ice was broken.

The ice breaker was Kinta, of course. She pulled Marshall up and showed him how to hold his hands around her as she led him through a bouncy-rhythmed swaying of "Jingle Bell Rock." Once he stopped caring what anyone else was looking at and started focusing on her, he started to loosen up and move more naturally.

Things had about wound down, and I was taking a load off my feet when Bill approached.

"My daughter is about to sing. May I have this dance?"

"What's she going to sing?" I asked as I let him take my hand to lead me back into the makeshift dance floor.

"No idea."

She stood stiffly at the mic for a few seconds, and I started to feel bad for her. There was no band.

Then she began a heart-wrenching a capella rendition of the Carpenters' "Merry Christmas, Darling." Honestly, we danced about two-turns, and then we just stood there, her father's arm around my waist, and we listened and enjoyed it.

> *That I wish you Merry Christmas*
> *Happy New Year, too.*
> *I've just one wish on this Christmas Eve,*
> *I wish I were with you*

To hear this child deliver such a well-known song, with no accompaniment, and to do it so well, was just marvelous. And when she started to tear up toward the end, I choked back my own tears.

> *I've just one wish on this Christmas Eve,*
> *I wish I were with you*
> *I wish I were with you*

As we applauded, I looked over the Bill, and he was in tears, too. I had learned the story of his wife, and I again looked him over. The thought of me asking him back to my room, like we were all back in college or something flashed through my mind. Part of me ached for those days, that innocence—even as forced as it was at the time.

And all of me ached to be with a man again …

Instead, I thanked him for his dance, and I walked back to the table where Sally was also sitting. She was busily preparing the Secret Santa event, the de facto culmination of the evening.

Previously, she had appointed everyone an opposite to buy for, taken all the orders, and gone into town to do all the purchasing. At this moment, she was busily doing all the wrapping.

"No peeking!" she warned.

"Really?"

With a twinkle in her eye, she jutted out her round chin to beam a smile at me and kept wrapping.

So, still seated, I turned back around to survey the scene. Kinta had stepped down from the stage and was being hugged by her old man and—*Did she just glare at me?? Is she angry or something?*

I did a double take, and there was no mistaking it. Over his hunched shoulder, she was just staring at me, with a glint in her eye.

Every one of the nine of us in the so-called command team was paired up with a rank-and-file member of the gangs. Sally took a lot of orders for aftershave and keychains.

But, as chance would have it (or, maybe not … come to think of it; Sally never expressly said she picked randomly), I was paired up with Marshall. And Sally herself was paired up with Po.

Po's gift to Sally wasn't purchased. She took it from her purse (which, except for a few clothes, was all her worldly belongings). And when she produced it, you could hear most of the people in the tent audibly gasp.

"Oh, my lord. I *cannot* take this." Sally was as taken aback as any-one.

"He wanted you to have it."

Po had passed on what Chief Storm Breather, Ben's father, had gifted to her. His personal prayer book. He had written the Tribe's prayers in it, in the ancient runes of his people … supposedly passed down to them by the spirits themselves.

"Thank you so much. But I can't read it."

"We can meet afterward, Sally. I can help ya' with that."

Sally nodded, and then it was Po's turn to open her gift—Sally had gotten her a New Jersey Devils hockey team cap. Po gladly replaced her Santa cap with that.

"Are you a Devils fan?" Ruby asked her.

"I am now!" Po declared. And the room erupted in laughter.

"Open yours!" This was Marshall.

Mine was a flat square. Some sort of picture?

"Sally got me the frame …" Marshall led as I tore open the paper. And that revealed a hand-drawn sketch of …

"Is this Kinta?" I had to ask.

"No! It is you!" he pointed out.

And he was right; it did look like me. Except that he had drawn me smiling broadly … that was why I thought it was her, I realized. She was always smiling.

"Of course! Yes, I see that now. Thank you! Only, I have to say. I thought it was someone else because you have never seen me smile like that, not really."

"Oh, yes. I have."

"When?"

"The other day, when you were singing in the rain."

At that, the room got strangely quiet. I saw a few people nodding at me.

So, rather than explore that, I just thanked him again and nodded to Sally.

Sally walked up and handed Marshall the last gift of the night, which she officiously announced as such.

It was a small, small box. He commented that he didn't like rings, as he opened it. And then, there it was. He took it out and marveled.

Sally had bought a toy elf and removed the small, cloth hat. And she had sewn a piece of elastic on it.

"It is a Santa hat—" she started to explain.

"For LITTLE RICH! Now Little Rich has a hat, too!" Marshall had known instantly.

Then everyone laughed, with Kinta squealing with delight and hugging him generously about the shoulders as he kept smiling at the little cap. They both got up and left right away to go and try it on his pet turtle as everyone laughed and cheered.

Bill had a strange expression in his face as they left. Then he caught me glancing at him, and he smiled. *Maybe I do need to … but maybe this is not a good time, though …*

Then he walked back over to the turntable to play some more tunes. *Who knows? The night is young. Heck, where's some mistletoe when you need it?*

BOOK ONE—CHAPTER TWENTY

"If the whole earth is infinitely small in comparison with the sphere of the stars, what is man compared with all these created beings! How, then, could any one of us imagine that these things exist for his sake and benefit, and that they are his tools!"

—Maimonides, *The Guide for the Perplexed* (Twelfth Century, A.D.)

The Analyst was informed of an incoming call, and so he excused himself from his meeting and returned to his office. His blinds were already lowered. He mounted his ergonomic ball-chair and donned the headset. "Terminal—active. Zed zed one. Accept call."

The mole's face appeared on the screen in front of him. They were in the dark, under the cover of the forest overhead … far away from the camp known as "Barn Grier." The mole carried a small MyFi personal router for connectivity in the deep woods. Most of the others couldn't even use their phones in the camp clearing, let alone within the dense forest.

"Status," the Analyst demanded.

"Most of the commanders are here. Apparently, the Chicago office security was so lax the boy and the CEO managed to visit Mr. Reese."

"Yes, I have heard. The agents in charge are being brought to me for a … *debriefing.*" His thoughts briefly floated in the void, until they returned to the matters at hand. "Recommendations?"

"The plan proceeds. The boy is wavering. I believe he will help them. Same with the CEO."

"The boy will be there to help them." *I have seen it.* "And you will do what you must to trigger the distraction. There must be violence at this protest. We will have long since secured the current stockpiles of the drug. But our … inside man … cannot find the necessary information on the servers. Key data is missing. You must try to find where that data is hidden. My guess is the Indian woman has it stowed away somewhere. I will send a squad to assist you."

The mole privately thought how unlikely that was, but he didn't dare voice his doubt to this madman.

"That makes sense. I'll confirm."

"Report back when you do. We won't move until you've verified our target. No more wasted strikes on a shotgun approach. Assuming Brick knew was my mistake. He didn't. So now, we will find out who has that data before we strike again. We are counting on you. Is that understood?"

"Of course. Out."

Satisfied, the Analyst mused: *Between him and the Regnant stowaway, something should shake loose.*

###

Rufepirts enjoyed the boy's, Butchie's, dreams the most. Tasty morsels.

The boy-who-was-grown-now was having a special dream tonight… *He sat with the other girl. They were eating … picnic.* The word revealed itself. He nudged the dream into a sexual encounter … the Master was always thinking of those. But somehow, Marshall's was turning out differently. Less violent. *The girl was condoning it, in the dream. Almost like an entirely different activity. They were … making love (new word).*

Then Rufepirts exerted himself so that the scene changed to:

The Server Room. Blue Rooks HQ. They are yelling as they move together, until the girl stops and realizes where they are at. She quickly dismounts him and starts to walk around the air-conditioned chamber of high technology. She doesn't bother to put any clothes on, but Marshall quickly pulls his pants back on. In the dream, he curses, filled with anger and embarrassment.

"Shhh," the girl says. And Marshall does as he is told.

Rufepirts didn't know who else to turn to. He couldn't ask the Mast—the Analyst. He would hurt Rufepirts with his anger if he found out that the dJinn wasn't making progress.

Rufepirts had already acquired all the data from these servers, but the Master wanted more. He said the key info was still to be found. He threatened Rufepirts. But Rufepirts had already done the task. If he did anything else, he risked exposure.

He may have looked like a normal, middle-aged man (with long hair and a long, bushy beard), and he always behaved meekly around others in the facility. And, thanks to the armed incursion a while back, the missing scientists didn't attract much notice. Local authorities believed them to be collateral damage. So, they didn't look too closely at the bodies that Rufepirts had personally shot. But if he started asking weird questions to the replacement scientists, now, that would look too suspicious.

So, Rufepirts settled on this.

Now Rufepirts was putting it into Marshall's mind ... in his dream: "Use the others." ... It wasn't always effective, but sometimes you could get, what to call them, after-images of possible futures from dream queries like this.

Marshall and the naked girl, Kinta, continue through the dream, and they come up to a large cabinet, like what servers where placed into many years ago. And they try to pry it open. Marshall has a little knife, no ... scalpel! And he uses that to pry it open—and inside is a woman. She's wrapped entirely in several layers of linens, all of which are covered with runes—NO! Cannot look! Rufepirts has to avert his eyes, and he ends up ending his connection with the boy's dream. But before he does, he is able to discern a single name. The person in the box. Her name.

A name for the Analyst.

"Sally!"

Marshall awoke with a start, gasping for breath. The back of his shirt stuck to him.

I dreamt of having sex with Kinta? he wondered. After what just happened earlier in the night, he knew that would never happen.

Marshall had just gone too far. She came back to his room with the little hat, and after, they played with Rich while she tried to get Marshall to agree to help with the mission. And Marshall (again) said no.

Then he tried to kiss her. But she said no.

Why did you do that? a voice asked him. Was it his own conscience? Marshall got upset and started tearing up right then, right in front of her. He felt some anger at her teasing. And he was ashamed that she was seeing him that way.

So, he asked if the one was contingent on the other. He knew that was wrong to imply before he even got done getting the words out.

Then, of course, she got mad and left. The walls of Marshall's room all echoed the lessons: *She is afraid of you. She doesn't care about your turtle! You would've raped her in the dream. Sicko! No one likes you. See?*

Before he even knew what he was doing, he swiped the keys to the car and was starting it up. He remembered driving down the driveway, eyes filled with hot tears. He had to get away from there!

He didn't know why he thought he could drive, speeding down dark roads just outside the encampment. But then the tree was there—in front of him, in front of the car.

And everything was darkness.

###

A couple of times he woke up in his hospital bed.

Each time, Palla was there, talking to him. He didn't hear her. He just wished she were Kinta. No, not Kinta. Grandma Marian.

Then Marshall closed his eyes and returned to the peacefulness of forced healing.

###

Back at Camp Grier, Po and Sally welcomed Palla Kalrajan into the darkened chapel. This room was so seldom used, dust and cobwebs offered another layer of refraction for the light coming through the small stained-glass window above the stage.

Palla was invited to sit on the other side of Po, in the front pew. Sally stood in front of them, holding the rune book.

"How is Marshall?" Po asked.

"We left Kinta there to look after him. The doctors say he is recovering," Sally answered.

"Dat boy's got a hard head. He'll be fine," Po informed them. "Did you bring the book?" When Sally said yes, Po offered Sally to kneel before her with it.

Sally smiled and knelt before the elder woman, a look of confusion on her face. She glanced at Palla long enough to see her shrug her shoulders, too. *Just go with it*, Palla silently suggested.

"Now, Miss Sally, open the book. Here, hold it so dat you can see da first page …"

Sally did so while Palla watched.

"Look at da symbols, Sally. Just look at 'em; open your mind …" Then Po reached out and touched the side of Sally's head, as though she were patting a small child.

"K'AAH!"

Sally's sudden gasp at Po's touch made Palla jump and yell,

"Are you all right?"

But Sally didn't answer. Instead, her eyes teared up, and she started to read, and she looked to one and then the other of the women, and then she peered back down at the book and began reading again, like a parched man finding an oasis in the desert.

Palla was just gaping at the say Sally was acting when Po turned to her.

"M'kay, your turn." Po said.

"OH no. No, no. That's okay, I'm fine. Thanks," said Palla as she backed away, arms extended.

But Po folded her arms and said, "Do you really wanna continue to be so unprepared the next time you face those bastards?"

Palla stopped at that. And then she looked over at Sally, who was still riffling through the old prayer book and smiling.

This is some kind of hypnosis. Well, at least I'm not suggestible like all of these other religious types, she reasoned. And she answered, "Okay," and let her guard down.

And so, Mother Po took a step forward and gently touched both ladies on their shoulders. She closed her eyes and muttered a nonword, and, like before with the rain, the very heavens seemed to open themselves up and shower Palla Kalrajan with all of their glory.

The first time Marshall woke up fully, Kinta was by his side.

"Hi."

"Hello, Kinta."

"Can I sit down?" She had already been sitting there, for hours probably, but she had stood up when she saw Marshall was awake.

Marshall nodded and added, just so she realized he knew, "So, they gave you a shift, too?"

Kinta smiled at his intuition, and suddenly, he stopped being mad at her. Her eyes were always so *big* when she looked at him. So pretty.

"I wanted to see you. I wanted to apologize."

"Apologize?"

"It wasn't right of me to leave the way I did."

"I am sorry, too."

She nodded solemnly and then gave a wry grin. "I have a surprise for you."

Marshall just stared, and then she brought out RICH from her purse!

"Rich! You took care of him?"

She handed him over, and they both smiled together. "Yep."

"How did you know how to take care of him?"

"Well, I am a naturally nurturing individual. Plus, you had a notebook full of about twenty pages of detailed care instructions for him sitting next to his terrarium, titled: 'INSTRUCTIONS FOR THE CARE AND FEEDING OF LITTLE RICH IN CASE I AM INDISPOSED.' So, there was that."

"I am planful."

She held her hand out for Marshall to grab. And he did, and she couldn't help but notice that when he talked to her, he didn't seem so preoccupied with the past or the future. She helped him live in the moment. The *now*. And, frankly, he did the same for her.

As chance would have it, right then Palla and Sally walked in.

He started to pull his hand away, but she grabbed it back with both hands and leveled a possessive glare at the other two.

"How are you feeling?" they asked in unison.

"Fine," Marshall answered.

"They're going to keep you for observation another night, but you are scheduled for discharge tomorrow. We'll come back and pick you up, then. Oh, by the way, thanks to some … persuasion by Sally, you are a *John Doe* to them. They just know that you work for the feds. So, there's no need for you to answer any of their questions about your background or any of that."

"Okay." But Marshall continued to give a puzzled look.

"What is it?" Sally asked.

"How did you get them to give me psychotropics?" Marshall's dull-around-the-edges feeling was unmistakable. He reached for a juice box that someone had left on a tray next to him, and Kinta passed it to him.

Palla replied again, "Sally did that, too. She is quite persuasive. Plus, I offered them a grant. So, two things, really." She paused for a moment and then added, "You had been getting worse for weeks, Marshall. And then you hurt yourself … I'm sorry, but I just had to do something."

Marshall nodded his agreement.

The two women exchanged a glance. And then Sally said, "Well, do you want the good news or the bad news?"

"Good news," Marshall said, not caring.

They both smiled, again, in unison, and then she added, "Well, Palla and I met with Po last night. Po had agreed to help Sally translate the book from the late Chief, remember?"

Marshall nodded.

"Well, now I can read the book," Sally announced.

"Okay." Marshall waited and when nothing was said, "And that is it?"

"Well, the bad news is that Po left us."

"She's dead!?"

"What? Oh, no, sorry. No, she just … left us. She wanted us to tell you … that she had us drop her off at a store on the way here. She says she's taking an Uber somewhere. Can you believe it?"

Marshall again nodded affirmation. Some things never change. Po never stuck around for thanks. She never said goodbye. And then, as the two ladies kept smiling, he had a new thought.

"You two are different now." He felt it to be true. Sally nodded.

"Well, she's better company." Palla was complimenting Sally?

"It is not just her. You are different, too."

"Well, I'm not great at reading the book, if that's what you mean. But, actually, I can when Sally is near … I think that's because … what was it that you called it, Marshall? An empathic connection? Sally and I have that now … Po did that."

You nodded your approval. *The wheel turns as it must, or it would fall over*, Marshall thought. Po used to say that.

Then the doctor came in and asked everyone to leave, saying that Marshall needed his rest. No one argued, but Marshall did have a problem when the doctor insisted that the turtle had to go.

"Don't worry, I'll take care of him. See you tomorrow when you get back to camp," said Kinta.

And so, for the first time in a long time, Marshall thought things might actually turn out all right.

BOOK ONE—
CHAPTER TWENTY-ONE

PALLA

###

"Marshall, what's wrong with the book? Too hard to read?" I said from the passenger seat.

"Impossible to read. Now, I wish Po had stuck around long enough to show me."

"I can help when we get there," Sally said from behind the wheel.

But I interjected, sort of mock-boastfully, "No way, I got this. Hm, let's see …" I crawled back from the passenger seat to sit next to Marshall in the back seat. "Okay, sure. Well, for one thing, this entire chapter is about the future."

"Why do you say that?"

"Hm?"

"Why do you say that this chapter is about the future?"

"Well, I mean …" Then I just sat there and stared at it for a few seconds. Finally, I had to admit, "I don't know. I guess it isn't."

Sally glanced over her shoulder. "No, you're right. It is. That is the dream vision prayer chant, the original version. The one that so many of our prayers in the Blue Rooks Church used as the template. Marshall, that was the primary spell for Marian, for—"

"Choicifering. Choosing futures," he finished. And he no sooner said it than Sally yelped out at the road ahead. She braked the car for a second, before continuing on.

"What is it?" we both demanded from the back seat.

"Just now, as you said that … I saw it again. The camp. In smoldering ruins, just as before." Then she looked at Marshall and asked, "Before—that wasn't a trick of the light, was it?"

"No, it is going to happen," he confirmed.

"Oh, my goodness. We need to hurry!" And Sally gunned the gas pedal.

And then Marshall and I both said the same thing: "No, wait. We need a plan."

Once Sally's practice prayers (with Marshall's odd coaching—he kept saying things in a fake Jersey accent, like he was Mother Po) were complete, we did, in fact, "floor it" to get back to the camp as soon as possible. And when we were about five minutes out, I called the authorities. We didn't know what we were getting into, and having the cops and fire department show up to sort it out after a bit seemed like a good plan.

This time we slowed and saw the very scene that Sally had described before through that gap in the trees. The camp was in ruins, smoldering.

As we approached, we saw several black minivans parked where the various bikes used to be. Scores of fully-armored soldier-agents were gathered under the mess tent. All the smaller huts were ashes, and the barracks were actually still on fire as we approached.

Those of us that thought to look behind us saw another black van there, cutting off our escape.

Marching out from under the tent was a large man carrying someone else over their shoulder. The body being carried was tied up and we were still too far away to make out who the large man was. But as we parked, we could see that the man was none other than … Bill?

Oh, god, oh, god. NO. Bill.

I made out with an agent! *That fucker.* At least we didn't actually have sex. It was fortunate that I was on my time. Deep down, I knew that I probably would've said yes.

Mustn't *puke.*

Then I focused on the body that he'd thrown to the ground. *It was Ruby! She was dead! Was she dead? No …* she just lay there, still on the ground, bound and gagged, eyes closed.

Bill was flanked on either side by agents who leveled their rifles at us as we exited the car. More agents encircled us at slight angles from behind as we approached him.

"Palla, Ms. Radisch. Young Marshall," he greeted us each in turn.

"What did you do to her?" Sally asked him.

"She has been subdued. I knew better than to expect her cooperation. But the two of you, I am more hopeful that you will comply."

"Comply with what?"

"Marshall is going inside, under the custody of Federal Marshals."

"On what charge?" Palla demanded.

Bill didn't respond but rather just nodded to one of the agents. A signal was given and two of them closed in on Marshall, easily overcoming his awkward attempts to resist.

For his part, Marshall was not only resisting, he actually was trying to fight. But that consisted of him mostly leaning into various blows to the head and sternum from the agents. But in-between getting pelted with blows, he did take a moment to yell out instructions to me and Sally. "Now!" he barked. "Do it!"

The plan was simple: Marshall wasn't going to do the spell—he was under the influence of his prescription meds, still, and was exhausted besides. No, instead, he would distract them, and Sally was going to spancast: she was going to slow time so they could escape. She had spent a lot of time working with Marshall and looking at the appropriate spell in the book. She had already started the mantra to herself as they walked up. She was already trying to gather her *chi*.

But I could see it in her expression: it was no use. She looked at me like she wanted to wail …

But Bill didn't even seem to notice what she was doing, he was focused entirely on Marshall as his agents did their task: a black bag was placed over Marshall's head, and he was shackled and dragged away from the scene.

The next few agents moved to corral Sally, too. *This is too fast!* my mind screamed. *The local cops won't get here! But the feds will have jurisdiction anyway …* all this went through my mind, and, ultimately, I decided I had to be the one to delay things.

I jumped in front of them and madly waved my arms. "Wait!" I shouted and then cried, *"UGNGH!"* as one of the soldiers quickly stabbed their rifled butt into the side of my head, knocking me down.

Stunned, I eventually forced myself up to a sitting position. I looked around and everything around me seemed to grow darker, like storm clouds had suddenly moved in.

Is it a concussion? I thought, because suddenly I thought I heard singing (*singing?*) off in the distance—like a music box, high-pitched and harmonic. The crackle of the barracks fire was audible, too. In fact, I could hear everything.

Bill (Agent Ironfoot, I heard someone think of him) also looked around and a look of shock replaced the confidence that he usually projected. His heart was pounding madly. He was murmuring *no* and starting to back up toward the tent.

I could hear his thoughts, now, too … he had been planning to torture Marshall to get the location of Sally's server from one of us. *They wanted that data!*

The soldiers just looked confused. They were awaiting further orders and now their lead agent was freaking out. A couple of the senior soldiers asked him what was wrong, as a gentle rain worked its way into framing the scene.

I couldn't see them. I still couldn't see them. But I could hear them. Their voices started to converge and coalesce into a single note. That note spoke to the soldiers, only. The all stopped and looked around, as if waking from a dream.

Then, as one, they all collapsed like puppets cut from their strings.

And I *felt* it. I felt their minds snap into darkness from the touch of power.

NO! I screamed to the voices to stop.

And they did. I don't know if it was me or not, but I could sense it: the soldiers weren't dead. But they were *out*. And incapacitated.

Marshall stumbled to the ground. Sally and I ran over to him to try to free him. Sally searched the forms of nearby soldiers for keys to his shackles, while I just freed him from his hood, so he could see what I could not.

Bill had just frozen in place. He tried to concentrate, *to summon his own chi I guess*, based on what Marshall had been teaching me and Sally. But then, just as quickly, he remembered he couldn't, due to the Blue Joy.

He blinked once in realization, and then he simply reached for his gun.

He pointed it at us with a sneer. I stood up between my friends and him and raised my hard as a ward, with a shout of *No!*

As if in response to my voice, I heard the other voices again coalesce into another note …

But before he or the *Others* could pull the trigger, I heard "Daddy!" Kinta had emerged from one of the vans, where she had been asked by her dad to stay until this was over.

At that, he stopped. He still pointed the gun at us, but his grip had relaxed, and the look of fearful rage was gone. He just looked at his daughter with a forlorn expression. That expression will always haunt me because the dJinni finished their job then.

The sound of them swooping in on him was audible, at least to me. In a few short moments, Bill's entire frame was covered by a strange *blackness*, like a slate blanket.

Later, Marshall told me that they literally aged the air around him, until it was no longer breathable. Something about using the energy of light and the nearby plants, using up oxygen.

But what I saw was Bill's disorientation and, finally, horror, as the blackness slowly crept over him, until it covered even his face.

Then the shrouded form that had been Bill dropped to its knees and grabbed its throat. It convulsed wildly, clawing all around it, more and more frantically … until eventually, it collapsed. Then the blackness left and all that remained was the lifeless form of Agent Bill Ironfoot.

It was so horrible. *Did I do that?*

"NOOOOOO!" Kinta ran at the prone form of her father, laying there in the mud. Then I could hear her sobs over the steady rainfall as she hugged the corpse of her father.

We were safe. For now. But what was next?

That was the question, as we all heard fire department and police sirens approaching down the road.

Sally grabbed me by the shoulder. "You okay?"

"Um, yeah." I was having a bit of trouble tracking. My head was pounding.

"Ruby is alive. She was only drugged. She's still out."

"Okay," I said, numb through the pain.

"Why did you kill him?" Sally asked.

"What? What do y'mean?"

"I mean, wasn't that you?

"No! What do you mean? Doing what? You mean killing him?"

"Yes."

"No!"

"No, you did," Marshall offered as he walked up to us, "I have never seen so many act so quickly, not even at the funeral, without so much as a warning. They were following instructions, from someone."

There was the music. That was the warning. The instruction. I thought to myself, but I didn't say anything.

"Ruby?" he asked.

"She's okay, I think. She needs medical attention."

"That's coming" I reminded them as the sirens got louder. You could see flashing lights off in the distance.

"They are starting to wake up, too," Marshall noted as certain sol-dier-agents started to stir.

I said, "The authorities'll all be so busy—between questioning each other, figuring out this scene, and putting out the fire … quick! Follow me!" I took the lead running off behind the barracks as I wiped the blood from my face. Sally and the still-handcuffed Marshall trailed behind.

We dove into the deepest woods, high-stepping as a solid two feet of underbrush covered all the ground between the trees.

By the time the flashing lights descended on the camp and the bar-racks fire was put out, we were deep in the woods.

###

"We should not have abandoned her," Marshall insisted as we tried to navigate the foliage.

"She needed medical attention and, even though they are taking her into custody, she will at least get that attention," Sally (again) patiently explained. She was walking way out in front of us, somehow nimbler now than I had noticed before. Ever since she'd read the book, she was changed in so many ways. We both were. She was conversing with Marshall, who trailed along behind her.

I was even farther back, like I lacked iron or something. I felt fatigued and just wanted to sit down.

"You could have saved her! You can do that!" I had tuned out their arguments, trying to think of what to do next, so it took me a few seconds of a pause until I realized that that had been directed at *me*.

"W-wait, what? Why does everyone keep accusing me of shit? I can't do anything!"

"You're a liar!"

"Okay. That. is. ENOUGH!" And I stepped up to him and put my finger out in front of Marshall's face for emphasis, "You are not going to talk to me like that. Is there something happening to me since our little mind-meld with Po that I don't understand? Yes, clearly. But I am not—"

And then Marshall, in an attempt to dramatically ignore me, pushed my hand aside and kept walking forward, trying to catch up with Sally. And even though he barely pushed my arm, I actually stumbled to the ground.

God, I really am so tired, I was thinking.

I landed in the underbrush with a thatched thud. But I didn't notice that because the music in my head was now again rushing loudly. The music box was now trumpeting in my brain. And I just sat there trying to not let the thunder of it make me scream.

"THIS CANNOT HAPPEN!" And the stormsong just repeated, "CANNOT! CANNOT!

CANNOT!"

Marshall and Sally heard it, too. Both spun around as a rushing wind blew leaves and branches into them both. Sally, maybe ten yards ahead, was knocked off her feet. But Marshall was unbowed … no, wait; he wasn't falling because he was suspended! He was off the ground!

His jacket, the black windbreaker, stretched far above his head, as though on an imaginary hook. You could almost hear the tear as Marshall deftly allowed himself to slip out of the jacket, and then it was blown away, too.

He fell to the ground and gathered himself until the rushing wind stopped.

Gradually, Marshall stood up. And when he stood, he looked all around, in amazement at the various beings that (apparently) had gathered near him.

Dang it, I still could not see them! And except for the music, repeating the same message over and over again, I couldn't hear them either.

"CANNOT!"

"CANNOT!"

The blood from my head wound had now fully run down my face, mixed with sweat, and its salty taste was bitter as the winter woodland breeze. I pressed my palm to my forehead and then gazed upon the shiny red covering my hand.

And I fainted …

… Into a dream. A dream where I could hear everything now:

"It was okay. We weren't in any danger," Marshall said with his typical straight face; he was just standing there in his dirty white oxford, his glasses akimbo. He was speaking to them as though to an old friend over a quiet cup of coffee.

But this phalanx of dJinni dwarfed the one that assembled for Benjamin at the funeral battle. Their large forms filled the forest in all directions, filled the sky … Marshall's thoughts betrayed him: He was in awe at the very sight.

And then the assembled beings … laughed.

It was so loud it rumbled like an erupting mountain. My own pain was strangely gone, but Sally and Marshall both collapsed with yelps at the splitting headache the laughter caused them. Sally was knocked out. But Marshall and I continued to hear the multitude laugh.

Then the lead voice spoke up:

"WE ARE NOT HERE TO PROTECT YOU. WE PROTECT HER, THE UNITY. LEAVE THIS PLACE AND THINK ON IT, THAT OUR NEXT MEETING WILL BE MORE IN HARMONY," said a voice. From Marshall's thoughts, I knew her name: the Demi-urge. She was already familiar to me, somehow.

And then, as suddenly as they all had appeared, they were gone.

Marshall was obviously horrified. They LAUGHED! They laughed at him!

Marshall's thoughts raced backward, like an old reel-to-reel, reliving all the tragedy in his life, all the death. And I could feel the bottomless pit of sorrow and grief and despair and chaotic fear well up and overtake his defenses. He no longer knew where to look for answers. His own voices, the ones from his illness, they often laughed at him. But not the dJinni. Not the others. Not his friends. Never before had they mocked him.

But before the dream ended and I slept, I was afraid that the de-mons' laughter had done what all the tragedy in Marshall's life couldn't. It had finally broken him.

BOOK ONE—
CHAPTER TWENTY-TWO

"… and this was my portion of all my labor."

—Ecclesiastes 2:10

Sally knelt on the ground next to her friend's body, listening for breathing, feeling for a pulse. *Yes, there it is.*

She then picked up Marshall's jacket and placed it over Palla's prone form. She was still taking in all the situation when she was started by the voice of Kinta, emerging from behind a tree:

"Don't move!"

Sally froze and automatically put up her hands when she saw the gun.

"Is she dead?"

Sally just shook her head.

"She should be! After what she did to my father!"

"It wasn't her. They did it on their own, they were protecting Palla."

"You're lying!"

"No, I am not. I understand you are upset, but please, they nearly killed Marshall for merely pushing her. And you saw what they did back there … please, I don't want them to hurt you, too. You are not in any danger, I promise you. Please put down the gun."

Sally had actually been in one or two scrapes, when she volunteered down at the shelter in rural downstate Illinois. She was younger, but even back then, she instinctively knew that projecting calm strength and promising a safe environment were the first steps in active shooter situations.

"Marshall? Is he okay?" She lowered the gun.

Sally shrugged. "He seems to have left us. I was out for a minute, and when I woke up, he was gone." Sally regarded the girl's hopeless expression then and decided to give her something else to focus on. "The armed forces, the cops, all of them, back there. What are they doing?"

"I watched from a safe distance for a while. Mostly they were talking on phones. After about a half hour, they finally assigned teams to start searching the perimeter. If you … if we stay here, they'll eventually find us. She really didn't do it?"

"No."

The girl put the gun back in the front of her pants. She seemed pretty comfortable with it. "It didn't really look like it. But I didn't know. I don't know anything … why?"

"Your father was just doing his job. He thought he was doing right."

"The way he threw Ruby to the ground. It's like he wasn't even acting like himself."

Sally took a long breath and looked askance for a long while, as though waiting for inspiration before speaking. She twitched her nose and then said, "He was separated from his own spirits, Kinta. Now that I've had a stronger taste of it, now that I have truly heard them, I can tell you … that would be a horrible feeling—like losing all of your senses at once. Deprivation."

"Marshall was right when he said that some people call them demons. Maybe they possessed my dad. But ever since my mother died … he has changed. I didn't want to see it, to admit it. But I knew."

"How did your mom die?"

"During childbirth."

"You were to have another little sibling?"

"The only one. It was … unexpected. And the entire tribe also gossiped, well they knew—it wasn't just gossip … it wasn't really his. The timing was all off … he had been away on assignment during the key months. But he claimed it as his own and was prepared to raise it. As time went by, I saw how it ate at him … how he felt he had lost Mom, lost his wife, twice: once when she betrayed him and a second time, giving birth to a child that wasn't even his …"

"Does anyone know …?" Sally started to ask.

And Palla answered it as she sat up and looked at Kinta:

"It was Ben Storm Breather's child."

Kinta nodded, with tears in her eyes.

"And you were right. The need for revenge against his oldest friend, Ben, ate away at him. But he never let on. Bill had struck a deal, a deal with the Analyst and his agency, the Extirpacy. He would infiltrate them, help them lead and warp this so-called protest into something that the Extirpacy could use …"

"He was *bad.* Just like my mother," Kinta said, with the moral clarity of youth.

"No, your mother *admitted* her wrongs to Bill and asked for forgiveness. And because he loved her, he forgave her, but he never could extend that to Ben. But his strongest feeling was a simple one. It wasn't revenge or hate. It was love. LOVE, for you, Kinta Ironfoot. His little *perfect raindrop.*"

Kinta wept openly. "H-how did you know … that he called me that? He never said that—he only said that to me, in private …"

"I could hear it in his mind. I am already starting to forget, but, for a little while there, I could hear everything," And Palla just reached out and took the weeping young woman in her arms, holding her steady as she shuddered.

"What now?" Sally asked as she walked forward and set her arms around them both.

Palla Kalrajan just stood there, holding her new friends, not sure how to answer anything anymore. And yet knowing full well what needed to happen.

Running through the forest is stupid. The voices notwithstanding, Marshall sprinted as quickly as he could. And he fell. And sprinted and fell, again and again. His arms were scratched badly, and several times, his hands were punctured by sharp rocks or small, broken off tree branches that raised welts on his palms and caused them to bleed.

His eyeglasses and the flip-shades were lost somewhere in the dense forest behind him, where the dJinni host had shamed him.

That first day wasn't so bad. Running became walking. He counted his steps, and that helped pass the time. But then, one time, he did not like the next number that followed: one thousand, one hundred and eleven was wrong. *Not eleven,* he decided. *Onety-one.*

For how long did he walk? He had no way of knowing.

Ti-i-ime is on my side. No, it isn't. His thoughts started to speed-jumble again, *My watch! It is not even on my arm. Who is on watch? To arms! To arms!*

Marshall Lastpost held his arms up as the rain started. He looked directly into the storm, sitting down in the mud, watching it wash the blood from his hands and listening to the raindrops as they imprinted fresh messages on his mind.

###

Eventually he got up and found a road. The mud was caked onto the rear end of his jeans. He thought of those assless chaps from the one routine that one comedian did, Grandma's costar.

He stuck his thumb out, but nobody stopped. He kept walking. As night fell, he decided he'd had enough, so he looked for shelter.

Marshall snuck into an abandoned barn way off the road and found some old hay-covered blankets. They were moldy and uncomfortable and perfect. He found a sharp-edged tool to cut his plastic handcuffs.

Then he sat down. He slept even though he didn't want to, because he knew that the world of dreams contained the perfect environment for the voices to return.

But there were no voices that first night. Just a cold that had him coughing the next several days.

His dreams had been filled with memories. Grandma in the coffin. Slinker being shot. Ruby on the ground. The host … the host of the *Others,* they were alien again, he could still hear the *Others* laughing. Their laughter was the laugh track to all of Marshall's memories now.

His foster parents in flames? Cue laughter. The Analyst ordering Ben killed? Laughter. More laughter. *No, no, folks; save your applause until the very end.* Just more laughter. Laughter at him.

He kept waking up to the sounds of coyotes off in the distance. One time he thought he felt a snake and jumped up and tried to stomp every square inch of the barn, his heart pounding in the pitch blackness, as though trying to kill it using the law of probability. As the seconds wore on, his expanded his circle of destruction, trying to calculate how far it could have gotten in the meantime.

Eventually, he fell over some pieces of lumber and hit his head, with a whimper.

The snake was the real trigger. It brought the voices in a big way. He hadn't heard them consistently since he had gotten the meds from the hospital.

Shh! Stupid. Someone heard you. Herd like sheep. You're going to bleed to death. Shear the sheep. Shear stupidity. Shka-mah-la-THERN!

The "la-Thern!" was made by flicking his tongue in and out, like the snake. He used to make that noise over and over again when he was very small. *La-thern! La-thern! Shka-ma-la-THERN! That* was the snake in the darkness. *La-thern! La-thern! See, like a snake! See the snake, Be the snake, Danny! La-thern! Na na na na na na na na.*

He was too mentally exhausted to fight them, so he just listened, the ideas cascading down upon him. Non sequiturs, advice, chiding, hateful insults … didn't matter.

Nothing mattered.

The creaking of the barn door didn't wake him. It was the cocking of the shotgun.

"GET UP!"

Marshall did not panic or even get up at the farmer's (probably the barn-owner's) request. He was too exhausted to do much of anything.

"Could I have some water, please?"

"Lord, boy! What happened to you? You a drug-ee?" The farmer was a stern man. No nonsense, through and through and, apparently, not willing to shoot first and ask questions later. "Where's your home? Where are you from?"

"I-I came from Barn Grier."

"What? That place. I thought they closed it down."

"They did. But I was there visiting it, and then the government came and … they shot my friends."

"The feds. Yep, that sounds about right. That place was messed up. But the feds aren't much better. I was one of the folks who marched inta' there and told that church to get out. I had a grandniece that was there for a while … it was supposed to be a religious camp. But they did bad things there."

"I know. I am not with the people who used to run it," Marshall lied. "I just—I just got caught in the middle …"

"Okay, okay. You need to get fixed up. I don't think you're any danger to me—but I don't want you to leave this barn, okay? I will bring you some water. I mean it. I see you outside this barn, and I'll shoot your ass. Got it?"

Marshall nodded and the farmer left.

After he had brought water and a bit to eat, Marshall (and his voices) conspired to a new set of facts—not a lie, really—just clever omissions so he only told this kind farmer what he needed to hear. Marshall was a member of the nonprofit that was running the place. But the federal government wrongly thought he were part of the old church group that used to run it, and they attacked. And he ran to safety. Yeah. Like that. *You're too stupid to lie.*

This farmer appeared politically suspicious of anything related to the federal government, so he took Marshall's word for all of it. He even added some details of his own to the story that Marshall didn't bother correcting.

The key thing was that he gave Marshall Band-Aids and sustenance. And a place to sleep for a few nights—right there in the barn. He still didn't trust the young vagrant enough to let him near the house. But he made a point of hanging out outside, in line of sight, during the day, so he always knew where the stranger was.

As for Marshall, the voices grew in volume and quantity. As the days went on, the food became unbearable for him to eat. Every bite activated all of his neurons, firing all at once, trying to tell him that it was poison, that he had to reject it. By day three (or was it four?), he was vomiting all of it up, only keeping the water down.

And the voices were too prominent to allow much sleep, even though he had gotten used to the barn.

But on day five, he decided to spancast a search of the property, do a recon. Much of that evening (which was only a few minutes in their time) he spent looking through the farmer's house. *Let's go here,* he kept telling the voices, again and again as he entered each room, in response to their warnings about what he was doing.

The farmer and his wife, Marcia, lived alone. Their kids had long since moved away. Marshall sampled several of their foods (teeny tiny bites, so as not to get nauseated), took a shower, and grabbed some spare clothes to hide in the barn, for when he ran away. During that illegal entry, he also found out that Frankie—that was the farmer's name—cut hair part time as the town barber.

The energy that it took to do that spancasting exhausted him enough to get a decent night's sleep that night, without the voices arguing about it.

Marshall hid the clothes in the barn, and the next morning, when the Frankie brought him breakfast, he asked him where the nearest barber was. The farmer of course proudly offered to give him a trim in exchange for the spare change Marshall had in his pocket.

While he cut Marshall's hair (which had grown way over his eyes and past his shoulders), he asked Marshall about his plans, probably wondering if he was a mooch that he'd eventually have to call the police about.

But the younger man had had plenty of time to think about it. Marshall said he was going to hitchhike to Vegas, and he meant it. But the farmer just laughed.

"No one hitchhikes any more. But I have a friend who's a trucker. He might enjoy having company, if you're willing to do some honest work. Sometimes his runs take him to Vegas …"

"Work. Like what?"

"Wash and wax the cab. Run errands in towns where he parks to sleep. Help load and unload where needed. Like that."

After the cut and shave, Marshall looked into the mirror and didn't recognize himself. He had told the farmer to leave the back long, like he liked it, but now his mullet was even more pronounced, because the rest was buzzed short.

He had a crew cut.

A crew cut!

"Thank you," he said to Frankie the barber, and he meant it.

Later the farmer called his friend, Dicky, and they agreed to take Marshall on Dicky's next run—which was going to be in a week. *Great,* Marshall thought. Now, he had the chance to sneak Frankie's clothes back into his room until he offered some to Marshall of his own volition. Oh well, it was better that way anyway.

###

Marshall hadn't actually slept in days. But Big Dicky didn't realize that at first. Before they both left for Vegas, Dicky had spent a long week of days training the newbie how to drive in a very basic way. The plan for the trip (which was to be nonstop, over two days and two nights), was that he was going to allow Marshall to take the wheel on the long stretches of empty, straightaway freeways in Colorado and eastern Utah, so Dicky could nap in the middle of that second day.

Marshall actually picked up basic manipulation of the rig pretty easily. Steering, watching the RPMs, watching the road. Even the gear shifting was fun ("Upshift, clutch, clutch, gas; *or* clutch neutral, gas, clutch ninth, clutch neutral, gas, clutch eighth …"). He tended to excel at anything that involved repetition.

But the real key was that he practiced the various motions he learned over and over, continuously, for three straight nights. All night. He could envision the smell of the cabin—the musty combination of cigarette smoke, sweat, engine oil, and lemon-scented hanging pine-tree air fresheners. In his mind, he settled into the vinyl seats, feeling the beaded seat cushion and the towels strapped to the seat behind his back for extra support. And then he would drill himself, again and again, on what he had learned.

After all, this was far preferable to sleeping, now that the voices were in full force. Better even than counting; this particular repetitive, combined-mental-and-physical regimen was an excellent way to stay mindful.

The trip: Day one was uneventful. Big Dicky was chatty. At first Marshall answered his questions. (Carefully avoiding anything true, he made up an entire life story on the spot. He was an out-of-work orderly who had been wrongly accused of assaulting a patient—so he was starting over in Vegas … like that.) Later, it became annoying how talking interrupted the various internal dialogues he maintained, so Marshall just shut down and stopped talking out loud altogether.

If this spooked Big Dicky, he didn't show it. He turned up the radio and ignored Marshall right back the next few hours.

Late in day one, after two Iowa stops to pick up the loads, as they were entering Colorado, Dicky offered Marshall a joint. Marshall politely refused, so he put it away.

"You are not going to smoke it?" Marshall asked.

"Me? No, I'm not gonna piss hot and lose my license. But you looked like you could use one."

Marshall knew his eyes were extremely bloodshot. His stubble had grown back in and his skin was shiny for some reason. The secondhand smoke and an entire day of fast food was also making him feel nauseated—Marshall missed Frankie's ubiquitous bacon and eggs.

On day two, in the middle of the night, not long after I-80 became I-76 and they entered Colorado, Dicky pulled over and offered Marshall the wheel.

Marshall pulled the truck out onto the empty highway as Dicky oversaw his driving for a bit. He ordered Marshall to slow down ("clutch neutral, gas, clutch ninth; clutch neutral, gas, clutch eighth …") and then speed back up. He told him to pull over quickly, just to test him. And then, satisfied that everything was going to be okay, he told Marshall to wake him if any other traffic appeared or if he needed anything. Then Dicky settled back into the passenger seat for a nap. He set his phone for some period of time; Marshall didn't see what.

He pulled forward and concentrated on the yellow dotted line whizzing by the cab as the large truck barreled forward through the desert night. They moved too fast to count …

###

"Hey, kid? What the fuck?"

Marshall woke and nearly hit his head on the roof of the cabin.

He remembered now. The consensus from everyone he heard was that he should sleep. He argued with all of them for a while, but at the end, he realized he really was going to pass out asleep and go off the road.

"What's wrong with you? Why …? How long were we sitting here?"

"I have not slept in a week," Marshall informed him instead of answering.

He shut his mouth and just stared at you. Then he staggered back to the passenger seat and asked, "Why didn't you tell me?"

"I get this way from time to time."

"So, you got insomnia. That part of your mental issues? My wife, she's bipolar. I have her sister come by and check in on her every day while I'm gone …"

"Schizophrenic."

"Multiple personalities?"

"No, that is a myth. Schizophrenia is when a person has psychotic episodes, hears voices, hallucinations, that sort of thing."

"You on medicine?"

"Not currently."

"Well, Jeezus. Listen, you can't drive. But also, I don't know about this. I mean, Frankie said you were cool. A little quiet, but cool. I figured maybe if we hit it off, I could recruit you as a driving partner, but now?"

The younger man regarded him for a long time. He was about to throw Marshall out. But then Marshall instinctively said the one thing he thought could earn the other man's trust, based on everything he had observed up until then:

"I would like that joint now. Perhaps then I can sleep."

Big Dicky seemed to relax at that. But then his eyes narrowed. "You sure that is good for you?"

"Marijuana is used to treat some psychotic conditions." Which wasn't entirely a lie. *You're going to get caught. Go to Jail. Go directly to Jail. Do Not Pass Go. Go Go Gadget arms!*

So then, Marshall smoked his first joint as an adult… and it had absolutely no effect. The burnt, tarry air made him cough, and the smoke that had already plagued the cabin now seemed to seep into every one of his pores.

But he could not say that it had any sort of major effect. *You must not be doing it right. Don't get all out of joint. Get another one. Maybe you're double-jointed?*

Dicky nodded. "Yeah, the first one doesn't take." He chuckled and gave him another one. "Try another."

So, Marshall did. And that time was different.

Marshall woke up several times without opening his eyes. Each time, he drifted back to sleep without acknowledging the truth. Finally, he woke up and looked around. And then he realized it. The truth that he was trapped, there in bed.

Strapped down to a bed. In a room.

The smell of latex and disinfectant was familiar. He was in the hospital. A hospital.

At that, he panicked. He started to yell, but only an abrupt croak came out. No one heard.

Marshall wanted to struggle, but he couldn't move his arms except in only the slightest way. He was helpless.

He thought he might cry then. He could feel the phlegm begin to gather inside his sinuses and run down his throat, as his eyes watered with despair.

But he gathered himself, snorting the mucus and swallowing it harshly so as not to choke.

Marshall turned his head to one side and saw a medical cabinet, and a curtain (mostly drawn). He could see past the foot of the bed, but he turned his head the other way, past the gap in the curtain. And there saw another bed, an empty bed. But next to that bed was an old man sitting in a wheelchair, looking much as he had when he'd last seen him in the federal lockup.

It was Uncle Brick.

Marshall started to smile, but he had a gravely sad look on his face. Marshall waited for him to speak.

He wheeled up to the younger man and leaved over his form. His big head blotted out the harsh hospital lights. "Hello, son. How are you feeling?"

Marshall started to answer, but then remembered that he had no voice.

"Well, it doesn't matter. It will all be over soon. Remember this will hurt me more than it hurts you …" Then Brick reached up and placed both hands around Marshall's neck— *WHAAAAT?* Your mind was on fire.

And then Brick Reese carefully squeezed.

It wasn't going to take long. With his enhanced strength the only reason Marshall was still alive was that he was hesitating … throttling him slowly instead of simply snapping his neck.

Marshall felt the cartilage in his windpipe start to give. He couldn't move. He was going to die.

NO. Marshall reached out with his mind and screamed the song that he heard during the battle between the Analyst and his friends, the one that killed, the one that stole another's *chi*.

There was a fulcrum moment … the precarious spot where Marshall was at the demarcation point between life and death. And at that moment, just as he was cut off from his own energy, he felt Uncle Brick's energy plug into that very slot.

"NO!" Now it was Brick who panicked. He attempted to remove his hands, but he couldn't …

The battle was short and fierce. Marshall tore through the other's mindspace much like he had, years earlier, shredded the dJinni at his son's deathbed. Then he felt the other person break. And the scene fell away like the straps on his arms. Like the hands at his throat.

Marshall sat and gasped, back in the cabin of the truck, in the passenger seat.

He stared down at Big Dicky, lying across his lap, whose dead eyes stared ghoulishly back at him.

Marshall felt his own neck. It still hurt. *Had he been choking me? He* had *been choking me.*

Marshall lifted Dicky's head and felt *his* neck. No pulse. He *was* dead. Marshall had killed him.

And in a wave of realization Marshall also realized he was largely rejuvenated, filled with all of Dicky's life force, his *chi*.

Marshall vomited all over both of them then. And he did it again, as he opened his door and staggered away from the truck.

He drugged me? To kill me? Or did I pass out and kill him in my sleep? What just happened?

Marshall laid there on the ground for a long time, waiting for a voice to give him some answers. But no voices ever came.

There was plenty of water in the truck. Apart from the occasional car, no one even passed Dicky's semi on the highway beside which they were parked. If any troopers drove by, it might be another week or two before they came back around and saw that they had not left yet. So, there was time.

I always have time, Marshall thought. *Sometimes I wish the* chi *would burn out of me. Just one spell too many. I don't want it anymore. That was why. I had the right idea: stop all dJinn, just stop it. I had the right idea back when I cared about anything.*

Eventually, Dicky started to stink.

Fortunately, the trailer was a reefer. Refrigerated.

Marshall stayed there for a week. Day after day, he sat and imaginarily drove his unmoving truck with the shameful evidence of his deed haunting him, not twenty yards away, on ice.

The police will return. You're a criminal! Killer. You said you would stop the magic. Liar. You have the right to remain silent. Silence is golden. Golden Pretzels. Pretzel Logic. Logic is the beginning of wisdom. It's so obvious …

Let's go here, you insisted.

But it was an empty command, devoid of purpose or hope. No one was going anywhere. It was just something to say.

We're on a road to nowhere …

Marshall kept smoking what was left of Dicky's weed. It removed much of the stiff joint pains that all the hours of riding and sitting in the truck had given him.

And with the smell of burnt leaves rushing all along the surface of his body, the voices decided to recede. Now, they just hung around the back of his mind like when he knew he'd forgotten something.

"What happened to you?" It wasn't concern but rather awe from Sally.

Palla smiled at the question while keeping her eyes on the road. She was driving the rental car that the church had called and arranged for her once they emerged from the forest and got cell service. She didn't try to hide the purchase. She wasn't hiding anymore.

On the drive, she, Kinta, and Sally had been talking, and Sally had been explaining some of the history to young Kinta. She spoke of the Revelators, the Blue Rooks Church, and even went back to the Wild Bunch days.

During the conversation, Palla barely spoke. But when she did, she always said what Sally had been thinking in her heart.

And then when Sally asked her where they would go next, Palla recited it like a mathematician recites an absolute proof.

This prompted Sally to ask her if she was a cleric now.

Wow, what a perfect question. Well I can't play coy, forever, she thought. *She is ready to hear a bit more.*

"I've been given a gift."

"What is that?"

"It's gone away. But, just for a few hours I was shown who I really am."

And who is that? The unspoken question hung in the air.

Like Shams reportedly said to Rūmī the first time they met, "I am the Money-Changer of the World," Palla thought to herself. But instead, she explained, "Behind all the songs from all the spirits that they have ever sung or ever will sing, there is a wondrous background chorus whose singing never begins or ends. It just changes."

Sally just stared at the apparent non sequitur. So, Palla added,

"Um, that's me."

Through the entire week in the truck, Dicky was still with Marshall. *What a pal!* thought Marshall. Although, truth be told, Marshall didn't much enjoy their conversations. Dicky was always so opinionated.

He wasn't that way when he first died. But each time Marshall went back there into the reefer trailer to talk, he got feistier. *He's just another one of your voices. The strongest one. Like what SHE used to be, from the others,* someone said to you.

But Marshall wasn't having any of that. *No. Big Dicky is my friend.*

Marshall slowly climbed out of the cabin and carried his notepad and a small penlight back to the reefer, where Big Dicky was sprawled out like Michelangelo's *Pieta* over some crates. Marshall kept the door cracked so he didn't freeze to death.

"Hey, Dicky, let me read this to you. Now, be honest with me … friend to friend. Does this haiku sound good?"

But before he could start reading: *Can I be your friend, too, Marshall?* a voice interrupted. *I already know you very well.* Marshall looked all around the trailer, his breath vapor trailing circles around his head. When he didn't answer, it continued:

Listen. Let's be friends. And I will start with my name … it's RUFEPIRTS. Pleased to meet you (again).

Marshall didn't understand. None of the voices, ever, ever, used a name. And "Rufepirts"? What in the world kind of …?

And you are Marshall. You will be the Champion. The Unity sees that now. It is all coming together. I am afraid that I can't explain it all to you. But I can help you get to someone who can. To make up for what I did to you. I hurt you and your friends when I told the Analyst that Sally had hid the formula. And where you all were. Of course, the Unity wasn't in any danger. But you've been hurt. And no matter what my Master tells me to do, She will never forgive me if I don't at least try to help you.

SHE? Was SHE the Demi-urge?

Her, too. But I was talking about my host. You will see. Even after we are severed, we are bound to our hosts. Listen, we don't have much time. They are almost there. But look, just remember—OH my! So soon! Hello, Palla—

SCREEEEAAAAAAACH'UULLLLLL!!, the sound of the trailer door opening the rest of the way made Marshall drop the penlight, and it fell, breaking on the floor of the trailer, next to the crate where Dicky was laying (What, you were asleep again?) and several guys with guns and a much stronger flashlight climbed in.

"Man, I told you this would be easy. This truck has been here all week, yo."

"Yeah, okay. C'mon, let's just see what we can get and—"

"What the fuck, there's a dead guy here! He's frozen! Wait, there's TWO!"

Marshall held up his hand to ward off both the flashlight beams and the headlights of the car that was parked behind the semi.

"Keep your hands up! Jeezus. What kind of sick fuck are you, fella?" Marshall just squinted with his arms up, mutely.

"Never mind him. Is there anything here?"

"These crates are all full of frozen foods."

"Not if we keep standing here with the door open, jackass! Just grab a couple so we can get home. Steaks sound good to me tonight." That was the leader?

"What about this guy? Is he gonna talk?" From his squinted eyes, Marshall could see something reflecting light in his mouth. He had two golden teeth, right in the front, top.

Marshall wanted to get a better look, but the other one made sure he didn't. He chopped a gun across Marshall's face so hard that he felt his jawbone crack. It felt like he'd bit through his tongue.

They continued to beat Marshall. Kicked his ribs. Collapsed several crates on top of him. And hit him several more times for good measure. Pain shot through every nerve of Marshall's body before they were done.

"Okay, okay. That's enough! Before you waste any more energy or a bullet. He never got a good look at us. And, anyway, he's already packed for going on ice." That was the leader again, the clever one.

Marshall laid there in a pool of blood and heard the screech of the door again. And then the sound of several latching bolts closing.

And then he was alone in the coldest of black places, preparing himself for the Inevitable.

BOOK ONE—
CHAPTER TWENTY-THREE

PALLA

###

It is because they mostly only remember the pain, the thought occurred to me. *That's what keeps the world in arrears.*

My brief knowledge of all that pain should've broken me.

But that was only part of it. I also felt all the love, the happiness, the silly wants and needs, and all the glorious desires (which were all the better fulfilled for having never being spoken). I felt all of that from everyone. It was remarkable what humans were capable of. All the heroism.

Thankfully, I could only remember the faintest hints of what all I had experienced. Prolonged exposure to all of that was quite impossible for this human mind. I mean, my mind.

The church's assets may have been frozen by the feds, but my personal ID badge had not been erased from the building's security. Our midnight arrival permitted me and my friends to bypass any awkward conversations with bystanders. And since the building had been quarantined as a crime-scene, no security personnel were around to ask questions, either.

Ironically, the church's utter destruction (albeit a temporary one) was just what we needed for easy entry. As we snuck through the courtyard, I remembered the slaughter I had witnessed three months earlier at the funeral. But we'd also been moved from that timeline to another one, shifted. So that I could not be sure that any precise thing I saw or experienced was, in fact, in the Timespace we were in at that point.

But I had other means of perceiving reality.

For example, I had Sally, who was enjoying (with some mild frustration) her new and improved Choiciferor talents. I had asked her to pray about the best time to reenter the Chicago headquarters.

She said that we had five weeks to get things in place.

She got it mostly right.

But really it was nine weeks, not five. That was how long I had to: buttress the board, access our offshore bank accounts, pick the right legal team to win the show-cause hearing to unfreeze our domestic accounts, confirm with everyone that the convention was still on, and finalize the schedule and the arrangements for the attendees.

The convention was to be in nine weeks.

I should explain. I did this without spells or songs. It all happened during my time when I was seeing *all*. During my "revelation." For me, during that, it was like daydreaming. Only by smell. Okay, so it wasn't smell exactly, but it was like that. It was like when you smell that meat is bad even when it looks okay.

You understand? Okay, so during my *revelation,* I got to see a multitude of visions. And when a vision was unfortunate or highly unlikely, it just didn't *feel* right to me, and my mind would recoil. But when I saw one that passed that test, that "smell" test, then I went ahead and watched it play out a bit … to see how it might lead to the next one.

It was all much quicker, even, that what the Regnant did for Marian when Marshall was young—the way they showed her their *preferred* visions. Same function, but this was much more rapid. And more objective.

They wouldn't try to mess with me that way.

And so eventually I (gently) suggested one. This one. But forces were already at work. Even as I chose it, it was already changing, shifting. Choosing futures is so fraught. I should never do it again.

That's the mistake all the other one's before me made, maybe. So easy to feel like you have to do something … to just pick one.

But anyway, no. The almost five weeks was how long it was to be before we went to meet *him.*

I couldn't really see much beyond that, before I returned to my normal self.

Of course, I knew that I could never tell Sally just how extraneous her efforts were. I didn't want to shake her newfound confidence.

My *revelation*. Whatever that was, please do not misunderstand: I didn't know how everything was going to play out. I still do not.

I mean, I am not omnipotent.

Nor, clearly, was anyone else behind all of this.

If any of you were really omnipotent, I silently challenged the others, *we wouldn't be in the mess we are now, would we?*

BOOK ONE—
CHAPTER TWENTY-FOUR

بشنو این نی چون شکایت می‌کند ** از جدایی‌ها حکایت می‌کند
"Listen to this reed, telling a tale of separations—"
(translated from Persian)

—Jalāl ad-Dīn Muhammad Balkhī
(a.k.a. "Rūmī")

###

Well, this is it. I am really going to die. This made sense. Marshall had killed … truly killed an innocent man.

After several attempts, Marshall finally managed to sit up against what must have been another crate. The pitch-black trailer smelled of death, perhaps a sign of what was to come.

Marshall turned to where he imagined Big Dicky was nearby in the darkness. "This is another fine mess you've … hhhuh." The air from your lungs ended before your impression could, but then a voice concluded it.

"Gotten *us* into." And there was a third being in the trailer with them both.

"Who?"

"It's me. Pick me up! Don't you recognize me?"

Marshall reached out in the direction of the voice. It was a hard, rocklike, curved—

LITTLE RICH! HOW COULD THIS BE? Marshall picked up what was, impossibly, his pet turtle from his perch atop the dead man's sternum and held him in front of his face.

It was pitch black in there, so he could not see him. But he knew it was him. In fact, in his mind he could see, as though standing outside in the noon sun, every scale, the claws, the colors of his rough shell. He was so awesome.

"You have much to say." The turtle spoke the truth.

Marshall shook his head. No, he was shivering. Freezing to death. This was all an illusion. *I am quite mad.*

Still, it is good to see Rich again.

"Focus, Marshall. You have much to say. But you have to get it out."

"Get it out?"

"C'mon, Butchie. Like your Kleinian talk therapy sessions with Grandma Marian as a boy. Talk. Talk to me. What are your thoughts?"

Marshall sat there, frozen.

Literally, HA HA ha, yes. Quite mad.

"Why are you alone, Marshall?" Little Rich's voice took a more formal tone.

"I kill. Everyone. Around me." And he nodded his head toward the dead body next to him to help make his point. "I kill with my thoughts."

"You haven't killed anyone. Just because you have visions doesn't mean you caused them. *You cannot see beyond a future you haven't reckoned: wherefore.* Remember? That's the first Precept of the training, Marshall. You have to understand what is happening before you can see what's next or choose. But you are assuming that understanding then means you understand the now. Not true. Anyway, this is all because you weren't weaned properly. You suckle Timespace threads like milky tits, ya' big baby."

Marshall winced. "Do. NOT. Laugh. The *Others* ... laughed at me. I am going to destroy ... the link between us and them! No more clerics! Prayers can just be. Words."

"You are just jealous. They have the power and you want it. Your own voices laugh at you, too? I don't hear you complaining about that. You just want all of them to love you, like I am supposed to, right?"

"You. Do. Love. Me."

"Jury's still out, son. Anyway, you still haven't really answered my question. You are alone. Why?

"I am the Precept."

"What did you say?"

"If I have to understand it ahead of time, then I am the Precept. The future that gets chosen; I have to understand what I want to happen. If I don't, then it is not my responsibility. That's what the rule really means."

"Now you are bargaining for love. You still make choices, Marshall. What choice do you need to make?"

"I need … forgiveness."

"Good. From whom?"

"From God."

"Touchê. That's as good a starting place as any. You know what to do."

"Do? I. Am dying. Probably. Already."

"You want to be dead because that is easy. Cold. Unmoving. Like you. But there is a fire in you, Marshall. You brought it once before. When you sent him away in anger. But you can do it again."

"Will it. Burn. You?"

"I certainly hope so. Turtle soup is delicious. Open the book, Marshall. Read between the lines!"

Now instead of Little Rich, it was the little book of Shaman prayers, open to the last page. In the pitch black of the trailer, the runes were still legible in Marshall's mind.

But he still couldn't read it. But maybe he didn't have to. *Come visit, Marshall. We're expecting you.*

HER voice was unmistakable now. *So, that's who … Little Rich? Hilarious. SHE did a fine impression, too,* you decided.

But she laughed at you before …

Stop being a child.

He felt warm all over. Did the trailer stop working? Were you going to be okay?

No, you realized. It was just hypothermia.

This was the end.

Bring the fire! SHE demanded.

Flashing in your mind: Everything you had gone through. Prince. Grandma. Brick. Rich. Ruby. Ben. Slinker. Kinta … *you had failed them all.*

But did you have to?
Did you have any choices?
NO CHOICES!
It wasn't FAIR!
DAMN IT … the faces flashed in your mind, No. No. NO. Over and over again NO, until your anger NO and anguish NO welled up NO like a NO … like a … like?
Drowning. Smothered by time. Breathing. No more?
No.

Then, with his very last breath, Marshall Lastpost screamed in flames that tore asunder space and time.

###

Sometime prior to that.

In his lab in Chicago where he worked (and lived, though no one knew that), Rufepirts moved the mop back and forth to the rhythm of the music in his mind. From time to time, he would place his forehead atop the end of the broomstick and dance around it, until he got dizzy and fell over. Each time he fell, he hoped he would hit his head on the floor. That was the best.

At that precise moment he was cleaning up his own blood, from all the falls. He could make sure his physical form healed quickly, but the blood always remained behind.

When he sensed the temporal disruption behind him, he yelped, expecting his Master. Instead, he turned to find a familiar form, beaten and bloody, laying on the floor.

"Master Precept!"

Marshall was unconscious. The dJinn dropped his broom and rushed to Marshall's aid. After a few moments, he was able to divine what had happened:

"Ah, you tried to get to the Unity, but you were still tied to me, through our visit. Or rather the one I'm about to have with you. Mmph. That's not fair, you beat me to it. But I like your spirit! Still, you cannot stay here. The Master will kill us both if he knew … plus, you might've actually gone *back* in time, technically. Pretty sure that's against the rules …"

Rufepirts thought for a while then, as he gently petted the unconscious form of Marshall. He concentrated on the problem so hard that he momentarily failed to maintain his human form. He leaned back and rested on his powerful hind legs and tail as his dragon-eyes stared at Marshall's prone form.

Then he decided.

Seattle.

Yes, that was a worthy outcome.

Rufepirts summoned the necessary energy, closing the circuit. In a moment or two, it was over: Marshall was gone from the lab and was back in the Timespace that he had come from, at the point in time that he'd come from, and on his way to visit his brother.

Rufepirts sighed. Then he grabbed up the broom and returned to his task. He needed to clean the place. Spotless. That's what it needs to be for her visit. First impressions are so important.

Then he laughed out loud at the idea of "first impressions" for the Unity.

Seattle.

Heychuck began his prayers as he always did: *Dear Lord, please watch over and protect …*

Of course, he started with all the families of the one's he had straight-up killed. And then he extended it to his congregants. Both were relatively small lists, but his heart truly went out to all of them. Then he turned to his own desires. That was usually a much longer list. Some days he would write it down. But his list had been more or less the same for a while now.

A new location, with a legitimate job as a minister. And enough money to pull that off. He had some very specific items of clothing and vehicles that he always included, sort of like a little in-joke between him and God. He knew he wasn't going to get them … but he didn't want God to think that he was losing confidence in him, right?

They he usually prayed for a decent date.

By the time he was done, the knot that was his stomach, his life, was just a little bit untangled and smoothed out. It was always so weird how prayer worked like that.

So, he ended the prayer as he always did, by checking out Tinder. Chicks on the prowl behind their significant-others' backs always dug someone who could legit forgive them their sins afterward. Hooking up with a minister was like extra points on the slut scale or something.

But for some reason, another thought popped into his head right in-between consecutive swipe-lefts—

I should pray for my Marshall. *Now, why did that crazy mother suddenly come up in my brain?*

One thing that did was definitely kick him out of the mood. So, he knelt back down and, after some serious thought, went ahead:

"And, God, please look after my dumbass brother, Marshall Lastpost."

"Hey …?" a strained voice rose from the back of the room; the thick wooden door to the chapel opened.

He recognized his brother's voice. *Amen?*

Turning around, he then saw his brother unlike any time he had ever seen him before.

His brother's eyes were wide and glazed with a sheen of madness. His hair was … gone! Now his head was topped by a flat slate of salt and pepper; and now he had a beard, also speckled. But, most noxiously, his clothes were disgusting. His black jacket was gone. And he had obviously been wearing the same light blue-and-white pinstripe denim shirt for weeks, as it was stained with various and sundry foods and bodily fluids, like a tie-dye of misery.

Marshall could barely stand, leaning against the door for support. Heychuck ran up to him to grab him before he fell, and Marshall managed to utter:

"—Thuck, you got the time …?" Then he collapsed into his brother's arms.

The Be(k)nighted

BOOK TWO—CHAPTER ONE

REVEREND HEYCHUCK SMITH

###

"You don't get to think. You just do what we tell you. Right?" said Charlie. The streetlamp's flare of light was reflecting off his sunglasses, which he wore despite it being midnight. He was in the backseat of his limo, talking to me despite his head being pointed askew off toward something else, like he was blind or something.

I just thought you didn't need me for these small jobs anymore, was what I had said to him. Since Marshall had arrived at my apartment the weekend before last, I had taken a pass on any other visits to clients who weren't paying. Charlie's rackets including drugs and arms-running, extortion, and the occasional assistance on high-ticket theft (which were usually insurance scams). But you didn't hear it from me.

I was hired muscle to make attitude adjustments in people who weren't following the program. Despite my job description as an *enforcer*, I seldom had to use force. And it had been ages since I used deadly force.

But when an enforcer falls out of line? That, usually, is a one-way ticket. If Charlie got mad at me—or he found me no longer useful—it would be a race to leave town before he got to me first.

"I gotcha."

"You understand?" his oriental eyes then looking at me over the shades.

"I understand."

"You have someone living with you."

I didn't realize he was having me watched, but I couldn't be surprised.

I said, "That's just my … friend. He needed a place to crash."

He considered that and measured my answer, trying to decide if my visitor was a leverage point or not.

Then he concluded. "Your next assignment will be soon. Be ready to leave at a moment's notice."

And I nodded again as the tinted window raised until all I saw was my own reflection, frowning at my own life.

BOOK TWO—CHAPTER TWO

"Our religion is the traditions of our ancestors, the dreams of our old men, given them by the great Spirit, and the visions of our sachems, and is written in the hearts of our people."

—Sachem Si'ahl (Chief Seattle),
of the Duwamish Tribe (est. 1854)

"He's waiting in the conference room, sir."

"Thank you," the agent mostly known as the Visiting Analyst (or VA for short) replied to the desk agent. He wasn't pleased. He didn't like surprises.

He briskly entered the room, handshake extended. "Mr. Secretary. To what do I owe the pleasure?"

Secretary Itiorvic didn't look up from his iPad. "Your boy was on the move." The Analyst immediately realized that he meant Marshall Lastpost. He had heard that there had been a match of his blood to the Nevada truck murder. The Analyst withdrew his hand.

"I had no idea you were monitoring the situation so closely. I can assure you—"

"I don't want assurances. I want the occasional win, that's all. Other than capturing an old man and killing a couple dozen of his friends at a funeral we have nothing to show for any of our prep work. Despite their funds being frozen, The Blue Rooks Church just announced that the convention is still on. I thought they were shut down. Hell, I keep hearing about how that Kalrajan bitch's high-priced attorneys are outmaneuvering us in court. She's out on her own recognizance? On your federal case?"

"She's just back to work. It won't matter, the important—"

"The convention is back on. We were—*you* were—supposed to shut that down. Taking possession of that Blue Joy drug was supposed to be trivial. As easy as claiming evidence for trial. Now, it's a goddamn legal logjam!"

"If you would just—"

"So, what *is* the plan now, Doctor?"

The Analyst took a long breath and centered himself. He could kill this fool, but that would have longstanding ramifications to the plan. His visions were clear. The secretary would be there for End Day. The Secretary had presidential aspirations, just like Mr. Lee. They both planned to use the event to try and achieve inroads with the religious right.

"The plan, Mr. Secretary, has not really changed. We have only had to adjust our tactics, *mutatis mutandis*. My best agent is acquiring the specs for the drug manufacturing. And even though we weren't able to forestall the convention and secure the drug in secret, our task force within the protest is now bifurcated. One team will secure the drug and ship it to our secret facility in Kentucky. The other team will turn the protest into a hostage event and, therefore, results of the experiment, the taking of the Blue Joy by the event participants will now be broadcast live, thereby increasing the exposure of the drug's effects. That way, when the government contracts out the manufacturing deal, even greater market penetration will be effectuated. But I am sorry for not informing you of all this sooner, Mr. Secretary. I was planning to wait until the next meeting of the advisory board."

The Secretary sat perfectly straight in his chair, head titled slightly. He seemed satisfied by the answers. Without saying so, he stood up and walked toward the door.

Before he exited, he said, "Doctor, I am a fan of your work. What you have managed to achieve with this agency"—he looked around—"there are entire parts of the world that have fallen into line thanks to your agents. Even without the showy violence, our ... *soft power* ... is greatly enhanced with your operatives in the field. But there are about four levels of bureaucracy above you in the FBI who have no earthly idea what you are up to. And I would prefer it if we keep it that way. And this becomes increasingly difficult every time one of your task forces go shooting up some small town. So, the plan is the plan. Fine. But, other than that, all of these domestic incursions? They must stop. Are we clear?"

The Analyst nodded. "Understood. And even within the plan, our embedded teams are doing clean up, yes, but the actual operations are being done by individual agents. The drug schematics? As I said, my best agent."

"And the Hostage situation?"

"Well, it will be more of a demonstration than a hostage situation. You'll see. And for that? I am handling it, *personally*."

"So, I'm not the only one looking forward to some screen time?" asked the Secretary.

You have no idea. "Ah, well. I will just be the warm up act, sir. You will be the star. I assure you."

The Secretary stiffly nodded again in lieu of a proper exit line, like the former military man that he was, and left.

###

"Oh, my! So soon! Hello, Palla—"

She was doubly surprised, stumbling upon this guy. The CEO had snuck into the lab after hours, so there should not have been anyone there. Plus, the facility was supposed to be abandoned. No one *could* be here.

Oh, and this person wasn't in any of her visions, either. So … three things.

This guy was very tall and skinny, with a pot belly, and a short mop of red hair cut unevenly and standing straight up. His nervous mouth hung open as he breathed, with a small gap between his top front teeth to emphasize when he smiled. He had a ginger beard that was more close-cropped than his scalp, and his eyes were so bright blue they were nearly glowing. He wore a jumpsuit that seemed to have lots of colors woven into the pinstripes of gray. His name tag was blank where the name should be … no, he had taped a piece of paper over it.

"Allow me to introduce myself; I am Rufepirts." And the skinny stranger did a large, theatrical bow, like he saw on the television. He was there around the clock, alone, and got to watch a lot of TV. He especially enjoyed it when he recognized one of Marshall's impressions …

"Okay. Who ARE YOU?"

"I am Rufepirts ..." And he started to bow again.

She stopped him. "Yeah. No. I got that. I mean: Who are you? How is it that you are here? Who gave you access to this building?"

After some thought: "I work for the Visiting Analyst." It was, after all, the shortest answer to all three questions.

As he watched the wave of anxiety wash over her, he continued, "A federal subcontractor was the janitorial service vendor for this building. My mas—the Analyst, made sure I was on that crew. And then, even after the building was secured, I was switched to a security-shift detail. But I truly am just a janitor." He bowed again. "I have been preparing this space for your departure, Unity."

"Don't you mean *arrival?* Wait, why did you call me Unity?"

He tilted his head like the RCA Victor dog. "You don't know? But you do. Or at least you have caught glimpses." He bowed again as he asked the question. It was so hard for him not to sing to her ... to try to gain her approval ... the way he used to when they were both back home. But at this point, he could no longer sing those sorts of songs.

And she wasn't ready to hear them anyway. She needed an artifact. Some object to infuse with energy of the *other* realm, to help her focus her mind, her powers.

"Why did he want you here. To try and kill me?"

"Ah, no. No, no no." He kept bowing, which annoyed her, he could tell. "He left me behind to find the data on the drug. The 'Blue Joy,' I believe it is called?"

"It isn't here."

"Of course it isn't. Most definitely. I have searched extensively. But you're going to tell me where it is."

"I don't know where it is." Which was the truth, even if momentarily she had, during her visions. She had forgotten, well, everything, now.

"Well, you'll know after I help you depart."

"There's that word again. 'Depart' for where?"

"Home."

###

She immediately saw the truth of what he was saying.

"So, you're another ... magic-user? A cleric?"

"Ah, *Order,* no, Unity. I wouldn't begin to be able to learn all of those techniques. No, I am the opposite. Where I come from, we don't learn the magic. We … do it. The way you breathe. And cough. And wear clothes!" The last was with a sense of exasperation, as he referred to his shoes, even holding one up to show her, with a big goofy embarrassed grin on his face.

His shoes were untied.

Apparently, this was a point of ongoing consternation.

"Would you like help with those?"

He hesitated since tripping over them had been exhilarating any number of times. But this was as may be, the Unity, the firstborn from the dead, could not be denied. He nodded.

She knelt down and carefully tied them … it took a while since they were true work boots, with all the little pegs up either side of the front ankle.

Afterward, the gap-toothed smile he gave her was such an expression of pure love—it actually took her back a moment.

"Please, have a seat. This first time may be disorienting." He helped her to sit down.

Sally had told her to come here. This was one that Sally saw better than she did. She had said that she was supposed to come here on this day. She had seen her leaving with an important object. A trinket of some kind.

Clearly, she hadn't seen this Rufepirts. If he was beyond her vision, maybe … Suddenly, an insight.

"You're one of them!"

"Ah, Unity. Everyone is one of 'them.' Well, except you, perhaps."

He worked on the preparations, hovering all around her seated form as he did. "It will help if you have an anchor. What do you …?" Rufepirts felt all around her pants and jacket pockets.

"HEY! WATCH IT!" She had to slap his hands away. He yelped and put his stinging hands into his mouth for comfort, bowing again his regret but still smiling.

For her part, she was pissed. He had clearly copped several feels. She probably wasn't in any danger. But she did reassess the situation and took out a burner phone to text Sally.

> *someone here. one of the dJinni. he knows me and says i am the 'unity.' What 2 do?*

Sally replied a moment later:

> *b careful.*

Then she noticed what the weirdo was doing. He was setting up a small table with all manner of flickering candles and religious paraphernalia, crosses and beads and whatnot and—HEY, wait a minute! What is he … Oh no, he was holding her bell!

He must have had snagged it while he was frisking her.

"DAMMIT! Gimme that!" She grabbed it back from him as she put her phone back in her pocket, knocking over his table of candles and trinkets. He looked distraught but didn't fight her, instead retreating a good ten feet from her anger.

"But, Unity … it is perfect. Precious. Pure. It even makes a noise!"

"Perfect for what?"

"You will need an anchor in this Timespace. So, you know where to return to. From there, they all look the same, sometimes."

Palla supposed that made sense, at least as much as anything did. It was like listening to science fiction technobabble on a TV show. She handed it back to him, and he carefully placed it in the center of the weird little shrine he'd made on the coffee table in front of the waiting room couch where she sat.

She sat back down and took a deep breath. For Pete's sake. She literally could not wait to get back to her office … that boring job of reading reports and purchase orders and legal briefs … she started to ask Rufepirts (what a name!), *So, when is this going to start?* But she was already in the slender silence of the Regnant's home dimension …

"Are you the verderer?" a small dragon asked her as she walked past … She sensed Rufepirts—no, she sensed his energy, with her. The various dragons (that's what they looked like: tiny, fat, floating dinosaur-dragons) mostly ignored her as she walked amongst and through them. There were so many, they filled the air around her.

Eventually, their ranks thinned out and Palla stood in a large, open field of slick white stone. And on that field were … statues. Men. Women. Various ages and shapes.

She stopped at an especially detailed one and ran her hands over the surface. She asked Rufepirts, "Their faces. Why do they all look so … "— she searched for the feeling she saw—"disappointed?"

He didn't hesitate. "They all started out 'ap-pointed.' Like you. But they all failed."

"Failed?"

"To save the world."

She thought about that a while as they walked.

One of the statues spoke inside Palla's head. "You should be dead."

Another, with a pained accent: "You're full of judgment. You'll join us soon enough." Great, now I'm hallucinating my own voices and visions, *Palla thought.* It's like Easter Island for psychos.

Or for Marshall.

"Be the island you want to visit." That last voice was impossibly deep, resonating through the ground like a distant thunderclap.

But it was also familiar. Who?

After a bit more walking, Palla felt dead beat, through and through, the energy of this place … it was like hiking in the mountains, when you are just suddenly short of breath, with no warning.

"Yes, you are not cut out for this. But keep walking. You are almost there."

Palla felt as though it were uphill, but that couldn't be because she was approaching a shore. When she got there, her feet stood upon fine, white sand. And a clear blue body of water stretched out in front of you as far as she could see.

She looked back behind her and, sure enough, she had been walking uphill. It was like she had been slowly climbing a giant eyeball of some impossibly colossal giant who was lying down on their back. As though now Palla could just jump in the blue iris and swim away …

"Very perceptive," Rufepirts intoned in her mind.

Palla was moving then. She lost her balance. No, now she was on a platform that was moving … lifting her upward.

Off in the distance, Palla could make out, vaguely, the impossibly long distances. The mountain range wasn't any such thing. They were … tits?

And those black storm clouds behind … that was … hair?

As the colossus sat up and she capsized onto another surface, she realized that she was inside the giant's hand, being lifted up so that she could be studied. Oh Shit, Oh Shit, Oh Shit, Oh Shit!

Palla of course fainted dead away. But not before the features of the impossible giant-world that held her became clear. For the barest, split second, Palla recognized the giant …

"Listen for the bell! The ringing?" Rufepirts was screaming. "Do you hear it???"

… as herself. Her head was spinning, the clouds, her hair was spinning above her like a web, each strand was another thread she could grab onto and slide down, down into the ether …

"Come back!"

… riiiinnnnnnnnnggggg. She sat up from the waiting room couch and saw Rufepirts—*dear Rufepirts. It had been so long*—holding the bell as its final ring faded away. But while the sound was in the air, she once again was in communion with the frequencies of the universe— "Blua Regino" they will call me ("Blue Queen" in Esperanto), because of it— as she once again knew what was to come … at least for a while.

Rufepirts gently handed the bell back to her. "Well, that didn't go well." It was his honest assessment.

"It was fine," she corrected the Regnant. That's what they called themselves. Regnant. In Sally's vision, the one that prompted Palla's visit there to the lab, Sally had seen her carrying a small, precious object out. But she didn't suspect that it was something she already had been carrying around. They had both just assumed that this trip was integral to getting what she needed.

Well, in a way, they were right about that.

"Now you will show me where the data is, Great Unity?" he asked her.

"Yes, I suppose I will," she said.

Be the island you want to visit, Palla recalled, even as the memory faded. *Boy, I am clever, aren't I?*

BOOK TWO—CHAPTER THREE

REVEREND HEYCHUCK SMITH

###

For the first forty-eight hours, he was with me in my apartment. I nursed my brother back to health, cooked for him. He was on my couch the entire time except for bathroom and shower breaks (where I helped him walk to and fro).

Is still hurt for him to talk at that point. So, I went to the store and bought a bunch of notepads and had him write down everything that happened to him.

At first, I thought maybe he was still too crazy for me to get any fucking thing out of that. All the stuff he was writing was all codes this and poison that. So, I scored some of the right meds for him, from on the street. I had a friend at a clinic who owed me a favor … you know how it goes.

And by the end of the week, he had a couple of days of meds in him, and he started to rediscover his balance.

So, I asked him to explain all the stuff he had tried to write earlier.

And this time is was demons this and magic that. He explained it all, and now I was starting to get angry. I mean, the meds were obviously working. He was far less twitchy. He stopped acting spooked and his eyes were focused (even if he looked sleepy instead of sad).

But at some point, I told him he was going to have to put up or shut up. Either tell me the truth without all of this magic talk or I'd have to kick him out.

That was when he proved it.

He could have convinced me of the truth of what he'd been telling me at any point, I suppose. Maybe make a stapler disappear, or steal my life-energy, right? But he never did. When I asked him why he hadn't done that over the past few years after he'd gotten better, he just said that he didn't want to disrupt my religious beliefs.

Oh, and it is possible for clerics to burn out all of their own energy, which usually means they cannot even talk to the dJinni after that, either, he added.

He said he'd been proud of how I'd cleaned up myself and gotten out of the crime and drug lifestyle, and he didn't want to disrupt my religious beliefs. Man, that made me feel like shit, I can tell you.

At first, instead of demonstrating his powers, all he said was, "Wath' the newth. Nevada. Themi-truck sthory." His jaw was still healing.

And when wrote down a written description of the contents (including a dead body), in detail, of a sealed trailer two states away that was found on an interstate, I started to despair. I thought my guesses had come true. He had gone out and killed somebody. My first assumption was that Marshall had killed the driver and hitchhiked twelve-hundred miles to get to me. After all, on the news, the truck driver's wife described how the truck had left ten days earlier. That left a gap of about a week from when the truck had stopped. So, that could have happened that way.

So, I called the cops on him.

I didn't live in a neighborhood that the SPD necessarily saw as a priority. They didn't come at all the first hour. We were out of toilet paper, and so I stepped out to go down the block and get some. Was only gone a minute, you know?

And that's when they came to the door the first time.

Marshall didn't answer it, but they had announced who they were, and then, after they left, I returned and Marshall confronted me:

"You call'th policeth?"

"Uh, no, what? No, I didn't call no one."

He gave me a stern look and walked over to the table and picked up an empty jar.

He had caught a cockroach.

He handed it to me, and I took it with a confused look.

Then, after giving me another angry glare, he stood in front of me and the jar as I held it, and he raised both of his hands so they were on either side of mine.

Then I thought I saw a gold flashbulb go off, and the jar exploded in my hands!

My hands were burned, like freezer burn, by a quick pulse of energy from the … spell, I guess. And they were pretty badly scratched up from the broken glass that shot out from what used to be the empty jar.

On the floor in front of me was a kitchen magnet. I looked over at the fridge where it used to be, but it was gone—no, it was there on the floor, like I said.

"Sthorry," he said, "forgot to warn you about that." There was a spot or two on his hands that had gotten cut, too.

"H-how did you do that?"

In response, he just walked over to the table and picked up the unruly stack of all the narratives he'd been writing up 'til then—our childhood, the voices, the doctor, his *Grandma* Marian, the Wild Bunch and Revelators, the Extirpacy, how banishing works … all of it. And he threw it at my feet.

Then we went and sat down with a defiant stare.

Then I keeled over, and everything went black.

###

When I woke up, he was looming over me holding a cold compress to my forehead as I lay on the couch. He had expertly wrapped my hands (and his own).

That's right. I forgot. He was a home healthcare aide.

And, apparently, also some kind of damn wizard.

The scripture, *and the magicians did so with their enchantments and brought up frogs,* popped into my head.

I'm still dumbstruck to this day. All those years, and I never really knew my brother.

Right about then, there was another knock on the door:

"Seattle Police! Open up!"

I struggled to my feet. *What did he hit me with?* Marshall explained later that he had stolen a bit of my life energy to cast the spell.

I opened the door and assured the police that I had just kicked out a bunch of party guests 'cause one of them was getting unruly, including prank-calling the police. I really was a talented liar. They didn't fully believe me. But they also didn't give a crap, so they left.

Marshall and I spent the rest of that week catching up. And for the first time in my life, I talked to him as an equal, not some disabled less-than person, not some retarded individual. But just as a person.

Heck, from everything he told me, it was sounding more and more like he wasn't just a person, he was some kind of damn hero. And I told him so.

That is what helped me forgive myself for how I had thought of him all these years, and especially after our last visit. I had always looked down upon him, subconsciously.

For his part, he stayed the usual—emotionless. But I think it was about day five, he had an unmistakably sad look on his face. And when I asked, he just said,

"I miss Rich."

And I knew that it wasn't just Rich. It was all of them. So, I sat next to him and held his shoulders as he lowered his head and wept his thanks to me.

"You are all I have left," he sobbed as I held him close.

The next day, he officially apologized for killing the truck driver.

"Don't tell me, tell him!" I half-joked. I knew, you see, that Dicky's voice, among his "fake" ones, had become predominant for him. And then he did exactly that. It was heart-breaking for me to hear; Marshall was truly a kind soul. And then he, once again, made a point of asking my forgiveness.

I did him one better. I told him that God forgave him, too.

"You can do that?" he asked in all seriousness.

"Sure. I'm a reverend, aren't I? See, you're not the only one with powers," I said with a smile.

Don't get me wrong. He still looked (and felt) like shit. If anything, he probably was doing worse than before he did that spell on the cockroach.

He described it like the flu. A conversation would tire him out. Or walking across my apartment would necessitate a nap. He ached all over and had no motivation to move his way out of it. so, by week's end he was stove up even more.

I thought watching TV would cheer him up. I remember how he used to copy the scenes that he'd just seen … voices and dialogue, word for word. He had a very good memory, even as a kid.

But now he just ignored it, preferring to stare out the window. Eventually, I left the TV off.

The view from my apartment in Seattle's Chinatown consisted mostly of traffic, neighborhood youths, and elders doing errands, wearing their face masks; this along with a healthy dose of tourists headed toward the nearby Wing Luke Museum. Anything there was to see, you would have seen in an hour or two. But he stood there for endless hours, just looking. All day and into the night.

Finally, I asked him what he was looking at.

"Time," he said. "I have never actually stopped and watched it before."

###

The next day brought the rest of our team together.

But I don't want to get ahead of myself.

It went like this: The knock on my door was firm. We thought it was the cops again at first—but they didn't announce. Marshall and I exchanged glances as he started to bound off the couch. I don't know what he planned to do; just quickly standing up almost made him swoon.

I walked up to the door, grabbing the baseball bat I kept behind it. "Who is it?"

"My name is Sally Radisch."

"Sally!" Marshall bellowed, again almost falling off the couch as I opened the door. I didn't know Sally. But I knew *of* her from his explanations of what had happened before.

When I opened the door, I found a stocky, ample-bosomed, middle-aged blonde wearing a long, black overcoat and muted dark-red flats that had a sparkly texture.

I instinctively sucked in my gut, so I must have been attracted to her.

As the leader of a congregation, I learned early on to check out people's shoes. Shoes tell a lot. These shoes said she was practical and had style. But she hid her light under a bushel.

She smiled at me. A smile without subterfuge.

"Are you Reverend Smith?"

"Yes, come in, Ms… ?"

"Radisch," Marshall helped me remember, over my shoulder.

"Please, call me Sally."

"Call me Heychuck."

She grabbed onto my hand with her off hand, to let the handshake linger. "Hey-chuck? That is a wonderful name. It is a pleasure to meet you."

I added my off hand to the clasp as well and gave her my best smile, which tends to shine through my black skin and thick beard like a spotlight. "The pleasure is mine. Come in!"

As Sally moved inside and stepped aside to stand next to me, we could then see the small girl that stood behind her in the hallway.

Marshall froze. And from his deer-in-the-headlights expression, this had to be Kinta.

During his visit, he had mentioned her more than everyone else combined since his initial info dump. Whenever I broached the subject of what he wanted to do next, he would start to answer and then he would mention Kinta in some oblique way and abruptly end the conversation. I got the impression that he very much didn't care about the future unless she was in it.

And now it looked like she would be.

"Hi, old man." She grinned at him.

"Hey, kid," Marshall riposted. Their actual age differential versus their looks was apparently an in-joke for them. Nice. I didn't know my brother had it in him to flirt. I was gaining more respect for him every day. Especially considering how she actually *was* a very cute young woman.

I urged everyone in, and we all sat down to chat, in my crowded little apartment.

At the time I didn't notice that a beige sedan had been parked across the street where they could see the ladies enter the building.

I spent the afternoon eating cookies and engaging in a deep theological discussion with my new friend, Sally. Toward the end, after I had described some of my background, she asked about my small ministry there in the city.

I did the usual elevator speech, telling her that my focus was on the addicts and troubled youths in the neighborhood. It was a surface-level answer, designed to move the discussion along. But she took a deep dive right away.

"I grew up in a small town. And I've spent some time with various Chicago congregations. And I think it's a myth," she said, "that problems like alcoholism, domestic violence, and crime are worse in the city. It's just that it is all denser geographically, so the problems are more visible. And, of course, there is structural racism at work with regard to the story that the myth propagates.

"But the good news, I think," she continued, "is that, because you can reach more people with problems more quickly in an urban ministry, and those problems are more … on front street, so to speak, you can help that many more." I smiled internally at the way she used the idiom "front street" incorrectly. "I bet you can go out and ask anyone on the street around here where the alcoholics could be found, and they could come up with a list of places—bars, street corners, and shelter—to find them. But in my hometown, for example, back in rural Illinois, while there was no shortage of alcoholics, there *was* a shortage of people among the community *admitting* that there were any alcoholics. Just try getting any doggone thing done there." She winked at me as she took another cookie from the plate in front on her.

I nodded heartily. "I very much agree. You know I really wish you were around to talk to some of my congregants. You would make quite an impression, I think." *Yeah, like a naive USO dancing girl to a pack of troops overseas …*

"I would like that. If our schedules permit."

"Good."

"Or, you know, Heychuck, we are always looking to expand into new ministries. We have grants …"

"Why, Sally, are you trying to convert me?"

She winked again, as well as two small twitches of her nose, one to each side. She had done that once or twice earlier in the discussion. I liked it. It was cute. "You never know, maybe I work on commission?"

###

"I do not want to talk about it."

That was Marshall, again rebuffing Kinta's attempts to find out what really happened.

They were in the courtyard just off to the side of my window. The acoustics of the little courtyard between buildings was extraordinary. I was eavesdropping, I'll admit.

"Look, it's okay," Kinta said, "I've had time to think about it. But you've got to understand, I can't really process what happened to my dad until I *fully* know what happened. I can't see them, the spirits … only what they do. But you actually could see them, right?" She paused for him until he mumbled his agreement. "Okay, so … just tell me."

"I will not."

At that, I could hear the twinkle reappeared in Kinta's eye. "You *will*, Marshall Lastpost or … you … shall … TASTE MY BLADE!" And then I could hear her causing some kind of ruckus. I couldn't see it.

But they were laughing.

Then they quieted down, and I didn't hear anything for a while. Something was mumbled.

Then Marshall piped up. "I smoked pot. And I killed a man."

She wasn't fazed. "You'd killed before, right? So, that's not very impressive," Kinta teased. She had a dark sense of humor.

"No. Technically, all those times I killed as a kid … I was just asking the spirits to do it. And it was not even me, who had chosen, it was my grandma's vision."

Kinta thought about it for a while. They were lying on their backs on the ground in a small park outside the window of Heychuck's apartment. *Stay in sight,* Sally insisted, like they were children. *No, like you are being hunted by federal agents,* she corrected when they complained. *That is fair,* Marshall had said in agreement.

Finally, Kinta: "Marshall, I hate to tell you this. But I don't think you are getting off so easy. I mean, okay, she chose the vision. But all she did was chose a vision where you made the choices you made. But you still made the choices. You see what I mean?"

Marshall started to say something, then didn't. He thought about it. "So, I am a killer."

"No. You were just a kid. With impossible powers, and crazy responsibilities and parental figures with exaggerated senses of ego and mission, dragging you into shit that you had no business being into. Believe me, I know something about that ..." And then she got quiet.

"Your dad was a good father."

"I know." She closed her eyes and tears welled up in the corners of her squint. "But, back to you." She sniffed and continued, "Anyway, tell me about the pot."

And he did, leaving out nothing. He'd learned from the camp that the more outrageous and extravagant his personal failure was, the better she liked it.

"Just between you and me, I still have some in my pocket ... ," he confessed. I smiled to myself and decided to stop overhearing their conversation. I quietly closed the window and returned to my living room, where Sally was still napping on the sofa.

Or maybe not. "Really? Eavesdropping?"

"I don't get all my info through scripture or divine inspiration. Sometimes, I just gotta put my ear to the wind."

She looked like she was about to say something important when her phone buzzed. She checked it.

She sat up. "We have to leave, tomorrow."

"Why?"

"Time is running short. My boss just reminded me. But Marshall has a choice to make. Tomorrow we will ask him. I think I am going to go for a walk. Will you excuse me?"

I nodded and got quiet as she left. I felt like it wasn't my place to intrude on whatever plans she and the girl had. But I also had some very definite ideas about where Marshall was at. He was still healing. And even though I had started to think the world of Sally, the last time he traveled with her, he ended up beaten up, narrowly escaping death, and leaving the scene feeling betrayed. So, I was going to protect my brother.

When the kids (I couldn't help but think of them that way) came back, they were still holding hands. She had a guilty grin from ear to ear and his eyes had a glimmer that they had lacked the entire time he had been with me. I supposed their relationship had taken a romantic turn. Suddenly I was glad I had stopped snooping.

"Where is Sally?"

"A walk," I said.

Kinta tethered him by the hand as they sat down on the couch together, so close he sat on her winter jacket.

"May we have a cookie?" Kinta asked, and I said yes.

"I get all the raisin ones." Marshall started in, and they began pretend-bickering like a married couple. Like our parents did in their lighter moments. I wondered if Marshall was copying that or if it was innate. Regardless, they seemed content to sit there mumbling to each other and finishing off my cookies.

"Marshall, I was there. I remember when you refused to join in your Uncle Brick's plan for the convention. You were quite adamant. Do you still feel the same way?" Sally was sitting across from the couch, in my chair. I was standing off to one side, leaning against the window.

He nodded.

"Okay. May I ask, why do you feel that way?"

"I like the idea that it all needs to stop. No more interference from the dJinni, the spirits. No more dJinni."

Sally leaned back against her chair. She was deep in thought. She understood his position, but she hadn't seen it like that. And she still didn't agree. Not really. She didn't see them as demons, at all, of course...

It was then that I noticed the beige sedan across the street.

Shit! This would be my next job ...

I stood up straight and interrupted: "Listen, excuse me. Um, I know you all have important stuff to talk about. And I forgot that I had an appointment at the mission. Let me run over there and take care of it. Be right back, okay?"

No one argued or questioned. They were too intent in their own discussion. The heck of it was that I really did want to stay around and take part. But this took precedence …

As I walked past the sedan, I inclined my head for them to follow me around the corner.

Mac (the driver) scowled at me, but Charlie was in the back and so Mac did as he was told.

"So, now you come to me in person to tell me my assignments? What, we burnin' down Amazon's HQ?"

"There is something new in the wind. Someone is commissioning a hit on a minister. I thought you'd appreciate the irony of that. And they're here in Seattle."

I thought about how I really didn't want to be distracted from Marshall right now, so I just wanted to get this over with. Or better yet, avoid it altogether.

"Yeah, yeah. Whatever. But you've got people for plain body work." *I don't do kills anymore. I did my time for that, and now I'm just a strong man. A show.* That's what I meant with that statement.

"Well, they need to be surveilled first until they lead us to their leader. And there is other information that they could provide."

This wasn't sounding like anything I'd done before. More like spy shit than street crime enforcement. "This sounds really involved. Why are we getting involved in this?"

"There's going to be a new drug for the street. Whoever can accomplish this gets the business."

I sighed. "So, when do you need this done?"

"You're already doing it. The mark's name is Sally Radisch." And he smiled because he was just the kind of guy who liked watching people twist in the wind.

To my credit, I made my decision almost instantly.

"I'm on it," I told Charlie with a nod. "You need anything from the store?" Then I walked away as a sort of *fuck you*, not waiting for an answer, to get me a new pack of cigarettes. And to fucking think.

Damn it.

###

I reentered my apartment in the middle of the same discussion I had left.

"Marshall, whatever abilities we all have, we owe it to ourselves, to each other, and to the world, to use them for good. I am not going to try to tell you what to do. But I am going to say this to you: Palla is our friend, and she needs our help. The day before the convention she is going to go before the media and publicly resign from Blue Rooks and take up the mantle of the protest movement. She is going to publicly disclaim the Blue Joy drug; and then she'll be in the streets.

"We don't *exactly* know what the Extirpacy is going to do. But, Marshall, you have to know this: Palla has changed. This has changed her. She is now communing with the Angles ... she isn't *praying*, not exactly. But she does see the future. Better than I do, usually. And she believes we all need to be there, together. Will you come back with us?"

When he didn't answer, she added more.

"I am not saying you have to help with any specific action, or the protest, or anything else. But whatever is going to happen, is going to happen *there* ..." And she left it at that.

Marshall looked at Kinta and the girl nodded slightly and said with a sheepish smile, "Well, you never technically showed up for your first day of work at the Extirpacy. You might get the chance to exorcise some demons."

And he just sat there, silently thinking. Then I jumped in to say what he couldn't, to these two people that he cared about too much to disappoint. Actually, I *was* going to help them convince him. But first I had to say my piece. For my brother.

"You two don't get it. You keep saying this is all about praying. But from where I sit, it is reading the future. So, if I am understanding this right, his entire life was some sort of preordained vision of somebody else's. And, oh, by the way, that life was no picnic, all right? I know—I was there for a lot of it. And now, Sally, you are like saying, hey Marshall, come along with us, because we saw it in a vision."

Sally said, "It's not us; it was Palla. I wish she were here. She has changed. Oh, I am afraid I am failing at explaining this. But it isn't reading the future. The future isn't static, the first Precept—"

"I know what the first Precept is," Marshall broke in. That shut everyone up. He was actually curt, and any time he showed emotion, even in the most subtle way, it was like gravity shifting under your feet. We all sat silent.

Suddenly, Sally roused herself. Whether she actually forgot or she had meant to, Sally had reserved her best argument for last. As with so many things, it was the symbolism of the gesture that gave it its power:

"Oh, I almost forgot, Marshall. Palla said you would need these." And she reached into her knapsack by the door and pulled out two things.

It was Marshall's black jacket and his flip-shades and eyeglass frames.

Marshall's jaw slacked open as he accepted his belongings back.

Kinta piped up, "I sewed the rips in the jacket myself."

He put the glasses on as tears formed at the corners of his eyes. He held the jacket as though it were a safety blanket.

Then he gathered himself and seemed to make a decision. He reached up and flipped his shades down. He seemed to be trying to concentrate on something. This went on for like five full beats.

Then a frantic look came over his face.

"What is it, Marshall?" asked Sally. She'd already realized what this meant.

"My *chi*. It is gone," he said as matter-of-factly as you would say you were out ketchup.

But Sally put both her hands over mouth to indicate her horror. Kinta mostly reacted to his grip on her hand, which had tightened, and the tears on his face, which had increased.

###

We all just sat there.

Finally, Kinta added, "Now, are you going to yell at me, too, if I make a suggestion?"

Marshall shook his head, wiping away tears.

"Why don't you do your own vision quest?"

We all just looked at her, not having the background to understand. Marshall shook his head. "I am no longer a Choiciferor—"

"I'm not talking about all of that. I mean a vision quest. Plenty of regular members of my tribe used to commune with the spirits that way. If they'll talk with you, you can reestablish things with them. I mean, whatever you get, at least you know it will be yours."

"But how do we do that, I mean, what do we need?"

At that she reached into his pocket and took out the baggie of weed from Big Dicky's stash. "I dunno. Seems like we have everything we need."

Marijuana was legal in Washington State. But there was still an aura of taboo when you did it. So, I tried to make it as banal as possible. Before Marshall lit up, I walked to the nearest dispensary and purchased some for myself and Sally. When I brought it back, though, she politely refused, saying something about second-hand smoke probably being plenty. I assessed that she was probably right about that.

So, I offered to let Marshall use my purchased buds as well. "Bad juju to smoke a dead man's stash, man," I said with the practiced voice of authority of one who's seen his share of drug trips gone bad.

There, in my apartment, I rolled, and we lit up (except for Sally, who sat primly on a folding chair in the kitchen, determined to be an objective observer).

As the smoke started to fill the air, turning my place into a hotbox, Kinta sang—or rather chanted—some of the songs of her people.

It was so random and atonal, it reminded me of those videos I played from YouTube to help me fall asleep at night sometimes ("Relaxing Delta Waves for Deep Sleep." "Deepest Healing." "Binaural Beats."). Even Marshall started humming along. And, of course, just to be a sport, I joined in with a soft rhythm of slapping my leg.

I thought of all of it as extraneous … the weed would free his mind soon enough.

This all seemed pretty harmless. And it would put everyone at ease before I did what I needed to do.

Then he got a strange look on his face, and he flipped his shades down again.

I was pretty buzzed, but this time I thought saw a strange orange flicker of light emanate from the shades, for just a second. It was like the jerky flash of light just before a camera takes its picture.

At the same time, there was a rush of wind that we all could feel. Then, when our eyes adjusted, suddenly, he was gone.

We all exclaimed, but Sally was loudest, "What happened! Kinta?"

But Kinta was the most surprised of all. "I DON'T KNOW!!" She literally lunged at the couch and started turning the cushions over, like Marshall was so much loose change. His jacket was still lying there on the arm of the couch—he had never put it back on after receiving it.

Sally wanted to search the neighborhood, she reached for her coat and said to Kinta, "C'mon."

But I stopped her, gently grabbing her coat and locking eyes with her. "No. We need to go."

"What? Why?"

"You're in danger, Sally. You, too, kid," I said.

"Danger? From who?" asked Sally.

"From me," I admitted.

I heard their heavy footsteps coming down the hallway. It was about two hours after I had told the ladies that a hit had been put out on them. And now we were out of time.

CRASH! My door was kicked in. Two, no THREE men—*such respect*, I thought—bull-rushed into my apartment, guns drawn. I had been present for a few of their shenanigans. If they were involved, it meant that I hadn't been persuasive enough or that the debtor didn't care anymore if they lived or not.

"He's not here!"

"They're all gone!" the goons were yelling to each other from between my bedroom and kitchen. One of them got a comrade on his walkie-talkie.

"Did they come out the back?" This was Josh. The leader.

A muffled voice said something back over the channel, and he didn't give the answer Josh wanted. "They must've used the roof. C'mon!" And their footsteps receded down the hallway toward the stairs, then up and away.

They didn't search my bedroom very hard. If they had, they would've found the panel of false drywall behind the boxes of junk on the floor of the closet. Behind that panel was the neighboring apartment. My arrangement with the landlord was that I collected the rent and maintained the place. He wasn't aware I had carved out this portal between mine and the neighboring room, which the restaurant used for storage. Counters, chairs, booths, tables, and countless boxes of foodstuffs were in the darkened room.

Along with three scared people.

"It's okay to talk. Just don't yell or anything," I told the ladies.

"How long do we have to stay here?" Kinta asked.

"They're not wrong about the roof. That's the way we'll eventually take. There's a special way to lay some random pieces of sheet metal up there so that you can walk in between buildings. You both up for that?"

They looked at each other and then me and slowly nodded like two people in a dream, which reminded me. "Hey, we should get some shuteye. We'll sneak out around midnight or 1:00 a.m., okay?" I smiled through my beard at their two uncertain faces, trying to sound more confident than I was.

BOOK TWO—CHAPTER FOUR

*"In non-violent technique, as I have said,
there is no such thing as defeat."*

—Mohandas Karamchand Gandhi,
in a 1940 letter to Adolph Hitler

"My ears popped! Have your ears ever popped?" Rufepirts asked the lovely Brianna as she led him to his appointment with their Master.

"Yes," she replied with utmost patience.

"It was amazing."

"Was that your first plane trip?" He had just flown in from Chicago to Washington DC.

"The first one I was awake for. When I was flown out there, I had not yet mastered changing my appearance to your minds … so I was flown in secret. In a military cargo plane. It was all very covert. That's the word, isn't it? Or is it overt?"

"You got it right." *Idiot,* she thought. She could not wait until they were done with him. "You sure you have the data?"

"Oh, yes. All of it." He confidently patted his breast pocket for emphasis. "Thumb drive!" he whisper-hissed loud enough that *literally* everyone in the office heard him.

"Where was it?"

"On a standalone server in a basement of a small nonprofit in Illinois. Some town called Buelford. A place where Sall—where one of Blue Rooks's leaders used to work, when she was younger." His smile was broad. He was quite proud.

"How did you find it?" She had to try.

"Ah, I am only supposed to report to the Mast—to the Analyst directly. You understand, ice whore."

"What did you call me?" She spun around and grabbed his collar so fast he didn't even see it. Her other hand was raised, as if to strike. She could snap his neck just as quickly, he realized. He could feel himself wetting his pants. How wonderful!

"I said, I swore! I swore to the Master, the Analyst, that I would only tell him, report to him. You know!"

She stared him down, looked at his wet pant legs in disgust, and finally let him go. Then she held out her hand. "Give me the thumb drive, and then go wait in that conference room."

He started to argue, but then thought the better of it. That thumb drive was only one of the two messages, anyway. And, in truth, it wasn't necessary that the Analyst receive *it* directly. The in-person one, that message was more important.

He complied, and she rotated on her spiked heel and walked away, paying him no more mind.

Ice whore, he thought. He went in and sat down.

He didn't have long to wait until the Visiting Analyst walked in. "You'd best not anger Brianna again. I'm not sure we have money for all the adult diapers you would need in our budget, my friend."

Rufepirts felt some shame at that. He momentarily assumed his actual form, just long enough to reset the illusion and then returned to the ginger-haired simulacrum that he had been taught to assume, this time compensating and removing the wetness from the illusion. *I'm not your friend. I am your slave. Well, might as well get this over with.*

"I gave her the data."

"Yes, I know. She's extrapolating it now with our forensic data people. She was rather surprised when you showed up on her doorstep with the data." The Analyst sat down and leaned back, one arm over his crossed leg. The dJinn sat stiffly with his hands in his lap. The Analyst turned his chair around and looked out the window, now facing the same direction as Rufepirts was. From outside the window, they looked like air travelers seated in the same plane—only the VA was in first class.

"Well, Master. I knew what I had was important. I figured she was the best, safest possible *escort*." *Oh, how he loved calling her a whore as often as possible.*

His cleverness was lost on the Master. Over his shoulder, he said, "So, how did you find it? Our team in Minnesota failed to secure Ms. Radisch."

"The Unity showed me where it was."

The VA held absolutely still for several seconds. Rufepirts started to count them, one-thousand one, one-thousand two … and Rufepirts couldn't help but smile.

Yes, he had been sympathetic to the Master's plight when they met. And he helped the Master escape back to here, to his home world. And, yes, he liked the idea of a new place to live, himself. A new purpose. Why not be the personal assistant to the chosen one?

But since then it had become clear to Rufepirts, especially after he met the Unity, that he had been mistaken. She explained that there could be another chosen one. One that was less cruel. If he would help.

And so, he said *yes*.

"Really. And how did the meddling bitch do that? More dreams for the retard?" As he spoke, the room around them seemed to darken, as hosts of dJinn, unseen by anyone but them, started to gather, summoned instinctively by the Analyst's rage.

Rufepirts got uncomfortable and made a slight gargling sound, instead of answering right away.

The Visiting Analyst spun his chair back around. "Is that it? No, it's not. Not dreams. What then …?" Rufepirts was shaking his head, unable to maintain a proper lie. "So, what is it about dreams, then … wait—you!" He leaned back and mentally asked the hosts around him to answer the unspoken question. "You've been talking to him! In his dreams! Yes, I see it now. What have you been telling the little shit?"

"M-Marshall's a good boy."

"Answer me!" The Analyst leaned forward and placed both hands on the table between them and the table rotted instantly from that spot outward … disintegrating before their eyes, aging a millennium in a second. The now-unbalanced two ends of the table fell away to the floor with a *thunk!* on either side as the Analyst smoothly walked through the vacated spot, directly up to Rufepirts in his chair.

"Wait! Master, the—the Unity … has a message for you."

He stopped, his arms still extended for Rufepirts's head like a zombie. "I'm listening."

"She said, tell the Analyst I am coming to meet him."

The Analyst screamed power. But the rage that exploded from him was momentarily deflected by Rufepirts attempting his own power play. The creature, now in full-dragon form, attempted to reverse the Analyst's previous spancasting upon the table. If it had worked, the table would have reappeared and sliced his Master in half, through the thighs and groin.

But the dJinni loyalists dissipated the energy of the idea even as he formed it—and the Analyst was only momentarily distracted by the effort.

"You DARE?"

Rufepirts then tried to escape. He wanted to jump to another place, closer to the Unity.

But the Analyst held him fast, both with his power and with his own bare hands. He placed his hands on either side of the dragon's jaw and squeezed. Infused with the power of his pet host of demons, the Analyst had the strength of scores of men, and he could already feel Rufepirts' skull cracking. Rufepirts tried shifting from form to form, dragon, to ghoul to banshee to various animal familiar forms ... but his attacker held fast.

In fact, the VA was so filled with rage that he forgot that this was supposed to be an interrogation. He would crush the fool before he ever found out anything about what the Unity was up to.

Rufepirts was terrified but also grateful; his last act was to shift back into a human form: his bones splintered, eyes bulged, veins crushed, denying the necessary blood flow to his brain, he could no longer hear the sound of his own choking gurgles. There was even a ringing in his ears, like the sound of a shrill little bell ... nonetheless he thought, *Thank you, Unity. Death in this body is a remarkable experience ...*

... before he disappeared in a burning flash.

###

Marshall laid on his back, in a puddle of oily, inky water.

Except that there was no ground beneath him. The water wasn't there either, rather it was a feeling of resistance, pressing against his shoulders, his skin, all around but from behind, when he tried to move.

And he was vertical. That is, he was perpendicular to the ground, the ground being a black blank slate stretching out in every direction as far as his eyes could see. But he didn't move. Any time he tried, he was pressed back *up*.

He was still wearing his glasses. He reached to his face and flipped them up to see if it helped him see anything. It didn't. Just a black slate horizon, coarsely reflecting a light-purple sky.

He turned his head from side to side to try and get his bearings. Then he tried to take a step but couldn't. It wasn't that he couldn't move, it was just that the *step* was negated. His weight never shifted forward, and his foot just suspended out in front of him, until he gave up and put it back.

He was trapped.

His heart raced a bit, but only a bit. He bit his lip and kept looking about, side to side. Instead of panicking, he decided to experiment with movement. He found that he could float (sort of) in any direction, with his movement marked as being oblique to the ground by his own senses. This disoriented him even more …

"All that fidgeting is impressive. You shouldn't be able to move at all!" It was a female voice, from behind/above him. She kept on:

"But don't worry, I can take you where you need to go. My name is SanDu." And then her face appeared before him. Her features were human, but her skin reflected a cold alabaster, as though illuminated with blacklight. Her hair floated about her, making her entire head look like a human-faced underwater jellyfish. Luminescent and dangerous.

"Marshall Lastpost. It is a pleasure to meet you. I'm your biggest fan, I think it is safe to say. I've felt so much about you."

"How do you know me?" was the question he tried to form—instead he croaked. And then gasped for air, unable to find any.

"Ah, yes. Here." And SanDu did something and, suddenly, his gasps made the large noises of someone not quite drowning for air.

Once he collected himself, she spun him around so that they faced each other. He was like a floating board to her … the way she manipulated his form.

"In our place of existence, you would normally be here only after you died, or were sent by a greater power. Humans are very fragile; all pain, from what I understand."

"So, I am dead."

She didn't argue the point. "Bound to happen sooner or later, with the company you keep. C'mon. We don't want to be late, SHE is expecting us."

"The Demi-urge."

"Hey, HEY! Look at you! You're finally starting to piece some things together." He floated beside her as she walked along. He couldn't see what she was standing on. The "horizon" continued to veer off at an oblique angle.

"Where is this place?"

"Somewhere near a love handle. Maybe you can tell her I said that, someday."

Marshall had no idea what in the hell she was talking about and said so.

"What in the hell, indeed," was her self-satisfied reply.

Marshall rolled his eyes and tried asking a few other questions, but he didn't—couldn't, really—pay much attention to her answers. It was everything he could do to keep—

"Where do you suppose your voices went?" she interrupted his thoughts with the sudden question.

He still couldn't answer, even if he had known. But she was right. The *Others* were silent, as well as his own voices. He was still on the meds that Heychuck had gotten him, but, typically in a stressful situation, *somebody* would say something.

He felt very alone.

"The mad synergyte trained you well. Your banishing is effective but off-kilter. You can put things askew, but not realign them. Rufepirts taught you too much, too soon."

That name again! "You are a dJinn. A demon. And so is Rufepirts."

She didn't answer because, suddenly, they were sliding downward at a rapid rate of speed. He could actually feel wind in his hair, as they moved. But despite the fast rate of descent, he could also make out other figures, off in the distance, glowing shapes, all approaching and adjusting their course … to intercept them. Or meet them.

He was starting to get his bearings. "What is a synergyte?"

"Words are important to you, aren't they? Labels. DJinni or demons? All right, B—Marshall. I will explain what I can, just as I always have. But first, I need you to—ah! We're here."

She put her hands on his shoulders to steady him, and now he could feel his feet on solid ground … she indicated that he was to look off to the opposite side from her and she gently turned him. (For dramatic effect? Their entry deliberately delayed this view.) And he saw a large field of …

… flowers? No. Yes. It *was* flowers. But the pods, the buds, or whatever you would call them, were taller than he was, and large enough to fit a small tractor in. What in the …?

She was whispering into his ear, now.

"A synergyte. That is the word for the matching creature. For every human, there is one of the Regnant. One-to-one. You and others want to sever that link. But there is more to it than that. To prove that, I need you to accept a gift …"

And she spun him, gently, very gently, back to facing her.

"… I need you to take some of my energy. Add it to your *chi*. It's okay. It is better this way. You'll end up with all of it, anyway, you know. After you left and lived on your own, your personal code of honor was that you would only use your own energy. That was noble but stupid. It made you age prematurely. Especially now that you've been brought here. You're a dead man walking, without the rest of my energy."

"The rest of …?"

"Yes. My synergyte has died. Once that happens, we become one of the Lost. We're able to move back and forth between Timespace threads—and forward or backward within a single thread … in a limited sort of way. But why bother? Most of us just wander aimlessly. But this Holy War has given many of us a purpose. Look, she will explain the rest. You just need to see this. And this is the best way …"

"Why, why is it the 'best' … because you have *seen* it?" For some reason her shuttling him around this strange place reminded him of Grandma Marian's machinations.

"No. Because you haven't."

The expression on her face had all of the earnest love and despair that his didn't. But he felt it, too. At her unspoken bidding, she leaned him back and placed one hand behind him to support him, as she held out her other hand above his head, as if cupping water.

He closed his eyes and concentrated, and opened them to see that the entire sky was full of eldritch energy, all lifting from her form and falling back down, curling back like a magnetic field, and all reentering her like into a funnel in her single, cupped hand.

He rotated his head and locked eyes with Grandma Marian, with SanDu. *Of course! This is Grandma Marian's—what was the word?—synergyte dJinn! She must be powerful.* They locked eyes—and he nodded. And she smiled with love.

"Goodbye, Butchie."

She overturned her hand, and the energy of the ages poured over his head.

It washed over him and splashed about the landscape, and, indeed, he felt more energized than he had in years. After a few moments more, even his mind was at peace.

But that was not the most important gift. He noticed something else…

… as the energy left SanDu (where is SanDu?) and entered him, the fields of pods all glowed, in response to the energy. Like a reflection, deep purple light throbbed and turned inside the nearest pods.

One in particular, off in the distance, glowed the strongest. It seemed to leak violet streams of luminescence as it split asunder. The pod petals slowly peeled away. And several of those distant forms that were other dJinn now were attending to it. They pounced and converged on it and each grabbed parts of the pod petals, pulling with all their might…

… until a throbbing, pulsing, fluorescent-veined new baby dragon-shaped dJinn was born, tumbling from its birthplace, as the others rushed to gather it up and give it sustenance, in their way.

That was the lesson.

Their prayers. Their spells. Their visions. The movement of the energy … all of it, all of it! It had purpose—not just on Earth—but here, in the magical land of the Regnant, the homeland of the dJinni. *No, call us demons. We prefer that, maybe,* various voices from just out of sight corrected him.

And so, in his dream—*for this had to be a dream, did it not?*—Marshall sat alone for a while, right there in Hell, and he cried and cried, maybe transfiguring, just a little bit, all the tears of despair from all the times he had helped kill into tears of joy that he had also helped create some life.

Anyway, it was a lovely thought.

###

After a while, he looked up at the gathered horde, now no longer out of sight, all looking at him from the purple gloom.

And beside him sat the Demi-urge.

SHE was the most beautiful thing he had ever seen.

More beautiful than the quiet companionship of Little Rich. More beautiful than his baby boy or than his late wife had been. More beautiful than his own life. He knew, instinctively, that he would gladly give up his life for this one.

"What …?" Marshall began but could not finish.

"I can answer your questions, Master Precept. But, surprisingly, given who you are, time is short."

He considered all of that, ignoring the moniker, and decided to ask, "Okay, if I no longer wanted to end all clerics … would the Regnant support that?"

"Indeed," she began, "some would. And I would lead them. But that host of the Regnant is in the minority. We are a rebellion, of sorts.

"A dark bargain has been struck between the Regnant Lord, the leader of most of us, and the Mehkard, but that bargain is madness. The Regnant Lord wants this new drug to work, they want this realm to be cut off, no more prayers. No more newborn Regnant. They are helping the Mehkard's first choice as champion, allowing this Analyst to style himself as a new dark master, a sole *singular* cleric, to kill all the humans and, once we are all among the *Lost*, to be brought there, to your world."

"But why? If they rule here, why would they want to be brought there, to my world, just to be his slaves?" The Regnant Queen openly ruminated about the entire cause, as though to herself, like she'd forgotten Marshall was even present.

"He can command only the very weakest of the *Lost* at this point. It is … unclear … whether he could continue to hold sway when our leaders arrive there. They don't think so. They feel he is weak, despite being a *Champion of Order*."

Marshall was still digesting all of this. *And you disagree*, was Marshall's unspoken corollary. Marshall had so many other questions … *Why did you always call the Mehkard the enemy when you used to talk to me? What is his goal? What is yours?* But Marshall interrupted himself with a very specific thought that popped into his head. "Kinta and Sally. They told me Palla had changed, that she had become like a dJinn herself."

"This is truth. She is the Unity. And this place is the Unity, and we are its keepers. But, despite being the Unity, her mind is still human. We've managed to give her a tool, a talisman that focuses her energy and her mind, for short periods of time. So, her cosmic awareness will only be temporary and intermittent. Which is for the best, anyway, for what she will be needed to do. You, too, will be cosmically aware while you are here … but when you go back, you will not be able to recall all of this. It will haunt you, since here is where you were finally free of your voices, *cured*, as they say in your world."

Marshall looked down and nodded his agreement. He could feel that this was all true. "How did I get here? I didn't do this."

"Ah, no," SHE answered. "Many of my brethren sacrificed themselves to do this in a way that didn't require your death first. Just like the spell for your grandma's time to die … many sacrificed themselves for that, too, you'll remember."

Marshall remembered it differently. He remembered a certain glee in tricking some of the dJinni to help him with the final spell for his grandma, convincing them to take energy from their lesser brethren to complete the spell without killing themselves. But perhaps that had all been preapproved by the Demi-urge, too. *Yes, that makes sense.*

"The one you call grandma received visions … and in her visions, you joined forces with the Regnant to defeat the Mehkard, but you had to receive training. You had to live through death—the deaths of many—to be prepared to understand the stakes."

Marshall had no more questions. His mind couldn't even process all of this. He took several deep breaths, just like Marian had taught him so many years ago. Finally, he settled on first principles.

"What is this place? And, no, I mean, I know it is your home … dimension, or whatever. I mean, what is *this* place?"

"You stand within the Unity. It is a place that creates the next Unity. And it is created by each of the Unity, in turn."

Marshall asked, "Seriously?"

"You asked."

"You all are born from within the Unity?"

"At first, yes."

They are born inside a tautology. Okay, that was useless. Marshall's head was pounding. *Try again.* "You brought me here. Why?"

"As you have seen, we are … *bound* to protect the Unity. When that next happens, we will not be able to protect you. Despite our tumultuous ways, we are creatures of honor. We owe you a debt. Our fate is bound to yours. And, whereas the Mehkard chooses his Champion from a place of ignorance, we choose transparency. Not now, but soon, you will be in mortal combat. And when you are, we want you to have our help, in advance."

"You said when I go back, I won't remember any of this."

"True. But just as with the Unity, we are empowered to help you with creating a tool, for your future use. So that you can return here from time to time."

"What do you want me to do?"

"Think of an object. Something you care greatly about." And before Marshall could answer: "And no, it can't be the turtle."

Marshall felt a pang of disappointment about that and even started to argue. But at some level, he already knew that it had to be an inanimate object. So, he sat and thought long and hard about this.

The problem was, SHE was obviously impatient. Eventually, HER angst started to register upon his nerves, the *physical* contact of HER hands still over his.

"Young one, I need you to hurry."

He inhaled suddenly (he apparently had stopped breathing), and then, in a flash of inspiration, he decided.

"Show me the prayers, the songs, that have to do with traveling back here, as you say. With traveling *at all!* Quick!"

Suddenly a host, unseen a moment ago, in the shadows, sang. Marshall was able to close his eyes and *see* the runes in his head.

"Yes. Go on. Now, what of moving between Timespace streams, and all the rest? What Ben did? What Sally can do with the book … let me hear it all …"

"Young one, this song. Those harmonies. It will attract them even more quickly …"

But Marshall didn't stop. He kept requesting more and more examples. And, with each request, the songs shifted—the harmonics, the rhythms, and the various spells burned across his mind's eye, like a flickering home recording on a projector screen …

Now, to transfer them …

"Young one! They are here!"

Marshall could sense combat in the distance … some of the singers were being silenced. *Well, you started this, Demi. All of it! So, you will just need to do as I say.* "I need to speak to them!"

"WHICH *them?*" the Demi-urge demanded. She sounded like she was already in combat. Songs of violence were in the background, starting to drown out all the rest.

He opened his eyes and looked intently at the Demi-urge, as if he'd never considered other options—he meant anyone in his family … Sally, at first; but the question—does it matter? *Yes, no. This felt right, either way.*

"Whichever one is asleep!"

The Demi-urge closed the circuit instantly, linking his mind to the sleeper's dreams, as though it were the most trivial of requests, and then the Demi-urge turned back to fling impossible amounts of eldritch energy at those of his brethren who had been sent to disrupt this.

He quickly shouted instructions to Heychuck in his dream, and he even more hurriedly started showing him all the runes—but mere moments after the connection was created, it was severed.

And then Marshall felt himself being taken back. Back to his own Timespace.

Back home.

But just before—*WAIT, something is different*—Marshall could sense someone, some being, interfering … *where?*

BOOK TWO—CHAPTER FIVE

Reverend Heychuck Smith

###

Marshall is alive! was all I said to the ladies as I awoke. Apparently, I had dozed off. We were under a clear, starry sky, huddling for warmth under a tarp. This was one of my favorite hangouts, atop a neighboring warehouse roof.

At midnight we had climbed up onto the roof and accomplished a pretty acrobatic escape to a neighboring roof using a special ladder that I stashed up there for just this purpose.

We were supposed to leave town this next morning. But now we needed a detour.

It took me a while to find the nearest fabric store. I spent some time nosing around, inside the place, preferring to find what I needed on my own. But it was a low volume, high-end store near Occidental Square, sandwiched in between an art gallery and a boutique mountain-climbing gear / apparel shop. And I didn't look like their typical crowd. They were polite about it, but there's always a subliminal message to that "May I help you?" that dark-skinned people in this country could hear. The message is: *You don't belong here.*

The ubiquitous vagrants sleeping outside the doorways of these upscale "shoppes" didn't dress exactly like the hipster twenty-something girls who came in to the shop for the latest crochet classes. But to someone from another city, either would have looked more like the other than like me. My look was unique.

Instead of the standard-issue stocking cap that all males were statutorily required to wear in Seattle, I wore a ball cap with my church's logo on it. It was straight-brimmed (seein' as I wasn't a hick), and, similarly, I didn't own sunglasses because … y'know, like I said, my hat had a brim. Besides, we were in Seattle, so sunshine was seldom an issue eight months out of the year.

I preferred dress shirts and multiple scarves to the pea coat. And my jeans were clean and baggy, without any tears, blemishes, or other examples of *distress*, either earned or paid for. For shoes: work boots, steel-tip. With a blade hidden in each.

Like I said, you can tell a lot about a person from their shoes.

The ladies who ran the shop assured me that they didn't have what I was looking for, which was a paint pen. They started to refer me to the next nearest shop, many miles away, but as soon as I acted disappointed, they quickly gave me the one that they used. Anything to not have an upset black man in their store a moment longer than was necessary.

Or maybe they were just being nice. I was having trouble tracking our conversation as I hadn't gotten much sleep, and the dream images themselves seem to be permanently embedded on my brain. Like a song you can't stop humming, I just kept seeing the blasted symbols everywhere I looked.

But Marshall had spoken to me in a dream. I had to follow his instructions. He seemed to be in trouble. He was surrounded by demons.

Oh, Marshall. What have you gotten us into?

I paid them for the pen, over their objections, and left to go back to the nearby diner where I had left the ladies. I was glad to see Sally and Kinta still there, waiting for me with breakfast.

The day before, I had told them everything: My background as a hit man. The time I did. And how I still did low-level enforcer work and that they were supposedly my next mark. (If I killed Sally, I'd have to kill the girl, too, after all.) Kinta obviously wanted to run, but Sally just smiled at me and said, *You are a brave man.* And she asked me for help in escaping the building. I did maintenance for the building, so I knew that the trapdoor to the attic led us onto the roof, and, like I said, I had a special way to move from building to building once there.

You are a brave man.

But, truth be known, until I saw them at the diner—I mean, up until that very moment—I really hadn't known if they were going to split on me or not.

They asked me fewer questions than I probably deserved. But I had told them Marshall spoke to me in a dream, and so they gave me the benefit of the doubt.

Along with Marshall's jacket.

And, one by one, right there in the diner, I used the paint pen to transcribe the runes from my dream-images onto the jacket.

It was a painstaking process. Sally looked over my shoulder and compared what I was writing to what was in her little prayer book that she carried around.

Kinta asked her, "What songs is he writing?"

Sally said, "Not songs, I don't think. Just song. One long, very long song."

"What's it do?"

"I don't know," Sally and I both said at the same time.

It was painstaking work. I didn't feel like it was taking that long, but by the time I was done, it was late afternoon.

But when I was done, the jacket was covered, inside and out, with the same rune-language that was in the prayer book.

"Okay. That's done," I assured the room. "So, what now?"

Kinta and I looked at Sally for guidance. And the religious director for the Blue Rooks Church Foundation solemnly answered, "After dessert, I'd like to offer you both jobs."

BOOK TWO—CHAPTER SIX

###

"Wait here." The officer stood up from behind his desk that was behind the window, pulling his pants up from one height to another under his belly. Then he turned and walked away, back behind some file cabinets, down the hall, out of sight.

Brianna stood waiting outside the window in the lobby of the Las Vegas Metropolitan Police Department. The polygonal room felt smaller than it was, painted up to the chair rail level in a dark military green, and with wood paneling from before any of them were born the rest of the way up the walls.

She was dressed conservatively, in her field attire. Dark blazer and overcoat, slacks. Inside the jacket, her credentials—badge facing out—were clasped to her waist to one side of the large belt buckle. However, her large breasts strained against both shirt and jacket and her slacks were as well-fitted for clubbing as they were for field work.

The same officer opened a door on a nonadjacent wall. "Follow me. The Captain is waiting. Everyone else is here."

She did as he said, following him down the skinny hallways. She thought back to her time growing up in this town, or at least nearby. She remembered every weekend at the lake, and long bike rides with her friends in the desert. Out there, they would catch lizards and have rock fights … and at night, they had a few favorite haunts where they, especially as teens, could light campfires and "party" (which meant music, not drugs) 'til the early hours. And by early, that meant 6:00 a.m. Brianna and the other kids didn't even go out until 11:00 p.m.

Sometimes, it seemed like the only thing to combat the perpetual boredom was the potential of an endless horizon and cosmos overhead.

She remembered how she pretty much followed her parents' plans for her. Undergrad at UNLV, grad school at Stanford. All went according to plan, and she was fundamentally unhappy.

Then her daddy got killed. She remembered flying back and picking up her mom from the hospital morgue. And then they both drove to the police station. The police questioned them in a building very much like this one. Same feel. Same smell.

They said it was an accident; but eventually Mom opened up (to Brianna, not to the police) and told her that some of his business dealings were, in fact, tied to some mob activities and Mommy believed this was tied to that.

But then she asked Brianna to go through her dad's computer files, and that's when Brianna's world broke.

Child porn.

Including pictures from sleep overs, sleepovers with her and her friends.

He had drugged them. And then took explicit pictures, posing them in suggestive poses with each other. And him.

She remembered the headaches she used to wake up with.

Now she remembered the haunted looks that Mom used to give her the next day, too. Now she understood.

Damn them. Damn them both.

Brianna did what her conscience demanded. She conducted a full investigation and contacted the authorities to enable a special sting operation that captured many of the distributors that her dad had been selling to. She shouldn't have been surprised by how much overlap there was between the mob bosses and sex trafficking, but she was.

Brianna's mom was never the same after that, of course. She spent the next decade drinking herself to oblivion.

Brianna didn't care.

But Brianna did do two things to refocus her life. She obsessively took martial arts. And she applied for the FBI. She decided to devote her life to fighting the very criminals who had ripped her family apart. No, like what her family *was.*

The FBI wasn't what she expected. It was *all* bureaucracy and politics. She had blossomed in college into her supermodel-level looks and even higher-level confidence. She unleashed her ambition and coupled it with her willingness to leverage her looks and sex appeal. And all of that got her …

… nothing.

She hit the glass ceiling like a coffin lid. The pattern was soon established: she was given desk duties so that she was at the disposal of all the male superiors in a given field office. This gave them free reign to size her up and try to hit on her. And then, once that all played out, she was politely transferred to a different office. Like some kind of whorish Russian roulette. *Step right up! Place your bets, gentlemen and gentlemen! Which middle-manager's gonna get lucky this time?*

But one office was different. Not because the bosses were different, but because one day another supervisor from a special task force was visiting. He was an analyst from an obscure subdivision called the Bureau of Indigenous Security Enhancements, or BOISE (like the city) for short.

The strange *Man from BOISE* never hit on her. But he did ask her about what she wanted from her career. When she told him, he suggested she join his newly formed task force on religious exorcism. She laughed, but he was so sincere, she decided to give it a try.

Her first several assignments were typical two-bit con men, engaging in various variations of mail fraud. But then she came across someone who actually was an Innie, someone with supernatural abilities, someone who was attuned to the demons. This person was invited into people's homes to perform magical feats (seances, or exorcisms). But once inside, they would summon demons who would then force everyone to kill themselves. Then they would rob the house, which was seldom investigated since it always looked like suicide.

But the Master somehow knew about this miscreant, though. Further, he had trained her, helped her train her mind, to resist the effects of the magicks long enough for her use her own lethal skills. She was a full black belt in multiple martial arts by then.

She had posed as a distraught widow of a wealthy socialite. It was in Baltimore. And once she felt the *evil* of the magicks used, she knew she had to make it her mission to stop anyone who would use it, especially to enslave children.

She snapped Olan's neck during that sting operation. George Olan was his name. And the feeling of relief she had when she'd done it, even though it was her first "kill," meant everything to her.

This was "god's work." so to speak. There is a lot of moral "gray area" in federal police-work. (Hell, later she found out that the Man from Boise was *also one of them magic-users*, trying to make good in his own way, he said.)

Since then, she'd learned the truth about him, too. What Brendent, what the *Master*, requested of her … honestly, she just couldn't say no to him. It was so amazing. Every time. No matter who else was invited.

But after several years she had begun to suspect that she was being controlled. That magic was being used on her.

Or was she just trapped in the horror of her years with her dad?

She was just numb.

But she resolved to do something about it. Ask for a transfer, some-day. Maybe.

For now, she followed the police officer down some stairs that went to the basement. This wasn't going to take place in the squad roll center or in a board room. This meeting was in the furnace room. No cameras, no reporters, no accidental witnesses, and no one to notice that the meet-ing ever took place.

Various city and state authorities who had been working with BOISE were present. In the center of the room was a long folding table that had a map of the convention center where the religious conference was going to be held. Off to one side, she saw someone dressed in biker gear with a mohawk haircut. That was Agent Bard. His name during this mission was Pharell. He had been one of the agency's two moles in the protest movement. He had left with the group before the slaughter. He was the one they embedded to keep an eye on the other one, the turncoat who had met with an unfortunate end during the last raid at Camp Grier.

"Agent Carson," the Mayor of Las Vegas began, "it's about time you showed u—"

"Shut up and listen," she interrupted. That took him and several others down a peg. Then she took off her long coat, and her stunning good looks disarmed the rest into silence too.

"You should all know that our man, Pharell, here, will be instigating some selected small incidents during the protest. Several of the protest signs are fitted with cameras, all of which feed back to your command center, which will be a plain-marked truck HERE"—she pointed to a spot—"as well as feeding into special lenses that will be inside his motorcycle helmet that he'll be wearing. This is his op. Any calls get made, they will be from him. You all got that?"

Without waiting for agreement, she continued, "Sergeant, you will need to station your men HERE and HERE and maintain a perimeter along the entire back side of the park. The march comes through here, and the incident will be when it passes through downtown. The incident should stop the protest from ever reaching the convention center itself.

"Your jobs are to make sure that anyone trying to stop or prevent the violence is contained. Let it play out, and let us federal authorities take control of the situation. This is how we're going to 'smoke out' and identify those Blue Rooks sympathizers.

"Mr. Jones, you have made sure that all the major media outlets have gotten their 'anonymous' tips about the impending unrest?" Mr. Jones, the PR consultant, nodded, and the various law enforcement officials confirmed that they had received those same heads up from the media outlets, too. As they all wanted to do their civic duty …

The meeting continued like this for exactly twenty-five minutes. Then Brianna and Pharell excused themselves to go upstairs and exit out the back door into the officers' parking lot.

"The data was spiked with a computer virus," she informed Pharell of what Rufepirts had brought her.

"Yes, and the actual samples that he dropped off with me were tainted as well. The E-Dogs we tested them on … died." His hesitation seemed to indicate the deaths were quite horrible. Her annoyance at the news was obvious on her face, so he hastened to add, "But we have located where they transported the actual samples to. Do you want me to bring a team …?"

Brianna nodded. She knew this was going to be the case before she heard it. The Master had assured her she would have to handle this personally. "Yes. But I'll take point myself. Send me the location. Meanwhile, make sure the protest 'unrest' goes as planned."

###

Something is not right, Marshall thought.

The smell told him where he was even before he opened his eyes, even before he felt the leather restraints on his arms and legs, even before he felt the bedsprings pressing against his backside through the soft mattress.

This unique alchemy of odors—lemon dust, old people, and crisp, clean laundry—was what created *this* unique smell. It hit his nose like static electricity.

This was *Greenless Grove Healthcare Center.*

He was back on the *Fifth Floor,* the Behavioral Health Clinic.

He had spent large swaths of his childhood in this place. But he hadn't been bound like this since he was very small. Since before they had figured out his meds.

After forcing back a brief urge to cry out in despair, various workers went in and out to do various routine tasks. Lots of asking Marshall questions about how he felt.

Trapped, Marshall said, the first time.

The nurse just laughed.

After he complained of a sore stomach, they gave Marshall some meds for nausea and general discomfort. Later, they gave him another shot, and he slept.

The next day, after he awoke, he noticed various nurses come in and remove items from a tray inside a cabinet in the room, paying him no mind at all. After several of them did this, one finally noticed him, watching, and said apologetically, "We're low on supplies. We're expecting more on Wednesday, don't you worry!"

Like *that* was what he was worrying about.

He knew he should do something. He should cry. Or perhaps scream. Or he should summon his *chi (if he could—could he? Did he still have any from SanDu?)* ... he should do something. But every fiber of his being told him that it just was not going to happen.

Everything he could see, everything he could feel, told him the truth.

Marshall Lastpost was finally powerless.

###

"The doctor wants you to try a new medication," A nurse told Marshall, as she came into the room with a tiny little paper cup on a tray. "Please drink this," she said. When he didn't comply right away, she said, "Either drink it, or we'll put it in your IV."

He lifted his head so that the liquid could mostly spill into his mouth.

"Why am I restrained?" he asked.

"Oh, you don't remember? That's probably for the best. You got a little out of hand. So, we had to protect you. Then you had your 'break' and just went blank on us. But even out like that, from time to time, you still would rouse and start to walk around and knock things around. So, we just got in the habit of keeping you in them, there restraints. They're loose, though, you'll notice."

"How long was I out?"

The nurse's face got serious for a moment before transforming back into perkiness, and she said, "I was transferred here about a couple months ago, and you were already catatonic when I got here. Anyway, I will let the doctor know that you're having memory issues. But, anyway, welcome back!"

"Wait. Where are my glasses?" he asked.

"You don't need glasses," she replied with a puzzled look.

Well, she wasn't wrong.

His head fell back onto the bed, and he tried to rest.

###

"Now, he's gone, too?" Mason King's famous voice woke Marshall up. His famously handsome, dark face loomed over the bedside.

The nurse on the opposite side of the bed nodded. "Yes, well. He is expected to recover. He is just taking a while. He just regained consciousness a few days ago." Voice had a funny lilt to it. She was obviously a little starstruck.

"Well, if there's anything he needs, let me know."

"We will." This was another voice … male, deeper. "Do you know him well?"

"No. Marian would bring him on set every once in a while, usually for the shows that featured her making a guest appearance as the *Butterfly*. He was such a fan of her earlier work, too, he loved those callback episodes. But I want to do what I can for him. Y'know. That's what she would've wanted."

"Of course," the doctor assured. He had a handsome face, his skin so smooth and perfect, almost like a statue. He was so familiar …

Marshall drifted off again just as the nurse was asking for a selfie.

After another day, as they became confident that the meds were working, they took Marshall the restraints off and moved him to a chair. He still had trouble moving his arms and legs, so they needed to move him about, to the restroom, to the cafeteria, and so forth.

One time, they made a special trip, more than one of them. They strapped Marshall into a gurney and wheeled him to a different room.

It wasn't a room for patients … he looked to his side and saw a desk. Seated behind it was a tall man in shadow, since the lamp on his desk was pointed askew. He had a familiar face. Marshall couldn't place it, though …

"Hello Marshall. Here let me help you with that." *It is the perfect-face guy again. Who is he?*

The man—it was a doctor, he wore a white smock—stood up and moved to Marshall's side. He grabbed his patient's arm and gently guided him up. Marshall hadn't even noticed that the orderlies and nurses who'd brought him there had unstrapped him. After a moment, he was sitting up on the gurney. He wobbled with the effort.

"That won't do. C'mon." And the man helped him down and had him sit at the end seat, at one end of the table. His grasp was incredibly firm, *strong*.

The doctor sat down at the other end of the long table and looked at someone who had been standing at the doorway, and they wheeled the gurney away and left, closing the door shut behind them.

"How are you feeling, Marshall?"

The younger man in the hospital gown didn't feel like talking.

"You are ashamed of being here."

Marshall still ignored him.

"You are ashamed of what you did to get here."

"Mmm-nh." Marshall shook his head no.

"You are irritated that I interrupted your little fantasies of making love to the various nurses here."

"What? No! I just. Cannot." Just the effort to say that exhausted him. This was just like when he was back in Heychuck's apartment. He was just … spent.

But the doctor was being so outrageous, Marshall had to correct him. Which, of course, was the idea. "Cannot talk."

"Ah, yes. The new meds. Your speech will be affected for a while. But that's okay. For now, you can just listen. Dr. Akhem has assigned me to your case. I am Dr. Chase. Brendant Chase. I have been monitoring you for some time, Marshall. We were all quite worried."

"Doctor …"

"Call me Brendant. Please." He leaned in. "Do you remember me?" From his tone, the question seemed to have a singular significance.

"Akhem. Here?"

"Akhem? Ah, no. He is away. Out of the country. Has been for some time. Listen, Marshall, when you re-admitted yourself here at GG, that was a good choice. You were very close to what we call an associative break. The trauma of what happened to your grandmother was quite severe. Do you remember me?"

Marshall shook his head.

"We spoke once, when you first arrived here. And your break was soon after that."

Marshall just stared at him. "You. Are lying."

"Why do you say that, Marshall?"

When he didn't answer, the doctor offered, "You are saying that because everyone you've ever known has lied to you." Marshall's look hardened. "Okay, then. Who am I wrong about? Who has told you the truth?"

Marshall's mouth felt like lead, but he was still able to form the words. "Uncle Brick."

"What about him, Marshall?"

"Truth about you: Visiting. Analyst."

It really was him. Marshall could tell by the dark cloud of an expression that passed over his face. His face. Marshall just didn't recognize him without his cool shades. His eyes were black enough, though. *What else? Something about his face.*

"Well, why don't we ask him? Did you know tonight it is movie night at GG? You know, Marshall, I've arranged for a very special movie night. Sort of a family reunion. He should be here any second ... what is the damn delay? Hm, I'll be back." And then he got up and left, tripping a bit on his chair and cursing as he did.

Marshall sat in the dark, gray room for a while. He looked around and saw several white smocks hanging on the coat stand. One looked more like a robe. The pictures on the wall were all of the doctor when he was younger. *Something about his face.*

Then another orderly came in and removed Marshall from the chair and put him in a wheelchair to be taken to the entertainment room.

Marshall remembered the entertainment room. He spent many days there, watching TV and playing board games. *Sorry* was his favorite.

This time there were only a few chairs set up, and they had been scooted closer to the TV. People were already there, sitting in three of the four chairs. A man and two women. One woman was black and wore a dew rag.

Even before he saw their faces, he recognized Ruby, Brick, and Grandma Marian.

Brick looked as he did before. Less battered. But his white hair was still slicked back with some sort of gel, and his arms hung loosely on his arm rests. He also was in a wheelchair.

Seated in a wingback chair that was scooted over was Ruby. She sat by his side and held Brick's hand in hers. She wasn't restrained nor was she looking like she was under any duress. She seemed to be there for Brick, not as a patient.

Grandma Marian on the other hand, did not look well. Her face had shriveled up like a shrunken head and her hair was now under a cap to keep it out of the way. Her chair was actually a bed that he been propped up into a sitting position. But she was intubated and breathing on a respirator. Other tubes and wired were connected to her. Her eyes were shut. She might as well have been dead, but the beeping machine told everyone that the body still functioned.

Doctor Brendant Chase, the Visiting Analyst, moved around to stand beside the television. He held several CDs in his hands, but he drew a deep breath and fluttered his clasped hands in front of him. They came to rest on his waistline with his arms in a "V."

"Isn't this wonderful? A real family reunion. Although each of you has seen better times. But the wheel turns as it must, I suppose." He paused for a moment, as though confused by what he just said. Then he recovered. "Anyway, I have here several of the same CDs from the special collection that you, Marshall, stole a while back. The ones you took were so good, I felt like we should watch them again, together—how does that sound?"

No one said anything. Marshall stared at each of them for a response. The only one with any sort of response was Ruby, who just absentmindedly nodded with a tear forming in her eye as she looked at Brick.

The wheel?

Familiar theme music came on, the music from *Bastion Hill*. It was the number one show in the mid-seventies, and then it made a comeback with a reboot in the '90s. In the '70s, it was a cheesy production about a gang of vigilante bikers called the Wild Bunch and their superhero friends like Hell-Rider, the Butterfly, and so forth. But, in the '90s it was rebooted as an absurdist comedy, with Marian Michaels returning as the (past-her-prime) superhero and her son trying to get the gang back together again (according to the plot), while doing a reality show about their current lives.

So, Marshall and the assembled family watched several episodes of Season 1 of the '90s reboot. Of special note was a scene where Marian temporarily faked her death in order to collect life insurance to keep their show funded. The conceit of the show was that she was incapable of listening to the lukewarm eulogies being offered and rose from the coffin to correct everyone and settle scores.

At the end of the makeshift *festival*, the doctor simply walked from the room and left them all there to think about what they'd just seen. Ruby got up and gently kissed Marian and Brick each on the cheek, and then looked over to Marshall and said, "Now, you two take care of each other. I know Marian would've wanted you to do that." She spoke about him and Uncle Brick.

"What is wrong with Grandma?"

"She's in a coma. During her heart attack, she used her medical alert bracelet and help came, but you delayed them. You always ... why do you always have to fight them?" She referred to Prince, you reckoned. "Well, you have had a tough life, son. I know."

"Why did we ... watch all of these shows?"

"It was my idea. So, we can relive our glory days, I suppose."

"These weren't ... the way I remembered them."

"We all see whatever we need to see. Goodbye, Butchie."

As she walked out, Marshall could hear her exchanging pleasantries with Dr. Chase in the hallway, as though they were old friends.

Whatever we need to see?

His face? What is it? What am I missing?

The wheel?

One by one, each of them were relocated back into their rooms. But before they put Marshall Lastpost back in his bed, he was left in his wheelchair alone for a bit. Second time they'd left him alone. *Protocols have changed. For example, where was the bell that signified sleep time after movie time? There should have been a bell.*

###

He sat there in his room for the longest time, just thinking about it. *Those shows? They were all Hollywood productions!? Grandma and Uncle Brick weren't superheroes, but actors? I mean, she was always an actor. Did I just imagine all the rest? All those missions? All in my imagination? Am I really that ... no ... really?*

Finally, Dr. Chase returned to talk. He was wearing his longest smock, one that went nearly to the floor. Attached to it was a folded back waffle of fabric that lay behind his shoulders. What looked from a distance like a hood, was actually a plastic helmet that could be pulled over and zipped up, during infectious disease protocols.

He was carrying a clipboard. He wore a stethoscope over his neck.

A stethoscope. Help you hear. What did I hear? Marshall's brain churned.

"So, now that you've watched the shows from a ... different perspective, what are your thoughts?"

Marshall looked at him.

"For example, do you still think you have powers? Did your family look like they had powers in there, to you? Hm? Don't get me wrong. This is a common illusion, Marshall. For people with your condition. You know that, right?"

He stared at a wall while he remembered: *The stethoscope was invented in France, in the early nineteenth century. It started as rolled up paper, like the trumpets of the time that hard-of-hearing people used; but this way the doctor could hear the problem without having to touch the patient who, in this case, was an overweight female. Otherwise he would have had to place his ear between her boobs.* You remembered reading that in one of the encyclopedias in Greenless Grove, as a small child. And the picture with the listing showed a diagram of the physician standing over an ample-bosomed lady, holding the instrument. You remembered being aroused by the picture and not knowing why …

"If I may continue." Dr. Chase leaned in and moved held Marshall's head so he would be looking at him. "What I really need for you to do is to strap yourself into the bed. If you do both feet and your off hand, then you know it won't be too tight. And we can do the final strap, yes? Will you do that for me, Marshall?"

"Wh-why?"

"It's important. It's an important sign that you agree that you need to be kept safe. That you know that you are a danger to yourself and others. And that, just for now, this is best. The best way to protect you and to protect everyone else … you *have* hurt others, Marshall. Don't you *remember …?*" The last betrayed a touch of rage, below the surface.

Marshall didn't say anything. *We all see what we need to see.*

"They will come and do it anyway if you don't. You *will* be restrained, Marshall. But it would show me that you know that what I'm saying is correct. That I know best …"

I remain very still. Just like with bullies. I sense the danger. The wheel turns as it must, or it would fall over.

"C'mon Marshall! You need to do as I say. Now!" He was pointing to the bed, like Marshall was a dog. The doctor was almost seething.

But Marshall just kept looking at his perfect face… perfect… perfect…

Then several of his voices and Marshall all intoned at once,

"There is no scar."

Doctor Chase was taken aback. "Wh-what?"

That was it.

This isn't real.

"You forgot the scar." More voices from Marshall's illness, his intuitive mind, no longer tearing him down, but, at this moment, helping. He said the words, even though he didn't understand the meaning: "The one that I gave you, all those years ago …"

The doctor's facade fell away as a look of pure hatred replaced it.

"But this was good. Nearly fooled me. But I heard the clues. YOU HEAR ME? I HEARD YOU, PO. THE WHEEL TURNS. YES. I'M READY TO GO," he shouted to the room.

"Go? You idiot! You retarded fool. You DARE? You are going nowhere! I am in charge here, in my own mind. Just as I am in charge there. One reality is as good as any other. You cannot escape me—"

But he had no sooner said it than the bell rang.

The bell for nighttime? No, not quite. It sounded different.

The doctor looked up at the bell sound and mouthed a silent NO from the pit of his stomach. Then he lunged with a snarl at Marshall, with both hands extended. There was only murder in his eyes.

Marshall could feel himself being pulled away, just as before in the Unity … but this time he was being pulled by the sound of the bell—

"No. He's not getting away this time, you cunt!" screamed the madman in the smock, as though to someone behind him, over his shoulder.

But the VA's weight had shifted. Marshall had been wrong. He hadn't been lunging murderously at Marshall. He had been invoking another shift … out of the corners of his consciousness, Marshall could feel the life-force of a couple dJinn blink out of existence as Marshall was, again, diverted … banished forward, to another Timespace … shortly into the future, but to yet another place, another timeline. Just as Ben had done with him before …

He could hear the VA's voice in his mind, like a summative amalgam of all the schizophrenic negations he had ever endured. *"Ha. You have a girlfriend? Not in this timeline, you retard. You don't deserve one. You are nothing. Not a champion. Not a hero. Nothing! You hear?"*

And with a powerful wave of a dead demons' energy, wherever Marshall Lastpost had been aimed to go, he was being highjacked again, to be somewhere else. Some *time* else the Visiting Analyst controlled.

Palla Kalrajan parked several blocks away and let herself into the apartment that she'd just rented. It was a room, really—a podlike existence in a larger home. Each room was its own sublet. It was located maybe two dozen blocks away from the Blue Rooks HQ, in a residential neighborhood that was one of those unique Chicago realms in Pilsen: a place that had been predominantly Italian, before it became predominantly Polish, before it was predominantly Hispanic, before it was gentrified to be none of the above.

It was a long walk, but doable. At night, there was every reason for her to be afraid, but she wasn't. Even though it had been many days, the calm warmth from her last visit with the Unity still billowed through her like a narcotic.

From time to time some of the vagrants or gangbangers would make eye contact, hungry for whatever they were lacking. But despite her suggestive attire (a short overcoat and tall boots) neither her eyes nor bearing showed the slightest bit of fear.

So, everyone kept their distance. Which was good for them.

The HQ was under surveillance, probably constant. But she had learned from Sally that there were multiple tunnels like the one they used to escape. Sally (bless her) had mapped them all. And now Palla, about a block and a half away from the HQ, pulled up a manhole cover and entered the sewer.

This was what the boots were for.

The tunnel led to the parking garage maintenance shaft. From there she entered the building through the utility room. Then she entered the building proper and headed to the elevator.

There was no reason for any of this. She had been released on her own recognizance by the judge. She had every legal right to go there every day, entering through the front door, to go to work. And she did. She went to work every day through the front door.

Why, just this past week, she had lined up all the advertising, public relations contract, and vendors for the convention; she had placed ads in all the online job-search boards to staff the event (rather than rely on volunteers); she had sent invitations and personally called each minister-invitee from each of the sixty congregations to encourage them to take advantage of the event.

She put the percentage of invitees who referred them to talk to their marketing and business departments at close to 100 percent. And from those departments she got close to unanimous agreement. Yes, they all wanted to be a part of this event. But that was all earlier in the week. This was Saturday morning and she had a *very special* meeting to set up. She got out at the top floor and walked to a heavy, crimson metal door that led to the roof.

But this was a special event. It wasn't something that could be done with others around. She stepped out onto the roof. It was about 4:30 a.m. She looked straight at the few stars that were still visible and took a deep breath. The air was brisk, maybe fifty degrees, but the breeze made it feel much colder. That was the reason for the short coat. It was designed with many extra linings, so it was her warmest.

She brought out a blanket from under her jacket and placed it on the concrete of the roof. The corners of the roof were adorned with fake owls to scare away the various corvids that tended to congregate on top of the building. They were mechanical, the owls. Their little heads rotated to complete the effect, but their maintenance staff had discovered that moving the statues themselves was the most effective strategy. At this particular time, all of the owls were knocked over ... she took a moment to walk to each one and correct it.

Once they were all once again at their post, she returned to her blanket and sat down, cross-legged.

And she took out *Asha*'s bell.

For a moment, she hesitated.

A flood of the strongest possible regret overwhelmed her. *There are so many! How am I supposed to choose? This cannot be right. It is wrong to leave so many out ...*

She held the bell in her right hand, the weak one. She rotated it gently, deftly, with a finger interposed, so as not to let the clapper make a noise.

This is unfair! Do you hear? I can save them all! Why won't you let me? You claim I cannot handle it. But HE is harming thousands with his wars in other lands ... he will kill so many more before he's done! You give him hosts of demons; and I get a child's toy?

For a moment, she considered throwing the bell over the edge of the roof. It was metal, but the fall might break it.

But he isn't my *enemy, is he? Still, if I get rid of him, that would show you, wouldn't it? If I help you do that, then can I save them all? That's fair. Just let me stay there, next time, until I save them all ... yes?*

But the answer was with her as soon as she made the offer.

That doesn't work. There is no victory for me. Of all the players, my role is the only one with no freedom. I am the only slave.

Palla Kalrajan began to cry at that point. Or, perhaps, she had already been crying, always been crying, inside, her entire life. Yes, that was it. Her cries reflected in her inability to make friends, to retain intimate partners, to "succeed" at the cost of her life balance, to try to redeem the deep shame she felt. The pain. Her pain, reaching the surface from time to time, like a dormant virus, but only coming to the surface to act as a shield. A shield to prevent human contact.

But that wasn't the kind of contact she was meant to have.

My contact is going to be wholesale, not retail.

She transferred the bell into her left hand and lifted it up in front of her. It glinted in the glare of the streetlamps.

Well, that about does it: denial, anger, bargaining, depression, and acceptance. If we start a sustainable "green" rooftop up here, I'll call it Gethsemane. No, that's vanity, she could hear her conscience say.

Funny, *her* conscience spoke in Sally's Illinois, female nonaccent.

She rang the bell twice, and each time, she invoked the name of the person she was sending the prayer out to. Instead of the forty-eight names, this time she just said two.

Rinnng-a-ninng-a-ninng-a-ninnnnnnnng.

In that instant, it all came flooding back, like memories of childhood that are triggered by a pleasant smell. Like a kaleidoscope, she was able to see all of the people who were to be involved in the final scene at the convention, where they were now, where they would be then, with whom they would ally during the End Day.

She mentally blinked and the portal shifted in her wake, with each person with whom she had had contact that day, the gangbanger who locked eyes with her, going home to prevent his dad from beating his mom to death, again. The clerk at the convenience store, offering her extra lottery tickets, going home to watch reality TV in a stupor of manipulated outrage over the actor's choices of mates.

She blinked again and the tunnel shifted; now it was the Regnant. Their enemy and his forces. Dear Demi-urge. All those who had sacrificed themselves and how they were to return …

Yet another turn. She saw the apocalypse. She turned away in disgust at her impotence to prevent it.

Another view. And this was from those who were not able to be there … what!? There was about to be another shift! But this wasn't from her … so dangerous. *He would DARE? Ben did it out of desperation … but Chase, he does it merely to retain cruel control?*

She was momentarily grateful of being the Unity. This meant that she existed in all the timelines and such shifts didn't affect her. Still, with such a change taking place so late in this, should she change her absolutions?

No. Might as well finish it.

So, she invoked the first name before the bell's ring disappeared into the night sky. "Rufepirts."

She could feel the barometric pressure drop, her skin crawled with energy and the breeze shifted. The next moment RUFEPIRTS was, indeed, there, on the roof, his massive form lying next to her.

Satisfied—*remember to breathe*—she went ahead and did it again. *Rinnngn-a-ninng-a-ninng-a-ninnnnnnng.*

"Marshall Lastpost."

And as the ring died, she opened her eyes and saw … nothing.

He had not appeared.

The sound of the bell went away. And so did her cosmic consciousness. She couldn't ring it again right away; she was too fragile. So, there was nothing she could do.

They truly had him.

She just nodded. This probably meant it was about time for the Precept to be born.

BOOK TWO—CHAPTER SEVEN

REVEREND HEYCHUCK SMITH

###

I had put in a single call, to my landlord for the congregation hall, not for my apartment. I told the restaurant owner I was breaking my lease. When he asked me if I was ever coming back, I said I didn't know. They made a point to telling me that they would leave the congregation hall open for my eventual return. I said that wasn't necessary. I was a marked man if I ever went back. Some moves are permanent.

For the next several weeks, I was with Kinta and Sally in Vegas. Helping them coordinate the logistics of the on-the-ground preparations by day. And trying my hand at the slots by around the dinner hour.

Late nights, Sally trained Kinta and I trained in the ways of the Blue Rooks church. Sally would ask us to speak on a particular topic. I would go first, quoting scripture and giving my two cents worth. Then Kinta would try to come up with what her father might have said about it, which was very cathartic for her. And then Sally would synthesize it into a sermon and repeat it back to us. After a few weeks we all started to achieve a sort of symbiosis of philosophy. It was good for all of us, I think.

At the end of the three weeks, I was ordained as a full-fledged Preacher for Blue Rooks. Sally called it a field promotion.

During all that time, only Sally had had any contact with Ms. Kalrajan, but I was already being introduced to her.

The videos on the various streaming services were the beginning. I started binge-watching them during those several weeks. She really was remarkable.

In the videos, Palla just called herself the Bell Ringer. And her little ten-minute inspirational messages were so nondescript, so devoid of production value ... it was just her walking around, usually in a park, or along a waterfront. Shrewd commenters figured out it was Lake Michigan—so eventually she started to get a "flock" of followers who would show up just to see if she was streaming that day.

And those followers would also post and tweet and blog all about what Palla was doing—how inspirational she was in person. Apocryphal stories emerged about how people around her were healed by her presence ...

It had only been about a month, less than fifty streaming posts total, but she already had over seven hundred thousand followers.

Her messages were full of hope and love. But it was less about that than it was about the delivery. Her absolute confidence. From time to time, not overly much, she quoted Judeo-Christian scripture as though she'd known it her entire life. Or she told anecdotes about religious leaders from other epochs and other cultures like she had been there.

She mentioned her position as CEO of Blue Rooks and that checked off two other culture boxes: both the religious and feminists could get behind her.

And she talked about her background as a victim of sex trafficking. The #MeToo movement adopted her as a de facto spokeswoman within days.

And there was also the Bell. What was it about the bell?

It was her gimmick, right? I mean, it rang and she spoke the names of the people who were logged in ... and, even if it wasn't you, as you heard her ring the bell and sound off the names of the followers, you could just *feel* the power of it.

But most importantly Ms. Bell-Ringer Kalrajan connected it all to her audience's everyday lives: their hopes, their fears. Especially their aspirations.

It sounded so corny. I know.

And, of course, there were her looks. She was easy on the eyes. A different kind of cute than Sally. Palla was exotic and funny, sardonic, with a twinkle in her eye.

Sally was just straightforward girl-next-door *hot*. At least to me.

I crushed for Sally, sure. The entire flight back I flirted with her—y'know, with extensive theological arguments. Catnip for theo-nerds like us.

But I have to say it, watching those videos, I started to feel love for Palla, too. And not sexual love. But *love*. Real devotion.

Then we arrived in Chicago, and I got to meet her.

###

When we first arrived at her office, Sally went in first. Sally said, "*Marshall …?*"

To which Palla just said, "No." We all knew that meant he hadn't been found.

Then she gave Kinta a quick hug and a sweet forehead touch. Finally, she walked up to me and bypassed my extended handshake in favor of a long, and I mean *long* hug.

And in that hug, I felt the contentment and security that I hadn't felt my entire adult life. Honest. I didn't want it to end. *I mean, what the hell? Who was she?*

Well that was the question on everyone's mind, wasn't it?

After she met with us alone, she invited her crew in … not a camera crew, with her public relations manager overseeing, but just a bunch of kids. Whenever she gave the signal, they would take out their cellphones and live-stream different aspects of her day.

And that was how she operated from then on until End Day.

For example, every time she sent a subordinate away with a task to do, she allowed a member of that live-streaming entourage to follow that person and talk with them—see how it got done.

Same with all of her phone calls. This was especially true of any calls to other leaders within other congregations. If they rebuffed her invitation to the conference, they would soon here about it on social media.

She was a suspect in a federal case—but far from going into hiding, she had made herself into one of the most public personas in the country.

And she had singlehandedly overcome all the negative PR from the federal cases against Blue Rooks themselves.

But she also was very careful not to allow any of them to videotape our interactions. Sally, Kinta and I remained off the social media grid.

###

But that first meeting with her was so simple and sweet. It was her first words to me that set the tone.

"So, you're the one who's come to lead my church."

She didn't say it as a joke, but rather with a tone of absolute gravity. Reciting a fact, like the final score of a Seahawks game or the death toll of a plague.

I just felt embarrassed by the remark—I glanced over at Sally, expecting an angry glare at the idea that she would be supplanted by me. But Sally just smiled, gently nodding like she heartily approved. What had I gotten myself into?

BOOK TWO—CHAPTER EIGHT

"What I really need is to get clear about what I must do, not what I must know, except insofar as knowledge must precede every act. What matters is to find a purpose, to see what it really is that God wills that I shall do; the crucial thing is to find a truth which is truth for me, to find the idea for which I am willing to live and die."

—Søren Aabye Kierkegaard,
his "Journalen" (1835)

Mother Po enjoyed Buelford, Illinois. Sally's hometown had a population of only one thousand, three hundred and fifty, but it was close to the city that housed the campus of the state university, so it was sort of a bedroom community for the professors and other professional employees of that school. That meant that its townsfolk were arguably more intelligent than average.

This made things easier for her. For whatever reason, the more intelligent the audience was, the more effective her empathic abilities were. The increased intelligence led to self-empathy and awareness, which allowed her a greater bandwidth with which to tune in …? She didn't know. But she had convinced the first couple that she interviewed with in town to allow her to stay as a boarder in their guest room above their garage for a few weeks as part of her hiring.

And they even allowed her to store her "pod" trailer of personal belongings that she had shipped down from Chicago inside their garage, forcing them to both park in their own driveway. This was all in ex-change for her being brought on as a live-in nanny, to watch over their special-needs child while they both worked. Nice people.

She was also able to rebuff their occasional queries as to why the pod needed to be plugged in. She just told them it was for temperature-con-trolled vintage collectibles, art pieces. Sealed up tight.

They were satisfied with that because they preferred that to having to look for another nanny. Since she was so good at her job.

Of course, she was using her abilities on the child, too. To help keep him happy. They were amazed with her results.

Po never fully shared that the "collectibles" were a stockpile of po-tentially biohazardous pharmaceuticals that were themselves the subject of an intense criminal investigation by the federal government.

It was a sunny day just after lunch hour. It had been about a week since she sensed that Marshall had needed her help. She did her best. He was *so* smart and receptive … sometimes she thought he was miscast as a cleric. He could have replaced her. He had such potential. *Oh, well, he's young. There's time.*

At this juncture, Po was helping another youngster with a particular affliction. She was helping the resident teenager with the severe disabili-ties feed himself when the doorbell rang.

As the door opened, Po saw a stunningly beautiful female. The two women recognized each other, after a fashion.

Agent Brianna Carson recognized Po Minh Tât from her Extirpacy's most-wanted file. While Po simply recognized Brianna as a Fed. This was both from the fact that Brianna seemed to recognize her and because Po had interacted with enough of them over the years to sense it instantly.

"Yes?"

"I'm Agent Carson, FBI." She held up her badge, which Po ignored. "May I come in?"

"I thought FBI agents always traveled in pairs, especially when in-terviewing people?"

"I'm on special assignment."

"Come in, but please wait in here 'til I'm finished helping my young friend. He's a boy. I'll be with ya' in a few minutes." There was no special emphasis on this request. She was just talking. Nor did she wait for a response as she walked back into the dining room.

Brianna casually surveyed the room before sitting down as told.

When Po returned, he said, "What can I do for ya', Agent Carson?"

"Approximately two weeks ago, a subcontractor for the Blue Rooks Church shipped away scores of samples of new drugs, including a key one called Blue Joy, to a sister lab in Tennessee, for safekeeping. However, the invoices show one crate missing—the crate that held the Blue Joy. It wasn't the sort of thing that can just be tucked under someone's lab coat—it is quite large. It took some investigation, but we found the employee at the sister lab who had been bribed to remove the crate and divert it. His credit card records showed that he used a pod shipping company, and that pod was shipped to this very small town in Illinois where we are now—the home town of Blue Rook's religious director, it turns out—to a house matching *this address*. Camera surveillance along the route, and from some of your neighbors here across the street confirm that it arrived, as do the shipping records of the pod company."

She stood up and removed her coat, expecting the action to start soon. "So, what you can do for me is to tell me where the contents of the pod are."

"You neglected to mention that the drugs needs special environmental controls—so there needed to be a special battery retrofitted for the pod en route, and, of course, the pod needs to be plugged in now."

Po could sense that Agent Carson didn't actually know that. Interesting. "You think you're pretty cute, don't you, old witch?"

"I think I'm a-DOR-able, ya' little cunt. But before I take you to where we hid the drugs, you would like to have a cup of tea with me and discuss where the rest of my companions are."

Now this was an effort. But the moment came and passed as Brianna laughed.

"Your mind games won't work on me. The Master taught me your ways even before he showed me the ways of the *Others*."

The older women smacked her lips with derision. "If you really think of 'em as two diff'rent things, then he hasn't taught you much of anything at all ..."

Po sat opposite her and carefully placed her ancient looking wrinkled hands upon her skirt to straighten it as she went on. "You must get tired of that, don't you? He orders you around. He shows you only glimpses of the power. Someday he *will* ask you to be the very thing you hate, making an example of others in front of the cameras. You will have to think twice before following an order from him once he tells you to betray your ... father's memory, for example."

Brianna stood up and held a stun-baton at Po's throat before Po saw her move. "Shut up! I've had enough of these games. Take me to the stores of the drug. Now."

I guessed right. It's always daddy issues, Po mused.

"As you wish." She started to stand up, but it took her several attempts. Brianna assumed that the old woman was as frail as she looked. And she wasn't wrong.

But that wasn't why Po was suddenly so tired.

At any rate, Po led her into the garage and unlocked the pod.

Brianna removed a couple of the many vials in the container and confirmed the authenticity of the drug on the spot. And then she activated the garage door and took a step outside to make sure she had a good signal to call in the ops team to extract the drug.

"Did it work, I wonder?" Mother Po said to her. She had walked up to the agent's side. "Well, it's been a good life. Lissen, you are gonna' to have to do this out here, I want to die in the sun."

But Brianna just placed her hand on the old woman's shoulder and said, "Someone will be by for you soon." Then she walked away, down the sidewalk, and around the corner, out of sight.

Po was surprised. She went back inside the checked on the boy. He was still napping. Good.

She was exhausted, so she sat down and—*no, wait ... not tired. Something. Oh, of course ... the shoulder touch ... a pathogen. microneedle ...*

Brianna had poisoned her with a time-delayed poison ... just in case she decided to contact anyone in the time right after Brianna left. They were monitoring the land line.

But Po didn't call anyone. She just sat there as all the muscles in her body started to paralyze.

After all, I'm not a rank amateur, she thought, then she mentally corrected the tense—*wasn't a rank amateur*—just before she died.

###

As she rounded the corner to her car, Brianna touched her earpiece. "You got all of that?"

The ops center in the van (premarked as a furniture repair company) responded, "Affirmative." The van was parked two blocks away, in visual contact with the target house.

"Move in. First, secure the drugs. Then sedate the child and remove the body. Take as much time as you need. The drug has special environmental requirements. Have the local bureau office work with the town police to barricade the street, cordon off the neighborhood, until you're done."

The E-Dog on the other end of the channel: "Copy that."

Brianna got in her car and pulled it around to supervise the rest of the process. *I am also going to need a cooler,* she thought as she patted the inside jacket pocket that held the sample doses she still possessed.

This time, Marshall felt it was the real thing. Nothing was familiar. This was a recent installation, not the Chicago facility where Brick was. Walls, floors, ceilings: all white. The fluorescent lights infused everything with a sickly sheen. So, probably it was a healthcare facility of some kind. This could have been anywhere.

The cold, painful glow of the facility lights couldn't pierce the fog in his head, though. He hated that feeling. Was he still high? How long had it been?

And those visions! He was in the dimension of the *Others.* They said to call it "hell." *Really?* And the VA he pulled him away from … what? Something about his jacket … he couldn't quite remember … *would Kinta really not remember me well in this timeline …?*

Just as in the Analyst's illusion-scape, he was still restrained, but only his arms … via a skinny chain to his legs. He was seated in a chair. A wheelchair. He could stand, grab things, walk.

After he worked up the energy, he tested it: he could move, he just couldn't walk with anything more than half-steps. As he shimmied around his small room, he noticed that the ratio of healthcare workers to armed guards was about one-to-one.

And he was heavily drugged. In fact, it felt similar to other times when he had been incarcerated and the drugs had reached a saturation point. No voices. Nothing resembling clear thought. He had a funny aftertase in his mouth, a tar flavor just like after he smoked the weed.

He looked out the window of his room (cell). Is was just a plain yard, hardly any grass, even. No people. No activity. No life. The opposite of what he'd seen out of Heychuck's window.

###

Mess was twice a day, midmorning and late afternoon. The cafeteria was an orderly setup. None of other patients (inmates?) seemed to have any more inclination or energy to cause any trouble.

People mostly left Marshall alone. During the first week, other than the occasional chatty guard, no one tried to talk to him at all.

And, unlike in the VA's illusion, no one here would give him any information about how long he'd been here and so forth.

The time-shift wasn't apparent. It was meant to cover some nondescript amount of time that started whenever he had about to leave Hell and come back to rejoin his friends. Might have been days, weeks, or even years. Once Marshall was able to get to a TV and watch the news, he realized that it was the former. Only a few days from when he had been about to leave Hell. Of course, he had no way to know how long he'd actually been there in the first place.

The Analyst had done the same thing Ben had done once before, shifting Marshall into an alternate timeline. This meant Marshall really had three sets of memories. He had what he remembered before the funeral, then he had what had happened since the funeral through his time with Dicky and at Heychuck's apartment and in Hell, and now, he had however long he'd been unconscious when he arrived here.

Most troubling, he had no way of knowing how much of the other two sets of memories actually happened to him in this Timespace.

Ben's shift would've been a responsible one. He was skilled and conscientious enough that he would've minimized the changes. But the VA? He could've chosen anything. Or picked one, not caring.

For all Marshall knew, everyone he saw die was alive again in this timeline. Or maybe not, and even more had died … but he knew that something was different between him and Kinta. He had heard Chase's voice talking about Kinta. *In this timeline she hates me,* he thought.

Finally, he decided to stop thinking about potential timeline inconsistencies. Hoping for the something and finding out it wasn't so *or* imagining the other, would *both* be equally painful. And he knew that whatever happened, happened, in this timeline. He just needed to find out what that was.

It wasn't all bad news. It was the third day. Some stranger in the hallway, looked like an orderly, gave him a funny look and walked away with a purposeful stride. It must have been that guy who gave his old friend the heads up, because it was later that day, during the daily courtyard walk outside, when he appeared.

Marshall hadn't realized that he had been seated at the same table as his old friend the past few days. Once he even noticed him and locked eyes, but *even then,* he didn't recognize him!

Nor did he recognize Marshall, as he was apparently blind. To Marshall, he was just that guy in the shades.

Marshall didn't know. Maybe it was the drugs. Or maybe it was how different he looked. But, either way, there was no mistaking his gait when, after someone whispered to him and pointed in Marshall's direction, he cut, cane first, clear across the courtyard to interrupt his path during a walk. Nor could Marshall misidentify him after the distinctive greeting:

"Hello, Butchwald."

###

After that, it had taken several days' worth of rec time visits outside to get Boris up to speed about what Marshall remembered. And as each day added to the last, Marshall got more and more worried:

"But why hasn't he come here?"

"To do what?"

"To finish the job. To kill me."

"Well, m'boy, from what you've said, he wasn't after that. No, it sounds like you were already at his mercy. No, he wanted you to *strap yourself in.* It is curious."

Marshall was so comforted by being able to talk with someone about all of this. And he enjoyed the fact that Boris engaged no differently than he would were they sitting in his private drawing room in his Scottish castle, instead of in a (what they decided was a) federal black ops detention facility.

But it was striking just how different he looked: Boris's cheeks were still roundish, but now they were covered by a shaggy red beard with streaks of gray in it. His hair had grown long atop his head, too, and rather than the spiky look he had before, he now combed over like a politician. He'd lost maybe eighty pounds. Now he was nearly as skinny as Marshall. But with his broad frame, it just made him look sickly. Dark circles under his eyes made the gloom behind his dark shades seem even deeper.

At he was technically once a foreign dignitary, the British government was trying to achieve his release through diplomatic means. But this particular US administration not only didn't care about its relationship with the United Kingdom, it was decidedly vicious with foreigners of all types. So, it had been a long time with no progress.

Everyone in the facility called him Doc. He had befriended everyone who was civil service or a private contractor there ... only the hardcore E personnel wouldn't interact with him. Probably on orders.

And finally, Marshall could tell something else was different, too. Boris was now *not* tracking all the time. Sometimes he would space out for minutes on end. He was obviously on some serious meds.

"So, what happened in this timeline?"

"Well, I lived," Boris said with a grin. "That's utmost, you'll agree."

"Yeah." Marshall didn't smile with Boris but nodded and waited for more.

Boris shifted his ass on the metal bleacher seat and tried his best to summarize. "Well, from what you told me, the attack at the funeral was similar to what you remember, except that, prior to the start of the fighting, the three of you left immediately to go inside. By the fight's end, Brick and I were captured. Slinker and Ben both did die. Slightly different. My mum died, too, protecting me. But ... beyond that ...?"

"Your mother? Aunt Ruby?"

"Yes. Why are you surprised?"

"She wasn't there ... in the other timeline." Marshall didn't dwell on it. He could see it hurt Boris to talk about a different timeline where his Mom was still alive. Rather, Marshall asked, "What about the Barn Grier attack?"

"That's what I'm trying to tell you, m'boy, I have no real way of knowing what happened. We don't get news of that kind in here. But … I can tell you what *didn't* happen. He hasn't captured Palla since then."

Marshall caught his breath as Boris continued.

"Because she sends people to visit with me regularly."

"Can you get a message out to her?"

"I already have."

"So, she's coming?"

Boris didn't answer that question but rather returned to the first one. "He wants you to give up. He needs you to. Yes, that's it, my boy."

"Who? The Analyst?"

But Boris was gone now. He stared off into space for the rest of the rec time, and it took a couple of guards to carry him into a chair to wheel him back in, the cane carefully placed across his lap.

As he watched them wheel Boris away, Marshall tried to remember. He thought this was day seven since he awoke in this timeline. He tried to think back. Had he ever known when the convention and the protest were going to happen? *Wasn't it coming up soon?* Felt like it was.

Tomorrow he would start asking the orderlies if you could watch C-SPAN on the television. If a small religious conference with presidential candidates was going to be covered, it would be there.

He went to sleep that night thinking about Kinta. What was she like in this timeline? He listened to the barely liminal echoing and replying moans of his fellow inmates in their cells, and he fell asleep to them like they were frogs chirping in a swamp.

BOOK TWO—CHAPTER NINE

HEYCHUCK SMITH

###

The ladies got a tip from someone named "Boris" that Marshall was being kept in the same facility as him and Brick Reese.

As the Uber driver took me to the neighborhood where the federal facility was, I mentally reviewed what the ladies had told me about the facility I was traveling to, which wasn't much. But they had spelled out some of the logistics of the visits from their agents who'd previously visited the prior few months.

I knew this: I was going to the place where they were keeping Marshall. And it was important that I see him. Federal protocols allowed for the visit. Sally and Palla told me what to say and to whom. But mostly I just needed to sign in, and I couldn't carry in anything past the front staging area.

And it had to be me because, as his stepbrother, my visit wouldn't flag anything in particular. Whereas if someone from Blue Rooks showed up, especially one of the ladies, not only would the visit not be allowed, they ran the risk of being incarcerated themselves, on some trumped-up charge. I kept thinking about what I would say to Marshall. What I could say, what I couldn't …

My mind drifted to some of the lessons that Palla tried to share with me. Some were just basic mindfulness and religious training. She found me to be a quick student. But I didn't have a knack for any of the magic-use stuff at all. Apparently, I wasn't a sensitive. Plus, I just didn't get it:

"If clerics can see the future, why don't you just do what you gotta do? I asked her one time.

"What do you mean, dear?" Sally could be obtuse, sometimes.

"I mean, y'know … there's a bad guy on Main Street tomorrow at 9:00 a.m., so you go get him. Right then, y'know? Just to give a simple example."

Sally replied with a twitch of her nose, "Ah, yes. Well, here's how it was explained to me. And this was from people like Slinker and Brick, and the others who used to do Revelator missions: the spirits don't give us solutions … they give us choices. So, for example, one of the sibyls—like Marian was—if they see a future, well, that's what you want to avoid. The mission is to prevent that. And almost one hundred percent of the time, those visions are a bad outcome. That's partly why their communications are always seen in a negative light, and why the spirits are called demons."

While I took that in, she continued, "More importantly, this is why the first rule, the precept of our religion is: You cannot see beyond a future you haven't reckoned: wherefore."

"This essentially means that your interpretation of why what you're seeing is happening is the key to whether or not it happens. Wisdom precedes Intelligence. It's a remarkable gift, what the spirits share with us. But we have to be able to provide our own context to do anything helpful with it."

"So," I offered thoughtfully, *"the protesters are right … we really are demon-worshippers!"* After which, she attacked me with several pillows in an assault that could only be met with some more sex, or *lovemaking* as she would call it.

I tried my best to act calm while I filled out their paperwork, but I was so nervous I was having trouble breathing.

I took all my possessions out of my pockets and put them, along with my shoes (minus my knives, thank goodness), into a big round plastic tray, and they roughly dropped that tray on a shelf in a wall of cube-compartments in a little room behind where the guards were sitting (backs side the X-ray machine with the belt).

I took the jacket off and put it on the belt and then walked through a metal detector (which was set off by my belt). They watched me and, as I put the jacket back on:

"Why you wear that inside out?" The guard had a slight Southern accent, so I went with my instincts and flashed back to how I acted around countless juvie officers, careful to avoid actual eye contact:

"'Oh, come one. You never seen that? 'Cause it's legit, man. See, my brand name is on the outside now, back o' my neck. Magic Man brand." That's what it said on the tag. "You know? You oughta get yourself a Magic Man coat, yo. Maybe they come in camo, ya' feel me?"

That made him smile. He mumbled an *okay* and waved me forward.

They walked me into one of those rooms with the row of booths, just like you see on TV. I didn't see much of one when I was in jail. There was no one to visit me.

I sat where they told me, and I waited.

This wasn't busy like a county jail or juvie. I was the only one there. And I waited a long time. Probably an hour. I looked around. There was just a single guard on my side of the windows, sitting in a chair, not really paying much attention, it seemed.

I was about to ask them if something was wrong; but just then I heard Marshall enter, guided by a guard, through a door on the other side. He perked up a bit when he saw me. No expression, of course. But he stood up a bit straighter.

It didn't matter. *Oh* jeez, *take care of yourself, man.* Just once, I wished Marshall could make an appearance without looking like shit.

###

His most visible bruises were healed from when I saw him last. His jaw was no longer swollen, but one front tooth was now missing; his hair was all matted and tangled and sitting on his head like a fez, or a dead animal. And his posture was so twisted and hunched over, he shambled like a zombie.

As he sat down, I offered, "Got the time?"

"I still do not have access to it." I stared at him for a moment until my brain synchronized with his. *He's talking about his* chi. *He's telling me he's powerless.*

While I was figuring out what he meant, he went on.

"Boris has been filling me in on what's happened. We've all failed."

"The girls still want your help. You have to get better and get out of here." Like I was wishing him a speedy recovery from an appendectomy or something.

"Tell them … you can tell them that they deserve better help than me." And he dropped his head and looked down at his feet. Usually when he did that, he mimicked somebody famous or told a joke. But this time, he was just quiet. Ashamed.

I thought I should leave. I mean, finish my visit, sure. Wish him the best. But all this talk about prayers and powers … I knew, I KNEW, how tortured my brother had been. His entire life! And they wanted to drag him back into this … what? Some kind of magic war?

Maybe I would go back and tell the ladies that we needed to do this without him.

BOOK TWO—CHAPTER TEN

"If you want to control a population and keep them passive, keep beating 'em over the head and let them look somewhere else, one way to do it is have them—give them a God to worship."

—Noam Chomsky on *Democracy Now!* (2011)

Blue Rooks HQ.

"Okay. Explain why you want me to keep this, again?"

Kinta was sitting up straighter than one would think possible, the way a teenager does when they want to appear older.

The question was more than fair, since Palla and her creepy new friend, "Rufepirts," was taking up her time. *This goof keeps staring at me like he knows me or something,* she thought.

They just appeared in the doorway earlier that morning at Sally's place as Sally was leaving to go to work. Sally invited them in, and then they introduced this tall, red-haired creep (who was so weak he could barely walk). As Sally left, Palla and the new guy asked if they could talk to her.

Kinta's question was about a large vial, more like a skinny jar, or a thermos, really, of thick liquid. It was a translucent red, and it smelled like chalk.

"It's a special kind of antidote. And, with Rufepirts's help—he's been working in the lab—it's been specially crafted … for you. In case you get caught up in anything bad during the convention protests, we just wanted you to be safe," Palla explained.

"I don't know about going to the protests," Kinta quickly said. She liked helping Sally just fine. But the way Palla, and especially Marshall, had been a part of the way her Dad died. She was just very suspicious.

Palla sat back and nodded, like she already knew something. She always seemed like that now … ever since the camp.

But it was that Rufepirts guy that answered. "Young one. It is everything I can do … the emotion of seeing you. And you are *so* young … look, I know Marshall very well. Okay?"

Kinta paid attention, with a skeptical look.

"And, like him, and like your Dad did (I'm told), I also see futures…"

"He wasn't like Marshall! He does … *did* vision quests," Palla added, to explain. To try and justify.

"Yes! Exactly! So do I, then. You see. So, I believe that you will enjoy a long time together, with Marshall—together, like a team!"

Kinta just cocked her head, in a puzzled fashion, as though asking why she'd want that.

He continued, "But only if you accept this gift from me."

Kinta looked at him and at the potion and then back at him. And then she shrugged her shoulders and started to open it.

They both grabbed her arms.

"NO, no no … a hahaha. No, not yet. You don't drink that … now. That's only part of the gift. The real gift is this. Kinta Ironfoot, will you take my hand?"

Kinta looked at Palla, who nodded her assurance. So, she did.

His hands were cold.

He seemed to just melt with joy in his seat at the touch of her hand. *So creepy!* she thought—but then she saw it; no, it wasn't sexual. It was more like a hug from a grandpa, his expression. He was positively joyous.

Then, out of nowhere, Palla started to intone a song from the native Choctaw religion, "Shilombish Holitopa ma!"

How did she know that? Did my dad teach her that?

At first, she allowed the music to lift her spirits, closing her eyes and remembering all the good times she had with her parents and the other gatherings she'd attended as a child that included such songs.

Then the power started to flow into her. She felt it coming in from Rufepirts's fingers directly into hers.

In her mind's eye—*or were her eyes open?*—she saw that the man holding her hands wasn't a tall red-haired Caucasian man sitting in a dining room chair, but rather a short, squat-shouldered, raven-haired *Bohpoli,* standing in the woods, under a bright sky.

"Sing, little one."

And she did, her beautiful voice echoing that of Palla's, until they diverged into glorious harmonies and the power of the stranger washed through her, wiping away her doubt.

And then it was silent. She and Palla were just sitting there. Alone.

"Where did he go?"

"He is still with you." Palla reached out and gave the younger woman's hand a squeeze.

After a long pause to try and consider the meaning of this most powerful vision quest, finally Kinta held up the potion.

"So, when do I use it?"

Another squeeze. "You'll know when."

And Kinta sighed. "Somehow I knew you were going to say that."

This was unacceptable …

The Analyst, *the Master,* once thought he was another kind of master: a master of medicine. His peers called him *brilliant.* Men laughed at his every utterance, no matter how inane. He was awarded promotion after promotion, as though it were simply the natural order of things.

And women threw themselves at him. Some went to extraordinary lengths to try and secure his sole attention.

He became wealthy by the measure of most. Certainly, he didn't want for anything. And when he requested more money of the absolute wealthiest of local benefactors, for his own causes, they gave it to him sight unseen. Such was his standing.

And he thought that was power.

But since then, his eyes had been opened. Opened to the void. The Mehkard did that for him. After he'd been shunted away by the retard, the Mehkard brought Rufepirts to him. And he explained what Rufepirts was. He also explained who "the Lost" were, and, more importantly, the role they played in the order of things. The Mehkard brought him

Rufepirts. Rufepirts brought him the visions … and, in turn, Chase had convinced Rufepirts that all he needed was to talk to the leaders. He convinced them all, their entire council, of his plan. The plan where they agreed on one particular vision.

Of course, he knew they planned to betray him once he brought them all over. He had contingencies for that.

But first things first: first, the human race needed a good purging. And thus far, he had devised a well-reasoned plan and executed it with precision.

And now it was all at risk, because of that idiot Regnant. Rufepirts had betrayed him and, worse, then *somehow* escaped his due punishment.

Simply unacceptable.

As he stepped out of the elevator, he approached the commanding officer, who was standing behind the front desk, talking with the soldier-clerk sitting there.

"Agent Chase! So good to see you, sir." The CO was a jovial bloke. Mostly the VA found him annoying, but he was supremely competent as an administrative mind, and he was a loyal middle manager. The kind of officer he could work with. "You have to hear this joke. Corporal, go ahead and tell it to the Agent."

"Well, since it's Saint Patrick's Day, I decided to wear green and start drinking at noon. In other words, it's like every other day, except I start drinking later!" And they both laughed so heartily that the VA felt obliged to join in.

"Haha, yes. Oh my. Very good! Well, Commander, I am here to personally oversee the transfer into my custody of two of your charges: Wyskald and Lastpost, the Blue Rooks Church's boys. You can keep the old one, for now."

The clerk piped up, "Boris should be in his cell, but the other one, the kid, he's got a visitor. I think he's still there."

The VA said, "What? Who?"

The clerk handed the clipboard to the commander, who handed it to the VA, who read the relevant line out loud.

"'Heychuck Smith' … *brother* …? Why wasn't I informed? Blast it! Take me there. Now!"

BOOK TWO—CHAPTER ELEVEN

HEYCHUCK SMITH

###

"How is Kinta?" my stepbrother asked through the window.

"She's fine," I said to him, unsure of where this was going. In my apartment they had gotten into a big fight. At some level, she blamed him for the death of her dad. She thought he was powerful enough to have prevented it, and he hadn't. She was just a kid, after all.

"Tell me about her … about what I told you about her. In your apartment. And what we did, what Kinta and I said to each other, after she and Sally arrived there."

And so, I recounted the story he told me of how they met at Barn Grier camp; he broke in, "She and I never talked one on one, there at the camp?"

"No, she was too starstruck, you said."

His normally dull expression had an unmistakably despairing glamour. His eyes darted around, as though searching for a hidden passage in a dark place.

"And at your apartment? What did she and I say there?"

And then I told him of the argument. *You could have prevented it! I know you could!* she had screamed. Apparently Sally and Palla had never been able to fully convince her otherwise.

At that, he just hung his head and made a low moaning sound. I remembered it. It was the sound he made after he used to bang his head against the wall to try and go to sleep. Back when we were kids.

Like air from a balloon, the entire sense of *mission*, of *purpose*, that I had brought to DC all evaporated with that sound.

I thought a long time. Finally, I asked him what was wrong.

He told me that he and Kinta had had a relationship, but it was in another timeline.

And I really didn't know what to say. I mean, even if what he was saying about time-travel was true, the relationship probably *was* all in his head. My brother? A girlfriend?

Then again, he was married once. Man, he never got over Prince.

I decided to do what a big brother should do. Time to buck up the young buck.

"Hey, if you want her, you gotta do something to get her, man. Don't be a pussy. You know?" I said, pounding the little platform on my side of the window for emphasis.

I had to look back over my shoulder at the guard to assure him things were okay.

But when I looked back, Marshall was staring at me. I watched him thinking.

Then something changed in his expression. His eyes stopped being dead. His eyes were sad again, sure, but they were no longer empty. I think I saw tears forming for a second. He shook his head no for some reason, and then said, "You are wearing my jacket. Why?" He didn't ask it like he knew the answer.

Then I realized … maybe he didn't know!

I hissed the answer to him through the window. "It was a dream! Bro, you came to me in a dream and told me what to draw on it … symbols. Some of the same ones that're in Sally's book—but I don't know. All I know is until I wrote them, I got them out of my head. Y'know, like a song—"

And then he perked up even more. "That sticks in your head. Yes. So, it was real! Yes, that is right, like a song. Exactly like a song. Where are the symbols?"

"This is inside-out. Both Palla and Sally told me to wear it that wa—"

"Show me!"

I complied, taking it off and turning it back to right-side out. My activity got the attention of the guard, and he stood up. I said, "Just a little warm!" to assure him.

He actually smiled. As Marshall looked at the jacket, hungrily, he said, "Stretch it out, on the window."

I did so, but now I couldn't see him … but I heard him start to mumble something, like he was reading … then I heard him say his typical: "Let's go here."

"Say, what are you doing?" The guard grabbed me by the shoulder and spun me around, And I let the jacket drop from the window.

And then the guard gasped!

Marshall was gone.

BOOK TWO—CHAPTER TWELVE

"How can I help being a humbug," he said, *"when all these people make me do things that everybody knows can't be done?"*

—L. Frank Baum,
The Wonderful Wizard of Oz (1900)

And like a song, all it takes is reading the lyrics and the tune pops right back into your head. That was his thought, Marshall's thought, as his astral form stood behind the guard, free.

And he was no longer exhausted. In fact, he perhaps felt even a bit giddy. It had been some time since he experienced anything like *chi.*

Astral projection. Po tried to teach him this when he was younger. She said that this was where her area of expertise and the banishing spells of the Revelator clerics overlapped. She said that they even wrote songs about astral quests in their native song-language.

And now those songs were all compiled like a symphony of arcane knowledge onto his jacket.

This astral image wasn't Marshall, precisely. Now that he was experiencing it, he felt like it was rather an after-image of him. It wasn't spancasting or banishing—it was a hybrid. Spancasting and banishing always felt something like two sides of the same coin. Now, with this attempt, he better understood how they fit together.

With this one, he had *stopped* time locally while a physical after-image of oneself was *banished* to move about in this same, suspended timeline.

This spell-song sort of shaved one's essence, like when an MRI or a CT scan looks at you a slice at a time. With the runes on his jacket fresh in his mind, he felt like this was like taking a one-micron slice of his entire being and separating it (at least that is how he pictured it) into a sort of specter of himself, and then phasing that specter to another location—not too far away—while retaining his essence.

The specter (technically, a reverse-specter, he corrected himself) had physical appearance, it was solid and visible. But while it was separated, Marshall's essence, invisible and ethereal, remained in the chair.

In a flash, his mind summarized: *I am now a ghost.*

His reverse-specter had free reign to move. It could've physically fought with and overcome the guard but moving anything physically within the Timestream was an exertion, and this was already taxing to him.

This meant that Marshall's reverse-specter could move about while the scene was frozen in time and take guard's keys and unlock his shackles, unlock the door, and so forth.

In that way, Marshall's reverse-specter, his ghost, had its run of the place …

At first blush, he wanted to free Brick, Boris, and his brother! Then he would keep the jacket and use it to hide this way.

That was what he needed. To hide.

But then he thought about Kinta … she wanted his help. They needed him.

Marshall thought about sticking around and waiting for the VA. Eventually the VA would be back to investigate Brick's and Boris's escape. And then with a cold anger branching through his brain like freezing ice, he thought about how he would fight him, once and for all, to the death.

Probably Marshall's. He still had no *chi* beyond what SanDu had given him, and he had no idea when that would run out. Meanwhile, the Analyst had a host of the *Lost* at his command. It would be a short fight.

Oh, well. At least his failure of a life would be over.

His specter-form traveled down the first hallway into a T-shaped intersection, and no sooner did he turn to the left than he froze, seeing the stationary (in time) image of the Visiting Analyst standing right before him.

###

The VA was frozen in place and looking back over his shoulder, talking to the commanding officer walking next to him.

Marshall started to panic! *What could the VA sense with his powers? Would he sense what Marshall was doing? Would he, could he, stop it?*

Of course. Yes. Yes, to all of that. He had to assume so. This meant he might have no time!

Marshall quickly adjusted his plan.

First of all, he turned around the went the other way. His search for Brick and Boris would have to be on one side of the facility only.

He ran down that hallway and looked into every window. Opened every door. Eventually, he found Brick's room and (being ethereal) walked inside, right through the wall. Strange, Brick had some kind of comfort suite. It looked more like a hotel room than a cell. *No restraints on the bed. Separate bathroom. How can this be?*

Brick's room also actually had a glass door to outside, so then he was able to walk out there carrying Brick!

It took some doing, but he did it. But this mightily drained Marshall. But after some moments to recover, he moved Brick one more time, to get him into a relatively safe place, on the other side of a building corner in a nearby alley.

The he ran back into the building and continued to look for Boris. After some time, he realized it was no use. He was too exhausted … the spell was beginning to weaken. Back in the chair on the prisoner's side of the glass, his invisible, ethereal "essence" was beginning to fray …

So, Marshall's ghost form sat at the front desk and wrote two notes. One it took back outside and put in Brick's hand, telling him what he'd done and to stay put. Then he went back inside. He put the second note into the jacket pocket and carried Heychuck out to where Brick was, too.

At that point, Marshall had no energy left. He let the specter dissipate and reanimated (and made reappear) his substance back in his chair, sitting at the visitor's window. No sooner had he finished than his head collapsed onto the little table.

The guard on the visitor's side now looked around, seeing no visitor, but seeing you had reappeared, he called out on the walkie-talkie that a breach had taken place. And he did it just as the Visiting Analyst and his CO burst in, demanding answers from the terrified soldier.

BOOK TWO—CHAPTER THIRTEEN

HEYCHUCK SMITH

###

Marshall's notes were short but sweet.

> *This is Brick Reese. Do what he says, he was the one who came up with the mission that you are helping Palla with. When it all goes down, wear the jacket. Facing OUT. :-)*
> *—Marshall*

> *This is my brother, Heychuck. The one I told you about. He is a good man, and he will help you. He knows your plan for the convention.*
> *I love you, Uncle Brick.*
> *—Butchie*

I put the jacket back on, keeping it inside-out for now. And I threw away my note in a nearby dumpster.

"Mr. Reese? Wake up!" I grabbed the old man's crumpled form off the cold ground to try and rouse him.

And with a cry, he shifted his weight and flung me against the nearest wall like I was an attacking dog. "HYEAAAH!"

"UUNNNNHH!" I hit the wall at about chair height and crumpled to the ground. *What the hell!?*

He jumped up like a trained athlete.

I also scrambled up. I always tried to keep myself in peak condition; for me, high school basketball and baseball were only a few years in the rear-view mirror, while this guy was eighty if he was a day.

But I hate to a admit, when he closed on me, I couldn't stop him.

He took me down with another *thud* and put me into some kind of jiu-jitsu hold with his legs while his arms were around my neck.

"Who are you!?" he bellowed.

"Alghlhh!" was all I could say.

But I did manage to hold out his note.

He grabbed it and pinned me down while he patted me down for any kind of weapon. Once I realized what he was doing, I raised both hands just like he was damn law enforcement or something.

Then he shoved me away and read the note, occasionally glancing my way to confirm that I wasn't making any funny moves.

He finished reading it and put it in his gown pocket. Then he started to wobble a bit. He shook his head as though trying to stay awake, and after a minute or so of me watching him try to gather himself, he just looked down at me and said, "Yeah. Sorry about that, son. Welcome to the team."

And then he passed out, falling forward, right on top of me, just as I heard heavy-booted footsteps emerging from back across the street.

It was a good thing he was so malnourished. Made him that much easier to carry. Eventually I threw him over my shoulder like some kind of fire rescue and ducked down the alley. It had started drizzling, and my splashing footsteps and heavy breath seemed extra loud, but I didn't have time to be stealthy.

I must've lucked out … it sounded like they were right on top of me before I had even taken off. But I got several blocks away, and no one seemed to be following us. I was tired, and I tried to let Mr. Reese down gently but, in reality, I sort of dumped him on the ground, lading partially on top of him in the process.

I checked him over. He was breathing fine and awake, but totally out of it.

"Po, I thought I felt you die? Thank goodness, what are you doing out here in the rain?"

I maintained a full conversation with him, posing as this Po person, as I broke and entered our way into a boarded-up former drug store named Ted's Drugs. There were no drugs, and Ted had long since abandoned this as a going concern. But I wasn't looking for drugs, just shelter.

I pulled away some boards that were covering up one window. I tossed the boards inside and then Mr. Reese and I both got through the window. Then I scooted a file cabinet over to cover the opening.

"Very clever, Po," he complimented me, "but you're dead. I felt it."

Once inside, I took even more steps to secure the front portals, wedging chairs, stacking left-behind furniture, as well as some loose boards that had been lying round, against the front door. It was several minutes of doing that. I don't know. I lost track of time. But after I finished, I wiped my forehead with my jacket sleeve and took a deep breath: "All right, Mr. Reese, why don't you and I—?

But the room was empty.

I called his name, but soon, I heard a sound around back of a window being smashed. Then yells were coming from that way, too … I ran there to see what was happening, and I tripped over someone in a full suit of body armor as I fell forward into the hallway.

"UHNNNH!" The body was unconscious. The male form was covered head to toe in military-style SWAT gear; So, I grabbed a knife from his belt holster and ran into the back room to see …

Nothing. Brick Reese had easily subdued the unconscious man's two companions. He was still holding up one of enemy combatants by the collar of his jumpsuit. Each of the three of them wore helmets with a dark, shiny black faceplate.

"They're called E-Dogs," he explained, like he was showing me a specimen from a butterfly collection. "They are agents of a government group called the Extirpacy. That's who was overseeing my containment. How much do you know about them?" He was standing up straight, and seemed to not only be in good health but even hearty.

I shook my head yes, I did recognize some of those names from Marshall's notepad notes. But the look in my eye must not have been convincing.

He nodded affirmation. "Yeah, okay. We'll get you up to speed, eventually. What town am I in?"

"Chicago."

"What is the date?"

I told him. He said, "So, it's about a week away. Blast it. Okay. Well, we'll just have to get back in there and rescue Boris. Where is Marshall, anyway?"

"Back where we just came from, with Boris. I'm not sure going back is such a good idea, in fact I suggest we get the hell out of here ..."

"Hell ... ," he mused. Then he looked at the soldier he was holding and back at me, with a smile. "This guy looks to be about my size?"

I said he did, and he proceeded to take off that soldier's E-Dog (whatever that was) uniform and put it on himself. Before putting on the helmet, he just held it in his hands and stared at it for the longest time, like he was checking himself in the black-mirror faceplate.

"What is it?"

"I used to wear a costume like this. Ran around as a sort of vigilante ... only my helmet had a special symbol on it."

In a flash of inspiration, I reached into my jacket pocket and pulled out my final paint pen.

He smiled and took it, mumbling, "Hell-Rider rides again." And he drew a little pitchfork on it.

I swear, I would've laughed, except I had seen this guy's fighting ability up close. I figured, *This old fart wants to give himself a UFC nickname? Shit, go for it.*

"So, what's our plan?" I asked.

He put on the helmet, so I couldn't see his expression. "Your instincts are probably right ... some kind of rescue attempt won't work. We aren't enough ..."

"You aren't? Really?" I said, being serious.

"No ... my strength and speed, they're from a drug they gave me a long time ago, when I was your age. It comes and goes. Always has, even then. More so now. So, it's too risky."

"So, where we going?"

"The Analyst, he liked to brag to me about his plans, when we're alone, and he was ... torturing me. Like a cartoon villain. But *from that* I know that Palla and the rest are going to need our help in Vegas ... we're going to need transportation."

"You want me to call Palla for a car?"

"Ummm, no. Let's stay radio silent. Here, I'll put some of these cuffs on you, and we'll just walk away from this facility, as quickly as we can. But in a zigzag fashion. Up one block, down the next. So, if we're stopped, I can claim to be bringing you back. Here, keep the key in your hand. Okay, you ready to go?"

"Where are we going?"

"First, to steal us some transportation."

"What, you gonna hot wire us a car?

I could hear the smile behind the faceplate. "Well, honestly, I'd prefer a motorcycle."

BOOK TWO—CHAPTER FOURTEEN

"There's a difference between prediction and prophecy. These are two words in the English language that are easily confused with each other. Prediction and forecasting is saying: "Okay, in three months' time, this is what's going to happen because this is what the data leads us to conclude, logically ... "

A prophet does something different. And it's a word to be used with care, because it's often misused, it's often misunderstood. And it's like a Biblical term, and some people react against it for that reason. But what a prophet always used to do is to say: "Listen, if we don't wake up and we don't take action, then this is what's going to happen."

And the purpose of the prophet giving this prophetic warning is not to warn people that it will happen, but to say: "Listen, you've got to change something here. You've got to change the way you're doing things. You've got to change the way that you're being. You've got to change the way you're interacting with each other. You've got to change your whole attitude. Whatever it is that you change, then the purpose of the change is so that this prophesied event doesn't happen."

—Bill Ryan, Project Avalon
"The Anglo-Saxon Mission,"
as posted on YouTube (2010)

###

"What's wrong with him?" Marshall might have heard a voice say.

"He has pushed his mind beyond all normal strains … but I will not let him die. Not yet. He has to suffer. The Mehkard … he seems to think I have no choice but to kill him, but no. This one has to remain alive, to see my ascendancy. He will see me rise to power, destroy all his allies, and after all the Regnant have come over to me, I will send him away. Then he will suffer for all eternity—the way I did—banished and alone." That was the Analyst. He was pacing somewhere near your bed.

"So, what are you going to do with him?" It was some voice, coming over the VA's cell phone. Marshall glanced up and caught a brief glimpse of an Asian-looking face on the VA's screen.

"We'll bring him with us. Along with the Englishman. Have them neutered, along with the others."

"What do you need from me?"

"If you are the one to introduce me into the negotiations, it will seem less … self-serving on my part. And you will get the benefit of having had the idea, after I 'save the day,' so to speak."

"How do you propose I do that: introduce you into a hostage situation?"

"Well, probably someone in your government has received an invitation. If not, we can make sure you have a forged one. Either way, I think you should attend. As a participant. Don't you agree, Mr. Lee?"

But then Marshall might've fallen back asleep.

###

Palla was buzzed into the building that housed the studios for KANK, a small Las Vegas community radio station. She walked into their "great room" and took her place at the forefront of the assembled persons. A few of Palla's perpetual entourage were in tow.

The great room was just that, a large room lined with shelves and shelves of CDs, organized by genre. The place smelled musty, with a faint aroma of sweat. Some of the *airshifters* (what they called their volunteer DJs) were transient and spent the evenings there, too.

Palla recognized Pharell, in his mohawk, and a few other faces. Most of the crowd assembled, standing or sitting in front of her, had frowns on their faces.

Some of her cadre of livestreamers had already been meeting and talking with them. And they had reported back to her that the group was about evenly split into thirds. One group had been convinced of her sincerity and personal integrity by her video presentations. Those folks were ready to follow her ideas for how this protest could be used to reform the Blue Rooks Church.

Another group were inclined to like her personally but were not inclined to believe that the Church would reform.

But the final group, they either believed the anti–Blue Rooks hype, or were otherwise predisposed to hate organized religion. And, it turns out, most for good cause. They either were themselves survivors of toxic religious backgrounds—gays, transgendered—or some even had personal interaction with, or had family members who had been victims of, one of the rogue Blue Rooks satellite congregations that had left the fold and started using the religion for their own nefarious ends. A few were actually survivors from abusive congregations.

Or cults.

She started her talk with them with the most assuring thing she could think of. "What happened at Barn Grier, and in other locations, must never happen again."

"So, what's your deal?" Heychuck asked, while they stopped to gas up the motorbike that they had stolen. Reese had gone in to use the bathroom.

"What do you mean?" Brick Reese countered as he returned.

"Well, I read your book while I was studying for my ministry certification, you know. I … liked it. I mean, it seemed more like an advertisement for Native American animism as a philosophy—like "We are all nature, be one with it" sort of thing—than it did a religion, really. It *was* Zen-ish. But it became an actual *church*. How? Why?"

"Well, it's a hell of a tax break." He didn't sound to be joking.

"Okay, haha, yeah; so that explains why, but *how?*"

Brick smiled and playfully slapped Heychuck's shoulder with the back of his hand as the younger man finished pumping the gas. "Hey, man. We got results!"

Heychuck just had a puzzled expression as he replaced the gas cap, so Reese explained:

"Look, it was—god, was it really almost fifty years ago? It was the 1970s. I was out of 'Nam. Done with being an attorney like my dad. I had dropped out and was still running with a motorcycle gang, The Wild Bunch. I know that sounds frivolous, and it was. But, after a while, we all grew up a bit and balanced our partying with doing some public service. Word got out we did good deeds—for a small fee.

"So, we acted as security for music concerts. Or for celebrities. But our specialty was breaking up drug rings and helping deprogrammers."

"Deprogrammers?" Heychuck asked.

"Yeah, look, around that time, a lot of cults were springing up. Young kids, young boomers—lots of girls looking for meaning outside of their bourgeoisie middle-class lives—getting swept up into being groupies for religious fanatics. You heard a' Jonestown? Like that. Everyone in those places was brainwashed. The end was coming; you had to believe one hundred percent in the leader of the cult, and—oh, yeah, to be among his favored, you had to be in his harem. Coincidentally, all the cults had that as a requirement.

"Anyway, once a child, or even an adult for that matter, was brainwashed in one of those groups back then, the most effective way to get them out and help them was literally to forcibly extract them—like a military op—and then hole them up with loved ones. Then those loved ones did their best to try and turn them around, psychologically. Those folks were the deprogrammers. Get it?"

Heychuck didn't say no, so Brick kept talking.

"I was Hell-Rider ... sort of a low-rent superhero. That was when others were cropping up in big cities, too. They got all the press. But I was out west in the desert, on the coast. Not so much news coverage except some underground fanzines. We were like UFOs or Roswell, right? Okay. Anyway, the Wild Bunch, that motorcycle gang, took me in and had my back. We did those extractions together."

Heychuck nodded again, just to let him keep talking.

"Then in '79, we lost Animal. One of our extraction missions went sideways. He was the best of us …" Heychuck stood there waiting patiently. "And after he died, I shut down a bit. Since I had my, y'know, powers, I had come to think of myself as responsible for the group. So, I blamed myself.

"Anyway, Animal's dad was Chief Storm Breather of a splinter Choctaw tribe in western Mississippi. We went there for the funeral celebration and the chief shared many things with me, in exchange for stories of the exploits of his late son.

"I came to believe deeply in their religion. And we all had vision quests with the chief. In mine, I was like John the Baptist. My role was to prepare the world for the second coming, sort of. The Choctaw call it the *Long Winter*. Or the *Third Removal*.

"Others of our group were able to use those prayers to do amazing things. It was all so life changing!

"But I was never sensitive to the spirits like that. In fact, their drugs nearly killed me. I was in a coma … and then laid up after that, for months. But when I got better, I took it upon myself to write it all down, document the amazing things we were saying and feeling and seeing, but in a 'white man's' way, so that others might be able to gain from what we were learning. And I left out the part about magic miracles. No need to complicate it at that point.

"Not everybody liked that I wrote it. Even Ruby … anyway, the Wild Bunch broke up after that. But I kept doing extractions. A friend named Bill from Animal's old tribe helped me. And, over time, most of the old Wild Bunch rejoined me … but now I wasn't the only one with powers. Using the 'spells' from their prayers, various members of the team, Ruby, Slinker, and so forth, could all do amazing things. Especially Marian. She was … her visions were so precise. Look, she had dressed up and did the hero thing back when I did, too—she got some good press in Vegas. But she did it without any special powers in the beginning. Nearly died several times. So, it was gratifying to see her be the most powerful of us by the end. She deserved it.

"Anyway, we took to calling ourselves the Revelators. As we were doing that, with my own personal resources behind it to get it into bookstores everywhere, groups of Blue Rooks (named after the picture of the bluebird on our Wild Bunch jackets, from my picture on the back cover of my book) started meeting all over the country. I tried to meet the local groups whenever we were in the area on a mission, but it was all so haphazard. Finally, we met in Rosemont, near Chicago for a convention in 1984 for the first time. And by the end of the year, we had officially organized into a religion."

He took a deep breath. "So, to answer your question"—I am always amazed how old folks can seemingly meander, but really they are spelling out stories in more depth—"people came to us hurting: psychology, spiritually, even physically. And we helped them *truly* heal! No tricks, no bullshit. And there's no advertising like word of mouth, when you've got something that works. We were doing a good thing. Kept doing good things, for the next, what, twenty years? Cults fell out of favor, but international human trafficking kept going strong. And we kept rooting it out."

I would've let him stop there, but I knew there was more to the story.

"Until Barn Grier, and the others?"

He pushed his long white hair back from his face, while a kaleidoscope of expressions cycled over his face, eventually settling on hatred.

"By the time the Revelators set out, the government had also set up a special agency to try and collect and reeducate people who were exhibiting special powers. I mean, of course they did. All that power in the hands of people with no training? The agency was officially the Bureau of Indigenous Security Enhancements, but if you knew the true history of it, that was merely the official face of a centuries old secret society called the Extirpacy."

The younger man said, "I've heard the ladies, Sally and Palla, talk about the E."

"Yes! Yes, that's them."

"Well, it makes sense. A bunch of heroes springs up, you gotta' figure a big, bad government agency was going to spring up and be your enemy."

A pause. "Enemy. Right."

"Okay, so, what's the deal with this convention?"

"Listen, I will tell you everything. But let's hit the road, okay? I don't know how long this period of energy will last, and I am, on my worst day, a better rider than you."

"Hey, we only took that one spill …"

"Yeah, and nearly killed both of us. No, we're not that far away from my place, but we need to get going."

So, we climbed back aboard our stolen wheels and set out for his house in suburban Chicago.

###

"It was never our official policy to keep people from their families, Jane, Miss Bullok."

"YOUR SO-CALLED *CHURCH*—THE DAMNED GRIER HOUSE CULT KILLED MY DAUGHTER! She was sick, an addict, and needed help, and instead Reverend Grier wouldn't let her go to a doctor, wouldn't let anyone else communicate what was happening to her, and he subjected her to brainwashing and torture. He took her on strange trips to foreign countries where she was used as cheap labor and raped, repeatedly. AND! YOU! KNEW!"

Tears formed in the corners of Palla Kalrajan's eyes.

Actually, it was worse than that. All of that was true, but the daughter was also an impressive higher-order Spancaster whose powers Jason Grier used to commit several crimes and to secure his own international sex trafficking ring, ultimately enslaving countless others into similar circumstances. *She was me*, Palla had to admit. *Nonetheless, while our internal audit did find irregularities, still …* That was what the old Palla's reply was at the time. The company line.

Instead, now, the song had changed. And the world was to bring about change.

And it started here.

"Yes, I was the CEO of the mother organization, and many officers of the church knew. And, therefore, I should have been informed. Yes."

After years and years of legal battles by Blue Rooks to avoid saying those very words, the assembled group wasn't expecting the CEO of Blue Rooks to make a veritable admission of guilt, and while being recorded, no less. But the complainant was still fuming.

"And I know there's nothing I can say to make your pain go away, or even be any less. But I will promise you this, I am stepping down from my position as CEO. And I will join you in your protest. I have arranged a press conference for the lunch hour of the convention, right in front of the building for the day of. And this, here, right now, is being livestreamed, even as we speak. So, I am on record as I tell you this: at the press conference, any or all of you who wish to speak and are able, will be able to do so. But for now, I am here to let you know that I have summoned all Blue Rooks ministers to participate in the convention for a special announcement which will change the way the Church will operate thereafter. And that that will be my last official act as CEO."

###

Later, as Palla continued to address the protestors, one of them had asked, *So, you WANT us to wreck your convention?*

It was a good question. By way of answer, Palla decided to out the mole.

I said to them, "You came into this thinking that this church, or maybe all churches, are evil. With nearly all the denominations present, you saw this convention as a logical inflection point. You would make your stand here.

"Especially with regard to Blue Rooks. You've heard stories about strange missions with child abuse and individual congregations that are run like cults rather than community organizations. And I can tell you … all of that is true, in certain places.

"Plus, you've heard rumors about a new, *unsafe* drug that is being advertised, and even administered to test subjects, right there at this convention. And that is true, too.

"I can tell you that most all of this happened without me personally knowing. But now, believe me, that isn't the case. I am now aware of it all.

"So, I have step outside of it and tackle it head on from a larger platform. I don't do this as a loner. Ms. Radisch will take my place in the church and pressure it to do better from the inside while I help you from the outside.

"But there are powerful forces lined up that want this to go forward. The government is working to take possession of all the drugs and to oversee its distribution personally. They have even made knockoffs … our original formula had only mild side-effects. Truth be told, the talk about it being dangerous was overblown. But we found out, to people who pray to the spirits, it affects their mind so they cannot anymore. And for everyone else, the faux religious ecstasy that it promotes is so addictive … well there are no official studies. But it's long term effects on society would be profound.

"But there is someone here who knows far more about the government's plans than I can say to you. Perhaps he would care to share?"

And then Palla stared at Pharell. He had stopped leaning against the wall and was starting to look concerned, eyeing the exits.

"Mr. Pharell, you may leave and report to the federal government everything I've said. It's fine. There are no secrets between those of us who understand. But you don't share that understanding. So, you have to go. Now."

And Palla shared a glance with Sally Radisch, who edged closer to the biker as he said, "I'm not going anywhere, lady. What, suddenly you're one of the good guys?"

Sally Radisch was prepared for this moment. "Agent Bard … Tim. You want to leave, because you don't feel safe here, anyway … same for your two accomplices here." She indicated two other bikers who were also agents. "After you report back, you'll feel better because the Analyst will reward you. You want a promotion from undercover work, so that will be your chance. Go on." Palla winced a bit when she heard that. She knew better than that happening. But Sally was the eternal optimist.

Pharell huffed a bit, but he grabbed his keys and hurried out without saying a word.

Everyone looked around and as Sally went up to stand next to Palla, Palla said, "Nicely done, Sally. You all see why I am leaving the running of the church to her?" Then added to Sally, under her breath, "Po would have been proud."

"Yeah, well, I think I'm going to pass out," Sally whispered back. That empathy projection was brutal, and it was completely an act of faith to even try it. *Praise the spirits,* she thought.

After that bit of excitement, the discussion continued long into the night, with the various people airing their personal grievances by sharing their stories. Palla Kalrajan listened to them all and held their hands and cried with them, and then, at the end, she offered one last thing.

"Well, thank you all for sharing. I hope this has helped you all in some small way. It is getting late, but perhaps I can lead us in a small meditation, a moment of silence in honor of all those who have been lost?" She took a small bell out of her purse.

"Now that I know all of your names, let me begin."

Heychuck and Brick entered his estate, a large three-story mansion behind a gate and many acres, well off the beaten path, surrounded by similar homes off in the distance, and the sounds of several horse farms.

By the end of the trip, Heychuck had indeed had to switch places with the old man, as Brick was suddenly so lethargic he seemed almost ready to pass out.

But as the two men approached the house, the familiar surroundings seemed to rejuvenate Brick. By the time they climbed the third set of stairs under his front door, Brick was walking normally.

At the top of the stairs, Brick quickly punched in a code, and they entered.

Once inside, he yelled to the air, "You here?"

"In the pantry!" a female voice said.

We followed the voice and inside the small breakfast room was the most attractive blonde woman Heychuck had ever seen. She was dressed in a white jumpsuit, not unlike a feminine version of the E-Dog outfit that Brick still had on.

"You get a demotion?" the blonde asked with a grin, noticing the outfit.

Who was this? Some church employee? thought Heychuck.

Brick ignored the question. "Is he here, yet?"

"On his way." She looked like she wanted to say more but, instead, glanced over at me and kept quiet.

Brick indicated the younger man as introduction. "This is Heychuck Smith."

Heychuck walked over and held out his hand. She took it and said, "I know Mr. Smith. Mr. Smith, my name is Brianna. And you're under arrest."

###

Marshall was in the back of a limousine. He had been awake for a while. The Analyst had only given him enough *chi* to keep him alive. But he had no strength to do anything but dumbly stare at the images of what was happening around him.

They had stopped dosing him for several days at the facility before they left, so his typical voices were returning. *You really shouldn't ride with strangers. Stranger danger? You're not the champion. You're not even runner-up. Batter up! What's up, buttercup? Whoa oh whoa oh whoa oh.*

But now something was different. After his time at the Unity, and after his decision to try and make a difference, he no longer felt like the voices were some external force working on him. Not communiques from outside but from within. His voices were his own subconscious mind, warning him, shouting out his deepest fears.

The codes in the threads of the suits of his captors. he could ignore them for now. The bumps in the road were absorbed by the car's shock absorbers. And he could absorb them too. The danger was from overreacting.

It was all annoying, yes. But it does not have to debilitate me. He didn't have to be on alert all the time … he just had to keep calm. *And carry on! Where's your crown?*

Marshall sat in between the Analyst and Brianna, on their side of the backseats. They ignored Marshall, as they talked about the plans for the upcoming protest, and also because they were focused on the man sitting across from them: Sir Boris. He was drugged also, as well as bound and gagged.

Marshall realized, *From the tone in their voices, they respect Boris. As a true threat. But I am just an afterthought.*

On one side of Boris was an E-Dog, with a gun trained on him at all times. On the other side was Brick. Marshall could also see from the light show that passed overhead outside the windows that they were in Las Vegas. *Welcome to Branson!* a voice suggested.

But that wasn't right. He didn't remember the flight out there, but he know they were in Vegas.

He could hear them talking about Heychuck, as though he was near, too.

"Why did you insist that we bring him here?" Brick asked the VA.

"I want Marshall to see his brother suffer," the VA answered matter-of-factly.

"But you are letting him live? He's one of us, now. You promised—"

The VA waved his hand as if to dismiss Brick's concerns. "Yes, yes. They'll all live. Even Marshall. Especially Marshall. He will remain alive."

Brick knows Heychuck? He seems better now, so why is Brick not doing anything to save us all?

But Brick avoided looking at Marshall. Uncle Brick just had that same look on his face he got when he was losing at checkers.

It had been Marshall's very first summer visit with Uncle Brick. They broke the ice by playing checkers.

Marshall beat him ten straight games. And after every one, Brick would just sit there and stare at the board for a while. "HellFuck'n'Fire, anyway," he would say. Then he would get up and leave.

After which, he'd quickly return, usually with a new cigarette, and challenge Marshall to another game.

In that way, he taught young Marshall grit.

And all the games would start the same way. "I'll go first," Brick always insisted. And then, as he'd go to slide the first checker, he'd always say, "Let's go here."

BOOK TWO—CHAPTER FIFTEEN

HEYCHUCK SMITH

###

Once our private charter jet hit Vegas, I had been turned over to the local authorities, in the city lockup. It was early morning when I awoke.

I gathered that the convention was real soon—maybe even today—but in this cell, I wasn't getting news updates.

I was still sore from the beating that that Brianna chick gave me—it was bad enough to get my ass kicked, but to get it from a supermodel half my size like that was truly humiliating. Then I silently admonished myself for the sexist thought. *Perfectly fine that she was a girl.* Funny how my conscience spoke with Sally's voice now.

How I badly wished she was with me then, with her pure spirit and straightforward approach.

Not to mention her cool new Jedi mind-trick. For example, maybe she could convince my new cellmate to take a shower.

I was still thunderstruck by how much my life had changed since Sally and Kinta had appeared at my doorstep in Seattle, with their tales of Indian magic, Blue Rooks Prayers, and my brother. They spoke of (and Sally had demonstrated) powers far beyond what I could have believed. And my brother's final adoptive family turned out to have two superheroes in it? Just, wow.

###

My cellmate kept eyein' me. And he'd even tried to start up a conversation once, but I wasn't interested. I just wanted to sit. And heal.

When Kinta just casually strolled into the detention area, outside my cell, I damn near fell off my cot. She was carrying the keys and Marshall's jacket (which had been confiscated by the Vegas PD) as she casually opened the door.

My cellmate was just as surprised as me, but he was much quicker on the uptake. As soon as she opened it, he darted out and almost knocked her over, leaving the scene.

"Don't go," Kinta said to him as he left. He ignored her.

"What in the world?"

"Didn't you hear the bomb?" she asked.

I did. I mean, I was awakened by what I thought was thunder. Or a dream. It was sunny outside, so.

"Where the protestors were supposed to gather originally, a bomb went off. No one was killed, but all available first-responders have been dispatched. That left a skeleton crew here. And Palla told me what time to show up to avoid detection, where to go to get a set of keys, and where to get this jacket from—oh, and she told me to try and stop that guy because—"

Then we both heard gunshots, and I understood.

"C'mon, this way, quick!" And she led me to a side door that led to a stairwell. She unlocked it, and we went through. We ran downstairs, and two floors below she suddenly said, "This one!" She was still following her instructions from Palla.

After we went through this one, I said, "Here, let me see that key." And outside this stairwell door, I broke the key off inside the lock. Then I nodded to her and said, "Okay. Lead the way."

BOOK TWO—CHAPTER SIXTEEN

"We always rediscover our unconscious psychic contents in other people."

—Dr. Carl Jung, "Essay on Wotan" (1936)

###

WELCOME TO THE FIRST ANNUAL CONVENTION ON RELIGIOUS TECHNORAMA: 2020 VISION IN FAITH™, said the banner in the main hall. Sally's view of it was foreshortened by her vantage point, from inside the skybox that overlooked the scene from behind.

It wasn't a large building, by convention standards, but this single hall took up most of it. Capacity was maybe three hundred. And the walls were that soft, flat, light yellow so ubiquitous in modern chapels and cheap apartment complexes.

This wasn't to be a large convention. Representatives from about twenty-two of the thirty largest religious traditions in the United States had agreed to attend. Some of them were national figures, others were merely local ministers. But along with selected guests and the media it looked to be maybe a hundred and fifty people.

The chairs were set up fifteen rows deep, in a tripartite block formation. When Sally sent Palla a picture of it, Palla commented how it resembled a Roman Legion battle formation … she was so odd now, sometimes.

It had been a masterful tag-team effort just to get the entire event set up, utilizing Sally's personal relationships with the various leaders of other denominations to at least get them on the phone, and then Palla would be in on the call to generally seal the deal.

Sally thought about those calls and about how blessed she was to be helping *her* (she had trouble thinking about her as *Palla* since her ascendance) during these times.

The calls all went about the same. No other major church wanted to be left out of this remarkable business opportunity. That was to say, opportunity for outreach/recruitment.

The early results from the Blue Joy trials were promising. It was originally developed as a depression medication—and, for that, it worked fine. But the increased interest and intensity of religious feelings in those who took it were such a powerful and reliable side-effect that its usefulness as part of spiritual counseling was self-evident. And since nearly all religions faced actuarial realities in terms of drops in attendance and participation in church (as the baby boomers aged and died), no religion could afford to ignore it and miss out on the chance to be in on the ground floor of this new drug rollout.

Blue Rooks's behind-the-scenes pitch was straightforward. Through its third-party subsidiary manufacturer, they had already underwritten the development costs. It was FDA approved, fast-tracked (even unethically so, some might say). To this day, no one was sure how Brick managed to get the government to do that.

And now they planned to mass-produce and license it to any other churches who cared to use it.

Blue Rooks had made it clear: fail to participate in this event and you would not be considered for the distribution chain thereafter.

There were keynote speakers for day one. On the morning of day two, Blue Rooks was slated to make a presentation laying out how the upcoming afternoon was going to go—this presentation was open to the press.

That was Sally's big speech.

And then, that second afternoon, a simple double-blind trial was to be conducted. Each denomination in attendance were asked to bring at least one guest who had an official diagnosis of depression to participate in the study. One half of the participants (and anyone else who wanted). Just before dinner, Blue Rooks was going to make yet another presentation, this one designed to try and persuade the entire hall to convert to the Blue Rooks' religion. Of course, no one was expected to change religions based on this, but the questionnaires that the participants would be filling out at the beginning and end of day two would be tabulated to see if religious activity was, in fact, affected by this drug.

Sure, it was 90 percent publicity stunt (since there was already data in the professional sector about the drug's efficacy); but, as publicity stunts go, it was quite clever. The media loved the horse-race nature of it—*How many would convert? Which groups were more susceptible?*—and the idea that the scandal-ridden Blue Rooks church was trying to drug its competitors into joining them led to all kinds of fodder for social media comment. Blue Rooks favorability polled at an all-time low, but its Q-score was insanely high.

And, of course, by this time Palla's own social media presence was a factor. Was she the one who was emceeing this? If so, that's worth watching all on its own, was the buzz.

National media had started talking about how her livestreaming jaunts like this were all a precursor for her making some kind of run in politics. Yes, she led a scandalized church, but that just meant she had name recognition.

The whole scene added up to that old bromide: "No such thing as bad press."

Why am I so nervous? thought Sally as she walked to the side of the large window in the wall where she stood and looked down. *Because I am not up to this. I couldn't even pull off a funeral.* She walked to the switch and shut the light off.

Then she went outside, into the predawn darkness, and got into her rental car.

She sat there, waiting for Kinta's text, until it arrived.

I have him, was the message.

She took to the dark, empty streets as she continued to think about her role in the events that were slated to happen the next few days.

Can't you tell me what will happen?

Everything is in flux. But I know you will do what's right, Palla had told her.

Eventually Sally pulled the car alongside the old busses sitting quietly next to the abandoned warehouse. The faded letters formed "Clark County School District" all over their surfaces, but they had been decommissioned and sold off many generations ago. They had been found in a junkyard and refurbished just that past month. Palla's attention to detail continued to amaze Sally.

The bus windows were dirty, and Sally couldn't make out any silhouettes until she got very close. Sally tapped on the door, and it opened with a squeal.

The driver nodded as Sally came in, and then closed the door behind her before closing his eyes to get some more sleep.

Sally stepped up into the bus and was greeted by a waving Palla, who was still lying down in one of the front row seats.

"The hall is ready," Sally reported. "And I received an email saying that the protest route has been cordoned off. Do you need anything else from me? There any news to report?"

Palla just yawned and shook her head now, as she sat up. She looked so unconcerned it almost got Sally's dander up. Sally sat down next to her.

"The media will already be inside when we get there?" Palla asked.

"Yes, I think so … so, you're literally going to drive up in busses while the police are focused on the wrong street?"

"Yep," said Palla.

When Sally shrugged in wonder, Palla leaned over and kissed her.

"I am scared. I don't want anyone to get hurt."

"It will be okay," the darker-skinned woman intoned. "Don't worry. You'll feel better when Kinta and Heychuck get here." Sally nodded and they hugged affectionately.

And only during that hug did Palla drop her facade, letting her burden emerge, as her look of concern was reflected in the opposite window.

###

It was an odd thing. Brick Reese knocked on the hotel door so hard it nearly came off its hinges. Yet he was so weak that, when the Analyst finally opened it, Reese nearly fell into him.

"What can I do for you, Mr. Reese?" The Analyst wore only a towel and was covered by a glaze of oil. He had apparently been enjoying a massage from someone (*Probably that blonde*, Brick thought) back somewhere, in the bedroom.

Brick steadied himself on the doorway. "I want my final dose now." He was dressed in the clothes Brianna had arranged for him. A long-sleeve shirt and jeans. But under his arm was tucked a motorcycle helmet with a strange, bright-amber pitchfork-like symbol scrawled on. He clutched it like a talisman.

"Ah. Are you not feeling well?" The Analyst was obviously amused.

"Now! You promised me …" Sweat glazed Brick's forehead as his mind danced with fantasies of his superhuman strength suddenly return-ing right at this moment so he could snap the younger man's neck.

But no, not until I get my final dose, the old man thought. *And not even then.* Even if the strength returned, he had to let this play out. *I owe it to Marian.*

"I said you would receive the final dose upon completion of this operation. No sooner. Now, let's get you back to your room, Mr. Reese. Here, I will make sure to have someone give you something to help you sleep. You must get some rest. After all, tomorrow is a big day for you and your church. You both will resume your full power, no?"

Brick almost vomited his agreement. Not much longer, he swore to himself.

Full power, he silently agreed. *HellFuck'n'Fire.*

###

Religious Technorama seemed to mean different things to different de-nominations. Everyone had phones preloaded with their own church's online portals and e-books. Everyone was starting streaming services. And everyone who was anyone had the means to accept donations online.

But some had truly embraced twenty-first century technology: vir-tual reality sets, Fitbit-type devices (activated by making the sign of the cross or whatever). The most popular might've been the *Pokémon GO* rip-off mobile video game, which basically was a quest to capture relics and receive virtual blessings as you went about town. Sally wondered whether or not those virtual blessings were to be found inside, as well as outside, the local casinos.

But none of the devices were being presented yet. This first morn-ing, the booths were empty tables with only a few banners. This was because, while plenty of churches sent representatives strictly to hock their wares, the deal was still the same: attendance (and the vending booths) were to be permitted only on day three after the program (and drug-trial demonstration) had been completed.

The murmur in the great hall was growing. People who had been standing in the outer hallway gradually moved into the hall and sat down as the hour approached.

Sally sat at a desk in the small anteroom off to one side of the pulpit stage. The room functioned as a green room as well as, in a masterpiece of poor architectural planning, the main throughway to a larger room beyond where all the folded chairs and foodservice supplies were stored. So, her concentration was interrupted again and again by people walking to and fro right past her, bringing new coffee cups or whatever. She wanted to be with Palla right now. As nerve-wracking as this was, what made it the worst was that she had to this alone. And, even worse, she wasn't there to help *her*.

It's okay. I really don't need any help. Palla sounded quite sure, earlier in the bus.

And so, we all have to do our part.

It was okay. Sally had given sermons before. And, fortunately for her, she always ascribed to the axiom, "It's only a sermon if it makes you think of death."

Yeah. This qualifies.

She snuck a peak around the corner of the doorway to the stage and signaled up to the skybox that they could begin coming down and giving their speeches. Various dignitaries all stood up there awaiting the signal for their special arrival.

###

The mayor had been kind enough to kick off the ceremonies. She gave a humorous and rousing speech about how her faith had buttressed her through the travails in her life—both personal and political, although there was enough overlap, it was hard to tell which ones she considered which.

Then the owner of the new professional basketball team out of Las Vegas did the same (and best of all, Oprah-style, announced that all attendees would be receiving free season-tickets for their inaugural season that upcoming fall).

Then Blue Rooks's local minister, a wonderful man named Kevin Wilkersonn got up to say his piece and to introduce Sally.

"Ladies and gentlemen, it is my pleasure to introduce, in my opinion, the best nominee for *sainthood* that I could possibly think of, the religious director of the Blue Rooks Foundation, Ms. Sally Radisch."

As she entered the stage, she glanced up and saw a familiar figure standing in the skybox.

Standing there, in a well-tailored suit, was the unmistakable gray-haired form of Brick Reese.

She was so startled that she tripped and fell, as the crowd gave a collective "OOHHH" at her face plant.

She quickly scrambled back up to look again at the skybox, but the skybox was empty.

What? He just disappeared? That can't be. Did I imagine it?

As Reverend Wilkersonn helped her to her feet, she wiped the hair from her face and her eyes, all the while gazing dumbly at the giant empty window. *Then again, he can move fast sometimes.*

In her head, she balanced the desire to sprint off and try to talk with him against the speech she was committed to giving. Ultimately, she decided that she couldn't afford the distraction.

She arrived at the pulpit and the applause slowly built again, as though cheering her ability to stand.

"And I rehearsed that walk so many times, too … ," she said, glancing back at the floor, allowing the pent-up laughter to burst forth just as it needed to.

"Thank you. Thank you. And my thanks to my friend Reverend Wilkersonn, for that delightful introduction. I hope one day I get to meet the remarkable person you described." Her cheek twitches punctuated the joke well.

"You've all been very patient, and I understand that the caterers have set up the luncheon out in the hallway, so I promise to be brief. I just wanted to address the five-hundred-pound gorillas who are both lurking in this lovely room, First, what is the point of sharing and comparing technologies in religion. And second, just who does Blue Rooks think they are to be lecturing any of us about anything given all of their recent scandals?

"Yes, that's right. Well, I can answer the second one first. Buddhism tells us that once we let go of the illusion that we are separate from everyone else, our empathy not only rises for others, but also for ourselves.

"I am reminded of a short story. A recreant who had fled from a life of crime and shame in his younger years in order to start over, resolved to dig a tunnel so that villagers no longer need to use a road that hung over a cliff. This was to save the various people with carts who would inevitably plunge to their death each year.

"By day he would beg for his alms, and by night he would dig. After nearly twelve years he was very near his goal—the tunnel was a thousand feet long, and it was almost done. In fact, the story of his digging had made him famous throughout the region. People would come from far and wide, just to see the tunnel and to support him with charity.

"But, in his final year of the project, the son of a man he had murdered during his mis-spent youth arrives and tells him that he will kill him.

"'That is proper. Just let me finish my work before you kill me.' the older man says.

"And so, the younger man not only forebore, but he helped the recreant finish the digging, reasoning this would enable him to exact his revenge that much earlier. All the while, people kept giving to the recreant and singing his praises. For his part, the recreant always only accepted the gifts but not the praise, knowing that he had done much evil in his life.

"When the tunnel was finally completed, the recreant said, 'All right. You may exact your revenge, now.'

"But when it came to it, the younger man merely said, with tears in his eyes, 'How can I cut off my own teacher's head?'"

Sally paused for effect. "It is in that spirit, that, on behalf of the Blue Rooks Church, I am here to announce several things. First, we have reached settlement on all outstanding civil cases against our organization for negligence. We were wrong to not more closely supervise and oversee our individual ministers. Their preaching any kind of ministry which would condone child labor, child abuse, or the worshipping of questionable entities is contrary to both our teachings and to our future. We will root out any such remaining ministers that remain.

"Second, though our marketing partners, we will be offering the new pharmaceutical *at cost* to any other denominations and their healthcare facilities. We, as a nonprofit, obviously are not going to make any profit, and we never were. But in addition to that, all our supply-chain, from the manufacturing lab to the distributors, will also be transitioned to nonprofits. The entire process will be run entirely on donations, from now on. Now, that isn't to say that your partnering healthcare organization cannot profit from it. But we won't be.

"And third, I wanted to let you know that our CEO will be broadcasting a special announcement later during this convention. I cannot divulge her location. But it will be a profound statement. And I look forward to viewing it with you.

"Finally, I needed to answer the other question: Ultimately, what is the point of all this?" She waved her arms toward the assembly for effect. "The point is Blue Rooks isn't in this alone, any more than any of you are. And all of these technological advancements are really just more technical ways of doing what we, in the ole' religion business have always done: bringing people together. And so, we have to have empathy for one another, as people, and as churches. And if Blue Joy can help dig a tunnel through which all of the congregations can arrive at better outcomes, then I hope you all will join us in that effort.

"Thank you, and blessings to all of you. This is just the beginning."

And Sally walked off to strong applause.

This is just the beginning, she repeated to herself as she left the hall in a hurry to see if that really was Brick. Over her shoulder, she heard Reverend Wilkersonn tell the crowd it was time to break for lunch.

She didn't have far to go. When she walked out to the front lobby, she saw Brick stood across the street, in the small empty parking lot of a professional building. He was just standing there, sipping a coffee from a to-go cup, leaning against a big black van.

She smiled and waved and ran across the street to say hi. *This is so amazing! I wonder why she didn't tell me Brick was going to be here?* But as she approached, she felt the hairs stand up on the back of her neck, and she slowed. Brick's expression was unreadable.

What was going on? is what she asked as she eventually got to Brick and gave him a hug. He smiled, of course, but he didn't let go of the hug.

She thought she felt a pinprick on her thigh as Brick held her fast. She heard the van door open, and she smelled the odor of leather gear and equipment accompanying the shadowy figures who emerged … and then she was asleep.

###

She is the Unity. She cannot be opposed.

The Visiting Analyst's argument with the leader of the Regnant was by way of meditation … allowing his mind to embrace a theta-state while the half-heard, fractured voices of the *Lost* spilled snippets of "truth" to him. He hated doing this, hated doing it this way. But he had to know more about his enemy … he needed more data.

"She is just a woman," the Analyst whispered into the darkness.

She is the Unity, the Alpha, and the Omega.

No, she's not. She's a former child-whore who's powered-up now just enough to be a goddamned YouTube celebrity, he thought. But instead, he whispered, "You must know how to remove her." Of course, he knew that none of his thoughts escaped the notice of the Regnant Lord. But it helped him to whisper the direct questions, for emphasis.

In your form, in your Timespace, she is human.

The Analyst waited silently.

If the Unity were fully brought to bear in that form, her mind … it would fray.

"Fray? You mean, be driven mad … like me, right?"

And this time it was the Regnant Lord who said nothing.

It was okay. He knew what the Regnant thought of him. They all thought he was a tool. The Mehkard's tool.

Until he pulled each of them over and ate their fucking minds.

Bastard, he thought. *I can't wait until you get here, and we'll see who gets* frayed. *I can't wait to offer the Mehkard your happy, shiny, lifeless corpse as a gift, too …*

But first things first, the Analyst decided.

What an odd expression, the Regnant Lord teased, touching Brendant Chase's mind, ever so slightly, forcing a freezing cold shudder to run down the Analyst's spine …

Why would you do things that way?

Then the circuit was cut, with a strange knocking sound pounding the back of his mind. The Analyst slid out of the chair, which rolled away from him, as he collapsed in a heap on the floor.

He grabbed the handkerchief from his jacket pocket and wiped his clammy brow. The hotel room was dark. He had drawn the extra-thick curtain to prevent the sunlight. But now he rose to the window and flung them open, wanting to see the day. The window didn't open, but he breathed in deeply, as though it were a cleansing breath.

The knocking noise kept reverberating in the back of his mind.

He looked around. He had a view of the neighboring hotel and its own stacks of rooms. He hated the Regnant Lord. The Demon claimed to be a champion of *life.* But he knew that was a false promise. That *life* represented by the demon was merely another form of chaos. Brutish and fleeting. The strong feeding upon the weak, until they themselves were the meal of another … *I will beat you at your own game. That's what the Mehkard saw in me—I will bring the Great Death. And the Order that follows will produce true life.*

Another knock on the door. *Wait, that was real!* This one was tentative, probably wondering if he was waking his superior.

"Who is it?"

"A report, sir."

The Analyst opened the door to accept the electronic pad from the agent. Saying nothing, he closed the door and walked back into the room and sat alone on his hotel bed. He unlocked the e-pad and listened to the latest report from Brianna.

It was timed only ten minutes ago.

"Sir, an explosive device was set off along the route. All local first-responders are there, now. But it wasn't Pharell. He was outed and returned to our commend center. He said they still planned on using the route, but right now it is completely empty. They must have gathered elsewhere. But our chopper reconnaissance hasn't spotted them.

"And, sir, he reports that CEO Kalrajan has taken over the protest group."

The child-whore? he thought. *She's taking such an active role? That will help me with the Regnant Lord's idea. Fine then.*

"Hold for instructions," he typed back into the pad. *I don't care if I sacrifice all of them to overwhelm her … there will be plenty more Lost Ones to bring over, once I kill everyone here afterward.*

The Analyst quickly summoned one of the *Lost.* The dJinn dutifully appeared to stand before its Master, towering over him but with head bowed. The Analyst could *feel* the enmity emanating from the being, but it didn't matter. In fact, it just made him enjoy this all the more.

Show me, he thought, as he forced it to show him visions of Kalrajan, of Brianna leading her squadron of E-Dogs, it's on a street, but the images were jumbled—he never learned this skill … for him, it was always much easier to manipulate the raw energy. These fine-tuned manifestations, especially the choicifering. It all seemed so *pointless,* at least for one who had the power to make anything he wanted to happen, happen.

It didn't unfold for him the way it did for others. He knew that. But he caught glimpses. *Reese would attack some random Indian girl. Why? Then Brick would betray him. Of course. That was fine. We know who you really are, don't we? But that was too far. Back up a bit. An E-Dog bringing CEO Kalrajan into the hall. Someone watching a livestream of Kalrajan standing on an empty street, facing down Brianna … in front of big yellow what? Aha! And he tapped the orders into the pad, complete with his electronic signature.*

'File your undercover agents' reports vis-a-vis anti-terrorism protocols. Have the choppers look for school busses. Take your squad and cut her them off before they can reach the convention hall. Bring CEO Kalrajan to me at the convention, in custody. Disperse the rest."

Damn this Kalrajan woman! To think she can upstage me, who does she think—

Then there was yet another knock on the door.

"JESUS! Who is it?"

"It's me."

The Analyst opened the door, and Brick Reese stood there once again. And, once again, he was barely able to stand. The effort it took to meet with Sally, just routine walking, talking, that little bit of action—

even that wiped him out. Each session with the Analyst lasted longer than the last. But once these infusions reach a serum-level it was supposed to alter his DNA … he had his biologists explain it to him. It will work. It *had* to.

"It's time. You promised."

The Analyst let his head bow for a moment, before gathering himself and meeting Reese's gaze with his typical smirk. "So I did. You bring your gear?"

Reese showed him the truss and various arm and leg restraints.

The VA waived him in. "Very well. C'mon, let's get this over with."

As Reese went over to the bed to begin strapping himself in, the Analyst went to the closet and retrieved the IV unit that he had brought on the trip. He began assembling the metal stand and pulled the bag of the Q-101 prototype from his luggage.

The VA silently admired Mr. Reese's constitution. There was a part of him that thought he wouldn't survive the dosing regimen. Each one was more painful and dangerous … with this final one being the worst.

But after that, after the last one, Brick Reese should recover his full functionality. With no lapses. He'd still be in the body of an eighty-year-old, the enhanced strength didn't mean his bones wouldn't break, for example … but, for the first time in six decades, he'd have no more bouts of incapacitation.

Reese had fastened himself in except for the final arm and laid there like a junkie, barely able to hang on. The VA knew from experience that he would have to refasten all the gear due to Reese's trembling and frailty.

"Let's see, Mr. Reese. Where did we leave off last time? I believe I was regaling you with stories of just how much I was going to enjoy seeing your petty church be dispersed to the four corners of the Earth."

Brick's head shot up from the bed so he could see the VA's eyes: "But you'll let them live! You promised that. And you're precious *Order* won't allow you to break that promise. Boris, Palla, my godson. All of them. You will let my people live, right?" *Brick spoke from the certainty of the many visions Marian had had over the years, too.*

"Yes, yes. Neither I nor any of my legions of the others will harm them," the Analyst assured, as Brick let his head back to rest. *Of course, that just means they'll be alive to see millions, BILLIONS of others perish,* he thought. And the VA stood at the doorway with his eyes closed, trying to imagine all the glorious screams from the multitudes as they perished.

Oh, well, I'll have to settle for just these screams for now, he thought referring to Brick.

Then he closed the door, after hanging the sign: *DO NOT DISTURB.*

BOOK TWO—CHAPTER SEVENTEEN

HEYCHUCK SMITH

###

Next day. Sunrise.

I was still in my orange jumpsuit—it had been a long time since I'd worn one of those. I hated it. But after Palla asked me for Marshall's jacket, I gave it to her. So, I was back to my jumpsuit. I was visibly displeased.

One of my companions on the bus had loaned me a brown and black bomber jacket for normalcy. He was a kindly older African-American gentleman, former military. He said something about having plenty of other layers on, anyway. I thanked him, and he returned to his wife's side a few seats ahead of me.

The fellow protestors (thank goodness at least a few of them knew how to drive a bus) filled mine and the other bus, as both busses set out.

Palla had been talking to Kinta in the front seat. Eventually, she came back and sat next to me.

"How are you feeling?"

"Gee, I don't know, how should I feel? Damn it! I go there, risk everything to take that jacket to him. And he does some magic shit *just so* he can give it back to me. But don't worry, 'cause he tells me *trust Brick* ... and then I find out Brick is working for the government, too! And to top it off, I end up in jail for my trouble, only to be broken out and given the jacket back—which you then take!"

"This must all be so difficult."

"I trusted you!" Some people turned their heads to see why this upset convict was yelling at their new savior. *Fuck them.* "And now I've got a record again, my brother is no better off than before, and here I am, following you into what I hear tell might be a war zone!"

I knew that Sally would not have approved of me giving Palla the business this way. But I was righteously angry.

Thankfully, all the little phone camera paparazzi were up front, talking to themselves and giving Palla a rest. Or else all her followers would have had to confront my anger, too. A few of them did glance to see what was up.

"You're right. I had no right dragging you into this. But I am trying to do the best I can …" She just trailed off, shaking her head. For the first time since I had first seen her online, she was at a loss. And my heart panged at that. Like sometimes when you win an argument with your girlfriend—not really a win.

Then *SCREEEECH!* We both crashed into the seat in front of us as the bus's brakes hissed us all to a sudden stop.

It was a blockade. The other bus in front of us was stopped, too. We could see a few flashing lights from over in front of it, but we couldn't see details.

Palla didn't hesitate. She walked to the front and turned around, telling everyone, "Wait here." With a quick glance at me, she exited.

I personally was done taking her orders. Plus, I was the one on the lam. I decided to strategically remove myself, to get a better view, or to flee, if it came to that.

I left out the emergency exit in the tail end of the bus and slunk off to the side behind some cars, joining in with the bystanders on the sidewalks.

The blonde agent who kicked my ass, Brianna, was in front of the first bus, with a phalanx of black SUVs. She stood on one of them, rather dramatically. About a dozen agents wearing those full face-plate helmets were exiting their vehicles and assuming some sort of formation on the street in front of her.

Along with Palla, there were about a half-dozen protestors who had gotten out of the first bus, with more streaming out afterward. I saw that the bus behind them was following suit. Within a few minutes all hundred or so of the protestors were gathered in a big crowd behind Palla.

Two things I noticed: the kids in Palla's entourage were, of course, filming; Kinta was nowhere to be seen.

Brianna was looking at some sort of pad and talking to it, as though receiving instructions. Finally, she rolled it up and slipped it into her belt holster, with her other various weapons.

"Ms. Kalrajan, I am Agent Carson of the FBI. And you are under arrest! You are to come with me! My agents will process and detain the other protestors until local law enforcement arrives to assess which, if any, among the group, took part in the terrorist bombing along the actual protest route!"

"It was me! Only me," Palla responded. "And no one was hurt! The bomb, which I had built, was filled with pamphlets. Like this one!" And she held up a piece of paper. "Do you want to hear what it says?"

"NO! Agents?" Brianna ordered, and the E-Dogs started forward to arrest them all.

Palla took a step back. Not because she was afraid for herself, but because she was afraid for her assailants if they got too close. "It's only three short words: BLUE. JOY. KILLS!" And as she said that, the protestors began chanting those same words:

"BLUE. JOY. KILLS!"

"BLUE. JOY. KILLS!"

And as they chanted, they lifted their signs and began moving forward themselves, beyond Palla, eventually settling into marching around her in a circle, chanting their chant over and over again.

If the E-Dogs were going to get her, they had to go through the crowd and their revolving march.

Palla seemed to be continuing saying something, but she couldn't be heard over the chant. Probably it was for the benefit of the recording that her entourage was making inside the maelstrom of protest, I decided.

The edge of the swirling crowd was only ten feet or so from the row of E-Dogs. And another six feet behind that, Brianna looked over the entire scene.

I expected violence. Certainly, the crowd did. Even as they marched, they cowed as they approached the agents. But then the E-Dogs did something strange.

Rather than move forward and simply arrest everyone, they joined hands and began saying a chant of their own. I couldn't make it out at this distance, but after about a minute or two of it, the protestors started walking slower and slower. *Wait, it was another of those spells!*

Eventually, there was hardly any noticeable movement at all in the crowd. At that point a smaller group of four or five agents, guns drawn, moved easily through the crowd toward the ladies and the filming kids.

I instinctively started to move toward the group to protect them, but someone grabbed me from behind.

It was Kinta, holding my arm with both hands and shaking her head. She was wearing Marshall's black jacket, right-side out, with all the bright yellow runes standing out like neon signs in the grayness of the scene.

"No. Palla told me. I have to get you away from here!"

I pulled my arm free in anger. "I don't care what she said!" And I ran into the the crowd, trying to get to the center as quickly as I could.

But then just as the closest E-Dog grabbed hold of Palla, I could hear Palla's voice yelling, "No! Don't hurt them!" *What does she mean? Is she talking to the soldiers?*

Then I thought I heard distant thunder, and I saw Brianna suddenly bark out a *no*, and she started staring at the air above the scene like she was seeing something horrific. She was agog, looking at her troops.

Then she and I watched as the guard that touched Palla, and all of the other guards who had been advancing, suddenly fell to the ground like discarded puppets.

A couple of the kids who were quicker on the uptake than I was began bending down and taking the soldiers' guns. Thinking that was a pretty good idea. I helped them—

"No! Be careful, don't point those at anyone!" was Palla's urgent warning.

But it was too late, Brianna had leapt down from the top of the SUV and done a running vault from the font hood, doing an acrobatic leap and landing inside the circle with us.

She quickly disarmed the two kids with the guns and knocked them both unconscious.

I leveled a third gun at her, and she kicked it upward as my shot fired into the sky. Then she punched me in the throat, and I collapsed, gasping for breath, feeling lucky my windpipe hadn't collapsed.

Brianna quickly spun around to face Palla. But Palla was able to say something to her first:

"You took the drug, didn't you? You saw them! And they're watching you, too, Brianna. Everyone is."

Then Brianna looked where Palla was pointing, at the kids holding up their cell phones, recording her efforts.

And in that moment, Brianna seemed hypnotized. She was *frozen*. She just stared at the *cameras*. And Palla kept on:

"I *know*, sister. They watched me, too. The pictures,

the people *seeing* us,

naked,

alone,

angry,

scared,

so, we strike out, any way we can, to stop the pain …"

Then Palla reached up, and I could see Palla crying! And as Palla gently touched Brianna's cheek, she said, "How do you want to be *seen*, Agent Carson?"

And Brianna cried out, like a child. Brianna crumpled to her knees, holding her head in her hands and gently crying, "No, no, no no!!" Whatever Palla had done to her, it was still happening …

Other E-Dogs who had been back near their vehicles broke ranks and began knocking over the various people in the once again milling crowd. They were working their way toward their leader, thinking she was in trouble, and arresting everyone in the crowd along the way. But now, suddenly, it was dark all around us, like a fog. It was raining openly.

I could see the distraught look on Palla's face while the sounds of police sirens from off in the distance also added to the sense of dread.

"C'mon!" It was Kinta again, pulling on me. This was hopeless. I had nothing else in me.

I could see Palla nodding her agreement. "Go see Sally," she said.

And so, I dumbly nodded to Kinta. *Yes. Take me to her. Out of this.*

The last thing I heard as I fled was Brianna Carson's voice yelling, "I will KILL YOU for that!" The dirty-colored storm began to rage in response.

BOOK TWO—CHAPTER EIGHTEEN

"FUTURE PUNISHMENT: See PUNISHMENT, ETERNAL"

—Orville J. Nave, Chaplain,
Nave's Topical Bible (1896)

\###

Two hours later.

Bartholomew Richard Reese stood proudly before the assembled crowd to a long round of applause. It wasn't approval exactly, but it was more than just polite—this was because he was a true celebrity. Despite his advanced age, his notoriety was on a par with movie stars and political leaders. The resume said it all: Vietnam vet, attorney, playboy, super-hero, author, speaker, religious icon.

But that had been undermined recently. The scandals had not undermined the church, but they had marred his legacy. *I am the Church,* he had once told Palla in anger. But deep down he meant it. But because of his advanced age, the cycles of energy from the residual Q-47 in his system had become so erratic that he could essentially never be counted upon for an appearance, or an engagement. He was a shut-in, an invalid. And, therefore, unable to properly defend himself. The few times he did try to make appearances for PR purposes, even those he managed to sway treated him like a doddering relic, a symbol of a simpler time.

But that will all change today, he thought. He woke up feeling like his old self. He entered the hall hours early and mingled with the attendees with a vigor that became the talk of the hall.

Brick Reese is back. Hasn't he been sick? He seems good now.

"Ladies and gentlemen. Welcome. My friend and coworker, Ms. Radisch was not feeling well—and I was! So, I am more than happy to fill in. There has been a slight adjustment to the program, and that is why I had the doctors make their presentation first thing this morning. I believe you all would like to go ahead and conduct the Blue Joy trials *as soon as possible.* I say this because I have spoken to many of you, and this means that you all will be able to show each other your wares that much earlier, yes? So, I think we will just do that. Okay? Okay. Great.

"So, we have some of our scientific folks lined up to speak with you. And then, I have a special guest to speak with you in exactly one hour. After that, the trials can begin and perhaps even be done before lunch. And thank you again."

Brick excused himself to the sound of the light rock music playing over the loudspeakers. He walked offstage into the small hallway where Secretary Itiorvic waited.

"Hello, Stan. You ready for your big speech?"

Secretary Itiorvic stood in his black suit like a conquering hero. *Does he guess? I haven't told anyone I'm announcing my run for the presidency except family.*

"I am. Why, look at you! Dr. Chase told me you were doing better, but you look twenty years younger."

"Clean living. Where is your Secret Service detail?"

"I told them to hold back. With the Extirpacy here, they would just get in the way. Besides where could I be safer, what with all these believers around me?"

"Well, I'm the wrong person to ask. I've always been a professional catastrophist, Stan—lived in a world of worse-case scenarios since I don't know when. But maybe you're right. Maybe this is the beginning of a new dawn. Anyway, well, I will be back in a moment to bring you out." And Brick clapped the secretary on the arm like they were buddies, even as he held his tongue and walked past, thinking, *what a tool,* the entire time.

Doesn't he know Lee has all the inside party support already? And I saw Lee in the audience … that must be why he wants to announce to-day. To undercut Lee.

Brick went out back. Parked back there was the black SUV that he had arrived in, as well as two others. Seven agents, total, inside those vehicles. And leaning against the lead van was the Visiting Analyst, staring up at the sun through his fancy shades. He failed to note the sudden clouds gathering off in the distance.

Another unmarked, white van was also parked out back, off to the side. To a passing bystander, there would be no reason to include that vehicle in the scene. Two agents had slept in the cab, with two plain-clothes agents outside, in the nearby alley, doing surveillance.

Inside that van, three friends, two males and one female, were bound and sedated.

"It's about time to begin," Brick said to the madman, who paid him no mind.

Wake up, Marshall! You are needed.

You're trapped. They're gonna kill you. Will you ever stop being useless?

He had to admit: the counterpoint voice seemed to be more on point. Marshall squinted to make out his surroundings and replied, "Well, you are not wrong, Big Dicky. I am strapped to a gurney. I am in a truck. And I am too tired to do much about it." He said all that out loud, just as Grandma had taught him. Replace the assumptions you were hearing from the voices with *facts.*

Psychosis manifests as worst-case scenarios and conspiracy. *You might as well give up. Useless!*

But Marshall thought about it. And then he thought about the stakes. And he eventually decided: *No. I am not giving up.*

Good.

Sally?

And Boris, m'boy. Don't leave me out.

If Marshall could have, he would have wept with joy. Sally continued:

It was Palla, Marshall. Po studied her entire life, but she never had the advantage of studying under the Unity. She worked with me to teach me the prayer book. This means that while Po's abilities stopped at empathy, mine are stronger, purer.

You read minds?

For a short time. It's really tiring … but after I woke up in here, I decided to exert myself.

Butchwald, can you get us out?

Can't you?

No, he has already dosed me. Since right after I was captured. I cannot summon my chi, cannot speak to the others. Nothing. And then he's dosed me up with antipsychotics on top of that. You've talked with me! I can barely hold a conversation without tripping over my own drool.

He's that afraid of you?

As well he should be, boy, if I ever got free.

Marshall, listen—this was Sally—*he plans to dose you, too. In front of everyone. As part of the trials inside the convention. I caught a glimpse of their plans. He no longer wants to destroy the drug.*

The VA is planning that?

No, Brick.

And the thought of Brick's betrayal stabbed through Marshall's consciousness like a spike.

I know. I know. I still can't believe it … but it seems he's struck a deal with the VA. Their original plan—of the drug being distributed per normal—is moving forward. The deal was for none of us to be killed. And the Church can continue. And …

And what, Sally?

He's been returned to full health. The Blue Joy was originally created to be a way for his original Q-47 to become perfected. No more weak spells. It never worked quite right. But with more tinkering they developed a strand of drug that will fix Brick's intermittent weakness. He's obsessed. It's all he cares about.

Marshall had to digest this. But only a few moments later, *Listen, I have to tell him … the drug trial can't go forward. It won't just stop magic, it will kill all the dJinni! The magic is part of their reproductive cycle!*

A pause. *You're sure.*

YES!

Another pause. *He's going to take you in, Marshall. Whatever you're going to do, do it there. In front of everyone. I know Palla is planning that.*

And that's what Grandma had always seen. I'm supposed to save everything aren't I?

Yes, m'boy, Boris jumped in. *I never was told the details, but I do know that's why we pushed the envelope with you. You were to be trained. That's one thing you and I have in common.*

And then Marshall started to cry.

See here, lad! Breathing through these tubes is hard enough without all the blubber, yes?

But Marshall didn't stop. He kept crying. He couldn't stop. All the voices were right. All the visions were for nothing. He was no hero.

Sally had already stretched herself to the breaking point. The link she had established would have been difficult to maintain half this long, even under ideal circumstances. In this situation, her psyche was about to burst.

Marshall, listen to me. What do you fear?

I don't know. Myself. I don't want to kill anymore.

Marshall. I have a riddle for you. Ready? Five blackbirds are on a phone line and four decide to fly away; how many are left?

One?

No. All five are still there! They only "decided," you see: they didn't actually leave! Listen to me, Marshall, you are not a born killer, any more than you are a born hero. It's easy to get muddled, because we are always dealing with prophecies and visions. But our religion's precept gives you the clue: "You cannot see beyond a future you haven't reckoned: wherefore" means you give meaning to the futures you choose. But choosing doesn't mean anything until you ACT. Behavior is truth. The people who have acted with love toward you, they love you. Unintended consequences and all. Now, go do what you do.

What is that?

Love others …

But, Sally, what do I do about the Analyst?

Sally??

I waited, but Sally didn't reply.

And now I noticed: one of the machines was humming a steady *beeeeeep*. There was one less person's breathing sound echoing through the trailer. And while I couldn't hear his thoughts any longer, I was able to hear Sir Boris weeping for Sally's passing in the darkness.

BOOK TWO—CHAPTER NINETEEN

HEYCHUCK SMITH

###

We managed to avoid capture in the confusion, but Kinta just wanted to huddle in safety. I insisted we move on.

"Where are we going?" she asked.

"The convention."

"Why?"

"Whatever is going to happen, it's gonna happen there." *And Sally is there. I never should have let her go away.*

###

We had time to go into a deluxe gas mart that sold some Vegas touristy clothes. I had on UNLV sweatpants and a Vegas T-shirt with all kinds of brightly colored iconic images, dice, and Vegas strip signage silk-screened onto it. At least it was no more jumpsuit.

Under her Marshall's black jacket, Kinta was already wearing the polo shirt and khakis of convention personnel that the protestors had managed to obtain (with Palla's help).

When we got to the little convention center building, I noticed a suspicious cluster of black SUVs parked across the street in an empty parking lot. I suggested we walk together around behind the building to check it out what was there.

Back there was just this one white van. A group of vagrants, one was African American, the other three where white, were all leaning against the building alongside the adjoining alleyway.

"Okay," she said as started to walk away, toward the front to go inside and enact our plan. But I held onto her sleeve and just nodded for her to watch. And after a while, one of the vagrants lifted his hand like he was wiping drool from his mouth … and spoke into his wrist.

The other guy pressed what looked to be an earpiece and said something back.

Oh, boy.

She saw it, too, so I told her, "Go on in. Go to work, but let me in the front as soon as things start to hit the fan."

"But when will that be?"

"You'll know when," I said.

"I wish people would stop saying that."

Kinta suddenly sprung up and said, "That reminds me!" And she started rifling through her pockets, jacket first. She stumbled upon something, a thermos of something and then, "Here it is! Maybe you should take this?" And it was the book of prayers. Palla had apparently placed it into the jacket pocket at some point.

"What do I need that for?"

"To give to Sally."

She was right. I took it.

She was about to go in and start helping them set up, but suddenly, most of the black SUVs that were out front of the building pulled around to the back, near the back exit.

We both watched as some of the agents got out and went inside.

We kept waiting, watching. Some tall dude in sunglasses who was the only one *not* dressed like an agent, with the whole helmet thing, got out and stretched his legs, eventually settling into leaning against the lead van, like he was soaking up some sun.

Then I'll be damned if Brick Reese didn't emerge, and they began talking … they and two agents started toward the white van right as I felt it.

No. It was like a flood of emotion. *Sally.* Something was wrong. Something …

Next to me, Kinta actually had to stifle a cry of pain. *She feels it, too?*

Off in the distance, we could see that the VA felt it, too—he hesitated so obviously that the other agents and Brick stopped. And then the VA ran toward the van.

They extracted a female on a medical gurney from the back.

It WAS Sally. I knew this. She was gone. Tears started forming in the corners of my eyes as I thought about what could have been but now would never happen. Kinta wept openly.

We could also see Brick's form hovering over Sally's dead body for a moment. There was yelling coming from inside the van, too, and Brick looked up. The yelling sounded … British? Two agents stepped up in there to deal with whoever was yelling.

Brick angrily jumped in after them and the next thing I saw, their bodies flew out of the back of the truck trailer so that the VA had to duck to avoid being hit by them. He lost his shades in the attempt.

By this point, every single one of the remaining agents had taken notice and were hurrying to the VA's aid. With a wave of his hand, sparkly clouds gathered around him and the door to the back of the van suddenly slid shut, and then the VA hurriedly latched it shut.

The VA then turned to his agents and gave them various orders.

We then watched as they pumped some kind of gas into the van. They waited for a good ten minutes before opening the trailer and extracting Brick. His body was limp. They put some shackles on him. They also shacked some other old guy with a big red-and-white beard, who had been on a stretcher.

And then they brought out Marshall. They brought him out and started strapping him to a wheelchair that they hurriedly brought out from one of the black vans. Apparently, they needed him for something.

The VA barked a few more orders and went inside, with the entire company of helmet-headed E-Dogs following close behind!

Then one of the white vagrant-dressed agents finished strapping Marshall into his wheelchair, while he said something to another one, the black one, who kept his gun trained on the two sleeping old men.

I told her to take off Marshall's jacket and to run around the front and carry it with her inside. She should try to make it out the back door as soon as possible. And, while she was in there, she could maybe show Marshall the jacket the way I did in the facility. Either way, as she popped out, she would be a distraction for me, I figured.

It wasn't much of a plan, but she nodded and sprinted away.

I didn't know what else to do. There was no way this was going to work … I mean, I was a non-cleric with a spell book. They had semi-automatic weapons.

I just had to have faith.

I began purposefully walking toward the agents and their charges.

But then, before they even noticed I was walking toward them, the agents all took all of their charges inside the building, with the door shutting and locking behind them.

So now I had to go around front, too.

###

I had no sooner emerged from around the side of the building than an E-Dog agent in full helmeted regalia stumbled upon me and stopped to train his weapon at me.

"Put your hands up!" The voice was altered, scrambled like they were in witness protection or on *Dateline* or something.

I complied, and he proceeded to march me back toward a group of his comrades that were gathered in front of the building.

Brianna stood among them.

And next to her was Palla!

I smiled at her, but she avoided my gaze, looking instead intently at Brianna.

When another agent who had gone around the other side of the building returned from his reconnaissance, Brianna gathered them all around her.

Brianna seemed poised for violence as she looked at her companions. But from time to time she would exchange a glance at Palla, and then she would visibly relax. She seemed indecisive about something.

"Gentlemen, I have a very special mission for you. It is this. I need you to stand down. By my count, there are six covert E-Dog operations taking place around the world right now. A total of eighteen agents. You five are with me. So, that is less than two dozen total, other than those who are currently inside with the boss.

"If you set foot in that building, the Visiting Analyst will order you to take a drug. And that drug will remove your ability to speak with the *Others*, make it so that you are unable to use your powers. It is his intention that all E-Dogs no longer have powers."

"I am asking for your loyalty. I mean for you to stand down. Holster your weapons, turn over your comms, and then stay out here and stand guard, let no one in or out, until I give the order. What is your answer?"

They all looked at one another. One started to say something but then thought better of it. Finally, the oldest one raised his weapon ever so slightly and said, "I'm sorry, Agent Carson, but I need to get verifica—"

Brianna disarmed him and caved his helmet's faceplate in with the butt of his own rifle before he could finish the sentence. Per their training, two more started to engage here, more or less due to muscle memory, not because they really wanted to fight, and she dispatched them with similar moves, while Palla cried out for her to stop. I'm telling you, they were dead in less time than it takes you to read my account of it.

Then I watched as Brianna stood there in a battle crouch. She turned to face the remaining men.

They, on other hand, had not moved a muscle. Whether they were too terrified or too wise to move, it didn't matter. Their lives were spared.

Palla stood with her head in her hands, and I think I saw tears forming in the corner of her eyes.

"I need to know their names."

"The dead ones?"

"No … no, I mean these two."

Brianna told her, and Palla took out her bell, assuring them that everything was going to be all right.

I didn't know how it happened or why. And I remained skeptical … what did this mean? *Did Brianna join Palla? Was Palla always working for the government? I could only think, Just what the hell is going on?*

###

When we were about ready to go inside, Palla made a point of giving me an out.

"You really do not have to go in there. Whatever will happen will happen either way."

"So, what's going to happen?"

"Many people will die. And a new religion will begin."

"Your religion?"

"Either as savior or martyr: One way or the other, yes."

"Did you know Sally was going to die?" *I can't let it go, damn you.* She shook her head but said, "Yes."

"How can you just let people die?"

"That is always the toughest question. The answer of course is that it isn't up to me—everyone still has free will. Like with sports: I am just betting on the game, I'm not fixing the outcome."

"But you are. You going around hypnotizin' people to do what you want."

"No! Oh dear, no, Heychuck, please don't think that. No, never that. I just help them to feel better about what they already intended to do. It isn't some kind of mind control. You know that. You were around Sally and saw how it worked. You heard about Po ..."

"The one who taught Sally? Yeah, I was around Sally! I was around her a lot. But see, I was still surprised by her death. But you weren't, were you? You knew Sally would kill herself, right?"

"No! Sally just made the choice I believed she would make. Her sacrifice was notable, but anyway, it is her cleverness that will save us in the end. Similar to you: your ... righteousness is notable, but your faith is what will be determinative."

"I don't have any faith in you."

"I didn't say *in me.*"

Brianna had stopped typing into her pad and glared at us threateningly. "You two: SHUT. UP. You are giving me a headache." Then she rolled the pad up and put it away and said, "Are we ready then?"

And then Palla looked at me, the weight of the world in her stare.

BOOK TWO—CHAPTER TWENTY

"Of this allow,
If ever you have spent time worse ere now;
If never, yet that Time himself doth say,
He wishes earnestly you never may."

—William Shakespeare
The Winter's Tale (1623)

Kinta Ironfoot had been walking around the place, carrying Marshall's jacket for a while now. She didn't want to attract too much attention to herself, so she didn't walk around front at first. But her hovering around the back looked even more suspicious.

Whenever anybody asked what she was doing she told them she was returning a jacket. It wasn't a lie. But, finally, somebody suggested she walk around front to get a better view, and she was forced to agree.

That was when she found him.

Kinta was surprised, but he was literally sat right there in the front row! Kinta had only met Marshall briefly at Camp Grier. She was so starstruck; she had heard so much about the *Minko Puskus*. But when she actually met him, she was underwhelmed. *Sickly looking guy with a stony stare.* Sure, he cleaned up nice for the Christmas party. There was something about him.

But he didn't seem that interested in her anyway.

But now he was totally out of it. He was sort of slouched down, which was why she hadn't seen him from behind—he had been hidden from view by the other attendees seated behind him. But now she saw him.

Kinta looked around. Some businessman-looking guy in a suit and another strange-looking dude in track sweats holding a white cape, both kept peering out from that little doorway near the back of the stage. They seemed super ominous. They poked their heads out often enough that she didn't risk walking right up to Marshall.

Then someone shouted, "EVERYBODY ON THE GROUND!" and everyone in the hall started standing up and/or briefly running, so that it gave her the chance … she quickly ran up to the man in the wheelchair and collapsed onto him.

"UUUUURGHHH!" She pushed on him and pulled on one of the wheels until she finally managed to knock him down to the ground, per the gunman's instructions. As everyone around her eventually also started lying down, she just laid there next to this enigmatic figure that she had heard so much about and wondered what it was about this guy that everyone was fussing so much over?

Then he opened his eyes.

And she saw love there. It was unbelievable, yes unmistakable. He even smiled.

"Hi, Kinta."

"Quiet. I'm gonna try and get you out of here"

"That is very nice of you." There was more shouting from the lead terrorist, or whatever. But he didn't seem to care. Talking with her seemed more important to him.

Then the windows above and behind the hall exploded, and they both had to look.

But Marshall couldn't.

"Oh. Sorry." And Kinta quickly unstrapped him.

Suddenly more agents, the ones with the helmets, were rushing in.

"Hey, Kinta?"

"What?" she hissed, looking about nervously.

But Marshall just looked at her, finally breaking through her worry with a question: "Is that my jacket?"

Right about then, an E-Dog walked past them and dumped two bodies on the floor. *It's Brick and Boris!* Marshall saw.

"What are we going to do?" Kinta shivered in terror. But Marshall sat up and grabbed his jacket and covered Kinta with it, as though to offer her comfort.

"DO NOT FIRE!" said the Visiting Analyst in the background as he strolled out in front of them. He was wearing sunglasses, so you couldn't be sure, but didn't seem to bother to look down. So, he seemingly was unaware that they were there.

But Marshall just looked at her, from over her shoulder. "Don't worry, Kinta. I will protect you." And he intended to.

"How are you going to do that?"

"Well, let me see my jacket …"

###

Minutes Prior.

This is it, thought the Visiting Analyst. *Everyone is nearly in place.*

Secretary Itiorvic and the VA were both waiting in the wings. The VA ordered the Blue Rooks flunky to ask everyone to return to their seats, and then to introduce the Secretary. The Secretary looked forward to hijacking the event by announcing his candidacy for President of the United States as an Independent. *Idiot,* the VA thought.

The VA looked to see—yes, there he was. In the front row, in a spot earmarked for the disabled, and Marshall Lastpost was unconscious and still strapped to a wheelchair (under a blanket so no one could question).

Not far from him was Mr. Lee, seated as one of the normal attendees.

The media was off to one side.

And, of course, everyone was carrying a phone.

Finally, Brianna sent an update. She was arriving with the CEO child-whore.

Yes, everyone is nearly in place, the VA thought.

After he was introduced, the Secretary confidently strode out and began addressing the crowd. During his walk out and the ovation, the VA looked up at the skybox and nodded to the agents hidden here behind the drawn curtains.

The Secretary: "Thank you! Thank you. And thank *you*, Reverend Wilkersonn, for that introduction. My friends, people of faith, all. Let us rejoice in the simple pleasure that we have been chosen for a singular task, to celebrate our savior, and to promote a world were all people of faith can shine their light in their own communities and help lead this world into and through this period of severe darkness we find ourselves in—"

"EVERYBODY ON THE GROUND!" The plain-clothed agents dressed as vagrants stormed into the main hall, brandishing their weapons at the crowd.

One agent, the largest, carried both Sir Wyskald and Brick Reese over his shoulders in a fireman's carry. As two of the agents stayed back behind the rows of now-empty seats, two others stormed the stage, and the last one dumped the two older men onto the floor before the lectern. One of the ones on the stage, Pharell his name was, trained his gun on the Secretary and told him to sit in a nearby chair. The Secretary, for all his bluster and military background, cowed in shock. *Guess he never actually saw combat*, thought the VA.

Pharell said to the crowd, through the microphone: "EVERYONE STAY ON THE FLOOR! EXCEPT YOU—YOU, THE CAMERAS, YOU'RE THE MEDIA, RIGHT? GOOD. WE ARE THE ANTI–BLUE ROOKS RESISTANCE, AND WE ARE HERE TO TELL YOU THAT THE DRUG IS NOT WHAT YOU'VE BEEN TOLD. IT IS DEADLY. IT KILLS MANY AS SOON AS THEY TAKE IT. IT WAS NEVER PROPERLY TESTED. BRICK REESE GOT THE FDA TO SKIP ITS TESTING AND APPROVE IT. AND WE ARE NOT GOING TO STAND DOWN UNTIL WE GET THE CEO HERSELF TO APPEAR AND ORDER HER COMPANY TO UPLOAD THE FORMULA FOR THE DRUG TO THE INTERNET SO THAT IT CAN BE PROPERTY TESTED."

The VA turned to his E-Dog agents who were waiting in the wings with him, and gave a nod.

Just then, a small explosive device they had planted in the skybox detonated, showering the gathering in broken glass and screams. This was just a distraction, at that point the E-Dogs all ran in from separate entrances, including the hallway in which the VA stood, to point their weapons at the undercover agents in a stand-off.

The VA's men, on both sides, had been ordered not to fire at each other, of course. But they all did a bunch of shouting at each other. The screaming continued.

It was a very tense scene.

Now, everything is ready, thought the VA as he strode out onto the stage and said, "DO NOT FIRE!"

Everything paused as he continued his walk to the podium. The time for his ascendancy had come.

"Your men will stand down!" Pharell screamed from the stage, where he held the Secretary in a headlock and pointed a pistol at his head.

The VA agreed, "YES! Yes! Stand down, everyone. Everyone can calm down. This situation is well in hand. We thank you for doing our work for us, young man. The federal government has been tracking and cataloging the criminal activity of this church for some time. But now it is obvious … I mean, look at this, everyone here is at risk. A member of our cabinet. All in danger. This so-called church is nothing but a criminal enterprise. But you aren't helping."

Pharell played his part well, quite convincing. In fact, in all his undercover work, only Sally and Palla had ever discovered him. He still didn't know how. But it didn't matter, he kept reciting his lines:

"We need the CEO to upload the specs for the drug to the Internet. To confirm that it is dangerous!"

Every time he made that claim a murmur ran through the crowd.

"No, it isn't. Was it created immorally, with the church testing it on children and other congregants? Yes. But the subsequent FDA trials were conclusive, it's safe."

"PROVE IT!" Pharell screamed.

The VA paused and lowered his shoulders, as if in thought. Then Mr. Lee, from the audience, just as they had planned, said, "Excuse me. But I have a thought. My associate will volunteer. After all, I came here to find out. And my companion is quite ill and has already signed a waiver. As I'm sure most of the participants here have. But, apart from anyone who still volunteers, but Agent …?"

The VA straightened. "Chase."

"Agent Chase, why don't you have some of your men take it as well? That would be a show of good faith."

And like a scene from a play, it was concluded. All parties agreed to disarm, while all but two of his men volunteered for the drug trial. The two men who remained armed kept their weapons pointed at the alleged *terrorists*, who were all herded up on to stage-right, the opposite side of the exit door they had all been using.

Everyone decided that an hour was plenty of time. After that, the media interviewed the participants who had been dosed. And once they said that, they felt fine. It was suggested that all the Blue Rooks ministers, nearly all of whom, nationwide, were in attendance do the same. They had already been ordered by Palla some time ago to do just that.

Finally, after they all were dosed, the VA said, "I think that has put everyone's minds at rest. Where is Wilkersonn? See here now. Go ahead and have the staff go ahead and conduct the trials ... whatever way you were going to before."

Everyone was asked to set their chairs back up and to reseat themselves and stay seated. And then, like the audience was taking communion, they began walking the pills to everyone.

BOOK TWO—CHAPTER TWENTY-ONE

HEYCHUCK SMITH

###

Brianna asked us, "Are you ready?"

Then Marshall stood there, outside the building, right in front of Palla and me.

He had moved so quickly, he wasn't even a blur. It was as though he teleported, the way he was suddenly standing in front of us.

Bro' finally managed to sneak up on me, after all.

Brianna lunged at him with a debilitating blow, but she passed right through him like he was a ghost, and she fell to the ground eve as Palla was shouting for her to stop.

Meanwhile, Marshall ignored the blonde who tried to kill him. "We need to talk," he said to Palla.

She nodded. But instead of talking, she took out her bell and gave it a slow, steady *rrrrriiiiinnnnnggg*.

Meanwhile, I tried to catch up. "Hey, bro. You okay? Lost some weight."

"Hello, Heychuck. It is good to see you alive in this timeline. I am fine. This is just my spectral image. Right now, my real essence is unseen, but alive, and next to Kinta, inside. Palla! She is in great danger. Everyone in there is. But I had to talk to the Unity. Palla, what …?" he just trailed off.

Palla spoke with a deeper tone now. "Yes, she is the *Ward*, Precept. I know. Hear me, I know you think you have … time … all the time you need to hear explanations, but the ones who are coming, the Lost of the Regnant … they won't respect the boundaries right away. We must all go in there, now."

He sneered at her warning. "I am always running out of time. You know, I could try to kill him. But I don't know if that is the right thing to do. I cannot see the future anymore. What is going to happen, Palla?"

"You must go back in. Keep him talking. We will be there, and I will confront him. I will attempt to try and get him to concede his error."

He paused then and cocked his head; he was hearing all his voices, garnering a consensus. I had seen it many times before: "You can't be serious."

"I have to try, Precept." she affirmed.

He stared at her for what seemed like a long time. "Fine, then."

Marshall then turned as though heading back into the building, then he literally disappeared.

Palla said to the group, "Let's go."

Brianna looked at us. "Wait. I have an idea."

BOOK TWO—CHAPTER TWENTY-TWO

"Consumers want heroes, but heroism is contingent on the hero's willingness or ability to emblematize an audience's psychic and libidinal needs."

—Prof. Steve Salaita,
Blog: "An Honest Living" (2019)

"Say, Mr. Boggs, it looks to me from here that not only is the comic supplement to lose two precious lives, but four. Exit Joy. enter horror. O horror!"

—*Chicago Sunday Tribune*,
"HUGO HERCULES SAVES
FOUR COMIC SUPPLEMENT
LIVES" (November 2, 1902)

After nearly everyone in the room was dosed, Marshall started to walk back in to set the scene. But then he remembered Ruby's words, all those years ago, *Think tactically.* He looked at the small sign over one stairwell, "To Balcony," and thought, *That might help.*

Once up there, he saw a bombed-out room with torn drapes in front of a large picture window that he shattered outward. From that perch, he could oversee the entire hall.

He saw the last of the doses being administered to the various volunteers (and even the E-Dogs?).

And he saw Brendant Chase in front of the crowd making a speech. At some point, Chase had donned his white burnoose again. Its cape and hood were both drawn back, revealing his handsome frame. He held his shades in one hand, waiving them about for effect.

He said: "The rest of mankind that were not killed by these plagues still did not repent of the work of their hands; they did not stop worshiping demons, and idols of gold, silver, bronze, stone, and wood—idols that cannot see or hear or walk. Nor did they repent of their murders, their magic arts, their sexual immorality, or their thefts.

"For those of you who are unfamiliar. That is from the Book of Revelation, nine twenty."

Marshall looked at the front row, and he could see the hunched over form of Kinta, still wearing the black rune-decorated jacket … and holding his invisible essence, while the VA continued.

"We do face a literal plague right now, out there in our streets. And I'm not talking about sexual immoralities, or of crime, or even of literal germs—although those are all on our doorstep, to be sure.

"My friends, I am talking about something far more sinister and serious. The true face of evil. I am sharing with you today those who practice what the Good Book calls *their magic arts*. Some, like these Blue Rooks false prophets, do it under the guise of Native American religion. Others bring it to our homeland from other disgusting, barbarian foreign places. And until recently, they have always been in the shadows witches, voodoo queens, secret societies.

"But these days, it is right out in the open! Yes, now they have TV infomercials and Internet pop-up ads, and no matter how many documentaries or exposés are written concerning their scandals as a haven for child abusers and criminals, they just parley that into more media exposure. No such thing as bad press in this wicked world!

"Well, I have dedicated my career to stopping those *magic users,* those purveyors of evil. I know what they look like! Indeed, one of them tried to banish me from this world, many, many years ago. So, let me introduce you to one of them; she is the leader of this organization. And no, I do not mean the old man, Brick Reese. As you can see, he is no longer a threat to anyone. No, I am referring to the CEO—born as a foreigner, raised as a child-prostitute, she has been in charge of this organization while it sheltered and promoted these *magic-users.* Bring her in!"

And the VA pointed toward the back of the room, where the main entrance doors were. Everyone turned to see Palla Kalrajan, plastic straps wrapped around her wrists, being brought in by two figures. Each one held an arm. On one side, a tall blonde woman dressed in white, form-fitting militia gear. On the other side, one of the helmeted E-Dog soldiers.

As they slowly walked up, the VA continued with a grand smile, "Miss Kalrajan, thank you so much for joining us. The federal government has already begun seizing your church assets, including the manufacturing of this Blue Joy drug. You and your pimp, Mr. Reese here," and he indicated one of the two unconscious old men at his feet, "will be tried for your crimes. But I am not only here representing the government. I am here representing the forces of *Good*. There is a higher law than the laws of man. I am talking about the law of God. I want everyone to see what God thinks of you! Come up here, Miss Kalrajan. Bring her, Agent Carson."

As the three newcomers walked down the center aisle, the various people in the audience were getting noticeably sedate. As the effects of the drug took hold, they started to stare forward, following the VA's voice as he narrated.

"Ladies and gentlemen, I beg you. Watch the air around us. If the Good Lord deems my mission worthy, there should be a sign."

And even as he spoke, sure enough, the air around them seemed to darken …

Marshall, from his perch, heard their song even before they appeared. The VA's cadre of the Lost, appearing once again at his bidding.

The three continued to walk toward the stage. As Brianna and her E-Dog brought Palla in tow, the two old men who were lying nearby suddenly roused.

The one with the beard flailed blindly at the E-Dog who clumsily lost his grip and let Palla fall away.

Meanwhile, Brick sprung up and faced off against Brianna. She was strangely hesitant, and so he even landed a rib-crunching strike against the woman in white.

Brianna rolled backward and stood up. She flicked her wrists toward her belt and a stun-baton emerged from each hand. Matching her battle stance, Brick ordered the nearby crowd: "Get back!"

The first several people in the rows on either side of the center aisle once again dumbly scurried away, just as they had done earlier. But their reflexes were slowed by the drug. Most were in a haze. And depending on who they were, they saw one of two things: all the former Revelator priests and the E-Dogs simply saw the figures near the stage battling; while the regular, non-magic-sensitive members of the audience also saw the gathering gloom and the glimmering outlines of the dragonesque figures overlooking the scene, as well.

A couple people stumbled over Kinta and Marshall's invisible corporal form.

Marshall decided he needed to be down there, so he ran down the stairs.

Brick, meanwhile, had grabbed one of the metal folding chairs and lifted it, as though it were a weapon, and then, rather than engage Brianna, he turned and flung it with all his might at the Visiting Analyst.

The VA flinched, instinctively raising both his arms in a X-shape as he commanded the nearest dJinn to banish the chair away … and replace it with the probability of—anything! And a cup of coffee that had been sitting on the floor smacked into his face, splitting his lip and spilling its contents all over his face and torso.

Brianna grappled with Brick then, putting him into a *jiu-jitsu hold, which he broke free from thanks to his brute strength.* He smacked her twice, a punch and an elbow strike—stunning her—and then flung her up onto the stage, past the VA.

But before he could refocus on the VA, the two armed agents (and several of the phony "protestors," who had taken advantage of the confusion to re-arm themselves) aimed their rifles and pistols at him and shot him several times.

Boris heard Brick's scream. "NO!" Boris cried out, as he broke off from the E-Dog and lunged toward his old friend on the ground.

In his past decades as Hell-Rider, he had faced down armed gunmen hundreds of times. But that first year or two after he assumed that costumed hero identity, he was lucky. And after that, he had Choiciferors like Marian "the Butterfly" Michaels deciding on futures for him. That was how he managed to survive …

In reality, guys in tights going up against guys with guns get shot.

And so, Bartholomew Richard Reese was bleeding out.

Boris held Brick, and the silence of the room held them both. Boris asked him, "Brick, why? Why go along with it?"

"He promised to keep you all safe. To keep the church going. He was to be a *Champion of Order* … it never … so never thought he'd lie. But"—he coughed, and more than a little blood came out— "'s okay."

Boris held his friend, waiting for the inevitable.

"Means … he's … gonna … lose."

But Dr. Chase stood there, hovering like a ghoul, in response. "Wrong answer, Hell-Rider! But that's understandable, isn't it, folks? You haven't received your judgment yet." *You haven't received a … proper debriefing!* The VA had to act quickly, before Reese could die. He had dropped to one knee, as he spoke and summoned all his *chi* …

And Brick Reese disappeared in a flash of light. Only this was more than a typical debriefing … Brick's synergyte wasn't a run of the mill Regnant. And so, this flash was more than just light.

This banishment feedback detonated like a pipe bomb.

Boris screamed, burnt by the energy on his face and hands. Even Kinta was close enough to be damaged. And, from the doorway, where Marshall had been entering, the outpouring of energy shredded his span-casting spell … as his specter disappeared and he, once again, became visible, screaming with the pain in Kinta's arms, as they both were blown away by the blast.

The dozen closest convention participants were killed summarily. The rest screamed silently, fully under the spell of the drug and Dr. Chase's visions.

Palla crawled on all fours (the plastic wrist wraps weren't fastened) over to Boris to try and see if he was okay.

But he was dead.

She couldn't stop weeping. *So many dead. And it isn't over, yet.*

Then Reese reappeared. His eyes were blank, but he was still alive, barely.

This time he was no longer on the floor. Now he was held aloft by a pair of dJinni.

These two appeared to the nonsensitives in the crowd as demons or angels or ghosts or pixies … each person saw them in their own way. But no one will forget what they saw next. As all of the *Others,* the entire host, descended upon Brick Reese and tore him, limb from limb, disemboweling him before their very eyes.

Now, we will see! The Visiting Analyst's mind screamed with power as he finished the gambit that he had been planning for so long. Behind him, he felt the typical rush of eldritch energy, the sense of deity …

And behind him stood the Regnant Lord, dressed in bejeweled sparkles of silver and white chain.

It was he who was Brick Reese's synergyte among the dJinni. He who was the Champion of Chaos.

"Fool," the silver Dragon-Wraith chimed with a voice deeper than the abyss, with his head turned to aim his cat's eye at his summoner.

But, before the Regnant Lord could mount any attack, the VA lifted both hands to his head, preparing to commence his assault against the Regnant Lord, for lordship over the Regnant. It had all been meticulously planned, he has seen this play out countless times … in his visions he had sacrificed countless of the *Lost* in order to rehearse the battle. And he set about drawing the *chi* from all the *Lost,* every single last one of them that already had been brought over, tapping into their *chi, killing most,* in order to bring their "Lord" in tow.

And then, after that, using her to attack Kalrajan, the Unity, to drive her mad. He would be the last one standing, as soon as he completed this … he summoned all his power and thrust his hands toward the Regnant Lord—and nothing happened.

Through his vision, he stared first at his hands, then finally he took off his shades and relied upon his own human, visual senses to look around and see.

Brianna was lying next to his feet, hypodermic in hand. She had snuck up and injected the Blue Joy into the Visiting Analyst's heel … after she'd been thrown to the stage.

"Sir?" Several of the agents ran up as though to assist—and the Regnant Lord dispatched several of the dJinni from the shadows to touch them, making them collapse to the ground as lifeless husks.

And then the Regnant Lord turned his attention, his rage, toward the audience.

But before he could unleash anything else, Palla stood before him, supported by young Kinta and Marshall:

"Stop! It's all right, MiNëtor, *Ba'al,* and all of the other names you have earned—Highest of the Exalted. Mightiest of the Heralds of Chaos. You are safe."

"Oh, forsooth! I am the Apex, the Chaos-Bringer. There is not one among you who could end me. But now I *am* trapped *here.* Thanks to *this* recreant." It pointed its tale and the fallen VA. "This pretender who would be champion."

And the VA was lifted off his feet, suspended in midair. His burnoose ripped off at the clasp, as Brianna was lying on part of it. The VA tried to scream, but the hot air inside of the Regnant Lord's enchantment burned his lungs.

MiNëtor said, "You asked for judgment, petty human. Perhaps judgment should be rendered?"

Palla said, "No, this is unnecessary. It changes nothing. Let him be, MiNëtor."

"Is he under your protection, Scion?"

She shook her head. "That is not my place. You know that."

"Then he is mine."

But then Marshall moved forward and grabbed the burnoose from the floor. Though she could barely move from fear at what she was seeing play out in front of her, Brianna rolled aside and stood up, maybe in awe of this man-child and what he was doing.

Marshall just stood there, holding the cloak. He realized that this poor, wretched man was merely mad as a result of his own actions. "No, he is my responsibility. I am sorry for everything I have done and everything I haven't done. But I will no longer run from it. I do take responsibility for all of it." Mentally, Marshall knew he should be preparing for battle. But his soul told him different.

"And who are you?" the Regnant Lord asked.

Palla chuckled. "Look again. Do you truly not recognize this one?"

At that, the Regnant Lord peered more carefully at this poor, damaged human whose song was so discordant, yet strangely familiar.

But Marshall had his own answer as he donned both the white burnoose and the shades to replace his own lost ones. "I am the Precept. And you are welcome here, as long as you do not kill any of this world's inhabitants. That is true for all of you. I understand the balance; I understand how the magic is used by the Regnant. I now want things to remain."

And then the Regnant Lord laughed, bringing back the pain of the earlier incident, when he knew even less about what was going on.

"So naive! You lecture me about life and death, even as you set your feet upon the path that will bring about your end and my victory." Then he dismissively moved through Marshall's form to stand directly before Palla and Kinta.

"Very well, Unity! Of course, you and your little acolyte here may continue." Strangely, when he said *acolyte*, he pointed at the stray E-Dog, the one who brought her into the hall, who was standing off to the side, "I won't interfere. In fact, I rather look forward to your success. One day in the pits of your despair you will look for my kindness and you had best hope you not find it wanting.

"Before I leave, know this. This changes nothing. With every passing day, more on this world pass, and, even from here, I can continue the work. Eventually, I and my Regnant will hold sway. It is inevitable."

Then the E-Dog who hadn't drawn a weapon, the one who the Regnant had referred to, said, "Therefore rejoice, ye heavens, and ye that dwell in them. Woe to the inhabiters of the earth and of the sea! For the devil is come down unto you, having great wrath …" Then he took off his helmet, and it was *Heychuck*, "because he knoweth that HE HATH BUT A SHORT TIME. In other words: piss off, Demon!"

Then on cue, behind the dragon's form, Marshall lifted both arms and recited a portion of the jacket's prayer-song. The runes on Kinta's jacket seemed to glow like embers in a long-lost fire. He understood, with the runes in front of him, that the Regnant, even one as great as this one, were still inhabiting the astral plane when they were here on Earth, In this Timespace.

And so, he simply sent them away.

Not a banishment. Nothing forcible. No mind control or violation. No soul-rape like what Brendant Chase manifested.

But rather an invitation, a portal. After all, he had had a lifetime of experience hording the chaos of his internal voices and helping synthesize and synchronizing them into action. *Of course*, he thought, *Who else could manage this?*

Let's go here.

###

Then the Regnant Lord's eyes opened wider for a moment, realizing the truth of the trap he was in. And he suddenly stood erect, the way someone does right after they've tripped in a public place, to save face. To keep their dignity intact.

The he faded away.

The VA crumpled to the ground, and Brianna rushed to his side. To cuff him.

Kinta was the first to speak, "Is the shiny dragon dead?"

"No, I am afraid not," answered Marshall. "But he will think twice about messing with us, as long as that jacket you are wearing exists. The rune-prayers of your people act as a ward against him and his kind. With those spells I control astral travel of all kinds, so I can move them about, or trap them, at will. And they know it."

"So, why do you look so sad?" she had to ask. And it just made him more said that she had to ask. The old Kinta understood him …

"Oh, no reason," he lied. Truth was he wanted to hug her, but she obviously had no memory of their relationship.

"Brother, you were amazing!" Marshall disappeared inside a hug from his larger brother.

"As were you. Thank you both for being here."

"Marshall, how could you stand up to him and face him like that?" Kinta was still genuinely awed. She looked at him like he was a superhero.

He hated it.

But he answered her. Marshall thought about it and formulated his ultimate truth. "In the end, he was just another voice."

"What do we do now?" he added.

At that, Palla walked up to him and gave him a short hug.

"You are the Unity." Marshall declared.

"I'm fully aware," said Palla with a knowing grin.

"That's what I said," Marshall joked, in his own voice, not an impression.

Palla smiled warmly. *He will be fine.* And then she turned to split from them.

She hobbled up to the podium and produced a small thumb drive and inserted it into the laptop that was hooked up to the projector. Then she started a very special presentation.

This was Sally's parting gift. She had prepared the appropriate runes as part of a slide presentation.

By now, the major media networks were all streaming what had been happening … the local media had recorded the entire thing, too. In a sense the world was watching and, rather than say anything, Palla Kalrajan turned on the slideshow and sang.

She sang a song of life and death for the entire world to download, and she knew, somehow, that both the Mehkard and MiNëtor, the Lord of the Regnant, were listening, too.

Tears streamed from Heychuck's and Kinta's eyes as Heychuck instinctively put his arms around her and Marshall.

The song rose through the hall and out to the Internet, and beyond.

The world would never be the same.

Then in a *I'll drink to that* flash of inspiration, Kinta remembered the strange red liquid in the thermos in her pocket.

She took it out and, smiling at her companions, took a swig …

… the liquid that Rufepirts had prepared was a potion infused with his memories … and the memories of those he had touched, the memories of his synergyte: herself.

In an instant, her life experiences, from across timelines, flooded into her mind, filling her senses with the feelings she had had, and that they had shared …

And then she turned to look at Marshall.

To Marshall's delight, there was once again love in her eyes.

THE END

The Be(k)nighted:

EPILOGUE ONE

"This was the story told by Si-Osiri before Pharaoh, the people of Egypt attending to his voice, Setme his father seeing everything, the head of the man of Ethiopia being held towards the ground. And he said, 'By the life of thy face, my great lord, that man that standeth before thee is Hor the son of the Negress whose words I have been relating and who hath not repented concerning those things which he did at first; for he hath come up to Egypt at the end of fifteen hundred years to cast sorceries therein …'"

—"THE TALE OF KHAMUAS AND HIS SON SI-OSIRI," from *Stories of the High Priests of Memphis*, F. Ll. Griffith, ed. (1900); as referenced in *Egyptian Religion* by Siegfried Morenz (1973)

###

God and the Devil. He still hears voices, of course. Even mine.

And why not? I am the Mehkard and the Precept is my chosen Champion of Order.

You may see this: In this glimpse of Timespace I have shared with you, he still takes minimal doses of medicine. Not so many that the voices cannot be accessed. But enough so they don't distract him when his special attention is needed. It is a constant balancing act.

You may feel this: Chaos has always been necessary for proper Order. That is what the insane human, the former Dr. Chase, still doesn't understand, sitting in his cell at Greenless Grove.

Marshall has been balancing in that way his entire life, and he has help now, with his beautiful Kinta.

Both he and Kinta enjoy their night jobs. He is proud of how she is a better home health-care aide than he is. She is good with people.

By day, they often sleep in, through the noon hour. But day or night, they are never far from the special satchel, the one that used to belong to Kinta's father. In it is a black jacket, a white burnoose, and two sets of sunglasses. Marshall still had the VA's, and when they are on assignment, she wears the new flip-shades. The ones he got her as a wedding present.

Usually, the two of them are not needed. From time to time, Heychuck calls them, to give them an update on how the things are going. But Heychuck runs the church under its new auspices: The Blue Queen Assembly.

And he works closely with Brianna. It's different from the old days. Now, they had the full backing and intel of the federal government. And BOISE's leader, Brianna Carson, was their field leader, also. Her code-name was RA, which stood for Resident Analyst.

No more E-Dogs; only students. No more drugs; only training in community centers—mostly located on Indian reservations.

It wasn't a perfect system. There was still a lot to figure out. But it was a good life for Heychuck. He was making a real difference, both for normal folks and for the few remaining sensitives, like his brother.

And his testimony helped put away several criminals back in Seattle.

But, sometimes, those calls from Heychuck involved an opposing force, some rogue magic-using cleric, or other super-powered villain. And then Marshall and Kinta have to take a leave of absence in order to complete an important "outreach junket." And then they meet up with Brianna.

When they did that they were better known (and feared) on the Dark Web as the Precept and the Ward. Or, collectively, with RA: the New Revelators.

They thought they would live happily ever after.

But that is because of their myopathy. Such limited creatures.

Except for the Unity. She understands.

If they all saw how often she sat alone and cried, they would tremble. She knows there is more.

She knows the Regnant Lord wasn't wrong in his final warning.

She knows there is still one synergyte unaccounted for. Was there not one more who died? Did you catch it?

The Unity knows that every song has a final note.

Beginnings and Endings. Hear me. For I am the Mehkard and you are among the blessed.

The Be(k)nighted:

EPILOGUE TWO

*"Jesus knew their thoughts and said to them, 'Every
kingdom divided against itself will be ruined, and every
city or household divided against itself will not stand.
If Satan drives out Satan, he is divided against himself.
How then can his kingdom stand? And if I drive out
demons by Beelzebul, by whom do your people drive
them out? So then, they will be your judges. But if I
drive out demons by the Spirit of God, then the
kingdom of God has come upon you.'"*
—Matthew 12:25–28

###

Mr. Lee was circumspect.

He knew that the others at the convention and around the world
had simply missed the point.

They saw the event at the convention as the beginning of a new era.
End Day it was being called. Some more so than others, but in *every* sect
of every Western religion, it demarcated a new beginning for their religion. In every denomination, there were those traditionalists trying to
hang onto their own power structures in the face of what had become
obvious: everything had changed.

And on the other hand were the reformers, those who followed the
Scion, Palla (i.e., the second coming), and her prayers of the indigenous
populations of the world, those ancients who had originally been plugged
in to those higher powers, they held the key to the future.

Some formed a new religion, the *Blue Queen Assembly*, now the fastest growing religion in the world. The Preceptor H. L. Smith, was their leader. Most of the previous *Blue Rooks* churches had converted to this. Many other denominations around the world did the same.

But they were all wrong. Now that Mr. Lee had seen the ancient dragons of wisdom, the *Lóng,* up close, he knew only that he had been put on this Earth to worship them. And to bring them back to their glory.

He knew. This time marked a return to the ascendancy of *Eastern* religions.

His government's forces had intercepted the stores of Blue Joy. And destroyed them.

At least that was the official policy. What the Escher painting of bureaucracy in the Chinese government actually did was an open question.

But he dared not attempt to capture and/or recreate the Blue Joy formula, for fear of his own cadre of magic-using clerics, his *Wu*, discovering it and preemptively rebelling against him. He never dared use it. He had seen that was a dead end.

But, by the same token, he had become obsessed with how dangerous the continued use of these magicians was to normal humans. In order to retain control, he would have to study, to learn, to master himself so that he could master the *Lóng*.

How long would that take? For the first year, he despaired. Despite putting his own political ambitions on hold for it, his progress was so minimal as to not be mentionable.

Then he met *WërweJay*.

The man had hair down to his waist and, apparently, had spent the last many years traveling the wastelands in the mountains of Tibet, performing wondrous miracles to keep himself alive and safe.

The stories from the locals said he could slow time, much like his own *Wu* could. This would be key. Then he would have as much time as he needed.

So, he traveled to meet this stranger.

When he finally found him, he was just sitting under a small tree, in the snow. He was mostly naked, an emaciated Buddha. Several of his toes had been lost to frostbite. He was covered in rags and filth. He had apparently taken to cutting himself.

He was quite mad.

But Mr. Lee took in WërweJay and nurtured him to health. He tried to speak with him for many days without any luck. It was many, many weeks before the being started to use verbal language.

No, the first communications were mind-to-mind. Like a voice in a dream.

First was his name: in traditional Chinese, pronounced "Way-Yar-Jee-ay-EE" (Wēi ěr·jié yī), or, in English: *WërweJay.* It meant nothing. So, Mr. Lee reasoned it must've been a name.

But the next thing he kept hearing in his mind from the strange man *did* translate. It puzzled Mr. Lee, but it was clear. "Wah-men shee-Zhunee" (Wǒmen qù zhèl?).

Or, in English, it meant, *Let's go here.*

The Be(k)nighted:

EPILOGUE THREE

"I got you, babe!"

—Palla Kalrajan and Bill Ironfoot,
performing karaoke at Camp Grier

Palla was seldom seen after End Day.

After burying her friends, she retired. She didn't need to do anything. Literally hundreds of organizations and businesses sprang up, all based on the burgeoning worship of *her*. Some thought she was holy, a prophet. Or the Scion. About the same number thought she was a phony. Both types tended to devote their energy to church-related cottage industry with about equal zeal, she noticed. Except for the occasional speaking engagement, she stayed home.

She slept. She wept. She prayed. Mostly, she prayed. Prayed for a world she couldn't save, except for one bell ring at a time.

Am I the Scion? Close, but no cigar.

Well, maybe a cigar.

She laid down and petted Sebastian, who reclined beside her, playfully pawing at Asha's bell. Her naps had grown, in length and frequency. Therefore, so had Sebastian's.

Thus it was, ever since Palla Kalrajan discovered that the VA's final banishment/time-shift had accomplished one other side effect.

She touched the roundness of her stomach and closed her eyes.

www.ingramcontent.com/pod-product-compliance
Lightning Source LLC
Chambersburg PA
CBHW061345190726

48288CB00005B/1603